MARYSUE
RUCCI
BOOKS

THE
MYTHMAKERS

A NOVEL

KEZIAH WEIR

MARYSUE
RUCCI
BOOKS

NEW YORK • LONDON • TORONTO • SYDNEY • NEW DELHI

MARYSUE
RUCCI
BOOKS

Marysue Rucci Books
An Imprint of Simon & Schuster, Inc.
1230 Avenue of the Americas
New York, NY 10020

First Marysue Rucci Books hardcover edition June 2023

MARYSUE RUCCI BOOKS and colophon are trademarks of Simon & Schuster, Inc.

For information about special discounts for bulk purchases, please contact Simon & Schuster Special Sales at 1-866-506-1949 or business@simonandschuster.com.

The Simon & Schuster Speakers Bureau can bring authors to your live event. For more information or to book an event, contact the Simon & Schuster Speakers Bureau at 1-866-248-3049 or visit our website at www.simonspeakers.com.

Interior design by *Yvonne Taylor*

Manufactured in the United States of America

10 9 8 7 6 5 4 3 2 1

Library of Congress Cataloging-in-Publication Data has been applied for.

ISBN 978-1-9821-8958-7
ISBN 978-1-9821-8960-0 (ebook)

For my parents
and for Dan

PART I

ONE

I read the story on one of those spring days in New York when the world seems to rise out of hibernation. Music trailed from cars, pop and rap and oldies mingling with the Doppler whoosh of traffic. An early geysering fire hydrant. The chatter of starlings. The pages of the short story were crisp like new bills and my heart sped up when I turned them.

It was Friday, and Hugh—a waft of peppermint as he kissed my temple; the click of the front door—was at work. By the time I got up, sunlight flooded our tidy apartment. While I tend to leave half-finished books butterflied on the couch and deserted sweaters over the backs of chairs, Hugh is so fastidious that a stranger might imagine I lived in the apartment alone. Being there without him, as I often was those days, made the place take on a cinematic quality, as though I actually were that alternate version of myself: single, independent.

It was easy to slip into that fantasy, to trade the comfortable monotony of my relationship with Hugh for the solo artistic pleasures of a fellowship in Tokyo or a retreat on the Spanish coast. In college I used to picture our hypothetical life together with longing: the postcoital breakfasts in bed that have in fact happened; working together late into the night, he on his painting, I on a novel, which has not. Nearly six years out of school and two into cohabitation, I was prone to imagining us apart, so maybe by the time I boarded the Greyhound bus that summer I'd primed my brain for escape, the way tennis players visualize their backhands. I once read that the inability to distinguish between fantasy and reality is a hallmark of psychosis, but I think healthy people trick themselves into believing daydreams all the time.

Our apartment was on a quiet, tree-lined block on the south side of Prospect Park. Hugh paid most of the rent, because he made nearly three times as much as my salary at the magazine. The year before, a clothing conglomerate bought the start-up he worked for, and something blah blah equity, et cetera. When we passed brownstones with FOR SALE signs posted in what passes for a front yard in Brooklyn, he'd started looking up the asking price on his phone.

That past December, amid headlines about our country's nuclear pissing contest with North Korea and a wave of sexual abuse allegations, my job at the magazine had changed. I was a decently paid staff writer straddling our print edition and the website, but the features director I'd been hired to assist soon after graduation still asked me to make his restaurant reservations, and the website had recently instituted a soul-sucking quota system—these were the primary subjects of what Hugh called my "Hamlet lite monologues" during which, wineglass in hand, I'd complain about how my job left me no time to work on anything important.

"Just quit," Hugh would say, exasperated, but too much of my identity revolved around the title in my email signature, and giving up my paycheck—despite, or maybe especially because of Hugh's implying he could cover my meager portion of the rent as long as I needed—was untenable. After much hand-wringing, a compromise: the magazine allowed me to trade my health insurance, more than half my salary, and the illusion of job security (Hugh, that January: "Does anyone in magazines have job security in 2018?") for a contributing editor position, under contract. I had a reasonable annual word count to hit and the freedom to write whatever I wanted; if the magazine didn't like the idea, I could take it elsewhere. By spring this arrangement had produced a profile of a mysterious playwright, which I'd put to bed a few weeks earlier. I was proud of the piece, but even I had to admit it wasn't exactly the kind of ambitious reportage worth quitting a job for.

By the time I found the short story, I had been in search of a truly worthy idea for nearly four months. Embezzling philanthropists, reclusive painters, obsessive collectors; thus far nothing had panned out. I was supposed to be hunting for material that morning in late April, too. But there was a stack of magazines next to the front door, which was Hugh's tacit threat of impending disposal. I often let them pile up without so much as cracking the covers. (To cancel the subscriptions would be to admit defeat.) Now, with my own work to do, they offered procrastination under the guise of research: reading the good work of others was work for me, too.

I relocated the stack to the coffee table and settled on the couch, where I thumbed through a *New Yorker*, a *Vanity Fair*, and then reached for the most recent issue of *The Paris Review. Look*, I imagined telling Hugh. *I'm reading it.* I scanned an interview with the novelist Charles Johnson and a few short stories. Words, words, words.

Then my eye hitched on a familiar byline. Martin Scott Keller. I felt a pang of fondness, as though a childhood friend had called my name down a crowded subway car. I met Martin at a book launch soon after moving to the city. I'd been out of place, too young for the party, until he plucked me out of the crowd. I hadn't thought of him in ages. The story was called "Such Are My Stars." I scrunched a pillow behind my neck and lay back to read.

"Because the engines of our lives run on a fixed track," his story began, "there is no use dwelling in the hypothetical past tense. What might have happened does not matter, and so for the girl and I to meet as we did, when we did, can only be called fate." I skimmed the story, distracted by my phone and the anxious sense that I was wasting time, and then came to this line: "I was once again alone in the crowd when I realized I was holding, like a talisman from a dream, the girl's silver rose."

I sat up and propped the journal on my knees. I had a hiccuping sensation in my throat, the same one I'd get before pitch meetings. "What?" I whispered, the syllable tapping off my teeth. I leaned down close to the page, as though to climb into it. It was the strangest thing. The story he'd written, this story I was reading, was about me.

To be clear, I don't mean the story so captured my psyche it was *as if* it had been written about me, a sensation well known to anyone who loves reading fiction. I mean it was actually based on Martin's and my evening at the New York Public Library six years earlier. I started again from the beginning.

His narrator is a married writer who meets a colleague's teenage daughter at a literary salon, hosted by said colleague, and becomes infatuated. He goes home and gets in bed next to his wife, who refused to go to the party because of a petty fight, their backs to each other, "a pair of confused parentheses." He considers waiting until the girl's older, leaving his wife for her, and if the story had ended there it might have been almost hopeful. Instead, in the last paragraphs, the man begins fantasizing about the girl's life without him in it. He will think of her forever, and she will not think of him at all.

He'd lifted certain details straight from reality. "She is my Laura, my Nora, my Dark Lady of the Sonnets," he'd written. We'd talked about muses and their makers, about love preserved by literature. Here was the amused way he'd watched me, as though he knew me. He'd plucked the silver rose barrette quite literally from my own hair. As I read the story again I cycled through confusion, giddy excitement, nausea, pride, and eventually a creeping sense of ownership, though that might have come later. Vladimir Nabokov wrote Véra love poems soon after they met, which he published in a journal he knew she read; here was my own call across time and space. It was true that Martin had shifted our ages—I'd been twenty-one and he was in his seventies when we met that night at the Forty-Second Street branch—but the taboo transposition only added to the frisson. He described the girl as wiser than her age, more comfortable around adults than her peers. He wrote about the ambition that emanated from her. (From me!) It was as though I'd had part of an elusive tune stuck in my head for the last decade, and a car passed by with that very melody floating out through an open window, the radio host's voice making its way back to me with a name, the answer I hadn't realized I'd been looking for.

I sat back on the couch. I recalled Martin taught at a college upstate. I would track him down and pull up to his house unannounced, where he'd be sitting on a porch rocking chair with a novel in his hand. He'd glance up and his shoulders would loosen as if in a sigh. *Ah. Here she is.*

However. But. Alas.

I had not been a careful reader. I'd skipped the story's introductory lines in favor of jumping into the narrative. It would've saved a few minutes of excitement, because when I searched his name two sharp dates appeared, a beginning and an end. He had died in January. The story was posthumous.

———

SIX YEARS EARLIER, before leaving my apartment for the reading, I nursed a Corona and surveyed myself in my roommate Georgia's warped mirror. It was the middle of July: she had an air conditioner in her bedroom window, I did not. Georgia had invited me to the reading, but she was coming from her job uptown and so we'd planned to meet at the library. I wore a sleeveless dress I hoped projected an air of sophistication. Getting ready alone, I worried that its length was frumpy rather than refined, and spent half an hour manipulating my hair into slight variations on a dull theme. In the end, I clipped it back with a small, rose-shaped barrette, a long-ago gift from my mother. Georgia and I had only lived in Brooklyn for a month, and the subway remained an unpredictable and confusing experience—I was always working myself up on the platform about whether I'd find a space in front of the map, and once I was in the car I spent the ride craning my neck to check the station names through the window—so I left nearly an hour before I needed to.

The New York Public Library. Stone lions and Doric columns. By the time I met Georgia at the entrance I was more relaxed, having arrived early and killed time at an old boxing bar up the street. Next to Georgia's bare face and wide-legged trousers, my dress was too considered, but not terrible. "You are going to dazzle the literati tonight," she said. "Think of this as your grand debut." Georgia, an assistant at Sotheby's, loved networking and disapproved of how I'd spent our first weeks in the city. Through a friend of my mother's, I'd gotten a job as an unauthorized Central Park tour guide, a desperate choice I pretended was purposeful—time to write, interesting encounters with strangers—but between my newfound freedom following four years of academia and the tequila-Tecate specials at our neighborhood dive, I hadn't been getting much writing done. We linked elbows and made our way inside.

Regretfully, my enthusiasm for the event was engendered less by its literary promise and more by the prospect of meeting a future boyfriend. Georgia had started dating an editor almost immediately upon our move to the city, a serious man with a vested interest in his magazine's softball team who left trimmings from, I hoped, his beard in our bathroom sink. He was the one who'd given her the tickets to the reading. I don't know where he was that night, but I had the idea there might be others like him in attendance. I imagined falling in love under the iconic reading room ceiling, painted with clouds.

In reality, the event took place in a wood-paneled antechamber off a quiet hallway upstairs. We found two empty seats in the rows of folding chairs. Both the red-haired author who was launching her book and the blonde interviewing her wrote about the banal ebb and flow of life (babies, boyfriends), which they complained landed their novels in the Women's Fiction section of the bookstore. Stories by men about anxiety and having sex with younger women do not get a special section, the red-haired author pointed out to an appreciative chuckle from the audience, they are called Literary Fiction.

Afterward we filed like schoolchildren into the adjoining room. Plastic party platters covered one table in pale imitation of a Dutch still life: marbled salami wheels and rosebuds of prosciutto, sliced cantaloupe, a few anemic bunches of grapes. At another table, a pair of boys around my age poured wine into rigid cups and ogled my friend.

I was used to Georgia overshadowing me; she is a person to whom eyes are always drawn in a crowded room. Because, for years, men have felt moved to say very stupid things to her, she has adopted a remote air that makes people want to impress her. We met off campus the fall of our freshman year, right after I'd watched her dance barefoot on the hood of a parked pickup truck, all legs; she needed a partner for beer pong. "You're fun," she said when I landed a shot with my eyes closed. Her parents had their names on the walls of two New York museums and an elevator that opened into their apartment. The private girls' school she'd attended, her summers in Cape Cod, stood in stark contrast to my own childhood in the Colorado mountains, itself an idyll of ponderosa pines, ski lessons, and a main street flanked by pretty red-brick buildings, though I hadn't yet learned to describe it as such and instead found it embarrassing and provincial. Georgia was the most glamorous person I'd ever met.

While Georgia wasn't dancing on anything that night in the library, she was involved in a witty repartee with an interested stranger, the adult equivalent. I felt my smile calcifying as they discussed a museum show I hadn't seen. Waving my empty glass around, I murmured something about getting more wine.

I walked a slow circle of the room before arriving at the drinks table, where a boy refilled my cup, and then I made myself a plate of melon and fat green olives. I was hovering by the table, having realized I couldn't hold the wine, the plate, and also eat, when a man next to me said, "That looks bleak, doesn't it?"

I looked cartoonishly to my right, for whoever it was he was speaking to, but no one was there. The man withdrew the long white finger he'd been pointing toward the prosciutto. "Frayed at the edges, as though someone's nibbled at it," he said, fixing me with a mellow, generous gaze. "Who's your best guess?"

"Sorry?"

"The culprit," he said, and as he lowered his voice I, instinctively, leaned in. "Who do you think it could be?"

Tinted rectangular glasses perched grandfatherly on his nose below a pair of unruly eyebrows, and though his mouth at rest pulled into a serious straight line, he had a mischievous air. I scanned the room. "Him," I said, tipping my chin toward a goateed man explaining something to Georgia, blithely oblivious of her efforts to escape.

"Indeed," the man said. "He's had his vulpine snout all over this spread. Still, is there anything more pleasurable than prosciutto?" He gave the word a hint of a rolled r as he made up his own plate. "Even the bad stuff?" He folded a cantaloupe square in a tissue-thin slice of the meat and popped it into his mouth. "So," he said, chewing. "Who are you? Tell me everything about yourself."

Between the wine and the whiskey gingers I'd downed at the bar, the room had started to glimmer with possibility. It wasn't difficult to seem precocious around much older men, I'd learned from my mom's parties back in Colorado, her small house full of the wealthy outdoorsy types she often attracted. You only had to ask questions, make direct eye contact, and laugh.

Martin Scott Keller—though I didn't know his name for much of the night—looked and dressed like so many of the erudite men who populated my postadolescence. They had presided over classes in contemporary literature, postwar politics, the *Iliad*, the chemistry of water. After graduation, their opinions were the ones I would learn to turn to in the important pages of important magazines when seeking a way to think about the world. A parade of heads like polished oak finials, ad infinitum. They were my men, and my desire to be not just like them but of them was as strong as lust.

Tell me everything about yourself.

"There's not much to tell," I said, trying to hide my delight that someone, anyone, was talking to me. "My name's Sal."

"Such a petite name." I could smell his musky cologne, and his shoulders under his sweater and collared shirt looked strong, despite his age. I wanted to lean my body into his. "Just Sal?"

"Salale, actually."

"*Sa*-la-lay," he said. "A little waltz."

"My mother had only ever seen it written down and she botched the pronunciation. I think it's supposed to rhyme with 'Halal.'"

He chewed an olive, contemplative. "I know you, don't I?"

"I don't think so."

"Not my student?"

"No," I said, with regret.

"She was my student, one of my best." He pointed to the nearby red-haired author, now holding a red-haired baby. She lifted the baby's hand to wave at him, and he saluted. He turned back to me. "So, Salale. What is it you do? Don't tell me: you're a writer."

"I'm not anything yet." I felt small in comparison to this favorite, whom he'd come to see. "I just graduated. I give tours of Central Park to Italian tourists."

He reeled off a few lines: *fiori et felici*, something about Madonna.

"Mm." I didn't want to explain that I gave tours to Texan and German and Chinese tourists, too, that I didn't speak Italian. I waited for him to translate the quote, but instead he launched into an anecdote about Laura, Petrarch's muse, and I batted back something about Dante's Beatrice, which made him chuckle. It's the tenor of the conversation rather than the content that stuck with me. My lasting memory is of feeling that, though I had no real idea who this man was, I was exactly where I needed to be. I wished he'd been my teacher, that he would attend one of my own future readings and, from the audience, give me an encouraging wink.

We talked for an hour, maybe longer, as the party orbited our bubble of two. "You *are* a writer," he said at one point, and at first I laughed, but he looked so serious that I closed my lips over my teeth and felt myself nodding vigorously. "You have to reach into yourself and rip it out. Be selfish. Break rules. Choose work above everything."

The red-haired author, sans bébé, stopped by to say that she and her friends were going for drinks. "Go, I'm too old for all that." He kissed her cheek before turning to me. "Don't you leave me in my decrepitude."

"Never," I said, only half joking.

The author put a hand on his arm and said, "Martin, I meant to tell you, I read *Evergreen* again. It gets more beautiful every time." *Martin, Evergreen,* I willed myself to remember.

After she'd gone, he said, "My first. Nobody ever tells me they've reread my more recent novels."

Instead of pretending that I had read his more recent novels, I was drunk enough to ask, "Why do you think that is?" while holding an imaginary microphone up to his mouth.

"Not many people read them to begin with," he said. *"The Executioner's Song* came out the same day as my second book. Blew it out of the water."

This was solid ground. I knew Mailer. I knew Roth. Updike, Nabokov, Cheever. I'd spent the better part of the last four years reading not just their fiction but, with voyeuristic glee, their correspondences and fat biographies.

"Kicked off sort of a wild year for Mailer," I said.

"The Pulitzer," he agreed. "That business with the murderer."

"And then he also divorced and married twice."

"Ah yes, the six merry wives of Norman Mailer. Just like Henry VIII."

"Not *just* like him," I said. "Henry did have two of his killed."

"Was it only the two?"

"Two's not enough?"

"Well, Norm did give it the old college try." He raised his eyebrows and sipped his wine.

Just then someone knocked a bottle off the table behind us and as the dark liquid spilled out over the hardwood, Martin, ever so briefly, put his hand on my back to guide me away from the flow. Flashes: Georgia flitting by to say she was meeting the editor in Chelsea; the boys from the drinks table dumping crumpled napkins and smeared plates into trash bags; Martin standing in an old wooden telephone box in the hallway, pretending to make a call, me pretending to answer on my cell.

And then he and I were out on the sidewalk, a car pulling up in front of us, and he was looking at me with, what, a challenge? An invitation?

"So," he said. "Where to?"

I wiped my hand across my mouth. My upper lip was damp with sweat. "I'm heading to Brooklyn."

"This train doesn't go in that direction." He smiled. He reached toward my face. For a bewildering moment, as he cupped my skull in his hand, gazing at me with startling intensity, I was sure he was going to kiss me. The ease between us had come, at least in part, from our age difference; the interaction seemed devoid of any real chance of sex, and I'd been performing more freely than if he'd been a more viable romantic prospect. For the first time since our meeting I was anxious, but then there was a tug at my scalp and the twist of hair I'd pinned back fell down by my cheek. "Your clip was loose," he said, holding up the little silver rose. It disappeared into his fist. "And now you've lost it."

"Look at that." Maybe I was wrong to dismiss something more happening between us. Maybe this was the kind of turning point that would define everything that came after. But I waited a beat too long and anything that could have occurred evaporated into the warm air.

"Salale," he said, "I am sure your life will only become more beautiful than it is now." And then he was in the back of the car, the door closing behind him. The black sedan, or maybe it was a taxi, merged into the rows of other black sedans and yellow cabs and I was alone as bodies passed around me, smelling of liquor and perfume and cigarette smoke, the stoplights lit up with their Christmas tree colors. I bought a hot dog from a cart, and when my front teeth popped through the skin, the juice ran down my wrist and the bun caught in my throat like a pre-tears lump. I hadn't eaten meat in five years.

While I did consider sending a note to Martin Scott Keller, care of the college, instead I merely looked without success for

information about him online and ordered a cheap used copy of
Evergreen that, by the time it arrived, I never got around to reading.
The night did trigger a certain shift, though. I started applying
to writing-adjacent jobs in earnest—entry positions at publishing
houses, literary agencies, the *Times*—and a few months later I became
an editorial assistant at a legacy men's magazine in midtown, where
I transcribed interviews for the feature writers and filed expenses
for my exacting, British boss.

Martin's glow dimmed in my memory, but I did think of him.
When I published my first piece, a two-hundred-word interview with
a minor pop star, I indulged in a brief delusion that Martin would read
it, track me down at the office, and offer himself up as my mentor. In
other fantasies I made my own pilgrimage out to find him. But I never
saw him again.

———

A LOCAL NEWSPAPER upstate had posted his obituary online a week
after his death:

> Martin Scott Keller, author of three novels and longtime pro-
> fessor of creative writing at Linden College, died at his home
> in Linden-on-Hudson, New York, on Sunday, January 7. He was
> eighty. The cause was complications from heart disease, his wife,
> Moira Keller, said.
>
> Mr. Keller gained recognition for his debut novel, *Evergreen*,
> in 1974. One review of the book, which traces the emotional

decay of a young couple, observed, "Keller comes across not so much as an explorer of the human psyche as a rambunctious vivisectionist." But what detractors viewed as cruelty, admirers regarded as brave realism, and the first effort was widely lauded as a triumph. "That book was nothing like Martin as a person," said Mrs. Keller, a physicist. "He wrote it as if possessed, scraping up darkness and churning it into prose."

Mr. Keller was born in Connecticut to German immigrants. As a teenager, he waited tables in Manhattan before joining the staff of Grant Aikens Books, which would go on to publish all three of his novels. His previous marriage ended in divorce. According to his wife, Mr. Keller was writing a fourth novel at the time of his death, an excerpt of which will appear in the forthcoming spring edition of *The Paris Review*. He is survived by Mrs. Keller, their daughter, Caroline, and their beloved basset hound.

A novel? I thought. *There's more? More of me?* I called the Grant Aikens publicity department to ask about the book. The chipper girl on the phone put me on hold and then returned to say that while they'd been interested in the posthumous work, there wasn't going to be a publication.

"Why?" I cried.

"Um," the girl said thinly. "I guess the executor of the estate decided against it?" And though I pleaded for more information, for the executor's contact, to speak to Martin's former editor ("This is so sad, but he died in 2015"), anyone, it was no use. "I hope I've been of some assistance?" she said eventually. "If there isn't anything else . . ."

"There is something else," I said, trying to keep my voice steady. "There is the original thing." But the line was dead.

Either because of Martin's death or because of the general digitization of archives in the six years since I'd first looked him up, there was more to read about him online: a short profile in *GQ* from 1974, a glowing *New York Times* review of *Evergreen*. A brief report of a launch party given for its release, which took place at the home of Martin's father-in-law, a literary agent named Emmett Nelson. Almost a decade later, a few tepid words on his sophomore effort, and then nothing for his last book, which came out in the early aughts.

I was suddenly desperate to find my old copy of *Evergreen*, and located it in a box under the bed. I was reading when Hugh came home. He was acceptably invested as I explained, with backpedaling and breathless tangents, the events of the day, but when I asked him to read the story he said his brain was "fried." When I pointedly reopened the book without replying, he said, "I'm not saying I don't want to read it, just that I can't right now," and pulled my favorite chili jam out of his backpack. Point: Hugh.

I emailed the story link to Georgia, writing: "Remember that party at the library, you were dating Bennett (!!) and I talked to that old author? I think . . . he wrote a story about it?" Two hours later, while I washed dinner dishes that Hugh dried, I got her response: "Sal! You're a muse! What does this mean, tell me more? (I think Bennett used to manscape his pubic hair into the sink.)"

Over the following weeks I slipped Martin's name into conversations like a teenager with a crush. One evening, while Hugh was working at his huge desktop computer, he said in a benign monotone that I was being "a little obsessive." I thought about how in college he made enormous abstract paintings, explosions of color against multilayered, shiftable grays. He drank too much coffee, worked with devotional mania. Now he spent hours in front of his screen, his face calm, almost beatific, designing marketing materials for a sock disruptor. I stopped talking about Martin, but as Hugh did push-ups in the living room or browsed one of his plant-based cookbooks, I'd lie in bed, my laptop propped on my stomach, and stare at the black-and-white photo of Martin that dwelled ghostlike on the Linden College literature department website.

I imagined where he might have been when he died: in bed, unlocking the car door, jostling logs for a fire. In those last seconds—amid all the spilling forth of memory that survivors of near-death experiences describe to researchers and church leaders, amid images of his wife's face, memories of bending over blank pages and white screens, of the smell of spring rain, of first frost, of snow—did he, in that final short and infinite moment, think of me?

There is a version of my life in which that was the extent of it: late-night musing and a good anecdote. *It was surreal*, I'd say at parties. *I opened up the magazine and there it was, a story about me.* If my profile of the Playwright hadn't culminated in such an embarrassing disaster, or if Hugh hadn't left, maybe that's all it would have been. That's so much of existence, I guess, puttering stretches of buildup leading to a split-second decision, monumental only in retrospect. The imperceptible trajectory of a life veering off course.

TWO

E ven now, thinking about the Playwright engenders a cringing, full-body shame, perhaps particularly because I worked so hard to secure an interview with him, this secretive sensation who never gave interviews. I wanted to talk to him because his play, when performed in a workshop production, was described by a *New Yorker* critic as a "slow burn, high raunch thriller that just might bring the youth back to the theater," and besides rumors of early tragedy in his life, he possessed the aura of an enfant terrible. Serious men of his age made for good profiles, since you could poke some fun at, while also reveling in, their seriousness. Spangled with humor, these did well online. This was what I wrote in my pitch for my editor. What I didn't include was that I was always interested in talking to people slightly older than me who had done what I had yet to; that is, make a deep impression with their words.

I wooed him. After the press rep from the Brooklyn theater putting on his off-Broadway debut declined my interview request on his behalf, I found a recording of a workshop rehearsal online and called the Playwright's agent, letting her believe I was an ardent, early fan, which didn't work, either. Finally I typed, on the old Olympia Georgia used to court collectors, one line of a Noël Coward quote ("If you're a star you should behave like one") and scrawled my name, number, and magazine affiliation at the bottom of the page, sending it to his personal publicist. I didn't know if it was the note or the persistence that did it, but I got an email from the Playwright himself, gravely agreeing, for the first time, to sit for an interview.

The Playwright suggested I come to a table read, and that we take it from there. A sterile room, a ring of folding chairs flanked by Aquafina bottles. An assistant handed me a copy of the script and the Playwright barely acknowledged me. True film stars had been cast as two of the three leads, the woman's angular features even more architectural off-screen, the male actor's laugh stentorian—I first heard it after he made a joke about the fifteen-minute scene that he and the third main character, played by a quiet young woman not yet graduated from Juilliard, would execute in the nude.

Afterward, The Playwright came over as if noticing me for the first time. "Let's do this," he said, shrugging on a weathered bomber jacket. He was a decade older than me, in his late thirties. As we talked, I clutched my digital recorder in one hand and he guided us downtown, pointing out the café on Jane Street where he said he'd written most of the play over one fevered week.

"Have you been to Forlini's, Sal?" he asked as we strolled through Washington Square Park in the fading light. My name in his mouth, gruff and charming, sent a zing through my body. No, I had not been to Forlini's.

Over my gnocchi, his veal scallopine, and a bottle of red, he showed me a picture of his ex on his phone; she had left him for a job in France. "Better to have loved and lost," he said. "Everything I make, I make for her." He'd gone to school for studio art, and when I asked whether he'd ever written anything else, he shook his head. His mouth was full, and he chewed and took a sip of water. "I never thought writing was my medium. This just came to me." He talked about how, as a teenager, he'd witnessed the death of a friend, which for complicated reasons led to an estrangement from his parents. By college, he no longer shared their last name. He was private, kept to himself. Still, at the end of the night he wrote his cell number on a cloth napkin. "If you need anything else," he said.

I interviewed the electronic musician who scored the play, the two famous actors, and the director of the theater, who all said variations of, "He is amazing and brilliant and deeply *about the process*." His college thesis advisor took a moment to place him—it had been some fifteen years—but said she wasn't surprised that he'd switched disciplines, because he was talkative in class and his sculptural work lacked originality. My emails to the ex-girlfriend went unanswered but, after a follow-up call with the Playwright, he forwarded me a message from her: "You know how happy I am about your success, but the relationship is still too raw, please ask the writer not to contact me again." The piece was due out in May to coincide with the opening of his show. I was proud of it, and of the way I believed I had captured his personhood but also his work, and how the two spoke to larger questions of art and art-making and the world writ large. Watching a preview of the play a few weeks before opening night, I felt so invested that I had to remind myself I hadn't, in fact, been involved in its creation.

I found Martin's story soon after closing the profile, and it proved a diverting rabbit hole as I waited for my piece to come out. I ordered Martin's other novels, *A Gilded Age* and *Back Again*, and was toying with the idea of pitching a story about him when the Playwright piece posted online. I sent a link to my parents (Mom: "Fascinating. Have you considered exploring the decades-long Republican siege on arts education and funding in America?"; Dad: "Great, sweetie, can't wait to read!") and settled in to watch the metrics site that catalogued page views, social media shares, and time spent reading.

"You're going to drive yourself bonkers," Hugh said that evening as he stretched on a yoga mat, grunting annoyingly to reach toward his toes. He played soccer on Saturday mornings. "The numbers don't matter."

"Are you kidding?" Watching him stretch made me self-conscious of my own gargoyle posture, and I straightened my back. "When you were running the marathon all you talked about was shaving off minutes. Page views are my time-per-mile. Numbers do matter."

"That's not the same," he said, and started talking about the difference between what is (physical performance) and isn't (the decisions of others) under our own personal control. I turned back to my screen. On the metrics site, residing well below a piece about Donald Trump's most recent tweet and one about a starlet's see-through dress, my article's page views went up in tiny increments, and something inside me deflated.

———

OVER THE NEXT week I wrote a new pitch for my editor: a posthumous profile of Martin Scott Keller that wove in my uncanny experience of seeing myself in his fiction. The limits of imagination. The fluid boundaries of art.

"It's interesting," my editor wrote back, "but since he's not a household name, without a contemporary peg or interview I don't know if there's a *there* there. Perhaps an essay for a women's mag?"

I was irritated but not devastated; there were other editors, other magazines. But then the next day *New York* magazine published their own piece about the Playwright.

I was walking in Prospect Park when a link to the piece showed up in my Twitter feed. I stopped on the path, only vaguely aware of disrupting the flow of leashed poodles and beer-schlepping new dads as I shielded the phone screen from the sun's glare—the better to take in the long inventory of the Playwright's personal and professional wrongdoings. He funded his own sculpture show with trust fund money, he mistreated assistants and old colleagues. The ex-girlfriend in France said he'd stalked her. There was no record of his dead friend. His parents, far from the psychologically damaging people he'd made them out to be, were a pleasant retired couple living in Connecticut; they'd paid for his education, and for the Massachusetts cabin where sources said he'd actually written the play—a play, it turned out, that bore more than a passing resemblance to a short film by a former classmate. There was more than cursory evidence to suggest that he had once shit on his MFA thesis advisor's swivel chair.

Then I came to the section, complete with an introductory deep-breath-in editorial line break, that specifically addressed my profile. There was my name, there were the quotes from my piece, there were the condemnations: "It is difficult to imagine how any journalist and her editorial machine could have been deceived so thoroughly by a man who, for the last decade, has been leaving a trail of nuclear breadcrumbs." The reason there had not been a profile of the Playwright before, the writer suggested, was not because the Playwright was so elusive, but because his agent had kept him from sitting for interviews, worried that his past might out. The PO box I had believed belonged to his personal publicist was registered in the Playwright's own name.

Over the next day and a half (punctuated by bouts of comforting attempts by Hugh and Georgia) I waited for a What the Fuck call from my editor, a passive-aggressive chewing out full of weighty silences that I would fill with apologies, after which he would tell me not to worry, because how could I have known.

As I scrolled listlessly through Twitter takes, my editor's number did indeed appear on my phone screen. It was Wednesday. Hugh, whose start-up offered the perk of unlimited work-from-home time, had escaped my moping by going into the office, and I was prostrate on the couch wearing the sweatpants I'd slept in. "I'll cut right to the chase," said my editor, for whom I had once purchased Imodium. "I'm sure I don't need to tell you what a headache the last day has been. Endless meetings with legal, the head honcho, you name it. The timing couldn't be worse given the way things are going. Tightened belts, shoestrings, candles burnt on all ends, you know the drill. You'll be getting official language from HR soon but I want to reiterate that you're not getting *fired*, we're not severing the relationship, but the upshot is that, for now, it's best that you and the magazine part ways, financially and contractually speaking. I'm sorry, Sal." I said that I understood. I laughed feebly at his feeble joke about how he was sure he'd see me at the unemployment office soon. I watched the shadows of the furniture move across the floor.

"I got fired," I said flatly when Hugh arrived home.

"You're kidding." He looked tired, but he sat next to me on the couch and pulled me into a hug. "I'm so sorry."

"What do I do now?" I said.

"Maybe," he said after a loaded hesitation, "this is a blessing in disguise."

I didn't say anything.

"Maybe the magazine was a crutch. Maybe now you can figure out exactly what you want to do."

"No, Hugh," I said slowly. "*This* is what I wanted to do. This was the plum setup. Now, forever, I'll be persona non grata."

"It was just a mistake." He stood up. "You'll feel better after you eat something. Salmon? Pasta with shrimp? Work isn't everything."

You can say that because you gave up on what you wanted, I wanted to say. *You sold out.* "I'm not hungry," I said instead, though I was.

"Then it'll be there if you want it later," he said in a pleasant voice that made my head feel like it was going to explode.

"I won't."

They never felt good, these quick, miserly responses that came easier than what I actually wanted to express: that I didn't understand why his emotions seemed to become less complicated over the years while mine became more so; that he was, I worried, someone who tended toward the path of least resistance. We had gotten together in college, broke up when he graduated, and started dating again at the end of my first year in New York. Just as it had been easier to give up painting in favor of graphic design, maybe he found it less difficult to continue the inertia of our relationship than end it. Maybe this bothered me because I suspected I did, too.

When I got into bed that night, hungry, he was already asleep. I wanted to wake him up, apologize, bury my face in his neck, have sex, anything. Instead, I lay on my back staring at the ceiling I couldn't see.

THREE

The next morning, following an encouraging text from Georgia (good deployment of Fitzgerald's Owl Eyes quote about sobering up in a library), I rode the train into Manhattan and opened my laptop in the Rose Reading Room. Tweets about the Playwright had given way to a backlash essay about plagiarism versus artistic influence, and another about the danger of judging artists' behavior rather than their art. The online discourse had since veered into arguments about Picasso and Woody Allen and Charles Manson, and no longer had anything to do with me. I should have been relieved and I suppose in some ways I was, but there was something disgruntling about the ease with which everyone else had moved on, the members of a raucous parade too caught up in the pleasure of their own noise to notice the body—mine! my body!—trampled behind them.

I typed Martin Keller's name into the search bar and waited for the results to load, worried, as I always was, I would find a recently published, revelatory article about him; that someone would get to him before I could. Small chance, given that his memory appeared to be languishing in semi-obscurity, but I've never known logic to drive anxiety. I pulled the dog-eared copy of *The Paris Review* from my tote bag and turned to the story out of habit before rifling backward through the pages. Interview. Essay. Masthead. There they were, the last great hope; I don't know why I didn't think of it before, except that everything is obvious once it's been done. I emailed the fiction editor, copying the associate editor and the intern general account. "I'd love to learn more about the story you published by Martin Scott Keller," I wrote. "I have some funny background information, if it's of interest." *Funny background information.* I cringed as soon as I sent it, the words glaring from the screen.

Against the odds, a response arrived a few minutes later. "Hi Sal," the associate editor, named Anna, wrote back. "It's lovely to hear from you. I'm so glad you enjoyed Martin's story and I'd be happy to speak further about the genesis of the piece. Martin was my professor, so it's close to my heart." In her social media photos she was gaunt, with huge features set on a tiny head. I chewed the thick skin beside my thumbnail: Had he taught every waifish literary woman on the island of Manhattan? I snapped the laptop shut. But once in the hallway, I tapped the number in Anna's email signature into my phone and, pushing through the heavy revolving doors, placed the call.

———

ANNA SOUNDED FIRST confused, then reluctant, then intrigued, and twenty minutes later I was waiting for her at an over-occupied coffee shop near her office, where she said she'd meet me as soon as she could get away from her desk. It was a coffee shop in name only, as the only drinks on the menu were coffee alternatives—astragalus latte, cinnamon turmeric cappuccino, reishi mushroom tonic. I ordered the turmeric and, not drinking it, settled into a cramped table in the back. I scanned an email from my mom about a lost humpback whale starving to death in the Mediterranean. When Anna arrived, her dark hair pulled back in a clean, tight bun, I held up my hand.

"Sorry I'm late," she said, somehow looming over the table, though she couldn't have been much taller than five feet. "We're about to have a changing of the guard. Minor chaos." She said this as if I should know what she was talking about, and I did; the previous editor's resignation amid accusations of sexual wrongdoing had sustained media gossip for months.

"Can I get you anything?" I asked, half standing.

"No, no." She pushed up the sleeves of her unreasonably white button-down. "I put in my order on the way over."

While she was at the counter I found myself tapping my fingers on the table like a cartoon character at a typewriter. I flattened my fingers against the cool wood. Momentarily, Anna returned with a mug full of dark liquid.

"Reishi?"

"What?" She looked alarmed. "Oh. No. They have coffee, you just have to ask." She glanced at my drink and I wrapped my hands around it as though I might make it disappear. "So."

"Yes," I said. "The excerpt. I assume his agent sent it to you, after he . . . ?"

"Died? No. It's funny. Well, not funny. More sad." She had a darting way of talking, pausing between some words and then speeding through the rest of the sentence, as though speaking over a glitchy internet connection. "He'd sent it himself, ages ago, maybe eight months before his death. 'If this interests you, please call me and we'll discuss,' he wrote, or something to that effect. But I sat on it—it's so hard to tell what's good when it's your former teacher, and I had just gotten the job a couple months before—and then everything happened at work, and Martin died. I brought it up in passing to a friend who works at the *New York Review of Books*, and he said they'd been considering reissuing his first novel, *Evergreen*. It was a big cult favorite in the seventies, but they ended up doing an old Dorothy Hughes instead. Anyway, I contacted his wife, Moira, and she put me in touch with a lawyer and it all went through him. I didn't do much editing. It felt sort of nonconsensual, you know?" She took a gulp of her coffee, grimaced. "So, you think it's about the night you met him?"

"Six years ago." She listened as I filled in the congruences I'd left out on the phone: the muses, the hair clip.

"It certainly sounds like the premise of the story," she said when I came to my inelegant finish, less concluding the anecdote than letting it fall with a splat between us. "I have no idea what his influences were, if that's what you were hoping to find out from me. We didn't ever get to talk about it. I screened his calls. I feel horrible about that now, obviously."

"And he just sent you the excerpt, not the whole manuscript?"

"Maybe that's what he wanted to talk to me about. Gosh, the regrets. If only I'd gotten back to him sooner. If only, if only. Makes you want to be in touch with everyone constantly, doesn't it? You always think you have more time with people than you do. My grandparents, my parents' friends, all these writers and artists. They seem so permanent, until they're not." She threaded her fingers together as if in prayer and rested her chin on them. Her hands were small, like a child's. "Listen. I'm not being totally straight with you."

Involuntarily, I stopped breathing. "Oh?" I whispered.

"I don't know if I would have responded to your email if I hadn't recognized your name, from, ah . . ." She pursed her lips and waved her hand as though clearing dust from the air. "Your troubles. Everyone in the office was talking about that story, and then you emailed me out of the blue. It wasn't schadenfreude, that's not the right word. Rubbernecking, maybe."

"Oh," I said again.

"And now I don't know why I told you that." To her credit, she had begun working a strand of hair out of place in discomfort. "I'm bad at false pretenses. I can't ever ignore the elephant in the room. I thought you'd be—I don't know, less hinged. But having that kind of thing happen with a story is everyone's worst nightmare. I hope your editor's backing you up on it."

"Yeah." I cleared my throat, pieces of dry wood knocking together. "I mean, no. He's not."

"Shit, Sal. I'm sorry."

I have a soft spot for people who use my name in conversation; maybe everyone does. "It's fine," I said, squinting over her left shoulder. "I think it's probably why I'm so obsessed about this Martin thing, though. Distraction."

"I probably shouldn't do this, but you know Moira? Martin's wife? I have her number." She blinked hard. "If you call, you didn't get it from me."

———

RUMBLING BACK TO Brooklyn on the 2 train, I tried to imagine myself as the person Martin Scott Keller had found so fascinating. "She's wise beyond her years," he'd written in the story. There was a nasty pinching sensation building behind the bridge of my nose. Too little sleep over the last few days, too much to drink of not the right kind of liquid. But today: progress. Beside me, a woman workshopped a text on her phone. "It was really nice meeting you yesterday," she wrote, and then deleted "really" and added, "Planning on starting *The Sopranos* tonight! Will give you a full report." I wanted to tell her that intimating her Friday night would be spent alone streaming early prestige television wasn't particularly alluring. How lucky I was, to no longer agonize over those kinds of texts. I thought of Hugh and felt contrite. I stopped at the market outside our station to pick up parmesan, shallots, the expensive fettuccine sold in a tiny burlap bag—he'd like cooking dinner together, and afterward we could go for a walk. In my head, my mother told me grocery shopping for a man was retrogressive, and in my head I argued back that partnership wasn't a power struggle, sort of believing it.

I could hear voices coming from our apartment before my key was in the lock. "Sally!" a woman called as I pushed open the door. And because there was only one person in Brooklyn who called me that, dread pushed in, too.

Hugh was canted back against the kitchen counter, a bottle of beer in his hand. Bonnie, his former colleague, turned hookup, turned pal, was across from him, leaning her elbows on the kitchen island. They both had the kind of good looks people call interesting, and mean it positively. Hugh was lanky, with thick lashes that made his French grandmother bemoan he wasn't a girl. Bonnie had sharp, mannish features and wiry muscles, like an eighties fashion model. Two years ago she had left her job in PR to become a spinning instructor.

"How are you?" She beamed at me as though she lived there with Hugh and I were a welcome visitor. "It's been a hundred years."

"Has it?" I gave her a one-armed hug. "Feels like just yesterday."

Over her shoulder, Hugh frowned at me. He knew I was jealous of Bonnie and he thought jealousy was a sign of insecurity, which it obviously was. I will say that my Bonnie-induced self-doubt was not without reason, given the specifics of our braided timeline. Hugh and I started dating at the beginning of my sophomore and his junior year and broke up when he graduated. He and Bonnie met and "had a thing" sometime between our breakup and when we got back together two years later. I'd once made the mistake of badgering him into telling me why things had ended between them. "She never wanted anything serious," he'd said, finally. "At some point the sex just stopped."

"I'm meeting people for burgers down the street," Bonnie said. "I was just telling Hugh that you guys should come." I imagined them naked, Bonnie in cow pose, Hugh palming her hips.

"I don't know," I said deliberately, making wide eyes at Hugh that I hoped telepathed how much I didn't want to go out. "It wasn't the best week. I'm pretty tired, I thought we could make dinner here." I held up the bag of groceries.

"No! Come out, it'll be fun. Drink the pain away!" Bonnie, who'd never consumed more than a single Corona Light in my presence, frequently referenced her wild college years and pushed shots on everyone around her. She took my hand and swung it like a jump rope.

An hour later I'd summoned Georgia and her boyfriend, Michael, to run interference, and we'd all installed ourselves at a noisy, homey place nearby, a couple baskets of tater tots dotting the long wooden table and everyone glowing in the light from the battery-operated tea candles. Hugh was tipsy and happy, his palm on my thigh. It

became evident that Bonnie was interested in one of the guys we'd
met there, which should have effectively defanged her; instead,
her flirting had ballooned to envelop anyone she interacted with,
including Hugh, who started laughing so hard at something she'd
said that I thought his convulsions might cause him to hit his head
on the table.

Georgia and I had fallen into our favorite conversational mode, a
rapid regurgitation of our friendship highlight reel. Depending on our
audience, this could either charm or irritate. Michael, six years older
and enamored of Georgia, fell into the former category. Hugh, who
had already heard or experienced firsthand our complete repertoire,
tended toward the latter.

"Remember when our downstairs neighbor in Bushwick knocked
on our door holding a dead rat by its tail . . ."

"Remember when we spent the weekend on the Cape and your
father couldn't figure out why his scotch was so weak . . ."

"Remember when you got chlamydia and . . ." (Me: "Georgia!"
Georgia: "Don't be bourgeois, it's just chlamydia.")

"Do you remember when we were in that class together on truth and
narrative?" Georgia said, and though I nodded, I wasn't sure where she
was headed with this one. "About how facts are disseminated through
art and media. Remember when we were watching the Guzmán movie?
Nostalgia for the Light." She turned to Michael. "We should watch it
together. It's a documentary about widows of Pinochet's disappeared
victims looking for the bones of their loved ones in the Atacama Desert, where a concentration camp once stood. But it's also the darkest,
driest place on earth, which means it's great for observing the stars.

So you have these women digging in the dirt together, juxtaposed with yawning images of, like, the Andromeda Galaxy."

"I do remember this," I said. "You started crying."

"Sobbing," she said. "Snot bubbles, red-faced, hyperventilation. And our professor brings the lights up at the end and says to me, 'You're feeling, not thinking. What are the narrative manipulations Guzmán used to elicit this reaction from you?' And of course that set me off even more. He kept saying, 'Think, Georgia. Think. What is the film *doing*?' And then Sal points at me and says, '*This* is what it's doing!' and shuttles me off to the bathroom. That was when I knew I loved you."

I stuck my lip out. "Oh, Georgia."

"But," she said, "the professor was right. I did need to learn how to consume art critically."

"And look at you now, my dispassionate critical thinker," Michael said fondly. "You two are sweet."

"We are." Georgia fed him a tater tot and turned back to me. "How're you holding up this week, my sweet little waltz?"

"Ha ha," I said. "I actually met the editor who ran Martin's story today."

"You didn't tell me that," Hugh said, tuning back in and putting a hand on the back of my neck.

I glanced pointedly at Bonnie. "I didn't have time."

"Sal thinks her professor wrote a story about her," he said for her benefit.

"You know he wasn't my professor, just a professor."

"It's lucky he's dead. I probably couldn't beat up an octogenarian. Morally."

I jerked my body out from under his hand. "Never mind."

His eyebrows and mouth crinkled toward each other and we both studiously shifted our bodies in opposite directions. A barback with a nose ring came by to collect our empty glasses and said I looked like I needed a drink; eyes batting, I concurred.

The evening progressed. Georgia leaned her head on my shoulder and Michael took a picture of us. I ignored Hugh. Everything became progressively more wonderful. At some point I befriended a woman named Chelsea, who had just turned forty. She wore a cockeyed pink crown that read BIRTHDAY PRINCESS, and we engaged the barback in a game of Never Have I Ever. Later, I saw Bonnie leave, her conquest trailing behind her.

Hugh appeared soon after. Chelsea and I were shimmying in front of the jukebox to "Dancing Queen," while Georgia, for reasons that made sense at the time, pretended to be an Australian music video director. "Thet's right loidies, move those heeps."

"Want to head out?" Hugh said over the noise.

I shook my head, still dancing.

He eyed the IPA in my hand. "How many have you had?"

"Too busy mooning over your ex to count my drinks?"

"Is there something you want to say? You've been at me for weeks. Just say it."

"Nope, I got nothing." I started to walk away from him, but he grabbed my wrist, maybe harder than he'd meant to. I wheeled around, furious.

"When did you get so boring?" I said. "When did you stop wanting to make things? You're not who I signed up for." I felt uncharacteristically invincible, his hold on me just cause for unleashing my pent-up angst.

"Nice, Sal."

"I mean it," I said, aware that my voice was loud, but not lowering it. "Why did you stop painting? We said we were going to do all these things together. Make art. At least I'm trying."

"Yeah," he said, dropping my wrist. "That's working out well for you."

I was too stunned to respond. He gave me a curt nod and made his way toward the front door. Chelsea hooted as he left.

Georgia had shed her affect and was looking on with concern. "What was that?"

"Fuck men, man!" Chelsea said happily.

"Thank you, I think enough." Georgia hunched to look at me. "Are you okay?" I felt my face contort into a position akin to the one it held pre-sneeze. "That's a no, then."

—————

MY PHONE WAS dead. My head was leaden. I was wearing the clothes I'd gone to the bar in, minus my jeans. With minor panic I took in Hugh's empty side of the bed, cool and rumpled. His duffel bag was absent from the hall closet; he had gone to his Saturday soccer game. When my phone charged up and turned on, it did not contain a text from him.

After the argument, the night had dissolved into a yawn of darkness. Vaguely, I remembered sitting between Georgia and Michael at the bar, trying to explain that my relationship with Hugh was split into two parts. "There was the college part and the real-life part," I recalled saying. The college part had been intense because I'd spent so much time with him and his family right away, on most holidays driving to their home outside of Boston rather than flying back to my mom's place in Telluride or my dad's apartment in Denver, both of which depressed me in different ways. "The second part, the real part," I told them, "I didn't choose. I was seeing other people after he dumped me. I was totally fine. And then he decided he wanted to get back together, and he swooped back in and got what he wanted. Relationships are ridiculous," I said gloomily as Michael laid a fatherly hand on my shoulder. "Except yours. You guys are perfect."

I'd forgotten buying a bus ticket to Linden, Martin's town, until I saw the receipt at the top of my in-box. "I'm going to go upstate," I'd said to the barback, who had at some point become a member of my audience. "I'm going to go talk to Martin's widow and I am going to see what he wrote about me in the rest of his book."

"Amen," he said, and slid me a shot.

I poured myself a glass of water from the carafe Hugh kept in the fridge, hoping it might stave off my impending hangover and accompanying existential dread.

From the kitchen window, I watched the cotton fluff of a dog who lived downstairs stand off against a squirrel. My mind did some mental gymnastics, trying to square what I knew I'd yelled at Hugh with the belief that I couldn't possibly have said those things. I sipped my water.

———

WHEN HE ARRIVED home, I decided, I would surprise him with a second bus ticket and an apology trip upstate. I'd book us a place for a night or two; he could go for a hike while I tracked down Martin's widow, and that evening we would eat dinner at an overpriced wine bar. I hadn't meant what I said, not really. I had just been drunk. The quaint college town (I assumed) would remind us of the start of our relationship; the trip would jolt me out of my funk. And just maybe it would be the start of something else, too. In the search for Martin's manuscript, I'd find a story so good people would take photos of certain paragraphs to post on Instagram, and email the story link to their friends. Maneuvering tabs on my phone with one hand, I felt clear, buoyant. I tapped in my credit card information and another ticket appeared in my in-box.

It was when I turned away from the fridge to pull a box of cereal from the cabinet that I saw the note. It was propped up on the kitchen counter, folded like a dinner place card. *I'm going to Boston*, Hugh had written neatly. *I'll be back two weeks from today. I don't think we should be in contact. We both need time to think.*

A cool vibration shot down the middle of my body, as though the water had solidified into ice. Had our argument prompted this, or was there something more? I had a sudden memory of the barback's face close to mine, but I pushed that away—surely nothing had happened, with Georgia there to stop it. (And surely if anything had happened, Hugh couldn't have found out so quickly.) I thought I remembered the backseat of a car, Georgia shutting the door, but I couldn't be sure. It was possible I'd been noisy coming home, or continued our fight once I'd found Hugh in bed, or waiting up for me. I let out a creaky, involuntary moan.

"Boston" meant his parents' house. Having *time to think* was not Hugh's idea. Someone, his mother probably, or Bonnie, had coached him. *She seems unstable right now*, I imagined Bonnie saying; she of the daily affirmations, the toned upper arms. *Maybe you just need a little break.* And his mother—I suspected she thought I wasn't quite good enough for him. Realizing he had harbored these feelings, meditating

on them for days, maybe longer—because who decided to leave for
two weeks after one drunken fight?—required a dizzying reordering
of what I'd believed to be the facts of our relationship. Hugh was not
supposed to airlift himself out of our life together. I was the one who'd
felt increasingly unsure about us. I was the one who daydreamed about
disappearing. If anyone left, it should have been me.

With a sudden mechanical calm I checked the schedule for the
bus to Linden. I gathered my laptop, a notebook, and my digital
voice recorder and stuffed them, along with a pair of shorts and a few
T-shirts, into one of the oversized canvas totes that my magazine—or
what had once been my magazine—gave away as a subscription gift. It
was early in the day but already warm. I felt suddenly festive, and dug
out a short-sleeved jumpsuit I hadn't worn for years. I thought about
writing my own note for Hugh to find, but realized with displeasure
that I'd be home at the apartment long before he would. I couldn't
afford two weeks away. I'd be home in two days.

A garbage truck hummed down the block, passed by a peloton of
neon cyclists. On the subway, a man stretched out across three seats,
his backpack below him. The car smelled sweetly sulfuric. A woman
sat at the other end, absentmindedly smoothing the braids of a little
girl asleep with her head on the woman's lap. With a few clicks on my
phone, I booked a small, dimly lit studio apartment in Linden for two
nights. Between Fourteenth and Thirty-Fourth Streets the car filled up
and a couple phones brayed an alarm: an alert for either a flash flood
or a missing child.

I bought an enormous water bottle from a vendor outside Port
Authority and called Georgia from the bus line.

"Good," she said, over a whirring in the background. The gym. "You're alive."

I wondered whether I should try to collect details about the night before. It might clear up the Hugh question—besides which, hearing secondhand about my drunken behavior often held a morbid fascination for me, for the same nebulous reasons I used to make my parents tell and retell stories about my sleepwalking as a child. That morning, though, it seemed wise to move forward rather than gaze into the murky past. "I'm going," I said. "To Linden. I'm going to meet the widow."

"You're not. Did you call her this morning? It's not even nine—"

"I'll call on the way." As I said it, the bus heaved into place at the curb. "I booked a studio for two nights. Pretty cheap."

"Oh, Sal."

Though I'd seen her hours before, I missed her then, missed our messy apartments in Vermont and Greenpoint and Bushwick. There was a porousness to our relationship. She, more than anyone else I knew, had shaped me, introducing me to important post-adolescent stalwarts: Georges Méliès's *Le Voyage dans la Lune*, Brazilian waxes, social cocaine use. I had rubbed her back while she cried after her mother had said with censorious malice that she was "looking healthy." We had once told each other about the sex we were having with the detailed remove of a sociology paper—*and then the naked human male tapped his penis and suggested I call it Big Boy*—but no longer, either because the sex had ceased to be worthy of narrative, or because loyalty to our partners' privacy trumped whatever glee we'd derive from the telling. Now there were whole days, whole weeks, in which she existed entirely separately from me. Terrible.

"You should come with me."

"Yeah, sure."

"I mean it," I said. "Let's have an adventure upstate. I have two bus tickets. I don't have to get on this one."

"I have work and, you know, life. Why do you have two tickets? Where's Hugh?" she asked, suspicious.

I didn't want to enshrine Hugh's actions in words, so I didn't say anything, just stepped forward in line.

"Sal," said Georgia. "What happened to Hugh?"

"I mean, I didn't kill him." The woman in front of me turned, critical. I smiled at her. "Hugh left. To his parents' house." I climbed up into the bus and its stale, circulated air, lowering my voice as I headed for the empty seats in the back. "I don't want to talk about it."

"Okay." I could picture Georgia stretching beside the elliptical, a white towel draped around her neck. "I just think—"

"I love you and I am grateful for your infinite wisdom, but they're about to check tickets," I lied, cutting her off before she could shoot down my hot-air balloon. "I have to go."

"Let's get dinner when you're back. That's a bribe. You have to come back."

"Yes, Mom."

I tapped out an email, writing fast and pressing send before I could edit it into oblivion. "Hi Anna, I'm on my way to meet Moira Keller and, hopefully, find out more about the book. Any chance I can spin this into a piece for you? If it's of interest I'll send along a detailed pitch. If you get pushback given my recent issues, tell them I said, 'fool me once . . .'?"

In novels and movies and magazine articles, people were always showing up on other people's doorsteps unannounced and receiving transformative life experiences in return, so for a while I entertained a fantasy that this was what I'd do with Moira. Still, I had a difficult time imagining what might happen past ringing the bell. I could say I was a devoted fan writing a piece about his life and work. More or less true. It was possible Moira would turn me away, but I reminded myself how often people are naively willing, even eager, to talk about themselves, the Playwright a case in point.

As the bus purred out of midtown my face warmed in the reflected glare off the high-rises. I was a kid, falling asleep in the backseat of my mom's station wagon as she drove me to visit my dad, the car smelling of eucalyptus oil. Fiona Apple was in the tape player. We were moving forward, and everything was fine.

––––––

I WOKE UP bleary an hour later, my forehead slick, the placeless smear of strip malls and truck stops and highway streaking past. Some of the spontaneous elation had sloughed away as I slept, replaced by queasy anxiety and the image of the barback's face from the night before. I drank too fast from my water bottle.

The romance of wandering around Linden asking townspeople if they knew where Moira Keller lived had worn off, too. I had her number saved in my phone—first name, Moira; last name, Martin Widow—and I scratched a fingernail over the seat fabric as I waited for the call to connect.

A woman, younger-sounding than I'd expected, picked up after the third ring. "Hello?"

"Hello, hi." I pressed a finger into the ear not pressed to the phone. "Is this Moira?"

"Who's speaking?"

"This is Sal Cannon. I'm a journalist. I was hoping to speak to you about Mr. Keller's work. I was only lucky enough to meet him once, but I love his novels, and I'd like—"

"I'm not Moira. One second." The woman must have cupped her hand over the receiver, because when she called, "Mom, someone's on the phone," it sounded like her voice was coming from inside a seashell. There was a shuffling as the receiver passed from hand to invisible hand.

"Hello?" The same inflection, two tones lower.

I ran through the spiel again. "I'm sorry for the cold call. It's just that I'm going to be coming through Linden this weekend. And I think he was underappreciated." I squeezed my eyes shut.

"He'd likely agree with you," she said. "And you're writing this for what outlet?"

"I'm—" A Subaru trundled past, a dog's nose pressed wetly to the window. "I'm independent."

The following pause was long enough that I felt my eyebrows rising as though someone were watching me wait for an answer. I could hear the other woman, her daughter, say something in the background.

"I don't think so," Moira said, "I'm sorry." And then the line went dead.

I redialed the number, but it rang through to voice mail. "You've reached the Keller residence," a voice, *his* voice, rumbled down the line. Through my shock, I considered hanging up and calling back just to record the message, but instead I left my name and number and said

I'd be around for two days, if she changed her mind. I thought about the money I'd wasted on the bus fare, the nonrefundable nights at the apartment, the time I could've spent writing or cleaning or trying to get hold of Hugh.

My body felt fluid, as though its disparate parts, right down to its atoms, were at risk of flying apart. I closed my eyes and imagined walking into the ocean until my feet didn't touch the sand below. The slow lift of my body into horizontal, the bite of the sea salt in my nose and throat, an endless blue.

I almost slept through my stop, an Amtrak station in a brown and gray city two hours north of the only city in New York State that mattered. It was early in the afternoon, but it felt like I'd been traveling for days as I waited for the Linden College shuttle under a plexiglass shelter with three obvious college students and a professorial woman who told me, when I asked how long to Linden town, that she'd let me know when to get off. After another half-hour ride on the fat white bus, bumping down sun-dappled back roads through tunnels of trees, she turned in her seat and said, "This is you," and, two hours before I could let myself into the apartment I'd rented for the weekend, I found myself in the parking lot of a steepled white church.

The town was indistinguishable from so many eastern towns, with a wide Main Street and tidy storefronts—purveyors of stationery, secondhand books, tourist mugs, overpriced antiques, bath products arranged sparingly beside taxidermied birds and glittering displays of blue morpho butterflies. Weekenders in sundresses and linen shorts dotted the tables outside a coffee shop called the Beanery. A signpost with a spray of directions pointed to Linden College (1 mile) and the Catskills (60 miles) and New York City (152 miles) and Boston (170 miles). At one end of Main, a small park, and a playground with a tire swing painted to look like a pink pig.

It was too early to go to a bar, but the bar was open. It was a sticky, windowless Pabst-and-picklebacks kind of place called the Last Resort. I ordered french fries and, for the drama of it, a merlot, which arrived lukewarm and nauseatingly sweet, so I traded it for a sugar-free ginger ale. The back patio was surprisingly tranquil, with gingham umbrellas shading three picnic tables and a ginkgo tree in either corner. A man sat alone reading *The Information*, so naturally I began to picture our life together, and then I felt my phone vibrate in my bag. I imagined Hugh, a day into his self-enforced solitude, ready to discuss his feelings. I turned back to my fries and let the call buzz itself out.

It wasn't until I climbed the back stairs to the apartment I'd booked and took out my phone to find the door key code that I learned the missed call and accompanying voice mail were not from Hugh but from Moira.

FOUR

The thermometer in the kitchenette was already pushing eighty degrees by eleven the next morning, but the sky was an ominous whorl. What appeared on the map on my phone to be a pleasant walk to Moira's instead became a muggy trudge and then trot down a country road as the first raindrops speckled the asphalt. Moira's address was marked by three metal numbers nailed to a birch, and a winding driveway led to a wide clapboard farmhouse with a mossy roof. I took breaths timed to my footsteps to trick my nervous system into calming down, and by the time I reached the front porch I had bludgeoned my psyche into something of a dream state: I couldn't be anxious because this couldn't be real.

I hadn't thought much about Martin's widow as an actual person standing before me, but still, I was disappointed when she opened the door. She wore a sweatshirt that had once been black, now faded to gray and splotched with bleach stains. Thin sweatpants cinched at her ankles. Ratty red slippers from a Chinatown dollar bin, gold knots clipped to her earlobes. Dark eyes, wide lower lids, age spots high on her fawn-colored cheeks. A gray bob. She was so ordinary, this woman in the afternoon of her life.

She wasn't paying me much attention, either, as she held a cordless phone to one ear and pushed a fat, gray-faced basset hound back with the other hand. *Come in*, she mouthed. The entryway to the house opened into a dining room on the left with a kitchen beyond, a book-stuffed living room on the right, and a staircase up the center. Moira waved me toward the living room and then walked away: I was expected, but not highly anticipated or even welcome.

"I wish we could send this rain out your way," I heard her say over the sound of a tap, the click of a gas stove. She had music on, too; something classical, a violin. "But it's lucky you flew out yesterday instead of today." The room was painted goldenrod with creamy trim, and on the only wall not covered by bookshelves hung three small oil paintings of fruit. A squat couch and a pair of wing chairs flanked the coffee table. I felt underdressed in my damp shorts and T-shirt, a camp counselor's uniform. I started to sit down in one of the chairs but, worried about leaving a wet mark, stood back up.

This was Martin's house. It was here that he'd written so many thousands of words. This roof sheltered the boxes of his typed manuscripts, veined through with his handwritten scrawls or—I tried to imagine his writing—sandpiper footprints, pointy and black. The long-handled umbrella propped in the entryway was like one he'd described in "Such Are My Stars": a glossy black raven, newly stuffed. The room smelled like citrus and some not-quite-identifiable spice. Nutmeg, maybe. Unseasonable. I bent down to look through a bookcase below a picture window filled with pines and birches. Hawthorne, Goethe, Hemingway, William Dean Howells, George Eliot, Charles W. Chesnutt. And then a row of editions in German and Russian and French and Spanish, a row of M. S. Kellers as long as my arm and furred with dust. It wasn't only relief that I felt as I ran my finger over them, these pieces of proof that Martin was not just important in my mind but generally; something kicked below my abdomen, something carnal, desirous. He had sat in front of all that verdancy, reading, thinking. Perhaps even of me.

"Can I offer you anything to drink?" Moira called from the kitchen. I found her washing a colander of fat dark grapes. "Water?" She glanced at the clock on the wall, that googly-eyed black cat with a swinging tail. "Is it too early for wine? There's something civilized about a glass at lunch."

"I'm all right, thank you," I said.

"No? It's good stuff, my daughter brought a case from California."

"Just water is great."

"Just water. Well, I'm having a glass, I hope you don't mind." She tipped the fruit into a bowl and set it, and her wine, down on the kitchen table, pushing aside a neat pile of papers. "Grapes two ways. So. Who are you?"

She'd been so at-ease that I was startled by the need for an introduction. I sat down across from her. "Right. Salale Cannon," I said, pointing to myself—*I, Tarzan.* "I think I mentioned I met your husband, briefly, years ago. He and his writing made a huge impression on me." The basset hound wandered over and nosed at my feet as though trying to bury them. I reached to scratch behind her long, oily ears.

"That's Blue," Moira said. "Blue, be a lady."

"I've loved his work for a long time," I continued, my voice hitching on the lie.

She waited, the smallest smile tucked into the corner of her mouth.

"I hear he was a terrific teacher," I offered.

"He was. A talented critic, too." And then she waited once again for me to continue.

I was thrown off balance. I was used to circumscribed interviews, where the transaction was clear and the parameters delineated. By the time I arrived in front of the subject they had prepackaged answers. I practiced, too, to make sure I remembered essential avenues of conversation, and sometimes I had to cut rudely into their stories to say I knew the punch line already, I had heard it in a television interview last year, and were they ready, did they think, to talk about the reports that they had recently separated from their spouse?

But I hadn't prepared for Moira, and because she was waiting for me to explain what I wanted, and I was uncomfortable with the answer, I found myself babbling. "I don't want to write anything intrusive. I just want to give his story a home. *His* story, I mean, not his stories—those have homes."

"It's not considered facile these days to want to know all about what the writer ate and where he grew up and what time he went to the bathroom?"

"Biography is important," I said slowly, unused to having to defend what I was doing as I did it. "The translation of life into art. Mapping influences. Turning up Easter eggs, like that line in the new excerpt about how lonely the narrator feels around anyone except his basset hound." I motioned to Blue. "That's sweeter now."

"I didn't get you your water," Moira said, and walked to the sink, filling a glass and setting it down in front of me. "It was a poodle."

"Sorry?"

"The narrator's dog is a poodle."

"Are you—?" I had started to say, *Are you sure?* "I so clearly remember it being a hound dog."

"Martin once promised he'd never write about our life together. I didn't want him to translate us into art, as you put it. Some minor details worked their way in, I'm sure, but none of his published work was explicitly autobiographical. Down to the dog."

"I guess I'll have to reread," I said lightly. I took my voice recorder out of my pocket and placed it on the table. "This is such a pretty piece," I said, pointing to the air as though musical notes were dancing over us, and then, in a quick aside, "Do you mind if I start recording?"

She peered, birdlike, at the machine and then waved her hand, *Go ahead*. "This is '*Spiegel im Spiegel*,' " she said. "The piece. 'Mirror in Mirror.' You probably like it because you've heard it before, it's popular in the movies. It's comforting, the way the arpeggios lead up and down but always return to that A. My daughter, Caroline, is a pianist and she likes to collect pieces with a distinct home note. There's little tension, and yet one feels such a compulsion to hear what comes next."

I nodded, sliding the recorder out of her direct line of vision. "It's sort of like breathing." I sat back, watching her listen, the notes poignant over the patter of the rain. A person's face at rest is so rarely at rest; the muscles at the corners of Moira's eyes and mouth twitched. "Maybe you could tell me about Martin's routine? How he worked?"

"We're both early risers," Moira said. "Martin started his mornings with a short walk, then wrote until lunch. Throughout the years he changed his schedule to accommodate breakfasts for Caroline, taking her to school; particularly when I was teaching at Yale and staying in New Haven three days a week. Eventually, he had his own teaching schedule to manage as well."

"Was he working on *Evergreen* when you met him?" Beneath the table, Blue settled with her chin on my foot.

"A kernel of it. He was an editor at Grant, but he quit soon after we met. Perhaps prematurely."

"Had he always wanted to be a writer?"

She tipped her head minutely back and forth. "I'm not sure about always, but he was a reader for a long time. He left home—"

"Connecticut?"

"Yes. His father was never in the picture and his mother died when he was a boy. His aunt and uncle—or rather, his grandparents' cousins—took him in. They were dairy farmers. He still has the letters Ilse wrote him in the years after he moved to Manhattan. He was just sixteen, working bellboy and waiter jobs."

"He didn't go to college?"

"New York was his education. He read everything: *1984*, *Ulysses*, the *Odyssey*, the epic poets. That's how he got the publishing job. He was a server at Portofino, and he overheard one of the diners talking about *The Waste Land*. When he brought out their desserts, he mentioned an essay he was reading by Eliot on Joyce's mythic allusions. The man was impressed." She put a grape in her mouth and spoke around it. "That was Grant."

"Of Grant Aikens." I could imagine a winsome young Martin, his voice cutting through the noise of the restaurant.

She nodded. "At the time his roommate was a poet, his friends were poets, but all he wanted was to write novels. He got a few short stories published, things I think he'd hoped to turn into longer projects. But he had trouble sustaining the work, while working as well."

"And you met him when?"

"I was twenty years old. We ran into each other in the elevator at his office building. My father's literary agency was a few floors above Grant Aikens."

"Did he become Martin's agent?"

"No, no. Someone else at his agency did, though Martin switched representation twice. He was poached after *Evergreen* and then that man dropped him in the long stretch between his second and third books. A lot of heartbreak in Martin's line of work. Laying yourself out on the page. But I don't have to tell you that. You're a writer, too."

———

IT WAS EARLY evening by the time Moira next checked the clock. The rain had stopped, and through the window above the sink, left ajar, I could hear the crickets outside—*Crepitating*, I thought, the word arriving from a distant memory bank.

Moira's answers were dashed-off sketches of Martin that bloomed in my mind as she spoke about their early life together, jumping in time from their apartment in New York, when Caroline was a baby, back to Martin's life before she met him, his mother traveling from Germany to London and then crossing to America just a few months before Martin was born. His "brief marriage" to a former ballerina who worked at a department store. A friend, in his early twenties, an "interminable so-called poet" who did "'This or That' performances, standing on a stage, droning on, 'You are on a bridge: you must push off,' big pause, 'your wife or your infant.' Blow up the Mona Lisa or a security guard. A hundred strangers or your lover." Moira sounded so annoyed that it took a moment to realize this was something she hadn't actually experienced herself; it was one of Martin's stories, repeated so many times Moira had subsumed it.

It was all fascinating, but my tired mind became preoccupied with the ticking clock and the question of how many glasses of wine it would take to get Moira up to the present, to a place where I might probe her for information on Martin's final manuscript, and the possibility of reading it myself.

"You've let me talk the day away," Moira said, checking her wrist-watch as though to confirm what the cat said. She stood up from the table, and I felt like Scheherazade, searching desperately for something to keep her interested.

"How much of his writing did Martin share?" I asked, standing, too, and carrying the bowl, now empty except for a few stems. "While he was writing it, I mean?"

"He was private. I saw the finished work."

"You weren't the secretarial wife, then," I said, jokey.

She let several seconds elapse. "Martin often repurposed my own work for his writing. He squirreled things away—equations, theories, papers he tore out of journals—and jammed them into his stories. For instance, while going through some of Martin's files upstairs, I recently found a set of my own discarded notes on the Drake equation, something I'd jotted down at a conference, which he'd overwritten with his own notes for a scene."

"The Drake equation . . ."

Moira stretched her fingers against one another, tenting them and then collapsing the tent. Two gold bands, one thin and fitted and the other heavy, held on with a sizer, were hard against the soft wrinkles on her left hand, a blue sapphire on the right. "It calculates commu-nicative life in our universe."

I squinted. "I don't follow."

"How many other advanced civilizations might exist."

"Got it."

"Martin loved those big concepts. Schrödinger's cat, entanglement. He used them as a framework to prop up his plots. The multiverse was his longest-running fixation. You probably noticed him playing with that idea in the new story."

"I'm not sure if I did, actually."

"There are various theories of infinite universes, and therefore infinite versions of existence: one in which you came to my house and stole my dog, and one in which my dog scared you away. Hillary Clinton is president, it didn't rain today, Martin is alive." I searched her face for signs of mourning, but she was impassive. "That was the construct for this last piece, the idea that the young woman and the narrator lived multiple imagined existences. But maybe that only came across in later chapters."

An energy built behind my shoulders. "That manuscript—" I started to say, but Moira cut me off.

"Yes." She looked amused. "I have to correct myself. After years of abiding by my rule, Martin did write me into that story."

I thought of the narrator's unflattering portrayal of his relationship with his wife. "Does that upset you?" I asked gingerly.

"Well," Moira said, arch, "I suppose he should be allowed one major lapse."

"No, what I meant was, the wife is not exactly—"

Moira laughed, a quick huff of amusement. "No, no, no," she said. "I'm not the older woman. I'm the girl."

I thought she was making a joke I wasn't getting, but as she watched me curiously I became increasingly confused. "What?"

"How funny. I assumed you wanted to hear the real story behind the story but you were being too polite to ask." I scrambled to keep up. It felt as if my wish were being granted through a kaleidoscope. "Martin loved origin stories," Moira went on, "and ours especially. He showed admirable restraint, actually, refraining from using it for so long."

"I thought you said you met outside your father's office?"

"Yes, but Martin had a favorite story he told about our meeting years earlier. He came to one of my father's holiday parties. When we ran into each other later, he thought it was cosmic. A certain type of person would probably find it poetic that this was the last story he insisted on telling."

"I'm sorry," I said, my mouth dry. "I don't think I understand."

I listened dully as Moira settled in, more practiced than she'd been earlier in the day; it was a narrative she'd heard and told before. As she spoke, I felt myself nodding, a hollow smile tacked across my face. Martin had crashed the party with his roommate, Wesley, and the girl he was seeing at the time, and at some point he'd broken off from the fray and found twelve-year-old Moira upstairs in her bedroom. They'd talked, he'd been called back to the party, that was it. "I was used to men loping around the house," Moira said. "My father attracted a lot of young acolytes in those days. And I don't know if Martin would have thought much of the meeting, either, except when we ran into each other all those years later he said he thought I looked familiar. Eventually he figured out why. It's no surprise why the story held such appeal for him. Fate is validating."

I tried to hide my creeping panic, scrambling for something that might illuminate and smooth over the disparities between what I understood to be true, and what Moira did. "Do you think I could look at the whole manuscript?"

"I don't think so," she said, as though indulging a joke. "As I mentioned, Martin was very private about drafts in progress. Now, I don't want to push you out, but I do have some work to attend to. Did you get what you needed, or shall we find more time this week to talk? I could go through his office, collect what might be of interest?"

"Yes," I said, barely hearing her. "I mean, let me lay it all out, have a think. I'll call you, or if you change your mind about the draft . . . ?"

She walked me to the front door and I was standing on the porch, torn between feeling guilty for lying to her—why would I come back when she'd obliterated the point of my being there?—and crushed that she hadn't given me what I'd hoped for. She tucked her hands into the pockets of her sweatpants, her gray bob bright in the afternoon sun. She was fragile, alone in that house in the woods.

"Goodbye, Sal," she said.

———

I PLODDED BACK to the center of Linden. A couple kids in their late teens and early twenties, maybe students from Linden College working on research projects or summer jobs in the area, wandered down the sidewalks, their pale shadows stretched long. The air smelled of cut grass and waffle cones, too cheery for my mood.

I looked at my phone for the first time in hours and watched the notifications bubble up on my screen. A text from Georgia, checking in. One from my mom with a link to an article. A slew of emails, including one from Anna: "Hi Sal, still intrigued. Can't wait to hear how it goes. I could see it working for the Daily. Let's chat on Monday." The polarity between what I'd imagined I might get from this trip versus what actually happened made my head ache. I was too dejected to send the only viable response: that I'd been wrong, there was no story to tell. I imagined returning to Brooklyn, waiting to hear from Hugh. I had so wanted the story to be my deus ex machina, lifting me out of my own tired plot.

It was a Sunday, and felt like one: The shops shuttered long before the sky began to dim. The Beanery was dark, as was the ice-cream shop; I bought chips and hummus from an overpriced corner market just before it closed. The library, a churchlike building with a high gable, was lit up, but when I tried the front doors, they were locked.

A few broadsheets fluttered on a corkboard beside the door. It was *The Northern Light*, the local paper that had posted Martin's obituary. I was looking through the classified ads—goldendoodle puppies for sale, a lawn mower repair service—when the front door swung open. I yelped.

"I'm sorry," the man said as he emerged. He looked to be in his late fifties, with a red, spongy nose, a newsboy cap, and a yellow bow tie. "I didn't mean to startle you."

"No," I said, "it was my fault. I didn't know anyone was inside."

"Burning the afternoon oil," he said, turning to relock the door behind him and then motioning to the board. "I'm glad somebody's reading."

"You work at the paper?"

"You could say that. You could also say that I am the paper, the paper is me. Editor. Writer. Distributor, when the Balfour boy doesn't show up for his shift." He stuck out his hand. "Randall Jenkins. Randy."

"Sal," I said, entertained. "You didn't happen to write Martin Keller's obituary, then, did you?"

"I did. As stated, one-man operation here. That's one of the odd parts of the job; you end up being the first call to your own neighbors, acquaintances, the checkout girl at the supermarket, whoever's next of kin to the recently deceased. You build what you imagine to be an intimacy and then, come Tuesday, you're buying coconut milk and bananas, and the girl says, four dollars, please, no clue who you are. Strange, strange."

"You know Moira, you mean?"

"It's a small town. She and Martin did readings at the library on occasion. *The Northern Light* office is upstairs. She's a nice woman, smart, but no, I can't say I know her. Some people really open up during the interview. Talking about the loved one can be cathartic. But Moira couldn't wait to get off the phone. And not many others left alive to talk about him. Editor, deceased. Agent, deceased. No family, except a daughter in California, who declined to speak to me entirely. You're a fan?"

"Sort of," I said. "I'm a journalist, too. I'm writing a piece about Martin."

"Oh," he said, surprised. "Where for?"

Out of habit, I said the name of the publication where I used to work. "Or," I said uneasily, "maybe *The Paris Review*."

"Ah. *Magazine* journalism. I'm newspapers all the way back, myself. Chicago, then a stint in Manhattan. My beat might not be murders and muggings anymore, but it's no less interesting. You're in town for how long?"

"I head back to the city tomorrow."

"Pity," he said. "I'm running to an appointment, otherwise I'd scrounge through the archives. I'm sure I have things on the pair of them, over the years. Can't promise anything revelatory, but it might give you a bit of color. Judging from my own call with Moira, you're not going to get much from her."

"Mm," I said, thinking of the hours we'd just spent together. "Maybe I could come by tomorrow? Before my bus?"

"Closed tomorrow," he said. "The big man took a day off, and so do I. Just not the same ones."

"Right," I said. "We're ships passing in the night, I guess."

Walking back toward the apartment, I felt newly energized by Moira's reticence to talk to Randy but willingness to talk to me. I looped around the residential streets off Main, the houses set back at the ends of driveways on sloping half-acre lots, and larger. I pictured Moira and Martin as they must have been when they met: he in his twenties and unsure of himself, as unsure and out of place as I'd been the night I met him at the library; she a knobby-kneed preteen, her hair long and dark and tied in a bow. *Fate is validating.* That I'd found myself in his fiction had to mean something. The story may not be exactly what I was expecting, but surely there was a story.

If I were collecting my own fated signs pointing toward sticking around, I thought meeting Randy was as glaring as I'd get—until, that is, I arrived back at the apartment and found a zaftig woman in a pretty blue dress lifting a baby out of a car seat in the driveway. I introduced myself, and she asked if I was liking the area and whether I had everything I needed.

I told her I was, I did. "You probably have people arriving right after me, otherwise I'd be tempted to move in permanently."

"I don't know about permanently," she said, "but we had a cancellation, so nobody's coming until next weekend. Are you interested in extending your stay?" The baby rubbed its chubby white hand against her freckled neck and looked at me, disapproving.

Too quickly, eagerly, I said yes.

PART II

ONE

Martin

L
ike so many fairy tales, Martin and Moira's began in inclement
weather. The year, 1964. The place, Manhattan's Park Avenue. The
first downy flakes were just touching the streets when Martin surfaced
from the subway, pulling his too-thin coat closer to his body, shivering
not with cold but anticipation. He'd heard about the Christmas party
thrown by the eponymous head of Nelson Literary Services—how it
flooded Emmett Nelson's uptown apartment with clients, their editors
and publishers, Hollywood bigwigs, the occasional foreign beauty.
A starlet once attended with a gibbering capuchin in a Swarovski
crystal collar on her shoulder, and the annual event had catalyzed the
dissolution of at least two marriages when non-present wives heard,
through the liquid grapevine, of their husbands' libertine behavior,
unleashed by Mrs. Nelson's famous punch. That year, the girl Martin
was seeing had been invited; Martin and his roommate, Wesley, were
technically gate-crashing.

Under a streetlamp, Martin watched three big flakes dot his sleeve,
their crystalline edges defined in the glow. "Come on," said Wesley,
who had been making sotto voce comments on the train about not
caring to catch frostbite for the sake of social climbing, and whose
nose and cheeks burned a miserable red. The girl, a poet, grinned at
him through her chattering teeth.

By the time the three of them arrived at the party it was already
in full swing. Dizzy Gillespie played from the phonograph. In the

foyer and the high-ceilinged living room beyond it, guests clustered in
threes and fours and sixes, the women poured into satin dresses, the
men in suits and ties, and everyone, despite the chill outside, looking
overheated. Wesley nodded at the couple who'd come up in the elevator
with them. The man, some two decades younger than the woman, was
helping her out of a decadent fur.

"She keeps him," Wesley murmured to Martin, making his lord-
of-the-manor face.

Martin mirrored his expression. "As in . . . ?"

"You betcha."

Martin's date saw a friend across the room and disappeared into the
crowd, leaving him to peer, distracted, at the actual staircase looping
up to what could only be more rooms, more space, above them. Around
him swelled the sounds of wealth and intellect.

"We heard he took up with the child's Russian tutor."

"—it's being held on a lovely old estate modeled after a Virginia
tobacco plantation."

"I haven't read *The Group* yet. Don't tell her. Is she here?"

"—don't want to hear another word about that bleak woman or
that bleak trial."

The rooms were insulated by heavy built-in bookshelves; Martin
wanted to rub his face against all that cloth and paper, inhale its animal scent. By the fireplace, half a dozen men wearing an assortment
of plaid suits and tweed jackets and pressed white shirts spoke over
each other: the bookmakers themselves, he somehow knew, the writers
and editors and agents.

Wesley led him in the other direction, to the bar in the dining room,
where he procured a pair of alarmingly orange drinks before leading

Martin back through the gaping maw and to a girl Wes had known in college. "I can't stand Los Angeles in December. We always come back to the city for the holidays," she was saying, worrying the strand of garnets at her neck. "Christmas doesn't seem like Christmas if it's spent by a pool."

"I don't know," Wesley said, leaning past her to wipe a clear patch in the window's condensation, succeeding only in reflecting the party back at itself. "Bikinis and palm trees don't sound so bad right now. I almost lost my nose on the way over."

"Maybe they'll shut down the subways and we'll all get stuck here. Can you picture it?"

"Stranded on Park," Wesley said. "What *would* we all do to amuse ourselves?" The girl swatted him.

Martin eyed the crowd. Everyone knew someone, except for him. He was jealous of Wesley, jealous of the girl he'd come with. He was twenty-four years old and he knew no one, had done nothing. After a moment he realized the man holding court by the fireplace, arm slung across the mantel, was Emmett Nelson. The agent had a gravitational pull to him, a magnetism Martin was sure he'd feel even if he didn't know his reputation as a literary kingmaker. The men around him were mixed in age, though homogeneous in tone: an air of wealth or importance or both, simultaneously bored and amused. Wesley fit in, Martin thought, and tried to arrange his features in an expression that might convey similar comfort amid all this money and knowledge. He longed to join that circle of men. He couldn't stand to look at them.

"This drink is disgusting," he said to Wesley, who was telling the girl in a stage whisper about someone's affair. "I'm going to get some more."

After first meandering into the kitchen as though he'd done so on purpose, Martin found the room with the drinks and pointed out the punch to the man hired to serve it. "Another of those," he said, with authority. Then, embarrassed: "Thank you very much."

He recognized some of the faces around him from the society pages: a Black comic with watchful gray eyes, a gossip columnist with blue veins lacing her limbs. The woman caught him looking at her and broke away from her conversation, reaching an arm toward him like a fishing hook.

"Hello," she said. "And who are you?" Over the next decade he'd grow to expect and loathe those words for their presumption, as though he should know who the questioner was, that he should be the one explaining himself. He believed it was always women who asked, until a girlfriend pointed out to him that men did it, too, just not to other men.

"I'm Martin Keller," he said. "I'm a novelist."

"Oh? Would I have heard of your work?"

"I'm unpublished," he said, with reluctance, "but I've had a few things in—"

"Ah," she said, and her eyes drifted off his face.

"I mean," he said, "the book's taking longer to get off the ground. It's complex, and I want to—" She laid a hand on his arm, leaning in. Coyly, Martin ducked his head close, too.

"You'll have to excuse me," she whispered, and caught hold of a woman passing by.

Martin stared dully at the place where she had been standing. Someone knocked into him. His heart beat against his breastbone. The room was bright and hot; perspiration sprang up along his hairline and at the small of his back, and he could taste the punch, gone sour, climbing back up his throat. He thought he was hallucinating: his date was now in the center of the circle of men, right next to

Emmett; she tipped her head back in a full-throated laugh. It was too much. He found the bathroom tucked between the kitchen and dining room, but the doorknob didn't give when he rattled it. He emerged into what he thought would be the living room but found himself once more by the front door and the stairs leading to a dark hallway above. He took them two at a time, never more aware that his heart was a muscle.

This was better, up in the quiet. He found another bathroom, which glowed with a dim night-light in the shape of a mermaid. In the mirror, the ghostly light cast shadows under his eyes, his nose (the former too wide-set, the latter too narrow). He looked like a goat. He took a deep breath, leaning over to rest his hands on his knees. He thought he might feel better if he could vomit, but when he tried, all the prodding at the back of his throat produced were two abortive convulsions that filled his mouth with saliva and his eyes with tears. He spit and then urinated and felt better, and then splashed some cold water over his face and cupped some into his mouth and felt better still. "Hell," he said to his reflection. "What a night, eh? Oh yes. Martin Keller. You read it, did you? Kind of you to say. It was a favorite of mine, too."

He stepped back into the hallway, fighting the urge to lie down on the thick carpet and take a nap. Farther down the hall, a sliver of light spilled from one of the rooms.

The girl was sitting on the bed when he pushed open the door. Maybe thirteen or fourteen, shoeless. A full suitcase lay splayed on the floor in front of her.

"Hello," he said, feeling a frank, simple pleasure at watching her look up, see him.

"Who're you?" Her voice was lower than he expected, coming from her small, pale face.

"I'm one of your father's friends. I'm here for the party."

"I've never seen you before."

"I suppose I've never seen you before, either."

She pulled her head back in an equine scoff. "Are you lost?"

"I needed a break from the noise."

She stood, her thick wool skirt catching against the bed quilt, and, collecting an armful of folded clothes from the suitcase, padded over to her dresser.

"Are you coming back from a trip?" he asked.

"Semester just ended."

"Ship you off, do they?"

She saw he was joking, ignored the comment. "Are you just going to stand there?"

Martin thought about what this would look like, should anyone wander by—him silhouetted in the doorway, the barefoot girl unpacking her clothes. "Just for a minute," he said. "I need to catch my breath. I didn't know they had a daughter."

"They do."

"Why aren't you downstairs enjoying the festivities?"

"I was when it was all Dad's friends who I know. Then I got sent up."

He watched her make another trip to the suitcase and then the bureau and back. "Why don't you pull it over?" He walked over to the dresser, touching the tip of his pointer finger to a tiny glass deer, a long-handled mirror in burnished silver, an enamel pin in the shape of a flower. "If you move the suitcase over here, next to the bureau, you won't have to go back and forth."

"I'm fine, thank you."

"Are you going to work on books, like your father?"

"No."

"What would you like to be when you grow up, then? A princess, I bet."

"No."

"A farmer?"

She smiled with one part of her mouth, more a muscle tic than an emotion. "No."

"A sailor."

"Closer. But don't joke."

A large print displaying the phases of the moon hung above the bed, and in front of the big picture window perched a long-legged telescope.

"Astrologer," he said, and then laughed. "No, not that. Astronomer."

"Astronaut."

"I don't think they let girls do that."

"They'll have to. I'm learning the math and science. Mr. Dalton says that what we're doing with the physics is time and space travel itself. That we don't have to go to space to understand space. I'd like to, though." She examined a bug bite on her upper arm and scratched at it. "A librarian in Greece in 200 BC calculated the circumference of the earth. In 200 BC!"

"Who was that?"

"Eratosthenes."

"Eratos," he drew out the word. He was a little drunk.

"Every time you look at the stars you're looking back in time."

"How *old* are you?"

"I'm twelve. How old are you?"

"Older than twelve."

"Whatever that means." She dragged the suitcase to her closet.

"Indeed."

She stretched to slip a dress onto a hanger. "Is something the matter?" she asked.

"Hm?"

"That face you're making."

That face, he imagined, broadcast everything that was wrong: his stories weren't selling, he hated New York, he didn't know his father or mother or home, he was poor. "What is—?" he began, grasping. "What is the best thing you've learned in your science class?"

She thought for a moment, tugging at the end of her ponytail. "I can't pick one."

"Pick one. Please."

"What about energy conversation?" She let out a short, barking laugh. "Conservation, I mean."

"What about it?"

"First," she said officiously, "you should know I don't believe in God."

"Sensible."

"My parents don't mind, they don't believe in him, either. But I do believe in something—well, in a transfer of energy. It's more a feeling than something I understand, so my teacher said someday I should find a way to prove it. I think it would have to do with Einstein's theory of how energy can't ever disappear; when plants and humans and animals die the energy has to go somewhere." As she spoke, her eyes darted back and forth between his face and other items in the room.

"Ghosts," Martin said.

"No," she said, delighted. "Better. The energy is absorbed by the universe. If a body gets buried its energy is taken in, either by the animals that eat it or the plants that feed off what decomposes into the soil. And if it's cremated, energy is immediately"—she snapped her fingers—"released in heat and light."

"You're young to be thinking about death."

"It's a biological process like anything else."

"I think you'll change your mind about that down the road."

She shrugged and turned back to her suitcase, as though being reminded of her age displeased her. "You know, I think I like chaos theory best."

Martin heard Wesley down the hall, hissing his name. "Sorry, kiddo. Save it for next time."

"What next time?"

He saluted her. "It has been an honor and a pleasure."

From the top of the stairs, looking down at Wesley's skeptical, amused face ("What are you doing up here, being sick?"), he felt a wash of unease, as though he'd forgotten something. Taken his watch off in the bathroom, maybe, or left his wallet in the girl's room. He held up one finger to Wesley, who started following him up.

"Listen," Martin said, realizing it as he leaned with both hands on the doorframe. "I never asked your name."

She had pulled her sweater off and was small in her white collared shirt. Her hair was disheveled and she smoothed it down in a gesture she would repeat in ten years, in twenty, in thirty-five. "I'm Moira."

TWO

Sal

"Welcome to Jupiter." Moira finished orienting the telescope and straightened up. The low moon, she had told me, was a waning gibbous; a silver glow shot up from behind the trees and, farther up, the stars shone so brightly they looked three-dimensional.

Moira stepped back and I took her place in front of the scope. In the viewfinder, I saw my magnified lashes like spider legs and looked beyond. "Oh," I said. "Wow." The realness of the little planet was peculiarly captivating; a copper marble on black velvet. I'd never seen anything like it, though I'd been looking at images of it since kindergarten; who couldn't draw a picture of Jupiter? The round rusty red, the tiny dark spot a never-ending storm. Three dots flared out along an axis, and these were moons. I never wanted to leave.

Behind me, Moira was quiet, and even as one part of my brain attached fixedly to that point 450 million miles away, another couldn't help imagining Martin over all those years, coming outside to find her in the clearing beside the house. They may have taken turns at the lens just months, weeks, days before the end, Moira wrapped in one of Martin's heavy coats, Martin supported by the walker he'd taken to using in the last years of his life, a reluctant addition following a fall on an icy step. I could picture the way he looked at her, because I know how, back in that room at the library, he'd looked at me.

———

THAT MONDAY I had called Anna to describe what I had in mind, a sprawling intellectual journey piece: a posthumous "Frank Sinatra Has a Cold" meets "Although Of Course You End Up Becoming Yourself." She had countered with and confirmed a neat twelve hundred words for the website, due in a month, after which I called Moira and scheduled a second interview. The next morning, I met Randy at the library. For an hour he spun like a dervish around his cramped office and its Seuss piles of old newspapers, notes, and past-due library books. He pulled a radio interview Martin gave while promoting his first novel, which he sent to me in an email, and two photocopied clips on their daughter, Caroline, winning a regional piano competition as a teenager and an award from the conservatory she attended for college. "I have more on Moira," Randy said, and when I'd expressed disbelief he said, "Come," and strode downstairs to the library, where he pulled from the shelves two books, *Always Present* and *To the Stars*, which I was surprised to learn she had written.

"It's almost a cliché at this point, cosmologists writing pop-sci," the librarian said, peering through her elaborate purple-and-green glasses as I set up an account and signed out the books. "But hers are so—I don't know, so expansive. Generous. You'll see when you read them. They're not Sagan- or Sachs-popular, but people seem to love them. Her other two are checked out." Randy handed over the stack of clips he'd compiled and shooed me out the door.

I took the books to the Beanery to read. At the counter, I'd started to order an iced tea when the person behind the cash register stuck out their hand. They were Black, with a buzzed head, and delicate hoops hugged their earlobes. "Hi, I'm Sawyer. Nice to meet you."

"Sal," I said. Their hand was soft and warm. I paused too long—it had been days since I'd touched another person—before realizing they were now waiting for my order. I let go. "An iced tea, please. Unsweetened."

"Coming up."

I spread my findings over one of the small tables near the counter, the marble top chipped with years of wear. The books and scanned papers made me feel collegiate rather than professional, which I didn't mind. "Do you do that with everyone?" I asked.

"What, say hello?"

"I guess."

"I fostered this shepherd puppy last year," they said, dropping a tea bag into a clear glass mug. Dark whorls unfurled in the water. "After a few months I knew the names of more dogs in this town than humans. I'd have whole conversations with people, get all this information about the intestinal troubles of their Lab-pitt mix, but nothing about them. So now, if there's time, I tell them my name. Usually they tell me theirs. We take it from there. Seems to work out okay."

A man and two kids came in. "Hi," Sawyer said, leaning over the counter to see the smaller boy. "I'm Sawyer. Who do we have here?"

In a good mood, I opened *Always Present*, an esoteric meditation on time interspersed with historical records of philosophy and physics, which Moira had written in the eighties. Reading it made me aware of my smallness within the universe, but also the vastness of the self. She explained the breakdown of predictability that occurred at the turn of the twentieth century following the discovery that knowing every possible aspect of an atom did not guarantee, with absolute certainty, a correct prediction of its future—order was not the steadfast thing science had previously understood it to be, and chaos and chance were responsible for more than anyone realized. I could see why Martin had wanted to co-opt these ideas for his fiction; reading Moira's book made me think more about myself and my own life than about the actual science it described. Of course chance was personal. Everyone played that game, the "if I hadn't missed that bus" or "if I'd gone to my first-choice school" or "if I'd been born a year later, I never would have met my husband" or "won that award" or "gotten in that car accident" game. If the Playwright hadn't agreed to an interview . . .

An hour passed. I'd powered off my phone that morning but I turned it back on to check whether there were any ride apps I could use to get to Moira's. A lone car circled the far edge of the map before disappearing. "No Uber up here, huh," I said to Sawyer, who was reading behind the espresso machine.

"Nope," they said, closing the book—*The House of Bondage.* "Two cab companies, Carl's Cars and Blue Line. The numbers are there"— they flipped a paper menu over and stabbed at the numbers on the back—"but honestly, it's sort of luck of the draw as to whether they show up." I started to leave, but they looked like they were contemplating further. "I don't think the instant gratification of modern life's any good for us," they said. "Ordering a T-shirt online and getting it that day? Wanting to go somewhere and, bam, there's a car and someone to drive it? It's better not to always get what you want, when you want it."

"Right," I said. "Well, cheers to not getting what you want."

———

CARL OF CARL'S Cars did not pick up, and the person at Blue Line
quoted me thirty dollars without tip to take me the ten-minute drive
from my apartment in town to Moira's, so in the end I walked again,
the heat prickling my shoulders. Though I'd been there just once
before, the journey to Moira's house was now familiar, and I noticed
more: a long-limbed praying mantis swaying on a brushy stalk by
the side of the road, a sundial at the top of Moira's driveway with a
child's handprint pressed into the base, a gutter hanging down from
her roof.

Before the sun went down, Moira hauled out a box of old photographs, a lifetime of memories spread across the coffee table. A
long-haired Moira, barely out of adolescence, holding up a pair of
Pringles tubes; Martin, arms crossed in a wicker chair, his first author
photo. "Here," she said, pulling an album over. "Wedding photos."
Her face was small and unlined under a short veil, his grin big and
dazed. In one photo she stood between her parents, a fragile-looking
woman and a man sitting in a wheelchair. Moira and Martin, white
frosting dabbed on their noses, as they cut a three-tiered cake covered
in fondant violets.

"Haircut," I said. It was lopped off at her chin, closer to how she
wore it now.

"Martin did that. I must have been twenty-two. Everything was
magnified. My father wasn't well and my mother was barely speaking
to me. Martin flew to Berkeley to help me settle in and never left."
She was stir-crazy in the tiny apartment they were living in. Martin
wanted her to ask him to stay, she wanted him to suggest it. Instead,

they'd been fighting. They were both up late working in the night-time heat, somehow amplified by the dark world outside, the warm lights in. *Cut my hair*, she'd said, an idea from nowhere. He'd been irritated at the disturbance but then: surprise, delight. He turned her bedroom into a makeshift salon, dragging a chair from the kitchen table and cloaking her in a bedsheet, adopting a bad Italian accent, not Italian at all. She was shivering with excitement by the time he found a pair of scissors, heavy and silver, which he wielded like the demon barber. Brown curls carpeted the pocked hardwood. They had made it through the war.

She showed me the album of press clippings about Martin's books, interviews and reviews, more than I'd been able to find online. "Many people would call him a success," Moira said, as though I'd argued otherwise. "Three published books. That's not nothing. He used to say that if *A Gilded Age* hadn't come out the same day as Mailer's *The Executioner's Song*, he would've had a different career."

"He said something like that to me the night I met him," I said, delighted by this congruence. Moira, though, winced. Maybe the idea of him sharing this private heartache with someone else, another woman, was painful to her. But it was far-fetched to imagine that Moira was jealous about that. Maybe it was Martin she was sad for, stuck in his old resentments. I moved on. "Do you have one of these albums for your own reviews?"

She managed a stilted laugh. "Oh," she said, when she realized I was serious. "No, of course not." I tried to segue into talking about her books but she brushed me off. "You're not writing your article about me."

I was still anxious to get ahold of Martin's manuscript, but my desire for information, rather than being sated with what I'd already received, had expanded. Because I didn't know exactly what story I was after, I believed it could be anywhere. Every detail was relevant, not least ones illuminating the woman Martin had spent his life with. I enjoyed falling into their lives, working out how their oppositional forces pulled them toward each other.

"It's quite clear out," Moira said a few minutes later. "I could show you Martin's favorite part of my job."

It was a perfect night, sharp and cool. Moira had given me one of her sweatshirts. Soft with age, arms that hung down to my thighs. A roaring came from the woods, insects and the tiny moss-green frogs that plopped through the grass in the daytime, empowered by darkness. "My work has taken me to observatories all over the world," she said. "Mauna Kea, Palomar, Stockholm. I always wanted to get to Paranal, in the Atacama."

"Oh yeah," I said, as though she'd mentioned a mutual friend. "I was just talking about the documentary filmed there the other day. It looks so beautiful."

She nodded. "Still, there's something special about what you can see from your own home." After Jupiter we looked at Mars, three satellites. Moira trained the scope on Spica, the sixteenth-brightest star in the sky: in reality two stars, she told me, a binary system so close in orbit a telescope couldn't pick them apart. A massive star, responsible for 80 percent of the system's light, and a smaller one beside it. "We used to play a game with Caroline," Moira said. "We'd pick a star and 'teleport' to it, and then look back at earth. From a star five light-years away, we'd be looking five years back in time, and so on. We'd look back at Caroline being born, or the Paleozoic Era, or Beethoven's last performance. Sometimes I still find myself doing it."

Out by the telescope, Moira told me about the summer she spent living with her aunt and uncle in Nassau Bay, Texas. It was 1968, and their neighbor was Buzz Aldrin. "I'd ask my aunt Celia about him in the years after he came back from the moon landing," Moira said. "She didn't have much to report, except that on some nights he'd spend hours in his backyard, staring up at the moon."

"Were you working for NASA when you stayed with them?"

"That's a generous definition," she said. "My uncle was an engineer there; it was the summer before I left for college. My father was sick, more sick than I understood at the time, and my parents needed me out of the house. My uncle knew I had childhood aspirations of becoming an astronaut, and he got me a job doing clerical work for one of his colleagues. Busywork."

"One year later, and you would've been there when we went to the moon."

Moira tilted her head slightly and, though she was not wearing glasses, made as if to look over them at me.

I winced. "Right. Obviously. You didn't go back after college?"

"Not to work, no. There's more than one way to explore the sky. Here. The moon's high enough to get a good look at it."

I squinted my right eye closed and peered once more through the lens. "It's getting farther away from us, right?"

"It is," Moira said. "Its orbit increases about an inch and a half each year."

"In college I read the Calvino story 'The Distance of the Moon,' and my professor told us that all the stories in that collection were based on facts. That the moon had once been closer and was perpetually straying seemed poignant to me."

"To Calvino, too, apparently." Moira took another look at the big white disk in the sky. "Ready to head inside?"

"I think so."

We broke down the telescope and walked back to the house, Moira's headlight guiding the way. Inside, Blue greeted us with a few low woofs.

"I'm going to run to the bathroom," I said. Moira nodded, already involved in a paper she'd picked up from the counter.

I opened the medicine cabinet but there was little to glean from the two mottled boxes of Band-Aids, a tube of antibiotic ointment, and bottles of vitamins: lecithin, lithium, B_{12}, fish oil.

I swung the mirrored door closed and was met with immoderate script reading MSK over my left breast, a monogram on the sweatshirt I hadn't noticed before. Moira, I thought, but then I considered the arms—Martin. I pulled at the collar and lowered my nose to it, tried to find his scent. Martin and Moira Keller. MK + MK. Fated, their love story. They had lived the life I had imagined, at age twenty, for myself and Hugh, a partnership dedicated to work, the pursuit of big things. They lived in a house full of books, some of which they'd written. The paperback editions, the row of translated copies, M. S. Keller, M. S. Keller, M. S. Keller. Martin, unless . . .

I ducked into the living room and found the books: *Théories de la Vie, En Teoria.* Translations of *In Theory.* And the others: *Die Gegenwart. L'Orrizonte Degli Eventi.*

"You have the same initials," I said to Moira, who was flipping through a stack of papers in the kitchen, drinking a steaming mug of what smelled like strong rosemary tea.

She pulled a paper out of a stack, flattened it with her hand. "Hm?"

"You and Martin. MSK."

"Yes," she said, "I took Martin's last name when we married. He didn't have a middle name and wanted one for the book. He chose Scott. Mine is Selene. Voilà."

"I thought all those translations in the living room were his novels."

"The foreign editions?" Her glasses had slipped down her nose, and she peered at me through them. "No. *Evergreen* did go into German and French, I think, and the UK split off for *A Gilded Age*—French, too? Long time ago. He has those upstairs, in his office."

I perched on one of the high stools at the counter and watched as she compared a piece of paper to the calendar she kept beside the telephone. She noted something in the month of August.

"It must be difficult, living here without him," I said.

She gave the funny, slow head tilt she was prone to when considering to what degree she disagreed with my characterization. "You go through life for some fifty years with someone beside you," she said. "And then you go it alone. I miss him. Terribly. But I have to admit that sometimes, the best and then the worst times, I forget he's gone. I assume, for a split second, that he's just in the next room. It's a strange sensation, as though something is always missing."

"Do you get lonely?"

"I have Blue," she said. "We're good companions."

I nodded hesitantly.

"You don't believe me," she said. "But I have friends, and I'm happy with my own company. Did I watch a kettle of hawks wheel over the house this spring and ache to find Martin so he could see them, too? Yes. But I'm no longer young. People die, move away. My daughter has lived far from home for so long that missing her is a permanent state. Even when we're together, I still often feel it. I long for Martin to be here—desperately, painfully—but I don't wish not to be alone." She made a resigned expression. *What can you do?* "Now, why don't you come back Sunday around noon? We can go through the manuscript boxes. Caroline threatened to give me that book about thanking your objects and then saying goodbye. But she's right: if I don't go through it she'll have to, eventually. And now you're just another reason to get it done."

"I'm not sure about Sunday," I said. I only had the studio apartment until Friday, but I'd been toying with the idea of finding somewhere else to stay until just after Hugh's return. Delicious, but costly.

"Well, just let me know," Moira said agreeably. "And how are you getting back to town? You shouldn't be walking in the dark. I'd be happy to drive you, though I do prefer to stay off the road at night."

"I can get a car," I fibbed. "On my phone." I hoped she might tell me to stay. I would have happily curled up on the couch under the itchy wool blanket that smelled like Blue, who smelled like corn chips. But, though I hemmed and hawed, patting my pockets as though to make sure I had everything, she didn't ask.

Of course I couldn't get a car.

I walked down the long dirt drive until it joined with the main road, feeling nineteen again. I used to leave off-campus house parties alone and wander out into the darkness, experiencing something of an out-of-body experience, drunk, young, lost. Looking back, I'm probably lucky I was never hit by a car or picked up by a nefarious stranger, but bodily fragility was never anywhere on my mind. Sloping fields, moonlit roads—maybe it was that shrugging off of my too-strong sense of self that made me do it in the first place. Or maybe it was the more embarrassing longing to be missed enough that someone would come after me.

For the first minutes of the walk, that's what I thought about, too; whether Hugh had any idea I was gone. I wished I could imagine him returning early to an empty apartment, but he loved schedules and order too much for that. He was still in Boston, surely, thinking his own thoughts.

Without the warm invincibility of Jose Cuervo, it wasn't long before those musings gave way to a full-body fear. Every crack and crunch was a murderous psychopath or a hungry mountain cat, and the few times the slow slide of headlights illuminated the pavement my breath became so shallow it seemed impossible I was taking in any oxygen at all. I started to run, and when I arrived at the edge of town, the streetlamps lighting the rest of the way, my heart was hammering in my chest.

At the apartment, after checking the closet for men and monsters, I boiled water for the licorice tea in the cupboard and shuffled through the pages Randy had scanned for me, before remembering the recording he'd sent.

It was from 1974, just after the release of *Evergreen*. The interviewer began with a synopsis of the book ("a remarkable first novel about the destruction of a young married couple") and a synopsis of Martin ("a former Manhattan dweller now living in sunny California"). It wasn't a long interview, just fifteen minutes, but Martin talked about his influences, about how he had labored on the novel for more than a decade until, a couple years earlier, the story cracked open for him; falling in love, it turned out, was all he needed to imagine the absolute worst things that could happen to a relationship.

"Yes, I understand that other congratulations are in order," the interviewer said. "You've been made an honest man."

"I owe everything about this book to my wife, Moira, though she'd be quick to deny that," Martin said. "But let me tell you, a writer could do far worse than to marry a burgeoning theoretical physicist."

"There are some girls you can't let get away."

"Indeed. My wife doesn't believe in destiny, but tell me: you meet a brilliant little girl and a decade later step into her elevator car and fall in love. What's not cosmic about that?"

———

THE NEXT MORNING, while eating a banana at the small table in the kitchen, I looked for a bike on Craigslist and found a woman's Trek for sale on the western edge of town. I sent a message asking whether it was still available and, a minute later, learned that it was. Could I come pick it up that morning? This had moved more quickly than I'd planned. I wasn't sure I was staying past the end of the week. I closed my computer. The sky was foreboding; I could see my reflection in the window. I called Georgia.

"Tell me about life in the big city," I said. "Is it gray there, too?"

"Very. I had a breakfast uptown." I could hear her footsteps on the other end of the line. "Popped in to see Felix afterward."

"You haven't done that for a while." She'd written her undergrad thesis on art created by incarcerated people: her inspiration was Felix Nussbaum's grim *Self-Portrait in the Camp*, which had haunted her since she first saw it as a teenager on a trip to the Neue Galerie with her father. Nussbaum had painted the work in 1940, and so Georgia assumed he'd escaped the Nazis and made his painting of imprisonment as a free man, which was true, but then she saw that he'd died in 1944, and a thick, dull dread fell over her.

The summer we moved to Brooklyn, the Neue was a frequent haunt; Georgia would get us both in with her family membership and stand staring at the portrait as I wandered among the Klimts and Schieles.

"I was in the mood to feel something," she said to me now. "But what I started to feel was guilty. The man was murdered in a death camp, and I'm visiting his self-portrait in between meetings so that I can feel more alive."

"Oh, Georgia, I don't know—"

"It's fine, I don't need to hand-wring about it. How about you? How goes the adventure?"

"Swimmingly, actually." I told her about the stars, and the assignment for Anna.

"I don't want to say I'm shocked it's working out," Georgia said, "but I'm shocked it's working out."

"Me, too, sort of."

"I hesitate to ask, but have you spoken with Hugh?"

"He's not back for another week," I said. "So, no."

"Will you be back before then?" When I didn't say anything, Georgia continued, in her concerned-parent voice, "Salale? What're you doing?"

"You know what I keep thinking about, with Hugh? I was okay when we broke up. I was dating other people, spending a ton of time at work. I was fine."

Georgia was silent on the other end of the line.

"What?"

"Nothing. It's just, this is ancient history. I don't get what you want from him."

"I want him to stay gone, and also to come back and beg to stay together. I want him to keep making the money he's making, but as a painter, so I never have to talk about socks"—I almost spit the word, and Georgia laughed—"ever again. I want to take a three-month break where I date other people and travel alone, and return to find him waiting for me like a good little eunuch."

"You know what they say about having it all."

"Don't I. But I don't think I can look at his face every day and figure out how I feel." It was one of those things that I only realized was true as I said it. "Do you have that, with Michael?"

"No, but it has also only been three years. Maybe I haven't had time to get good and confused."

"I can't even tell what Hugh looks like anymore. I can't tell whether, if I met him now, I'd think he was handsome. I think it's good for me, being here on my own."

"I'm sure there is a Sylvia Plath quote somewhere that would confirm that."

"Georgia, you're wonderful. I'll let you get back to your day. I have to go see a guy about a bike."

"A bike."

"It's sort of in the middle of nowhere, so if I don't text in half an hour—"

"I'll assume you've fallen in love with him."

"Right," I said, reopening my laptop to look for a new short-term rental. "'Bye."

The condo complex where I was to meet Bret-with-the-bicycle was half a mile out of town in the opposite direction from the woods and watering holes of Moira's home. On the walk there I thought of her during her own transformative, solitary summer. Texas, 1968. Soon I arrived at the address. Small windows plugged with dingy air-conditioning units, and walls that could use a fresh coat of paint. Bret, his heavily sunburned arms protruding from a shirt with the name of a vacuum repair company on its breast pocket, led me to the back of the building, where he disappeared into a shed, a blue tarp crumpled on the ground outside and a rusted padlock hanging open on the door latch. It was with some relief that I watched him reappear with the bike. It had been his daughter's, he said, and she bought herself a new one at her college in Florida. I wondered if he was lying, giving me a story he thought I'd like to hear, but then he took ten dollars off the price he'd posted online and told me to get a helmet soon—he'd give me his daughter's, he said, but she'd taken it with her.

THREE

Moira

The air was oppressive the first time Moira, at age sixteen, stepped onto the tarmac at Houston International. She carried a red suitcase made heavy by the five books her father had insisted she bring with her, incredulous that Radcliffe hadn't assigned their incoming students summer reading.

Her aunt Celia picked her up from the airport. She barely knew her father's sister or her husband, Dean, born in Texas to an old oil family and, after working on a bomb detection team during and after the war, was now at NASA doing "God knows what," her father said.

"Look at you," Celia said. She was just how Moira remembered her from childhood holidays at her grandparents' in Connecticut: hollows at her wrists and ankles, her hair tied low at her neck. She taught biology at Rice. "You look just like your dad." She pulled Moira into a gentle hug that smelled of perfume. "But your mom's in there, too."

Before she'd trained herself not to care, Moira used to stand next to her mother as she sat at her vanity, staring at the reflection of Nina's wide mouth. Her own features didn't coalesce like Nina's. Her eyes were too deep-set, her cheeks and jaw devoid of the dark shadows that cast such drama over her mother's expressions.

"How are they?" Celia said. "How's Nina?"

"She's well, thank you." Her mother was a crisp sealed envelope, her feelings tucked inside; who knew how she was? She was in Europe, and Moira was here, spending the three months between her high school graduation and her first semester at Radcliffe pawned off on family members like a Dickens orphan.

There was a time when her father had taken her to the Hayden Planetarium and helped her write letters to astronomers Jan Hendrik Oort and Donald Edward Osterbrock. Her mother had always been more remote—and increasingly, as Moira got older—but she had chaperoned class field trips to the Met and helped Moira map the stars at their cabin in the Adirondacks. When her parents fought, which had been rare, the verbal sparring used to end in embarrassing displays, Emmett slinking up behind Nina to nuzzle his face in her neck. There was little of that now.

During Moira's last visit home, that long Christmas break five months earlier, her dad was on edge: she made too much noise walking up the stairs, left wet boot marks in the front hall. When he found Moira and her mother flipping through an issue of *Vogue*, he accused them of whispering about him behind his back, and knocked a vase off the fireplace mantel. Then he canceled the annual Christmas party. Her mother spent the following weeks consumed by fabric swatches and wallpaper patterns, planning yet another redecoration. Her father was often at the office or in his study, where, one night, he dragged the family television, leaving a gouge in the hallway floorboards and a near-perpetual strip of light flickering beneath his door.

Years later, Moira found it hard to believe how much she didn't understand about that time. Why, when her mother wrote to her at school to tell her that she would be spending the summer in Houston, didn't she realize that something had to be wrong at home? *Celia could use help with the boys, and Dean has a colleague who needs assistance organizing lesson plans*, Nina wrote. *You should get to know your aunt and uncle.* When Moira reached her mother on the phone, it was hard to take in any information other than that she was being sent away.

"Babysitting and secretarial work?" Moira said without saying hello. "Organizing lessons?"

"Hello, Moira," Nina said. "Let's drop this petulant teenager routine."

"I *am* a petulant teenager."

"Frankly, I'm shocked. All you talk about is NASA and astronauts. I thought you'd be thrilled."

"Can't I go some other summer?" She was only sixteen and hadn't lived at home for four years. In front of her loomed the long unknown of college, and beyond that a bleak, untold future. She bit back tears. Nina couldn't abide sniffling through the airwaves. "I won't bother anyone."

"There won't be anyone to bother. Your father and I are going to be very busy at home before the trip to Europe."

"Why can't I come with you? We could go to museums and visit the Observatoire—"

"This conversation is costing a small fortune. It's not that kind of trip. Your father's going to see some of his clients, and then he has an appointment with a doctor in Germany. It won't be all fun and games."

"What doctor?" Her mother had said it as though it were an afterthought she was trying to hide.

"It's nothing to worry about. He has a referral for someone—Moira, this is all beside the point. We can't bring you with us and you can't stay at home alone; the city is in absolute chaos. You're fortunate to have an aunt and uncle who are happy to have you. Dean is the one who suggested we get you the telescope. You have him to thank for your love affair with the sky."

"But I don't know anyone there. I don't have any friends."

"You have Celia and Dean and the boys. And I'm sure you'll make friends."

"With who?"

"With the astronauts. Maybe they'll take you to the moon."

Moira placed the phone carefully back in the receiver. She imagined her parents, glamorous, listless, at whatever so-called doctor they were going to visit. Her father tracking down some loony deposed princeling whose story he would coax out and spin into a bestselling memoir while her mother lounged poolside, sipping whatever one drank in sanatoriums—digestifs?—and badgering the staff into bringing her a pair of sunglasses, something to cover her shoulders, a book she'd left inside. Later, in the final years of her father's illness, Moira would remember these bad thoughts and cringe, wishing she could take them back, trying not to think about what she might have done that night, had she known what was going to happen. She would have taken a train home, arriving at the apartment to find her father sitting in his study. She would have held his hand.

In the car, Celia made a humming sound. "We're certainly grateful to your parents for lending you to us. When was the last time we saw you?"

"I'm not sure," Moira said. She didn't feel like talking. She wanted to sleep. "Maybe Grandpa's funeral?"

"Your cousins were just babies. Now they're like hulking men."

Moira stared out the window. She thought about human growth, physical change. She thought about something she'd been reading the week before, the indeterminacy of particles, and how experiments attempting to predict the state of a quantum system could, even in retrospect, only do so correctly a fraction of the time. She imagined a single point with hundreds of branches, and then imagined choosing one branch and all the others disappearing, only to have a hundred more branches spring forth from the one she'd chosen. She felt wise and old because what could be a better visualization of life and the forward arrow of time than this? Celia, too, seemed lost in thought. Content, they drove on in silence.

Moira had expected a Texas cliché from her temporary home, highways and dirt, cowboy hats, slow drawls, new money. But her aunt and uncle lived on a pretty street with two-story houses spaced like gap teeth, their tidy circles of lawn dotted with hydrangeas and black-eyed Susans, a man-made lake sunk down behind the backyards. A French country home sat next to a Spanish Colonial next to Celia and Dean's English cottage, all so different from her own New York apartment and the sprawling suburban neighborhoods in Rye and Ossining she had visited with her parents for barbecues and birthday parties.

Dean was at work, Celia said, as they pulled up to the house. "Let me take you up to where you're staying. It's Billy's room, but he did neaten it up."

"I hope," Moira said, bleary from the drive, "he's not too upset that I've displaced him."

"He doesn't mind." The room was tidy, with sports trophies on a shelf and a plaid blanket on the bed. "He's at camp," she said.

"When does he come back?"

Celia pushed at the open closet door, which fell open when she let go. She pushed again, and again it swung ajar. "I'll see if I can fix that," she said, more to herself than to Moira. "When's he back? Not until August. They love it, can't wait to get away from us."

Moira was wide awake. "Sam's there, too?"

"Yes," Celia said. "Oh dear. Did you think they'd be around? You'll be just missing them. I know I told your mother that they would be away, it was part of the consideration—"

Moira was shaking her head. "No, I must have been confused." She wondered if there was a world in which her mother really had thought she would be babysitting her cousins, or if, to Moira's mind far more likely, she had decided that that was a more compelling excuse for sending Moira away—maybe she'd even made herself believe it was true. "How old are they now, the boys?"

"Twelve and thirteen," Celia said. "It's Sam's first time staying for the full ten weeks. I've never gone so long without either of them in the house. It's why I'm so grateful I have you." She lowered her voice. "I did always want a daughter."

Moira hoped her smile wasn't as thin as it felt.

———

TWO OR THREE times a week, Moira rode with Dean to the Manned Spacecraft Center offices, where he flashed his badge and left her in a small room with the physicist's handwritten notes she was to collate and retype into coherent passages for a set of lectures called "Astrophysics for Astronauts." It was helpful to have someone looking it over who was new to the concepts, Dean said as they clacked down the clean linoleum, since the astronauts would be, too. Comprehensible, he told her, but not dumbed down. Men passed by, a chorus of pressed shirts in pale yellows, blues, whites with thin stripes. He motioned into some of the rooms: wall-sized chalkboards with rickety ladders, rows of dark green screens that she imagined would light up with scrolls of numbers. But the sparse office where she was to work had just three metal desks and a row of filing cabinets against one wall.

She shared the space with one of Dean's colleagues, a recent doctoral graduate named Ted Danvers. "You should get to know the girls on the desks," he said, extending his hand; a soft drawl, a firm shake. "Though I don't know if you're the giggles and lipstick type." Moira nodded, uncertain as to whether he was laughing with or at her.

"We go way back, your uncle and I," Ted went on. He was shorter than Dean but broad, as though a tall person had been pressed down. "My big brother Drew was in his fraternity at Vanderbilt. The stories those two would tell—"

"And now," Dean clapped Ted on the shoulder, "lucky me, little Teddy's moved in right down the street and into the lab."

"He got me the job," Ted said. "He'd never admit it, but he's an old softy."

"Enough, enough." Dean patted down his pockets and extricated a packet of Marlboros. "Don't make me blush. Tell the girl about your research."

As Ted talked about their search for black holes, those sucking vortexes, he lost his goofy swagger and started sounding like a man in love. Over the coming weeks he'd become a fixture of her days at the office, whistling and strutting past the doorway like a Chaplin bit. "What's up, buttercup?" he'd ask, and then listen as she explained the concepts she was working through, giving her notes on how to clarify, and kicking his feet up on the desk. "She's a genius, folks!" She'd shake her head, pleased, but on the days he went straight to his desk with barely a nod, she'd find herself cutting her eyes over at him, bent over his work, feeling as though something were missing, like she'd forgotten her house key or to put on underwear.

Two weeks into her stay, her parents sent an anodyne letter, the first half written in her mother's spider script, the second in her father's perfect schoolboy's penmanship. She responded in kind. The work was interesting, the people were nice. Yes, she was looking forward to starting Radcliffe; she was sure these last months of summer would fly by.

But in truth, she was electric. Every part of her fizzed. Houston was a hothouse of outsized existence: the labs at NASA, Celia's work at the university, even their own little cul-de-sac was more sharply defined than the world Moira had encountered before. She'd finally met the physicist whose notes she was working on: Dr. Page, who wore an eye patch and drove a car he said had belonged to Erwin Rommel during the war. "Here are the bullet holes," he said around the pipe protruding from his mouth. At the grocery store, Celia pointed out the stoic young woman made a widow by the pilot program, holding a toddler in one arm as she dropped a package of chicken breasts into her cart. A Gemini pilot lived next door with a houseful of sons, and down the street there were girls around Moira's age who performed in the water shows at Sea-Arama, arriving back in the neighborhood with their blond hair slicked wet against their heads, a chain of linked limbs and echoing laughs. When Bobby Kennedy was killed, Celia and Dean were drawn and pale watching the news coverage and Moira felt that it was an attack against them, against Houston, against her, too; it had been his brother who'd promised they would make it to the moon, and now neither of them would see it.

She ate turkey and ham sandwiches from the cafeteria with Ted, sitting beside the men who made computer simulations of the earthrise over the moon, and women who churned out punch cards that somehow made this possible. They gossiped about the astronauts in line for the manned flights and talked about a secretive UFO panel held fifteen years earlier. "Your Dr. Page is trying to gin up enthusiasm for a new symposium on unidentified flying objects," Ted said, mocking. "It's embarrassing for a scientist of his caliber to be indulging paranoid fantasies from the unwashed masses." After work, her aunt and uncle argued about Wernher von Braun, the former Nazi scientist and so-called architect of the moon missions. Celia thought his campaigns for racial integration in Alabama were self-serving; Dean said it didn't matter, if it got the job done.

In bed, Moira read *Wanderers in the Sky*, which Dr. Page and his wife had coauthored a few years prior, and let the creak of floorboards, low murmurs, and the fizzy pop of the television coming to life lull her into the meditative mental space on the edge of sleep, which inevitably procured a rapid regurgitation of what she'd been working on that day. They were like near-dreams, as though she were scrolling a lecture through her subconscious or transcribing the scrambled notes into her brain. She could never recall them in the morning, these long elucidating narratives, though she had the sense the information was lodged somewhere.

ROGER PENROSE HAD, the previous year, proved what had previously been suspected: that when a large star collapsed at the end of its life it created an infinite gravitational vortex, a so-called singularity, where relativity and space-time broke down. For Moira, the mere knowledge of the discovery was thrilling; if phenomena of this magnitude were still being uncovered, she might one day do the uncovering.

For Ted, the Penrose paper was cause for intense anxiety and depression; he had spent two years circling similar research.

"I'm already twenty-four," he said, perched on a table in a computing workroom down the hall from their office, his legs swinging like a boy's. He was so like her father's young acolytes, the writers and editors who lolled around their apartment, raising their voices to be heard and all but shaking with ambition.

"Twenty-four," said Moira, bent over a row of numbers, "is pretty young."

"What if that was my sole contribution? What if that was my shot? Another month or two and I would've gotten it. It could have been me."

"But now you can build on his work."

"I don't think you understand," Ted said, standing up and stuffing his hands in his pockets. He had the affable demeanor of a golden retriever, and a tendency to make proclamations and then glance wide-eyed at whoever was near, checking for reactions. If they proved insufficient, he'd repeat himself. Now he shuffle-kicked one foot as he spoke. "You won't understand until someone comes and does the thing you're trying to do, takes it right out from underneath you. Ours is not like other professions. Only one person can succeed. Once they do, whatever simultaneous work anyone else has done all but disappears. All you're worth is a confirmation of someone else's brain. I was so *close*. I just needed time."

Moira sat back and crossed her arms. "How old is he?"

"Penrose? Thirty-four." He took the pencil perpetually tucked behind his right ear and flipped it in a whirring circle around his fingers. "By my age he'd come up with that stupid triangle already, with his father. 'Impossibility in its purest form,' all that."

Moira didn't know what he was talking about, didn't care. If it mattered, she'd find out someday, but today it was enough to sit in proximity to this man and his big aspirations with the quiet understanding that by his age she wouldn't be worried about anyone. She would be the best. She thought about patting Ted's head, ruffling his hair. Since she'd arrived in Houston, a dichotomous sense of calm and excitement had settled over her, a future spinning into existence. Everything was sparse and new, specifically attuned to produce the forward-reaching thought they were all doing here. Put men on the moon? Why not? Delve deep into space from the comfort of these clean white halls? Yes, all that and more.

"It's all so random," Ted went on. A rivulet of sweat ran down his hairline, and dark circles bloomed under his arms. "It's maddening. I wish I was born in fifth-century Athens, when everyone discovered something at age fourteen and no one knew what was going on anywhere else."

"You might have been born a peasant. Or a slave."

Ted snorted. "No."

"Life span was a lot shorter," Moira said. "Fourteen was more like thirty. And they weren't sending rockets into space."

"How can I make you understand?" He chewed on his pencil eraser. "You know who Alfred Russel Wallace is?"

"Nope."

"*Quod erat demonstrandum*. He discovered evolutionary biology when Darwin did. Separately. On his own. He was famous for it when he was alive, but now? Old Alfred's name doesn't pop up in elementary school textbooks. And why? Darwin's theory was sexier than his—and I mean that, because Wallace didn't make such a thing of sexual selectivity. Can you imagine being a genius like that, contributing to science writ large, and then in death getting erased, as though you'd never existed at all?"

"But you know who he is."

"You don't. My wife"—he had married that spring and said the word haltingly, as though getting used to it—"certainly doesn't. And *every*one knows Darwin. If that happened to me, I would be morbidly depressed."

"Not really," Moira said. "You would be dead."

A MONTH AFTER arriving in Houston, Celia suggested she phone her parents. "Don't worry about the charges," she said. Nina and Emmett had arrived stateside a few days earlier; Moira knew this from the postcards of an old castle and one of rolling hills, and the letters printed on crisp hotel stationery, which they'd sent from Germany, Italy, the last from London, announcing their return. She'd put off phoning, not wanting her mother's disapproval dripping into the bubble she'd created in Houston, nor the way her father sometimes asked her to explain something she'd told him the day before—he didn't listen to her the way he used to, didn't care. But maybe, too, she had wanted them to worry about how she was; she wanted them to call her.

Her mother was sharp and businesslike when she picked up the phone. "Oh, Moira," she said. "You might have found time to write more than that one card. Such a garish thing, too. Where was it from?"

"AstroWorld," Moira said.

"AstroWorld, of course."

"I've been busy."

"That's good. With what exactly?"

Moira twirled the cord around her finger and lowered her voice, aware of Dean reading in the living room. "I'm attempting to determine whether there is depth to a black hole."

"How interesting. I'm sure it would all be over my head."

"Undoubtedly."

"What's that?"

"Nothing. How was the trip?"

Her mother sniffed, a short hard sound that made Moira homesick. "Your father's not feeling as well as we'd hoped. I'd put him on but he's resting."

"I don't understand what the matter is."

Her mother made a ticking noise with her tongue. "I suppose it's better you know. The diagnosis is still unresolved, but the good news is that there isn't a tumor."

"A tumor?"

"There *isn't* one, Moira. They're crossing things off the list. He's young to be exhibiting these kinds of . . ." She paused, and Moira imagined her waving her hand in the dismissive way she did when talking about things that bored her: the weather, the children of Emmett's colleagues. *It's called small talk for a reason*, she had once said with an acid smile. "These kinds of cognition changes."

Cognition changes. Like a gear clicking into place, Moira could now name the uneasy shift she'd felt from her father in recent years. The irritability, the forgetfulness. It was an ominous relief. "Do they think he might be sick? What is it?"

"They don't know." Her mother sounded defeated, the crystalline sharpness so intrinsic to her voice melting away. "But the hope is that he'll be back at work imminently."

"He's not working? He can't not work. That's all he likes to do."

"Moira, don't make me regret telling you this, your father didn't want me to mention it at all. We are figuring it out. How's Dean? And lovely Celia?"

"They're fine," Moira said, feeling the kitchen's oppressive heat all at once. She pulled the cord over to the sink, pushed open the window, and breathed in the muggy air.

"What's that?"

"They're fine. Everyone's fine."

"I'm so glad to hear it. I'm glad you're having an enjoyable summer, I knew you would."

"Yes, it's great," she said with a sarcasm she regretted immediately. Her mother had that effect on her. Moira was always waiting to be made to feel guilty, waiting for her mother to explain, as she had before, how much better Moira's life was than her own had been, and just how much she'd sacrificed for her. As though those weren't choices her mother had made on her own. *I went to college*, Nina would say, *just like you're going to. And then I gave that all up.* She'd gotten a scholarship—her family wasn't wealthy, like Emmett's was—had loved history, philosophy, studied Greek and Latin. When Moira was a baby, she used to read the *Odyssey* to her until they both fell asleep.

They said goodbye. Moira placed the phone back in its cradle. For a minute she stood in the kitchen, her hands heavy. She heard Celia coming down the stairs and, not wanting to see her, pushed open the screen door and took a few steps outside. The grass rolled lush and green down to the lake, its glassy surface like a piece of sky fallen down.

"It smells like rain, doesn't it?" Celia said from the doorway. Moira closed her eyes against the rolling sensation of impending tears. "They call it petrichor. I love that smell. It's so clean, you can almost taste it."

———

THAT WEEK THE sky went murky with ash-gray clouds. There was talk of hurricanes, of storm systems over the Atlantic. The radio weatherman, excited by the violent departure from endless heat and sun, issued his report with anticipatory relish.

The NASA offices seemed emptier; between summer vacations and research trips, maybe they were. On quiet afternoons, Moira could hear two secretaries chatting down the hall, the pug-nosed blonde waxing poetic about the Doors show she'd gone to see, the other, a quiet Black woman, *mm*-ing over her typing. They were older than Moira, with long pink nails like seashells. When Moira walked by on the pretext of visiting the water fountain, they'd go silent.

On a dull Friday she was glad to hear Ted on his usual wandering rounds, flirting with the girls and calling a Hollywood so-long to someone leaving for the day. A moment later he appeared in the doorway, his shirtsleeves rolled up and a cigarette tucked behind his ear. "Moira, old girl," he said. "Dean around?"

"In his office, I assume," she said, going back to the paper she was trying to unpack. She'd gotten through the notes Dean had supplied when she'd first arrived; now he'd set her up with new papers to read and summarize, equations and formulas that swam in front of her. "Here." She underlined a sentence and slid the page toward the table's edge. "What does that mean?"

"Actually, he's not in his office and I have a question I hope someone might lend their brain to," Ted said. "Maybe you can help me. I've been going over this set of numbers all afternoon and it's not coming out right. I've been looking at them too long. You mind?" He waved a notepad at her.

"If you can't do it, I'm sure I won't be able to help."

"No need for modesty," he said. He was chewing a wad of pink gum. He blew a bubble, let it pop, and gathered it back into his mouth. "If I'm being honest, I went out for a beer. Mental lubricant. Maybe too much so."

She sighed, only half meaning it. "Here. Let's see it."

He pulled a chair beside her and ran the point of his pencil down a column of numbers. "This set shouldn't have such a wide variant."

She could feel him watching her. She knit her eyebrows and sucked in her cheeks to keep from smiling. And then she saw what was wrong. "See what you did here? These are transposed." She erased, rewrote.

Ted scanned the numbers. "Well, how about that? You little genius."

"I'm not," she said.

"You're smart. You know that. So . . ." He leaned back in his chair. "Now what?"

She tapped her own paper. "If you would read this, here, and explain—"

"Moira." He crinkled his forehead.

"What?"

"Listen, I'm going to tell you something." He leaned close. He smelled sharp, sour. "I didn't come back to see Dean. I came back to see you. What do you think of that?"

Moira laughed, and the sound cut through something in the room.

"Moira," he repeated.

"Ted." She stood up and straightened the papers she'd been working through, then her chair.

He stood up, too, a dopey seriousness in his expression. "Moira."

"Why do you keep saying that?"

"Why are you laughing?" He put his hand on her shoulder and then slid it down, his thumb pressing into the soft crook of her elbow. "Are you nervous?"

"No, but you're being, I don't know—don't."

"You've got such a little waist. I can put both hands around it, almost."

"Don't." It came out in a whisper, as though the rigidity in her body had also affected her vocal cords.

"Look at you," he said, his voice low. He planted his mouth on the bare skin where her neck met her collarbone, and then she could smell his hair, too, damp with sweat, and there was a horrible tension building in her tendons, in her nerves. "You're so cute. Has anyone ever told you that before? Or are you too buried in your books for anyone to notice? I bet no one sees it but me."

"Someone might walk in." She was rearing her head away from him, thinking about the girls at their typewriters, the girls who had maybe seen him come into the room. They'd smelled his beery breath, maybe. Maybe he'd tried this with them, too. Maybe everyone knew just what was happening when he brought her a plate from the cafeteria.

"What's that?" He had his eyes on her waist, he was holding her out at arm's length, admiring her.

"Someone might see."

"No. No one's here."

"They are. They're right down the hall."

"So what? What's there to see? Nothing's happening. Here, I'll close the door." His mouth was impossibly, wetly, pressed against hers, beery, mustard, his tongue squeezing between her lips.

"No. Don't." Louder. *"Don't."*

"Jesus," he said, pulling away as though she'd hit him. "Calm down. I'm just playing around. You didn't think . . ." His laugh was just as it always was, like a taut balloon. "I don't know what you thought."

She smoothed her hands over her skirt.

"I didn't think you were such a kid," he said, and cleared his throat. "Grow up."

He opened the door and paused, his hands in his pockets, his lips pursed in thought. She thought he might apologize. "You know, eight years ago this whole place"—he waved his hand up and down the hall—"it all used to be a cattle pasture." Moira said nothing. He gave the frame two firm pats and went out. She listened to his steps down the hall. "That's me for today, ladies, y'all have a nice weekend." She sat down and let her breath out in a rush; it was only then that she realized she'd been holding it. It wasn't possible that she'd misunderstood what he wanted from her. Not her brilliant mind, in the end. He'd put his mouth against hers. His hands on her body. She couldn't have made that up. They'd inched up, grazing her chest. But it was true, what he'd said, that nothing really had happened, and if she'd been somehow confused— She squeezed her eyes shut against the embarrassment.

THAT EVENING, SHE drove home with Dean, as usual, and baked a peach pie with Celia that bubbled and glistened with caught sugar. But as she lifted the dish out of the oven something flickered in her peripheral vision and then the world blackened at the edges. She put the pie down on the table and looked at her hands in their heavy quilted oven mitts. The darkness contracted around them and she felt suddenly terrified: she was going blind, or insane.

She said something to Celia about not feeling well. She didn't wait for a response. She pulled the drapes in her cousin's bedroom shut and lay down in all her clothes. Periodically she opened her eyes to reconfirm the darkness, until the sunlight itself faded. At one point the door swung quietly open, but she pretended to be asleep until it clicked closed. Snippets of Dean and Celia's quiet, impassioned conversations floated up to her: *consequentialism, self-serving, he, he, he,* she heard. Ted? Moira turned over scenarios. Ted had said something to Dean. One of the secretaries knew Celia.

Had she been needed at all that summer, or was the work she'd done for Dean and Dr. Page just an elaborate scheme to keep her occupied?

She imagined Ted pushing her up against the wall, shoving his hand up her skirt. Revolting, the heat in her groin. She touched herself. Pleasure, then sickening regret.

The next morning, her thoughts dim and shredded after a sleepless night but her vision restored, Moira rose early, her bare feet cold on the carpet, and found Celia alone in the kitchen. Without giving herself time to change her mind, Moira said that she was sorry for the inconvenience but she couldn't stay in Houston, she had to go home, and could Celia please help her get the next possible flight to New York? And after sending her on an errand to pick up milk so that, Moira assumed, she could call her mother, Celia did.

On the plane, her forehead pressed against the cool window, the world subdivided into squares of greens and yellows that broke into craggy mountain ranges or slipped out of sight below wisps of clouds. Everything she was seeing had already happened. All these images, these transfers of light, were snapshots of an immutable past. It was all so permanent, so inevitable. She had done whatever she'd done to make Ted put his hands on her waist, and now that moment was stuck there in the gummy maw of history.

It was tempting to imagine and wish for any number of alternate trajectories, but Moira had stopped believing in a shiftable continuum. In retrospect, yes, certain conversations leapt forward to take on new, neon significance. How he had once, while reading over her shoulder, rested his hand on the top of her head. How she had teased him for the way he spilled condiments onto his tie, blobs of mustard and mayonnaise. Perhaps if she had not done that— Stop. There was no other reality but this one; no hypothetical *what-if*. Each moment was predestined, not by some omniscient deity but by science, by the laws of probability, by biology and chemical makeup, by the forces of environment, by the lawless particles that made up the world.

Whatever happened was the only thing that could have.

On that plane ride home—and through years of mounting, claustro-phobic guilt as she turned away from her father's deteriorating health to instead bury herself in more solvable questions—she worked hard to remind herself of that.

FOUR

Sal

On Sunday, I was sitting in one of Moira's wing chairs thinking about how I might more successfully broach the question of looking over the final manuscript when, as if reading my mind, she called down from Martin's office.

"Help me with these boxes, Sal?"

I bounced to my feet, having the idea that I might poke around his desk for, if not the whole finished book, at least something that pointed to what it contained. Moira had said she hadn't yet touched anything in the room—the piles were overwhelming—and I wanted to get to it before she threw anything away. I had almost a week before Hugh returned to the apartment, if he stuck to his plan, and so I began to think of that as my deadline for obtaining the novel. On top of everything else, I didn't want him to ask what I'd been doing and have nothing to say.

The door was ajar, but when I got to the top of the hardwood stairs, which sighed and clicked under my sneakers, I saw just a glimpse of a heavy wooden desk and boxes of filing folders, notebooks, and loose papers before Moira emerged and pulled it closed behind her. "Just these," she said, pointing to the two cardboard boxes she'd already pushed into the hall.

I crouched down to touch the fat, markered words, repeated on each box: FOR POSTERITY.

"He was joking," Moira said.

"Do you save your notes, too?"

"For two years. Then digitized and into the trash. Why keep them around for longer than that?" She worked her jaw, as though probing for something caught in a back molar. "Maybe he wasn't joking."

I thought the boxes would contain early drafts of his work, but they were instead filled with neat stacks of black notebooks. "I suppose I should go through these before handing them over," she said, picking one up and flipping through it. "Though I think they're predominantly catalogues of his work rather than personal musings. Yes, here: *Wrote six pages of the new story, feel as though I am beginning to inhabit the psyche of the man, though not sure I like what I am finding—in him, or perhaps in myself.* Poor Martin." She went quiet, reading down the page. "He would think I'd lost my mind, showing you all of this. Back when there was some press for *Evergreen*, one of the magazines wanted to interview him at our home in Berkeley and I refused. I've never sat for a profile, either. I always pretended—to myself and others—that it was because I worried it would make Martin feel even more ignored, by contrast, but I think it was somewhat more selfish. I didn't like the idea of putting my story into someone else's hands. And yet." She motioned to me, a sweeping gesture that took in the boxes, the rest of the house, and then tipped her face to the ceiling. "I'm doing it all for you, dear!" she called, and then abruptly left, down the stairs, to station herself at the computer in the kitchen. She'd just received edits on one of her papers; something, from what I understood of it, on the nature of time. For an hour I knelt beside the coffee table in the living room, flipping through the notebook pages as she tapped away at her laptop. Blue hefted herself onto the couch and followed my movements with her rheumy eyes.

"Moira," I said, eventually. "How would you feel about me taking a few of these to my place? I could show you which ones and have them back tomorrow or the next day. Moira?"

She didn't turn around. "Yes, yes, that's fine."

I'd left the studio apartment two days before and moved into a Linden film major's furnished one-bedroom, which she had decided to vacate only days before summer began and so, unable to find another renter, was willing to have me pay week to week. I fell asleep under posters for *La Dolce Vita* and *Wanda*, and in the morning drank drip coffee from a collection of chipped statement mugs. Dried roses in old wine bottles, a surprisingly comfortable IKEA sofa.

The journals I brought back to the apartment spanned 1975 to 1979. Page after page of Martin's internal vacillations: progress and optimism followed just a day later by the depths of despair. He noted page counts achieved, stories he felt good about but abandoned, rejections from various magazines. He reread his own early work, hoping to transport himself back into the mindset he'd had when he'd found success. He wrote little about Moira, nor their daughter and friends, except in relation to his work. For weeks he couldn't write at all, and spent long hours reading at his desk or playing solitaire. *No pages . . . nothing, despite C. and M. at N.'s for the day . . . Scrapped all of yesterday's progress, which in the harsh morning light I could hardly stand to read.* Some entries were so long—meditating on various books he was reading; noting at length the ways in which his writing, its stilted characters and flat settings, failed to match what he felt were the brilliant ideas in his brain—that it was no wonder he wasn't making headway in his fiction. He was spending hours musing about himself.

"Hello," I called to Moira two days later, sweaty and red-faced, from the front door.

Moira's head emerged from the living room, the house phone pressed to her ear. She held up a finger and I nodded, wandering into the kitchen to wash my hands at the sink. She'd told me on the phone that she'd dug up Martin's early drafts of *Evergreen*. I was there for that, but I was also there for Moira. I enjoyed her company, looked forward to seeing her. She was so straightforward, with none of my own people-pleasing mannerisms—huge smiles; compulsive, agreeable nodding. Moira's relative reserve made me want to impress her, to be liked.

"What does Priya think, sweetheart?" she was saying. Caroline, then. "Seven*teen* percent contained, or seven*ty*? Mm. They're so far away. I know, darling, but you have to put these fires out of your mind. Watch that lovely video you sent me, the one of the man playing piano for the elderly elephant."

Caroline Keller was forty years old and lived somewhere on the outskirts of the San Francisco Bay Area. There were pictures of her in most rooms of the house: In the living room, she was a toddler sitting on a plastic push-car, round-faced with streaky blond hair as though her genes hadn't been able to decide between her mother's near-black and Martin's pale blond. Held up by a Kermit the Frog magnet on the refrigerator, she and a woman in a yellow sundress grinned by the ocean. On the bookshelf in the hallway upstairs, next to a bowl of smooth black river stones, a teenage Caroline perched on a park bench with an arm around Moira.

Moira reappeared and set the phone in its charger. "She's a worrier," she said. On the counter, she lifted the tinfoil covering a plate to reveal the final quarter of a cherry galette. "I was an anxious child, too, and I thought, going into parenthood, that I could protect her from my own difficulties." She cut the pastry in half, putting one piece on a new plate that she slid toward me. "You think you can avoid all the pitfalls, your own parents' shortcomings, but then you repeat them anyway."

"What was Martin like as a dad?"

"I was lucky to have him as a partner. He encouraged me to put my career first, to make sure that I had the time and space that I needed to work. That's rare, and more so in those days."

"I'm sorry if this is too personal," I said, "but did you ever think about having more than one?"

Moira frowned. "We did, but maybe that was one of those accidental repetitions. Martin and I were both only children. Do you have siblings?"

"No." I liked when she asked me about my life. She didn't do it often, but it made our interactions feel more like an actual conversation than the one-way interrogation that interviews often resembled. I had the sudden realization that I could say whatever I wanted, could make up an entirely new backstory for myself, if I so chose. "My parents divorced when I was seven, but I think things were bad for them for years before that." I kept my voice light and airy. "My mom did have another baby, actually, but she died. I was only four."

"That must have been incredibly difficult," Moira said.

"I barely knew what was happening. I got sent away to stay with a friend, and when I came back to the house I expected to have a baby sister, but didn't. It was a home birth. The cord wrapped around her neck."

Moira put her hand on my shoulder and squeezed.

"And your parents now? Are you close with them?"

"Sure," I said. My dad had called once since I'd been in Linden and we'd had a perfunctory check-in; I'd told him I was on assignment outside of New York, and he'd let out a low whistle and said, "I'm so proud of you, Sal," which would have meant more if he'd ever actually demonstrated having read something I'd written. My mom had been sending her usual barrage of texts and emails, information about pipeline protests and an impending nuclear war and weird, badly written news bulletins about factory farms and corporate malfeasance, which I sometimes responded to with an exclamation mark, but usually ignored. I hadn't told her I was upstate. "Good dish towel," I said in an inelegant pivot, pointing at the damp one Moira was folding.

She ran her hand over the *New Yorker* cartoon of an astronaut and a man in a tux floating in space. "If you feel compelled to get someone a gag gift tangentially related to their profession, a dish towel is one of the less objectionable outlets. You wouldn't believe how many planet-shaped pillows and Einstein mugs I've received."

"What did people give Martin?"

"Beautiful pens. Books. Much more useful. His students adored him and several of them went on to become working writers and artists. We have their photography and paintings and signed copies of their books." She opened one of the vitamin bottles she kept on the windowsill above the sink and tapped a yellow capsule onto her palm. Then she offered the bottle to me.

I examined the bland label, stamped with a cartoon sun. "What is it?"

She had popped the pill and swallowed it with a swig of water. "Choline, amino acids, nootropics. For your memory."

I shook the bottle like a maraca. "Worried I'm losing it?"

"We all are," she said. "All the time."

———

IN THE FINAL days leading up to Hugh's return to Brooklyn, Moira was busy with her own work, so I spent long hours schlepping Martin's *Evergreen* drafts between the library and the Beanery; it had almost seemed like Moira was making a point when she sent me off with them, demonstrating just how not precious she was. After comparing the manuscript to the finished book—whole pages and characters excised; transitions smoothed—I'd wander upstairs to hear the town gossip from Randy before moseying over to the café where I was, at least, paying money to loiter.

"It's taxi girl!" Sawyer said the first time I overlapped with their shift, a bright weekend morning following a night of insomnia. "You get where you needed to go?"

"Working on it," I said, delighted to be remembered. Sawyer wore a gold crucifix with four tiny pieces of turquoise at its tips, which I would have assumed was ironic—I didn't know anyone my age who actually believed in God—but while chatting on and off over the course of the day I learned they were pursuing an interminable PhD in religious studies, with a thesis they'd tentatively titled "Subjugation and Salvation." ("God and I," they said, "are *très compliqué*.")

"It's cool that you're, like, leaning into this stereotype of seeking validation in the male authority figure," they said the following Thursday, when both Sawyer and a barista named Ben had been assigned to a shift that ended up being rainy and uncharacteristically slow. Ben was popping a wad of gum, half listening to us, but Sawyer had started to grill me on what I was doing in Linden. "I mean it," they said, when Ben laughed. "I have friends who were boycotting any art produced by men, but then they had to whittle that down to straight men, and then straight white men, and then cis straight white men, but who were they to assume the actual gender identity of a person raised in the oppressive era of lobotomized housewives, yadda yadda. You can't reject something with which you refuse to engage—though there's certainly an argument to be made that as a culture we have engaged with heteronormative maleness, you know, enough." I couldn't tell whether they were making fun of me.

The night before Hugh was supposed to arrive back at the apartment, I couldn't sleep. Everything felt uncomfortable: the oscillating fan blew hot air around the bedroom, and my hair over my face; the T-shirt I slept in bunched behind my back. Finally I turned the light back on and tried to read over the notes I'd been taking, wondering how to nudge them into something other people might find interesting, but my thoughts kept weaseling their way back to uncomfortable subjects: Hugh and what would happen when he returned; the chubby, asocial boy I'd made fun of in elementary school; the way I could now remember the barback's eyebrow ring under my finger from my last night in New York. The Playwright, too. I often turned the details of our interactions over, wishing I'd done something differently. I hadn't admitted this to anyone, but it wasn't just that he'd duped me. *This is my very first play*, he'd told me, but I had dug up two instances when, in high school and as a sophomore in college, he wrote projects for the school theater department. I'd told myself at the time that it was a negligible detail, but it was also true that those early efforts didn't support the narrative I wanted to tell: the Playwright's burst from the blue, inspiration and success like a thunderclap. Had there been a twinge of suspicion, too, when he sent that made-up email from his ex? I fell asleep sometime after five a.m. and woke up a couple hours later, my muscles achy and my brain slow.

I knew I'd spend the day compulsively checking my phone, so I left it in the top drawer of the nightstand, next to a pack of tarot cards and a collection of Neruda poems, and biked to the base of a trailhead less frequented than others in the area. I locked the bike to a birch and set off into the woods.

I hadn't spent so much time alone since I was a child. What had I done for all those years, the long weekend stretches after the divorce, when my father transferred to the Crested Butte location of his law office, and every other weekend my mom drove me an hour and a half to the midpoint between our towns and I got out of her car and into his? When she let me quit piano lessons and the soccer team and I didn't feel like talking to any of my friends? I was only seven at the time but I remember feeling I possessed a gravity that they didn't—not imagining they might be going through things as bad or far worse than me. I'd once found a report card from that year in which my teacher had written, *Sal is engaging in some attention-seeking.* Talking out of turn in class, refusing to come out of the tube slide at the end of recess. But at home, I hid in my room.

What did I do?—a stupid question. I read.

The trailhead was swamped with muddy puddles, clouds of dronelike mosquitoes zipping above. I batted them away, and when I ran into a pair of hikers on their way down, the woman held up a can of bug spray and, gratefully, I let her mist my arms, the back of my neck. As I walked, fragments of the piece of music Moira had talked about on the first day looped in my head, and I thought, as I did so often now, of Martin. A boy from a rural home, a mother who died young, a father never in the picture. Maybe he'd been driven to write because he believed, if he became well known, his absent father might read one of his books and search him out. Becoming a writer: the ultimate attention-seeking behavior.

The wooded trail gave way to huge flat rock faces covered in lichen. A family with a three-legged dog was picnicking on one side of the clearing. On the other, steps chiseled out of the stone led down to another flat rock face. I kicked aside a few pieces of broken glass with the toe of my sneaker. The mountain range stretched out in front of me, old and sloping, nothing like the enormous young peaks I'd grown up hiking. So many trees, bright pockets of water.

I was exhausted by the time I arrived back at the apartment, my feet blistering in sneakers not meant for that much activity. I splashed cold water on my face, and then I took the phone out of its drawer and the screen lit up with notifications. Two missed calls from Hugh early that afternoon. Four texts:

> I'm back, are you around?

> Please let me know where you are. I want to talk, but mostly I want to make sure you're ok.

> Georgia told me where you are. It was juvenile to leave without letting me know.

> I'm not angry, just let me know when you'll be back.

An anxiety that had become so constant I'd stopped noticing it lifted. Hugh was home, where he belonged. I microwaved a package of macaroni and cheese and opened one of Moira's books, but I couldn't concentrate, more interested in workshopping a response. I wrote versions that struck an earnestly ambiguous tone ("Like you said, I needed some time to think"), and others that were more petulant ("I'm fine, why?"). But if I responded, I knew the anxiety would return. I'd start checking my phone every twenty minutes, and then every ten. I might fire off a follow-up message, making myself feel worse. That was not a productive use of energy. I peeled off my clothes and dropped them in the bathroom sink, filling it with water. Though I had accumulated two new T-shirts from a vintage booth that set up by the park on Saturdays, I still didn't have enough clothing to warrant using the laundromat on the corner, and had instead developed a system of hand-washing items and draping them over the Formica table in the kitchen to dry. I ran a piping-hot shower and stepped under the spray. In possession of Hugh's unanswered missives, I was calm. I didn't have to go back to Brooklyn yet. I had work to do. I felt better than I had in months.

FIVE

Moira

M oira viewed her life as a series of discrete sections with little over-
lap, from her childhood in Manhattan to her years at boarding
school, the blip of Texas and the stretch of college. Little followed her
from era to era; friends fell away, she seldom returned to the places she
left behind. Despite Celia's invitations, she didn't return to Houston
for nearly a decade.

At Radcliffe she'd been wary of becoming close with the women
in her program. During her first week on campus, on her way to the
dean of studies to petition for attendance in a course reserved for
upperclassmen, she walked through Cambridge Common and saw
four boys sitting on a bench, their legs kicked out in front of them.
It was September and the summer heat kissed against the chill of
fall. The young men were occupied, she realized, by a trio of girls
sprawling on the grass amid a mess of books and bags. Two of the
boys were murmuring to each other, chuckling and nodding, but the
last of them, the most handsome, had curled his eyebrows and upper
lip into an expression between amusement and distaste, staring in
silence as though watching animals in a zoo. Moira didn't realize she
was staring, too, until he snapped his eyes up at her. "Do you need
something?" he said—slow, sarcastic—and as she hurried away she
could hear them laughing behind her.

She didn't want to possess whatever weak thing it was they'd identified in those girls, and in the amplification of their femininity en masse. And so she worked through those years with a single-mindedness almost entirely unencumbered by friends or serious relationships. She did go on a few dates. There was an engineer who took her to a movie. At the theater, she said she was getting herself a Coke and would he like one; he scrounged in his pockets for change and, pressing enough for one belligerently into her hands, said he wasn't fond of Coke and sat stiffly through the film and didn't call her again. Two literature majors, one economics major, an aspiring politician—fumbling kisses, pressed doubly into seats meant for one; dark theaters and darker cars. At the beginning of her final year, an assistant professor at MIT sat down next to her while she was reading in the public garden and commented on the size of the asters, which she'd previously only noticed as smudges of purple. They wandered to Bailey's, where he charmed her by ordering a sundae with extra hot fudge. Three days later, when he arrived at her apartment to take her to dinner, she invited him in and she was that sad, hard little word—*virgin*—no longer.

She saw him a dozen times over the next few months, a cozy companionship of reading and writing and routine sexual activities that nevertheless left her feeling vaguely guilty. Then they slipped away from each other, he perhaps into some other relationship, she into her last stressful months of school: her quantum field theory tutorial, the final exam for her course in Euclidean vectors, a paper on stellar rotation.

She was accepted to Berkeley's astrophysics department. After college graduation—during which, because of an administrative error, her name was never called and so she never walked across the stage with the rest of her classmates, receiving her diploma in the mail a month later—she returned home for the summer. It was only supposed to be the summer.

She hadn't been back since Christmas, and in the meantime her mother had installed a woman named Rita in the guest bedroom, following Emmett's disappearance one afternoon in early April. He had been caught looting the pharmacy on the corner, walking out with boxes of razors and cold medicine in his pockets. The Columbia-Presbyterian doctor who examined him pulled Nina aside and described what others hadn't been able or willing to: the gradual but inevitable deterioration of brain function over time, the loss of ability to feed oneself, eventually to digest, to breathe. *He referred me to two mental institutions,* Nina wrote in one of the lengthy letters Moira received at school, *which for obvious reasons are undesirable, and so despite your father's protestations we have enlisted the help of a live-in nurse.* Moira wondered about these "obvious reasons." The condition of the facilities? The stigma? Emmett's name was still etched into the glass doors of his agency, though his colleagues had quietly redistributed his clients.

Depending on the day, Emmett summarily ignored Rita or treated her like an exalted guest, asking her to read Dante and Joyce out loud to him in his study, and waiting patiently for her answers—"It seems to me Mr. Dante's pity for the lost souls is a burden to him, Mr. Nelson"—to his endless, musing questions. That was where Moira found them that May evening, lit by the Tiffany sconces that threw faint watercolors over the walls, Rita trailing behind Emmett as he stalked back and forth, hands clasped behind him.

"Dad," Moira said, after watching him in confused silence. "I'm home."

He glanced at her and turned back to the shelves.

"Is this a joke?" Moira said, talking to her father but looking at Rita. "No, *Hi, Moira, congratulations on graduating, so glad to have you home this summer, here's a manuscript I'd like your read on?*"

He turned to her, hands in pockets. "Yes, welcome," he said. "You know your way to your room? Have everything you need?"

Moira's eyebrows came down so low she could see them. "I'm going to borrow Rita, okay?"

"Her? What do you want her for? She's useless, doesn't know her arse from her elbow." He gave Rita an exaggerated wink.

In the hallway, Moira dug two fingers into the hard muscle at the back of her neck and asked whether it was always this bad.

"It comes and goes," Rita said. She had an unlined forehead and deep dimples. "Sometimes he doesn't have a problem in the world, and Mrs. Nelson tells me he's like his old self. Days like today, when his memory slips, she has a hard time with it. It's more upsetting for the family at this stage than for the person suffering."

"I see," Moira said. "And do you know where my mother is?"

"She goes on errands," Rita said.

"I see," Moira said again. Her hands and arms felt heavy. At the small desk in the bedroom she hadn't permanently occupied since she was twelve years old, she pulled out a piece of stationery paper. *To whom it may concern*, she wrote. *I would like to request a year's deferment on my acceptance to Berkeley's graduate program due to an unavoidable family medical issue.*

She took a research position in a lab at Columbia and spent quiet hours with Emmett and Rita reading and going for walks down Park and up Madison. Once a week she ate lunch with Nina at the diner down the street. She visited museums. Every few days, Nina would disappear for an hour or two and return, if not cheerier, at least more peaceful. At dinner, depending on how long Emmett's ever-lengthening stretches of confusion had lasted and whether Nina had left the apartment, the three of them could have conversations like the ones they used to when she was home on school holidays—there was a certain tautness to any interaction, as though each of them was waiting for the others to break in their own particular way, but they could joke about Nina and Emmett's old friends, tell stories about Moira as a child. Otherwise, they stared down at their plates and made comments on the food, the weather, the news, as though they were strangers.

Rita ate separately until one evening when, watching her cut up Emmett's meat, Nina waved her hand at a chair and said, "Sit down, for goodness' sake, this isn't the antebellum South." Rita, who had been heading back toward the kitchen, stopped where she was and turned her head to look out of the corner of her eye. "Sit," Nina said, waving with a jerk at a chair.

"I've eaten, thank you," Rita said.

"Then have a glass of wine. Or water. I can't stand this tiptoeing around each other all the time. Everyone in this house is always slinking around in the shadows. Sit," she said, pulling her crisp white napkin out of its ring. "Please."

Rita sat down and folded her hands in her lap. Nina took a small, bellicose bite of her steak. Moira opened her mouth, thinking she might say something, then closed it.

Rita turned to Emmett, who was not eating. "Are you enjoying the dinner tonight, Mr. Nelson?"

He toppled a limp green bean from its pile on his plate, looking bored. "No," he said. "Not particularly." .

Moira eyed her mother, half expecting her to throw something at him. Instead she started giggling. She hunched her shoulders and brought the napkin up to her face as though chloroforming herself, her whole body shaking. The sounds changed, grew wet. Rita remained unmoved, might not have been witnessing the scene at all were it not for her left eyebrow, slightly raised. Her mother straightened up. "I have to lie down," she said, and as her footsteps traveled down the hall Emmett pulled a face at Moira, looking , for a moment, like himself.

By January, between the end of the winter holiday season and the first soft lick of spring, the world came to a halt. It had never been warm before and would never be again, and the trees reached their brittle fingers up into the sky like doomed creatures pleading for mercy. She had been home for five long months. She was twenty years old. Even her time at Radcliffe was distant now.

Her father sent her on errands. Having read something in the *Times* he'd have her pick up a new book, or send her searching for a particular red scarf he remembered seeing, weeks or years ago, in the window at Bendel's. One bleak afternoon, as needles of sleet pecked the windows, he started talking about needing a set of files for one of his authors. "It's on my desk. Or next to my desk, in the filing cabinet. You'll have to search a bit, use your noggin."

She tried to get him to come with her; he'd have a better idea of where to look for it. But Nina, overhearing, said, "I think it's best you go on your own."

"Are you embarrassed about what the agency people will think?" Moira whispered as she pulled her heavy coat off the rack.

She expected her mother to deny it. But she just handed Moira one of her wool hats. "Of course I am."

It was late, the office empty but for a few assistants who didn't know her and barely glanced up from their typewriters as she passed. His office had not been appropriated, (as her mother had posited,) by Emmett's old ladder-climbing junior agent. It smelled the way it always had, an unidentifiable scent she'd come to think of as paper and tobacco and ink. She paged through his filing cabinet, through sales information and correspondences with authors. She tucked the mail that was still delivered to his desk into her bag and found, miraculously, the set of papers he had asked for.

On her way out she passed the financial manager, Alonse, locking up his office. He'd worked with her father for as long as she could remember. "Oh, Moira," he said, his face softening. She hadn't seen him in years; he was older, his cheeks and forehead creased with wrinkles. "How are you, my dear? How is he?"

Moira wanted to bury her face in this sweet old man's shoulder, to breathe in his scent of cigarettes and dry wood. *We are all falling apart.* Instead she talked about how much her father was reading, how well he was using the much-needed time off. "Can't keep him away entirely," she said, holding up the papers, and Alonse frowned.

"Tell him to rest. He must."

His sympathy cut a chink in Moira's forced nonchalance. "I think I've forgotten something on his desk." Immediately she wished she could take it back. Forgetting was the family ailment. "You go ahead, don't wait for me."

"You're sure?"

"Yes, it'll take a moment. He's so specific about what he wants." She returned slowly to Emmett's office and picked a book from his shelf at random. She stood in the dark until she was sure Alonse was long gone.

The agency had moved into the building a decade before; she'd loved riding the elevators up and down, watching the white-gloved men press the buttons, wheedling to push them herself. Now, stepping into the car, she wondered how she could make the ride last an hour, hating to go home.

Pause here on twenty-year-old Moira under the fluorescent lights, on the tiny tic that flickers under her left eye, on the way she taps the tip of her right thumb against the tip of her right pointer finger, then middle, ring, pinkie, in an anxious, infinite count.

She does not know that in seconds a man will step into the elevator, or that he will glance at her face and pull his wide-set eyebrows together over his wide-set eyes. He will turn back to her as though pulled by a string. "Thomas Hardy," he will say. "Bleak." She'll hold up the book in her hand. "My father's." He'll nod, looking as though he wants to say something else. They will walk out of the elevator and through the main doors, and they will both stand beneath the awning as the sleet falls around them. Then the man will say, "Listen, want to wait this storm out somewhere?" and first they'll be under a diner's bright lights and then the dim ones in his apartment. She doesn't know any of it, standing there in the elevator, and if none of what followed had followed, she probably wouldn't remember the man or his eyebrows or the way he rubbed the side of his nose, as though wishing he had something to say.

Afterward, their entanglement of limbs and bedsheets, a pretty wooden box and a bottle of cologne on the dresser: "Don't go," he said, kissing the palm of her hand. And while there was a certain temptation to stay, she realized it came more from what she was hoping to avoid than from what he was offering—the draw of his spare bedroom wasn't half as strong as the repulsion of what awaited her uptown, her mother suspicious, her father sitting on the edge of his bed in a dark room.

She couldn't analyze this reckless new version of herself while wrapped around him. His body was warm. He smelled like baby powder and, at his chest and neck, wet dog. She traced her finger over his eyebrows and the deep indentation above his lip and sloping lines of his jaw as though she knew him.

When she left, walking out into the charcoal evening, she was disappointed that the rain had stopped. It might have brought her back to herself, though the cold did help with that. A woman her mother's age hurried past, a kerchief covering her hair like a nun's habit. She locked eyes with Moira. Judgment? The wind whipped lank pieces of hair into Moira's face; she gripped opposite elbows and drew her shoulders up high to brace herself, straitjacketed.

But after a few steps she shook out her arms and flexed her fingers. She was determined not to let shame rush in to spoil the high. She thought about how, in retrospect, the hours of her day had gathered momentum as she and Martin hurtled toward each other in time and space, slowing into a more languorous temporality as he knelt to pull down her underwear. She'd experienced a bald curiosity at herself, at him, at this bizarre, benign situation, two bodies colliding.

When he pressed his face between her legs, she'd splayed her hands over her mouth to keep from laughing. This was new. She was supposed to be throwing her head back in ecstasy, but while there was a certain hot awareness building where he was touching her now, with his finger, it was nothing so monumental as to make her abandon her strong sense of presence. It was all absurd.

Once they'd fumbled their way into the bedroom, the soft bed, he kneed her legs apart and, breathing hard as he held himself over her, he said, "Do you want this?" She realized that he could hurt her, if he wanted to—but at the same time she had a sense that if she said no, he would disappear with a cartoon pop. She said yes.

When she arrived home her hair was a damp tangle and the apartment's warmth thawed red heat into her cheeks and fingers. Her mother, asleep on the couch, didn't wake as Moira crept by without bothering to move the half-full wineglass at the crook of her hips.

As she undressed in the bathroom, her arms sprung up in gooseflesh and her nipples accordioned inward. She washed her hair, scratching her scalp with her nails. She worked her way down her body with a bar of soap silked with slime and harshly floral, imagining that every square inch of skin was covered in a blue paint she was stripping away. She removed it from behind her ears and the webs at the base of her fingers and under her arms, their stubble of hair. When the suds had washed down the drain, she turned the water off and wrapped her body in a towel. She lay down on her childhood bed. Across the room the beautiful old print of the constellations hung on the wall. She'd told Martin about it and he'd said, "It's all so familiar. I must have met you in some other life," and she'd laughed at his earnestness. "I don't know about that," she said, "but it's been nice meeting you in this one."

Who was he? She played back the afternoon, grasping flitting images in an attempt to put together a picture. First they had sat at his red Formica table in the fading light and talked about his job as an editor, and her father's as an agent (*Former agent*, she tried not to think), and her studies and research. They'd talked themselves out. When he'd asked for her phone number as she left, she understood that it was perfunctory. If he'd wanted something serious they wouldn't have ended up in his bed so quickly. She tried to remember whether there were pictures on his walls and what the furniture looked like, but his bedroom had been dark and already the details were slipping into a sepia haze of translucent objects; had there been two bedside tables, or one? Maybe this was what life was like for her father. This grasping at memories.

She flipped onto her stomach. She'd be leaving soon. In seven months this apartment, that man, her parents, this whole year would be behind her. Even if Martin did ask to see her again, she would decline. Better to leave the evening siloed, a burst of color in an otherwise monotonous month.

He didn't call the next day, or the next. She didn't care. (She did wonder: Had she done something wrong, bad, distasteful? She tried not to imagine her own smells or noises.) He crowded into her thoughts during the long hours of the night, and when she grew tired of thinking about Martin she thought instead of Ted. An inoculation against pain. He had a child now, she knew from Celia, who wrote with updates about the boys and the neighborhood. She imagined a thousand versions of that night in the lab. She turned on her reading lamp and picked up the new edition of the *Journal for the History of Astronomy* she'd left open on her nightstand the evening before.

A week later, after a day spent studying, she skipped down the stairs, enjoying the feel of her palm on the wooden railing. Rita had left for the weekend; the house was silent and cool. Her mother had been at the apartment for the last few days, not making any of her usual clandestine trips away—an affair, Moira guessed, that had soured.

She brought some pages to the dinner table, not wanting to lose her momentum, not wanting to waste time, wanting to consume more than food. She said hello to her mother, kissed the top of her father's head, sat down. She was reading a paper on pulsar stars, lingering on the Wordsworth quote that prefaced it (*And now I see with eye serene / the very pulse of the machine*) when she felt the prickle of her mother's watchful eyes.

"Yes?"

"'Yes?'" Nina imitated.

Never mimic your children, Moira filed away, somewhere. She closed her jaw around a bite of lettuce and kept the leaf, paper-thin, on her tongue.

"Do you think I'm your servant?" Her mother was sitting up straight in her chair, her elegant hands holding the fork and knife above the plate.

"I'm sorry?"

"Do you think I yearn to wake up in the morning, do the shopping, tidy the house? Tidy *your* messes. Prepare *your* dinner. And then sit in silence watching you eat so that when you've finished, at your leisure, I might clear your plate? Do you think I like tending to my adult daughter on top of"—she waved her fork in a sharp circle—"everything else? Have I failed in raising you? Did I spoil you as a child?"

Moira glanced at her father, who was looking fixedly at the meat in front of him. "Do you want to talk about this somewhere else?"

"Your father doesn't need to be protected from anything," Nina said. "Emmett. Talk to Moira. Back me up, please."

"I can't . . ." he said.

Can't what? Moira wondered. *Can't remember? Can't help? Can't take it anymore, any of it?*

Nina sat back in her chair and pressed her fingers into the corners of her eyes, dragging outward. "Just clear the dishes," she said. Her mother, who served herself just a bite or two of everything, was the only one with an empty plate. The bones on her shoulders jutted against her skin; her rings were loose on her fingers. Moira left her father's plate on the table and took everything else into the kitchen, scraping food into the trash and running the plates under the tap. She stared at the pair of yellow rubber gloves her mother wore when washing up. Who was she protecting her hands for now?

The phone rang. Through the doorway, her father gazed into the private wonders of some middle distance; her mother looked at him. Neither reacted to the noise. It rang again.

"Hello?" Moira said, holding the receiver delicately, her hand covered in suds. "Hello?" she repeated.

"Moira," he said, so softly she might have imagined it.

She leaned her weight against the wall, her back to the living room. *Okay*, she thought. *It's an escape.*

SIX

Sal

How many times did I go to Moira's that summer—ten, sixteen? Because I thought about her life constantly, and because our meetings increasingly felt like coffee dates between friends rather than interviews between journalist and subject, it's hard to remember now certain specific instances of seeing each other. I got used to the way she trailed off, wanting to check on the dahlias outside, or make a fresh batch of hibiscus iced tea. I made hours of recordings, which I listened to while taking walks around Linden, and transcribed in the evenings, so that Moira's voice was a near-constant background track to my days. (The sound of my own voice made me cringe, and when I was with Moira I tried to keep my sentences brief and refrain from leaning into the word *I*, a particularly annoying tendency I'd only recently become aware of.) There's an intensity to spending so much time with someone all at once. It was something of a relationship pressure cooker; I became dependent on and attuned to the intimacy she was willing to share, and a particularly open conversation could leave me feeling elated for days, while a brush-off made me mopey and grim.

Moira sometimes suggested I accompany her on errands. We'd go to the farmers' market or the health food store in Bridgeview, a larger town half an hour southwest of Linden, on the Hudson River. The first time she asked me to drive, she said she'd had an ocular migraine that morning. "I'm sure I won't get another one," she said, holding out her keys, "but better safe than manslaughter-the-journalist." It had been at least a year since I'd driven, maybe more, and as soon as I was behind the wheel I felt like a teenager again, flying down the long empty roads outside of Telluride. A Christmas ornament shaped like a crescent moon dangled from the rearview mirror; Moira told me Martin had hung it there. I rolled the windows down, the air sweet and clear.

"I'm glad you're getting something from this arrangement," I joked as we turned onto the county greenway. "Your own personal chauffeur. It can't be *so* terrible to have me here."

"No, Sal," she said, as though indulging a small child. "It is not terrible to have you around."

"You've put up with me for a while."

"Three weeks," Moira said.

Three weeks. I'd emailed Anna the day before, asking for a deadline extension; the gist of the piece was expanding, I wrote, to include the story of their marriage. She'd responded, "Unless Martin made a practice of turning aspiring writers he met in passing at parties into characters in his stories, I don't think we're ripe for getting scooped, but I'd like to make this happen sooner rather than later. Who knows when MFA Twitter will get ahold of *Evergreen* and decide he's worth renaissance-ing—Great White Male or no. Can we say two weeks from today?"

It was a balmy day in late June, and Bridgeview's dreamy, diffused light made it easy to see why an entire school of painters gravitated to the area; even the CVS on the corner looked picturesque. After I bought a few new packs of batteries for my recorder, I found Moira browsing the cramped aisles of the health food store—vitamins and powdered supplements, packages of dried seaweed and mushrooms, rows of Epsom salts, a vegetal smell. I stood waiting as she compared the ingredients on two bottles, both labeled omega-3.

"Moira," I said, "I'd like to talk to other people in Martin's life. Caroline, maybe?"

"Oh, I don't think so," she said.

"Just a quick call?"

She put one of the bottles back on the shelf and started for the cash register. "You can try her, but she doesn't even think I should be talking to you."

"Why's that?" I asked, high-spirited, as Moira nodded to the woman behind the counter and held up a finger to me. I was interested in talking to Caroline about her parents, but for her to not want to talk to me—and to have her not want Moira talking to me, but Moira to be doing it anyway—felt like something of a win. I didn't like this one-upping, competitive part of myself, but there it was.

Moira paid and dropped the bottle into a canvas tote bag: INTERNATIONAL CONFERENCE ON NUMERICAL ASTROPHYSICS, 1998. "All the reasons you'd imagine. She's protective. A little suspicious." She made a face, as if remembering something funny.

I smiled, too, as I followed her out. "What is it?"

"She calls you the Interloper."

I stopped on the corner, the batteries hanging heavy in their plastic bag. "Oh."

Moira stood beside the Honda, hand on hip—waiting, I realized, for me to unlock the door. The old car was musty in the heat, and I drove in silence for most of the way home. Moira, unsatisfyingly, did not seem distressed by my quietude. As we rolled into town, past kids drawing with sidewalk chalk in front of Two Scoops and a woman wrangling a bouquet of Mylar balloons into the back of a minivan, Moira said, "I think I'll go for a swim when I get home. Is your apartment nearby? Would you like to get out here?"

"I have my bike at your place," I said, somewhat petulantly, as I turned down the road leading back out the other side of Linden. "And I'd like to at least try Caroline. Unless you think that's a bad idea."

"She's an adult, she can agree or decline. But I have a feeling—"

"I know," I said.

We bumped down the driveway, Moira gazing placidly out her window. Inside the house, she gestured to the landline on the kitchen wall. "Her number's the first in the speed dial."

"Thanks," I said. My stomach felt tight. "I'll just . . ." I motioned toward the living room. I didn't think I could talk to Caroline in front of her.

My mouth was dry as the phone began to ring.

"I'm watching the link now, Mom," Caroline said as soon as she picked up. She must have held her phone up to the computer; "Clair de Lune" floated out over the airwaves. "See? The elephant loves it," she said.

"Hi, Caroline," I said. "It's actually Sal."

There was a pause. "Oh."

"I've been interviewing your mom for the article about your father, as you know, and I was wondering if you might be open to speaking to me as well."

"It's not my thing. Sorry." It sounded like such an abrupt ending that I almost hung up, but then Caroline went on in a rush. "If I'm honest, I think it's predatory, what you're doing. I know my mom's talking to you because she thinks it's what Dad would want, but he's not here anymore. She's fragile. It hasn't even been six months, and she isn't thinking straight." She kept working herself back up. "And why now? Because he's dead? Why didn't you care before, when it mattered?"

"Caroline," I said, my voice catching, "I'm not going to—"

"I mean, at first she said you were just writing about his novels, and now you want to talk to me? And you've been there for, what, almost a month? I looked you up. I saw you got fired for making things up in that article about the director."

"I didn't make things up," I said, "he was a playwright—"

"I'm sorry, maybe you're a nice person. And my mother doesn't usually suffer fools. But it feels shitty, to me."

"I'm not—" I tried again, but the line went dead. Realizing Caroline had likely told Moira about the playwright, too, I felt a deep, sickening shame. Inside both cheeks I have what I'd long thought was permanent scar tissue caused by my nervous habit of chewing on the slick flesh there. Once I'd gotten Hugh to look at it with his phone flashlight, my fingers stretching my lips wide like a kid pulling a face. "Jeez, Sal," he'd said, and called me the Joker for weeks. Since arriving in Linden, without realizing it, the wounds had closed and the horizontal ridges I was so used to running my tongue along had almost flattened. I reopened a spot with my canine.

"No luck, I assume," Moira called from the foot of the stairs when I clicked the phone back into the charging dock. I shook my head, and Moira made an amused tutting noise as she climbed the steps.

There was an oscillating fan on the counter, with a piece of silver ribbon tied to the spokes of its protective guard. I was still watching that piece of ribbon flutter, chewing on the inside of my cheek, when Moira reappeared wearing a utilitarian one-piece with a faded bath towel wrapped around her waist. Blue trailed behind her, tail wagging.

"Sticking around?" she asked.

"I'm just going to put these away," I said, pulling a corner of the *Evergreen* manuscripts out of the tote bag I'd laid on the counter. "And then I'll head out."

I waited until I could no longer hear her footsteps on the back stairs. Then I slipped up to the second floor. It was an opportunity presented during a moment of weakness; maybe if Caroline had agreed to talk to me, maybe if Moira hadn't laughed as though at a private joke the two of them shared, I wouldn't have gone snooping around. Excuses, excuses. In the kitchen I'd been thinking about the Playwright, and how I had let him yank the narrative around, taking everything he said at face value. Maybe that was some justification, too. Of course, Moira wasn't the Playwright, and I wish I could say that the feeling I got, anticipating snooping through Martin's things, was one of guilt—maybe somewhere in my lizard brain, it was—but most everything was subsumed by adrenaline.

His office was in the back, overlooking the pond. The rest of the rooms of the house were painted shades of blue and goldenrod and dusty rose, but the office was a flat white. There was an armchair, smaller and in more ragged condition than the pair downstairs, and a row of three freestanding bookcases pushed against one wall. Papers covered a corkboard opposite, but they were just notes about other peoples' books: lesson plans.

Through the window above the desk I could see Moira, seallike, cutting a breaststroke through the water. The desk was heavy and wide, with seven drawers, none of which was locked. I slid them open quickly, some of them sticking as I pulled. Black Zebra ballpoints, yellow Post-it notes, receipts and bills and old magazines. On the floor of his closet, I found a box of photographs, older than the ones

I'd been looking through with Moira. One album contained family photos, faded images of his uncle Willem and aunt Ilse, who'd raised him, and one glamorous photograph of a young woman, Gertrud "Gertie" Keller, age sixteen, Martin's mother. I flipped through them and moved on to the next album, mostly pictures of Martin and Wesley, who I remembered was Martin's roommate. Martin broad and solid, hair swept back, his friend angular in a dark jacket and slacks, with his head tilted up and back so he looked down at the camera. Martin and Wesley shirtless on huge stones beside a lake, and one where they were wearing paper mustaches. Martin with old girlfriends: his arm around someone in a skirt suit and then, later, around a long-haired, hippieish girl in bell-bottoms labeled *Sarah-Beth*—someone, in subsequent years, had added *kicked her to the curb!* next to a photo where she was turning a cartwheel in the park. Several of a petite woman with a pile of red hair Martin had labeled *Lil*. Martin's other worlds.

I thought an old filing cabinet beside the desk might yield further insight, but when I next glanced outside Moira was toweling off on the dock. In a panic I checked that the room looked in order, and was downstairs and out the door before she made it onto the back deck.

———

I LOCKED MY bike to a NO PARKING sign down the street from the Beanery and found Sawyer at the counter. "Can I get an iced tea," I started to say, "unsweet—?"

"Sal," they said, collapsing onto the espresso machine in mock relief. "Thank Jesus, Hera, and Allah."

"Hera?"

"I like to spread the heavenly love, sister-wife got the short end of Zeus's stick. But seriously. I was so in my head this morning, I think I left my oven on. In fact I am almost certain I left my oven on, possibly on broil, potentially even with a tray of potatoes inside.

"I need you to handle the register." They ushered me behind the counter. "Don't make that face, it's not—what is it your scientist does—quantum mechanics. Here"—they scribbled something down on a Post-it and pressed it onto the counter—"is my number. You won't need it. But just in case. And the system's ancient, but it's easy. You just punch in the items, but scones and muffins are the same, and for orange juice you hit coffee twice. To ring up you hit the blue button, and whatever amount they give you, or a credit card—"

"I'm not going to remember this."

"Sure you will."

"I don't know how to make a latte."

"If anyone comes in, tell them the espresso machine's down. Make yourself an iced tea. Take deep breaths. You're going to be great." An absolutely sarcastic two thumbs up.

I watched them go, only realizing as the car jolted out of the parking space that I should've offered to go check the oven instead. The minutes ticked glacially along as I stared anxiously at passersby, willing them to stay away. And then a man came in and ordered a double-shot espresso and a scone.

"The espresso machine is down," I said with sorrow.

"Oh," he said. "Just the scone, then. And a regular coffee."

I got him a cup of coffee. I pressed the muffin button. The sense of accomplishment was swift.

Eight minutes later Sawyer returned. "Look at you," they said, "not burning down the store. And yes, the oven was off. What evolutionary purpose does it serve us to forget taking potatoes out of the stove?" They connected their iPhone to the speakers, silent in their absence, and started playing eighties synth pop.

"Hey, Sawyer," I said, "what if I filled in a shift here and there?"

"In what sense?"

"In a job sense." I pointed at the HELP WANTED sign. "I need the cash, you need the help."

"But as you said, you can't pull an espresso."

"And as you said, it isn't quantum mechanics."

Sawyer scrunched their lips toward their nose and ran their hand over their smooth head. "I don't know, I really don't feel like training someone. I don't mind doubling up shifts right now, it's an excellent excuse not to work on the thesis."

"Fine, fine." I sat down in the corner to drink my iced tea and thumb through the photo album I'd temporarily deaccessioned from Martin's office—Martin's pre-Moira life, his old roommate, old girlfriends. The former wife, perhaps. What better balancing lens than that of the woman who'd once but no longer loved him? I pulled my phone from my bag and searched a free database for marriage records; 8,137 results appeared for the name Martin Keller.

I closed the album on the Sarah-Beths and Wesleys and Lils and called out to a reading-bent Sawyer as I opened the door, "Think about my proposal." But if they responded I didn't hear, because, with an ominous buzz, Hugh's name appeared on my phone.

I don't know who you are anymore, his first message read, *and I can't believe you sent Bonnie that text.*

I didn't remember sending Bonnie anything, and at first I thought he was confused. But I do have an unfortunate habit of sending and erasing texts while drinking, and the last time I drank was the night before he left.

A follow-up: *This is fucked*. Hugh almost never swore.

I read his texts as though from a great distance, like something inside me had shut off. I was not a stranger to the feeling. When I was fifteen, after months of my mother pretending not to notice my sneaking out of the house several nights a week, a guy I'd been hanging out with had to call her from the hospital sometime after two in the morning. I'd tried to do a backflip off the monkey bars at the town playground and ended up needing twelve stitches on my chin. Released and somewhat sobered up, I was sitting cross-legged on one of the plastic chairs eating vending machine M&M's when my mother arrived in the waiting room wearing the drawstring pants she slept in, her hair in a graying braid down her back. In the car, we didn't speak for five or ten minutes. I was used to her silence, but the weight of it was still terrible between us. "I'm sorry—" I started to say, but as I opened my mouth she pulled the car to a dead stop.

"Are you an idiot?" she said, turning to stare at me. "Is there anything going on up there, Sal? There is experimentation, and there is pissing your life down the drain. Figure out which is which." I felt as if I were flying out of my body, as though her reaction had released me from my shame. It was the only time she'd ever come close to yelling at me.

As I walked back through town to the apartment, I felt numb and heavy, with none of the giddy elation that Hugh's first set of texts had instilled. I didn't want to open the photo album, couldn't read, and then it was evening again, and time to sleep.

SEVEN

Moira

For Martin, writing was an elusive occurrence possible only under precise conditions, the details of which he was constantly fine-tuning, like a biochemist overseeing a delicate chemical reaction. More than once, Moira had awoken to the sound of furniture being dragged over the floor and found him down the hall in his office sliding the desk away from the window, or spinning it to face the opposite wall, the utilitarian red clock flashing four forty-five a.m. "Perhaps a no-feng-shui-before-five rule?" she said once, to no avail. He tried writing on an empty stomach, after two hard-boiled eggs, on no caffeine, on three cups of coffee, following a long walk, following twenty push-ups, following twenty minutes of reading, with the fan on high.

Moira could write anytime—in a snatched fifteen minutes between a lab meeting and a thesis one-on-one, or in the hour between Martin falling asleep on the couch, mouth open and a book collapsed on his chest, and him waking up with a start and saying, "To sleep, my lady." It started after Caroline was born, when Moira , who had suffered a degree of tearing she hadn't thought possible, was sentenced by her doctor to weeks of bedrest. The nanny would whisk Caroline in for feedings, and Moira would hold her daughter's soft, strong body and smell her milky hot scent, her brain scraped raw from pain and sleeplessness. She wanted to eat Caroline. She wanted

to wrap herself around her. Also, she was tired. She was resentful
that it was her body and not Martin's that was required all those
many hours in the night. And yet she was glad it was her body.
Still, after two months she suggested they switch back to formula,
everybody did it, but Martin looked at her in horror, and so she and
her swelling, aching, leaking breasts, her nipples raw from teething
and the skin stretched taut and striped with blue veins, continued
to subsume all other functions but acting as food source to the tiny,
demanding human that the pair of them had produced. *Okay*, she
thought, breathing in the sweet hay of her daughter's head, *then she
will be the only one.*

The days were hallucinatory, but during the minutes she found
herself awake and Caroline asleep she felt driven to express herself
mentally, to remind herself that she was not solely an agent of reproduction and sustenance. She didn't want to write about Caroline,
had no desire to dredge her feelings out of their acute intangibility.
(One morning, with her nose and lips brushing the newborn duckling
softness of her daughter's head, Moira looked at Martin, who was
looking at them, and said, "As far as fiction goes, she's off-limits,
too." His face transformed with the hurt.) Instead, she wrote about
the theories she had learned as a child and a student, and her excitement for the discoveries being made right then, right at that moment.
The exercise reminded her of her summer in Houston. She'd loved
that work, too, the way she'd had to simplify concepts without losing nuance. In her notebooks—not the serious leather ones Martin
preferred, but the cheap spiral-bounds her daughter would one day
use in class—she wrote out descriptions of quantum mechanics the
way she had explained it to Martin all those years ago, holed up in

that downtown apartment; the way she might eventually explain it to Caroline.

She let Martin read whatever he wanted, whenever he wanted. He was a good editor, teasing out metaphors to demonstrate what she recognized were mind-bendingly abstract concepts. She felt a new kind of love for him, his generosity boundless, his brain almost visibly spinning. "I wish you'd known my father when he was well," she said, touching the back of his neck.

When, two months into Caroline's life, Martin opened the ivory journal Nina had given Moira in the hospital and saw that she had been recording Caroline's height and weight rather than more immaterial milestones, he told her she lacked sentimentality, and she wrote *A chronicle of the conversion of food and water into human mass* under the words *BABY BOOK* on the cover. The next time she opened it, the pages were spangled with his notes: descriptions of the popping sounds Caroline had learned to make, how she was terrified of cats but fire engines made her giggle. *You came into existence against impossible odds*, he had written. *So many circumstances aligned in perfect symmetry, from your birth all the way back to the beginning of time, to allow you to be here, now, in my arms.*

———

"CAN YOU GIVE it a break, Caroline?" Martin shouted from his office as their six-year-old daughter banged out the right hand of "Für Elise" and then the left, major and minor scales, arpeggios, a high trill over and over again.

Moira didn't recognize her husband's aversion to music until long after they married, thinking previously that Martin merely preferred story to everything else. They didn't go to hear performances in the first years of their relationship, and she only played records when she was alone, because when they were together Martin was working or on the verge of working, and when he was working there could be no sounds. Even the quiet chatter of people outside on the street made him glare out the window, as though trying to beam silence into them.

"What do you mean, you don't *like* music?" she said, six months pregnant, a Mahler record spinning on their underused gramophone, when Martin had said just that.

"I mean I don't like it." His voice was flat. Stretched long on the couch, he kept his eyes on the pages of *The Real Life of Sebastian Knight*. Outside, sleet fell in silver slants beneath the streetlights. "It's grating."

"Hold on," she said, hefting herself up from her chair. She tapped his ankle and he retracted his legs so that she could sit down. She took the book from his hands and placed it on the coffee table, a pinned butterfly. "I know you better than anyone in the world. How could I have not known that?"

"Is it such a big deal?" Martin said. "I don't hate it. It just sounds like noise."

In later years Moira had friends—doctors, neuroscientists—who explained that certain brains could not order sounds as they were meant to be heard, that the tones of a concerto arrive as individual, random notes rather than the patterned, climactic soundscape most people hear. "One can't, say, learn to appreciate the patterns?" she asked over forced department drinks at the dean's house or at the breakfast buffet in the faculty dining room. "No," they'd say before firing off follow-up questions with the ravening delight Moira remembered from her father's doctors: *Consider the research implications!*

Martin looked suddenly vulnerable, his brows knit in a child's frown. Together, they were too big for the couch, but Moira and her belly stretched out beside him, and he shifted to make room. She kissed his neck, breathed in the smell of him: yeasty bread, warmth. Six years. Had it changed in all that time? If it had, they'd never been apart long enough for her to notice. She inhaled again.

EIGHT

Caroline

As her cell rang with the tinny opening bars of a Chopin nocturne, Moira's ringtone, Caroline was playing the piano in the living room for the first time in weeks. Sound enveloped her all day, and when she came home she so often just wanted to eat an avocado mashed into toast and tool around on social media, looking at posts by her old friends about their accomplishments and pets and political gripes. But that afternoon the house was full of warm light and the piano was welcoming rather than reproachful.

She slid onto the bench and let the fallboard drop with a muffled thump. She breathed in, and on her out breath pressed her finger onto the middle E, letting three soft beats break the silence before tumbling out into one of her favorite pieces, which sounded like a childhood memory or being in love or breathing or something. She couldn't ever describe music in words, though she often found herself attempting it, imagining her father's voice coaxing: *Please, Caroline, try to explain how it makes you feel. It's a good exercise. Just try.* This would be followed by her slammed doors and his passive-aggression until over a silent breakfast the next day, they'd watch Moira scanning some new paper and pouring cream over her grapefruit rather than into her Earl Grey tea, and Martin would raise his eyebrows at his daughter, the equilibrium restored.

Caroline attributed the dynamic between the three of them to the story of her birth, a story that Martin and Moira never grew tired of telling. "Thirteen hours of active labor," Moira would say, peering over the top of her glasses at six-year-old Caroline. "And then a C-section, in the end, just like your daddy was."

"And he was holding me."

"Yes, you were this swaddled-up bundle, and he nestled you into the crook of my arm. I could barely move, I was so sleepy. But I looked down into your big gray eyes and your tiny, ancient face, and it was like something in my world had shifted. 'You are mine,' I said."

"Your mama got sick," Martin would tell her during their Sunday-morning ritual of retrieving bagels and cream cheese from Zabar's and walking them across the park to Grandma Nina and her sprawling, medicinally floral apartment—Caroline's hand disappearing into her father's larger one, the grocers giving her hard caramels that Martin made her pocket for a more appropriate hour.

Sick meant *a rending, a slow-healing wound*, Moira would explain as the three of them sat at the kitchen table during a power outage. They were in Linden by then, Caroline thirteen years old and wearing Moira's nerdy old T-shirt emblazoned with the Milky Way galaxy, the words YOU ARE HERE above an arrow that pointed to a tiny speck. They'd pulled out a box of photographs, lit by kerosene lanterns and long red candles. Caroline, small and wrinkled like a knobby vegetable. Martin holding her, eyes wide with exhaustion and joy.

"You had cradle cap. I was so anxious about that sad little head of yours. While your poor mom was on bed rest I'd rock you to sleep, wake up every time you needed to be fed."

"You did have a bit of help," Moira said. Hana, a brisk Serbian woman Martin said was so efficient he didn't trust her. Across the table,

Martin and Moira each sent Caroline private, half-joking glances of irritation. Your father. Your mother.

They both believed they knew her best.

Caroline had collected so many stories of herself. She had grown from a ponderous baby who bobbed like an owlet when Moira played records—Joni Mitchell, Tom Lehrer, Chopin, the Beatles—into a determined little girl who learned to read music before she could words. She discovered the baby grand at her grandmother's apartment when she was three years old, hefting herself up onto the bench and almost putting her eye out on its sharp corner. Her bawling slowed to sniffles when Moira opened the fallboard and showed her the beautiful black and white keys, pressing a long pointer finger onto one and then another, filling the room with a low *bong*. Caroline reached out her hands to starfish them down over the instrument. Then Grandma Nina sat down on the bench beside her daughter and granddaughter and began to play, and Caroline stared at her as though one of her beloved cartoon characters had been magicked into real life.

"This piano has lived in this apartment longer than we have," Nina told her in an accordion of memories. The previous owners hadn't been able to move it—it would have had to go out of the eighth-floor window, an idea Caroline found hilarious. "Rachmaninoff played this piano," Nina said, which only meant something to Caroline years down the road.

When, on Caroline's fifth birthday, Nina had an upright Steinway delivered to their Upper West Side apartment, Martin asked her, exasperated, "Where'll we put that? Who'll take care of it?"

"It's not a dog, Martin," Nina said.

That year Moira took Caroline to Brigitte Engerer's recital at Carnegie Hall. The dimming lights, the quiet shush of voices. And then the music—the tidal wave of sound. Caroline sat, a finger tugging absently at her lip. When Brigitte finished, she bowed and left the stage, but the applause didn't stop. Eventually she returned and resumed her seat on the piano bench. She smoothed both hands down her dress. She placed her fingers on the keys.

At home Caroline asked her mother for the program, which she'd seen Moira slip into her purse as they filed out of the theater. She wanted to know the name of the surprise final piece. "I don't think that one is on the program, my love," her mother said. "We'll find out tomorrow. We'll call the hall." But by the next day they had both forgotten.

When Caroline was ten, Linden College offered Moira a tenure-track teaching position. (That year a section of Brigitte's mystery piece floated into Caroline's head during her algebra class. When she tried humming it, it came out garbled and her sullen deskmate slapped her hand down on the test they were taking and glared.) In the early 1990s, amid concern about the effects of New York's light pollution on the Rutherford Observatory, Columbia University had partnered with Linden to create a graduate research lab in physics and astronomy on the Linden College campus. For two years Moira commuted the four hours round trip three days a week, occasionally staying over in a faculty housing room when she was required for a meeting or extra office hours, or during the snowstorm that raged through the state for three days. But then the college offered Martin a position, too. It was only a one-year visiting professorship with the possibility of extension, but that was more career stability than he'd had in a decade.

Caroline didn't care where she went to school, but she didn't want to lose Juilliard pre-college, which she'd started the year before. She waited all week for the subway ride down to Lincoln Center, the day spent in rooms meant only for music. The compromise: the family sold their small, perfect Manhattan apartment and moved upstate, and Caroline and Moira drove the two hours from Linden to New York every Saturday morning. Saturdays became Martin's largest stretch of uninterrupted writing time, and on those mornings he would glance periodically at the clock in the kitchen as Caroline thudded upstairs for the third or fourth time, in search of some forgotten item, and then stand in the doorway, wrapped in his thin blue bathrobe, waving with guilty relief as they pulled away.

Once, after an argument at the dinner table, Caroline flounced off to practice Beethoven's *Diabelli Variations*, and from the kitchen she overheard Martin say to Moira, quietly but not quiet enough, "It's like she does it because she knows it bothers me." Caroline played louder, because while she could not win a verbal argument against her father, she was talented in the art of musical torture: he had previously told her that when she played the *Diabelli Variations* it sounded quite literally as though a drunkard were slamming his forearms down on the keys.

Once, Caroline told Martin she hated him, and immediately burst into tears.

Once, when *The Northern Light* ran an "Our Kids Are Great!" column on Caroline, Martin went to the paper's office to request two more copies.

But she wasn't thinking about any of this as the call came in from her mother. When she sat at the piano bench, she didn't think about anything worth putting words to, just the millisecond in the future when she would play the next note, and the next.

———

IT WAS MOIRA who found Caroline's forgotten piece. On her nineteenth birthday, a brown box from her parents arrived at the post office. Back in her room the package released the particular scent of her parents' home, citrus and cinnamon. Her dad was always giving her novels; last Christmas it was Thomas Bernhard's *The Loser.* (She read the description on the back, took a painful gasp in, and ran upstairs as he, perplexed, shouted, "It's an incredible book about pianists!") This year it was *Lucky Jim.* Next, she pulled out a Tupperware full of snickerdoodles, a box of monogrammed notecards, and a CD. On a piece of paper taped to the front of the case her mother had written, *You were maybe too young to remember, but I took you to see her play almost fifteen years ago.* Caroline slid the disc into her CD player. It was a mature, self-assured Brigitte playing the Chopin Nocturnes. Lying on her bedroom floor, Caroline let the music eddy over her and then, twenty minutes in, the piece—her piece—began.

She sat up. It couldn't be the piece, this slow, enchanting amble. Surely she would have been able to remember this. But then there it was, the building, frenetic rise as Brigitte's hands climbed up the keys until they hit their impenetrable stopping point and fell crashing backward to rest on that last low note, a church bell sounding a death toll once, twice, three times, four, and then one step further down.

Caroline was coming apart. The music was sublime. She would never be able to play like this, would never be able to write a piece like this. When she had listened to it twice more, she called her mother.

"It's the piece," she said without waiting.

"You got the package. Happy birthday, darling."

"It's the piece, Mom. My piece!"

"I thought it might be. When I saw it, the Nocturnes rang a bell. Which one? I got myself a copy. I'd like to listen."

"Opus fifteen, number three. Twenty-five or twenty-six minutes in. Play it for Dad, too," she said. "You can't not love this music."

———

THAT EVENING CAROLINE and Julie—whom Caroline had started shyly referring to as her girlfriend four months and six days before—ate cheeseburgers at a sidewalk café next to the park. The streetlamps glowed down the street. The notes of a lone saxophone meandered across Rittenhouse Square.

Caroline had played Julie the nocturne when she came by her apartment before dinner. She'd watched her anxiously as Julie closed her eyes; absolute relief when she swallowed hard at the moment that made Caroline feel like the floor was dropping out beneath her. "Wow," Julie said when she opened her eyes. "Wow wow wow. I've definitely heard it before, I can't believe it evaded you for so long."

"I've heard it, too," she said, "I just couldn't ever pin it down. When I was thirteen or fourteen I was staying with my grandmother and she asked me to pick up some eggs from the store on the corner, and I was on my way back when I heard the music floating out of a second-floor window. I remember thinking it was like finding shade on a sweltering day, because I also remember making a note to tell my dad that simile. Whoever was playing wasn't perfect, but it was still so beautiful, and I thought if I listened long enough I might be able to transport it back to my grandmother's piano and plunk out some of the notes. But then this man passed by, very close to me, and he said something like, 'I've been watching you." I felt so sick. It was like he'd stolen something from me."

Julie cupped her hands around Caroline's face and, standing on tiptoe, kissed her forehead, her nose, her lips.

Caroline wished they'd had a more auspicious meeting than being paired to check each other's midterm counterpoint compositions. Julie was hopeless at the exercise, and Caroline spent a significant portion of the two-hour class pointing out hidden octaves and oblique motion and perfect consonances. "I'm a violist, I don't have to know this," Julie said, tucking a satin strand of hair behind her ear, the end curling at her jaw. "It's like teaching an accountant about Plato. Or maybe teaching Plato accounting. Though it is nice watching your brain work. Explain the thing about climaxes again." Caroline's face was heavy with heat. Then the hours spent sitting primly side by side on Julie's bedroom floor, watching MTV. ("You can't tell me you've never seen this, either," Julie said as the screen filled with a Smashing Pumpkins music video, a flickering, animated journey to the moon.) The first kiss, waiting for the bus back to Philadelphia after they'd spent the weekend in New York at her grandmother's grand Upper East Side apartment, sleeping next to each other, their breath sounding so loud.

At the music library, Julie went in search of a book on romanticism. A long-haired cellist in Caroline's year was working the front desk. "You can't check this out," he said, when he located Chopin's complete Nocturnes. "But you can photocopy what you need."

She nodded and, staring at the notes, sank into a chair. There it was, her piece. G minor, the key of Mozart's exquisite, mournful symphonies, of Dvořák's only piano concerto. She scanned the notes, the tripping waltz step of 3/4 time, and hummed as she followed the plodding dotted halfs into brief skips of eighths and quarters. And then she arrived at the section, her section, the place where the music slowed to that low, low C sharp and then, like a heart breaking, it opened into—oh, oh.

"Hey," the boy said. "You okay?"

"What?" She lurched up, disoriented. "Oh. I'm fine."

"I get worried when people come in late and look at the music the way you're looking at it. Like you want to light it on fire. Bad lesson earlier?"

"No," she said, touching her face as though to contain her enormous smile, "not at all. I've loved this piece for so long but I've never seen it written down. And here . . ." She brought it over to him. "Right here, which I think might be some of the most beautiful stanzas I've ever heard, Chopin has this: *Religioso*. Have you ever seen that directive before? That's just exactly how it makes me feel. Religious."

He turned the sheet music toward himself. "Oh, man," he said. "Yeah. I get that. That's dope."

"It is," she said, giddy to show Julie. "It is absolutely, magnificently dope."

———

FOR YEARS, WHENEVER Caroline was lonely or anxious, she had only to listen to that part where the melody split open; she would cry, and then she would feel better. When Julie spent two months studying in Vienna, Caroline became convinced that her girlfriend had fallen out of love with her. She listened to the piece to access that building up of tension, the expected and gratifying release. And Julie did return, and she did still love her.

She listened to it as a calming agent in the months of limbo after graduation, before Julie got her job and they were dog-sitting for a professor spending the summer in Austria. They both took whatever auditions they could, all over the country; she even had one in Toronto, and Julie in Berlin. The auditions were usually Julie's. All Caroline had ever wanted was to play in an orchestra, and the orchestral world needed more violists than pianists, Caroline thought, correctly and ungenerously. Julie practiced constantly, waking up at five in the morning to get her hours in before working a shift at an Italian restaurant and teaching lessons in the evenings. Certain pieces—the Brandenburg Concertos, the Tannhäuser Overture—didn't bother the dogs, but the second suite from *Romeo and Juliet*, which Julie liked to warm up with, sent them into paroxysms of crooning howls, bodies heaving, eyes squinted.

After Julie got the job in Pittsburgh, Caroline started limiting her auditions to nearby cities. She took one in Cincinnati and one in Baltimore, both unsuccessful. For four weeks she subbed on a Princess cruise that sailed from Miami to London, passing through Portugal and Morocco and back again. "I never want to look at a silk satin gown again," she said when Julie greeted her at the Philadelphia airport. She babysat, the hours flexible enough to keep in fine playing shape and travel if she needed to, and the pay better than the accompanist gig she'd had for a semester at Penn State.

Caroline had less need for the piece. She and Julie were happy. Yes, their apartment was small, too hot all year round except for a few brief weeks in the fall, when the temperature outside fell to a pleasant sixty degrees and the heat in the building didn't yet blast from the radiators. But Caroline had gotten onto the sub list with Julie's orchestra, and supplemented that sporadic income with gigs accompanying the ballet school and playing at a Catholic church in the neighborhood. When her maternal grandmother died, Caroline received an inheritance,

and with a portion of the money she hired expensive movers to extricate Nina's piano from the apartment before it sold—it went out the
window, after all—and put it into storage. Then she had her upright
shipped from Linden to Pittsburgh. When they had friends over, she
and Julie dragged the bench to the table and ate one-handed, for space.

One morning as she ground the beans for coffee the old familiar
impulse returned, a simple craving like any other, for sugar or sex or
wine. The world outside was quiet. Winter had descended, the light
diminished to a few short hours in the middle of the day. Caroline ran
her finger over the cold CD cases until she found Brigitte's. Julie was
still asleep, but she was hardly one to argue with waking up to coffee
and Chopin. The CD whirred and clicked as Caroline found her piece,
and the first notes spilled out into the hush.

Something was wrong. For the first time since finding it all those
years ago, she did not feel wrenched from inside. She sat back on
her heels, her hands on her knees. It couldn't be possible to love
something for so long, so deeply and evenly, and wake up one day
having lost it. She played it again, willing herself to react.

Julie padded into the room, eyes squeezed against the light of
their ugly treble clef table lamp. Caroline raised her arms, a ballerina
acknowledging her audience, and Julie folded herself into them.

"Are you leaving me?" Julie said, her bed-warm face pressed into
Caroline's neck. It was one of their dozens of patters, she couldn't even
remember the origin of this one. *Time is never time at all, babe*, Julie would
belt, at random. *Nice weather*, Caroline would say on a sunny day, and
Julie would reply, Pavlovian. *But we could use some rain.*

"Not today," Caroline singsonged into her hair, absentmindedly
completing her line. "Not today, not today, not today."

CAROLINE WAS TWENTY-FOUR and then twenty-five and then twenty-six. She kept an eye on openings, reading union magazines she got for a discount through the alumni network, checking in with her old piano teacher from time to time. He was the one who mentioned the position at the California Symphony Orchestra in Walnut Creek. California. She hadn't been since she was a child, when her mother had done a yearlong visiting professorship and they'd lived in a house in Berkeley with a lemon tree in the garden and begonias gilding pots on the front porch. Caroline asked Jeeves about Walnut Creek. Twenty minutes to the water. Forty to San Francisco. No more de-icing the car in winter. No more winter at all.

"I'm going to try, I think." It was Sunday morning, and she and Julie were at a coffee place a half-hour walk from the apartment.

Julie raised her eyebrows over her *Architectural Digest*. "Really?" she said. "California."

"We've talked about California before."

"Not since I got my job."

"We're never going to talk about moving ever again?" The door tinkled and a pair of men walked in. Caroline tapped out a Hanon interval pattern with her right hand. "Pittsburgh or bust?"

"It's so cheerful out there. It would be giving up."

"Having everything be difficult isn't necessarily the hallmark of a life well lived."

Julie closed the magazine, her finger marking her place. "Do you want to put yourself through all that? Months of prep? Not sleeping? The travel? You're no good at auditions."

"Thanks."

"I'm not indulging that. You know what I mean. You know that I know you're a beautiful musician. But you torture yourself. I don't want to see you upset for days on end."

"Maybe."

"You're mad," Julie said, reaching across the table to run her pointer finger over the back of Caroline's hand.

"I'm not." Caroline swirled her tiny spoon in the dregs of her coffee. "But I do think that if I don't try to do this, I'll resent you. I know I don't have a right to. But I will."

Julie, beautiful in her old L.L.Bean jacket, seemed to be turning scenarios over in her mind. "I get it."

"Do you?"

"I do. I think you should do it. I'll help all I can."

Julie reached farther, holding the fleshy part of Caroline's palm between her thumb and pointer finger. She went back to reading her magazine and Caroline looked down at her crossword. Forty-two down: *Cool, in the 50s.* "I might try to ring my parents before they, you know," she said, "go to church."

"Ha."

"Do you mind?"

Julie shook her head. Caroline pulled her backpack over her shoulder and, passing her chair, leaned down toward her girlfriend. Julie hooked her finger in the neckband of Caroline's ratty gray sweatshirt and pulled her in for a kiss.

NINE

Martin

M oira and Martin were quiet after hanging up the phone. They liked to digest their conversations with Caroline independent of each other, the same way, after seeing a movie together on a weekday afternoon, they indulged in a never discussed yet mutually appreciated period of silence while leaving the velvet darkness of the theater for the bright stimulus of the outside world.

"She sounds excited," Martin said.

"She does," Moira agreed. She'd carried the phone into the bedroom when Caroline, on the other end of the line, said that she had some news. ("You were conceived in Berkeley," Moira said when she told them she thought she'd like to try the Bay Area. "Oh my God, Mom," Caroline responded, sounding like a teenager, "stop stop stop.") Martin had been writing in bed, as he had done every morning for the past eight months. He'd strained a muscle in his back. He was almost seventy years old. The skin around his mouth sagged. A pouch had appeared on his abdomen six or seven birthdays ago, though his arms were thinner than they had been when he was young. Following some less than ideal cardiogram results and blood work, he was on a diet. He was losing fat, yes, but also muscle mass. Sitting up at the end of the bed, the phone on speaker between them, Martin could feel his wife surveying him as he spoke with their daughter, thinking, maybe, about how much both of their bodies had changed since the evening she first undressed for him.

"I don't want her to be disappointed," he said.

"It was hard not to tell her that."

He nodded. The skin above his eyes drooped under his lowering brows. It *was* hard. It was hard not to shout through the airwaves at his little girl that she should come home, that he would take care of her. There were so many other things she could be than this one thing at which she had (he hated to think it) already failed. She didn't need to sink all of her ambition into this one dream. "I want her to . . ." He waved his hands uselessly.

"I know."

"She's good, isn't she? You do think she's good, not as her parent but as a lover of music."

"There are a lot of good pianists."

"Maybe she'll get the job."

"Maybe she will," she said, and picked up the book he'd been reading. *The Wife.* Moira had purchased it after reading a review in the *Times*, and after she finished she'd handed it off to Martin. He was almost done. "We're not anything like them, are we?" she said gently, tapping the cover.

He was running his thumb back and forth along his upper lip, as he did when thinking. "Mm?" he said, his eyes refocusing. "Ah, no." He was embarrassed to hear how wistful he sounded. He snapped his voice to meet her cheery register. "No, thank what gods there are."

———

MARTIN THOUGHT HE understood obsession. Then they had Caroline. He'd never been so consumed by someone. It wasn't anything like the all-encompassing lust he'd felt on several occasions, different, too, from the perpetual yearning to know his parents, which he'd learned to bury. When Caroline was born all those other wants dimmed. For all he knew, she was his only blood relative on earth. "We have to stick together, you and me, kid," he whispered to her while she slept on his shoulder between bouts of screaming, her face torqued and red.

As a teenager, during the first weeks of summer, she spent long hours in her room listening to her tapes: classical, yes, but pop and jazz, too, a constant soundtrack that he worried meant she couldn't be alone with her thoughts. From mid-June through mid-August, starting when she was fourteen, she attended a music camp in the Berkshires, calling once a week and sending notes home with pressed flowers glued to their fronts, blue chicory blossoms and white snowbells. She spent so much of her life so far away from him, either in space or in thought. They should have had another. Surely they couldn't have produced two children with such a strong instinct to leave.

But it was just Caroline, always only Caroline. Caroline mourning being born after the golden age of vinyl records; Caroline saying, *Listen to this, I think you'll like it*, or, *Maybe this is something you'd be interested in*, or *This? Nothing?* Her hopeful expression fell as he listened dispassionately or reacted incorrectly, calling a piece "jolly" that she said was full of rage.

After she called to tell them about the California audition, he imagined her practicing, sitting pillarlike on the heavy carved bench he'd grown so used to seeing in their Linden home. He didn't know what she'd be playing for the audition but he imagined it might be that Chopin that Moira had played for him the night of Caroline's birthday all those years ago. Martin had strained to hear the emotion that his wife and daughter insisted was there, but nothing came. He kept his face blank, but his desire to feel *some*thing was almost unbearable, and he excused himself to the bathroom and sat down on the toilet lid, taking sawtooth breaths.

At the library in town he requested biographies of her favorite composers. Bach, Chopin, Strauss. They sat like old friends on the passenger seat beside him as he bumped back up his driveway. When he sat down at his desk to read, the stories of their lives moved him in a way their music never could—Chopin most of all, he was happy to find; his tumultuous love affair with George Sand, his illness, his premature death.

Sitting at his desk, the sun hitting the pages so they glowed, he came to a passage that made him slow down, reread. A good story. Twenty-three-year-old Frédéric, having attended a performance of *Hamlet*, wrote a beautiful piece of music. For Martin, seeing the play's name on the page was akin to how, when he read *Pale Fire* for the first time, he was almost brought to tears at encountering the loving, bumbling Russian professor from Nabokov's earlier novel. The joyous lift of familiarity. Martin remembered himself at twenty-three, deluded and unaware of the confusion, frustration, failure, heartbreak, and loss to come. To write something at that age, still admired two hundred years later. His own books were out of print.

The composer, the biography noted, had originally titled the piece "At the Cemetery," but moments before sending it off to the printer he erased the words. "Let them surmise it themselves," he said.

Let them surmise it themselves. Was that arrogance from a man so young, believing that his work could perform that magic of art: to transfer to his listeners, on winged notes, a piece of his soul? Or was it a wisdom so few young artists possessed: the discipline of pulling back, of leaving air for the thing to grow without its maker—the knowledge that that place, in the in-between, was where art resided?

Martin became the young Chopin. Here was the ink pouring from his quill, the headache from sleeplessness, the belief that he would never die. Greedy for material, he ordered a more recent biography. He skimmed through it, looking for a line that might further elucidate the story behind the nocturne. But instead of providing more imaginative fodder, in a few brief paragraphs it refuted the earlier story. There was no indication, it read, that Chopin had seen a performance of *Hamlet* while composing the piece, let alone anything backing up the fanciful anecdote of his racing home to capture the emotions it inspired. The story of the inscription, too, was impossible to prove, as the original manuscript was lost long before any scholar could see it.

The biographer posited that the piece had been ripe for the kind of mythical story it acquired because its disjointed construction was so strange, defying the era's musical logic: what began as a mazurka ended as a chorale, and the surprising final section, marked *Religioso*, leapt into a different key entirely. People didn't understand it and so they created stories to explain it, comparing one section to Hamlet's monotonous, waffling speeches, suggesting that the *Religioso* directive was an invocation of death.

"But in actuality," Martin said to Moira as they cut around the back road behind the pond, their ten-year-old Lab mix panting ahead of them, "no one knew what inspired young Chopin to write the piece. All that remains is the music."

Moira ran her hand down his back. "Maybe it was just an exercise. A flexing of muscles."

"Mm," he said. "That human impulse to reach towards that which hasn't been done simply to see if it can be. That irritating, delicious itch."

TEN

Moira

Twelve hours after Martin died, Moira lay in bed, her daughter beside her. Caroline and Priya had arrived that evening, Caroline a wild-eyed wreck, and the three of them sat in the living room with a bottle of wine and then another and then a kettle of tea, talking until around midnight, when Caroline fell asleep with her head in Priya's lap. They'd all been in the same positions less than two weeks earlier, for Christmas. Moira hadn't yet taken the wreath off the front door.

Like a sleepwalker, Caroline allowed Priya to lead her up to her old room, but a few hours later, as Moira read the same page of the same book for the fifth, sixth, tenth time, there was a tap on the door and then Caroline was climbing into the bed beside her. "I miss him so much already," her daughter said, her face crumpling.

Then Caroline was asleep again and Moira was time traveling.

Days earlier she had received a request from a biological anthropologist interested in discussing a survey paper she'd written on theories of closed timelike curves. "I ask that you remain open-minded, as what I have in mind may sound far-fetched." What he had in mind was a study on transtemporal travel and so-called unidentified flying objects, a theory with which Martin became immediately entranced.

Moira, losing time for a millisecond, found herself transported some fifty years into the past, to her months in Houston. Back then, Ted had talked derisively about Dr. Page's work with UFOs; he found it embarrassing, child's play. *What's he hoping to find? Little green men?*

All those years ago, as Moira lay on the verge of sleep and her thoughts rolled riotously through her consciousness, it seemed to her perfectly obvious why a man who had observed and reported on the atomic bomb tests at Bikini might be interested in seeking out fellow intelligent beings. If we are the universe's sole sentient occupants, and yet we still exact evil on one another—torture, slavery, mass exterminations, the everyday unkindness of closing an elevator door on a person rushing to jump in—what does that say? Of course one would long for the comfort of knowing that someone else might be a better steward of this place.

———

AND PERHAPS IT'S not Moira's sixty-six-year-old brain flicking through this information on the night of her husband's death, nor her sixteen-year-old brain as she falls asleep in 1968, but rather my own decades later, Linden left behind but Moira's voice still in my head, the information scrolling by.

"In the Drake equation," Moira said to me that June evening she set up the telescope to look at the stars, "a small flux in variables gives an exceedingly wide range of possible solutions. On the high end of the estimate, amid our network of a hundred billion stars, there's a possibility that around a hundred and sixty million planets in our galaxy alone support intelligent life. But if we bring the chance of any given planet developing life-forms down to a more conservative estimate, the likelihood of intelligent life currently existing anywhere else in the galaxy is close to zero."

"What do you think?" I loved her already, that night. How had I ever believed her to be plain? "Do you think it's possible we're the only ones out here?"

"Despite the odds," she'd said, adjusting a knob on the scope, "we exist. Why shouldn't someone else, somewhere else? Two weeks before *A Gilded Age* came out, a small literary magazine published a short story called "Game Theory" in which, just as in Martin's novel, a chess master attempts to order his life according to sets of calculations. Martin had long ago convinced himself that his greatest fear—that someone else would write the story he was writing—was ludicrous, and here it had happened. The concurrent germination of similar creative endeavors. Why not, too, with the random creation of life?"

I thought she was finished. I wanted to say something, but I didn't want to be trite or stupid.

She saved me, continuing: "Say that somewhere, on some distant planet, three-point-eight billion years ago, the first prokaryotic cells were gelling together within some alien primordial soup, just as our own building blocks were coalescing here on earth. Say some civilization, not unlike ours, exists within our galaxy. Say that they, like we, are transmitting hopeful signals out into space, and listening for our response. They are, in all likelihood, tens of thousands of light-years away. God's Quarantine, they call the distance between us and our heavenly neighbors. Even if they are sweeping the skies for signs, as we are, so many things can go wrong. A distant observer might miss our faint signal. If they receive the signal, it may take thousands of years to return it, and who knows where we'll be by then? We might be like two lighthouses on faraway shores, beaming our beacons across the fog, just out of reach."

That happens between people on earth all the time, I hadn't said then, but would now. *Even when they're just a few feet away.*

ELEVEN

Sal

On Friday Anna had called me to have a frank discussion about the piece: "Do you think it's going to come together?" I had assured her that it would, feeling increasingly unsure as we spoke. As if joking, in rapid succession I floated two ideas, the first that an essay might be interesting even if I never found the finished manuscript, because it could be an exploration of self-obsession and wish fulfillment, the second that maybe I could pivot toward Moira, to write about a woman using language to democratize science. "No," she said about the first idea, and, "Is she winning the Nobel anytime soon?" about the second. "If it's not going to work, it's not the end of the world, you know."

"No, no, it's all good," I said with manic cheer. "I think it's going to coalesce around his early relationship with his wife, and then the sort of mirrors and refractions of that, triangulating with my meeting him at the library, and then finally the fictional representation . . ." I trailed off weakly, aware of the stupid nonsense I was spouting. "Just need a little more time."

In an effort to stave off further anxiety-provoking contact of any kind, I'd powered down my phone over the weekend, going for a hike and a bike ride and working my way through a stack of books: *Pnin*, some cherry-picked Cheever, Martin's third novel, which was so dreary I abandoned it after the first couple chapters in favor of streaming *The Philadelphia Story* on my laptop while pressing my fingers into the sunburn I'd acquired during my outdoor activities. Then I made the mistake of checking my email. My mom had sent me an article about the California wildfires, which I read and thought of Caroline. It was already shaping up to be the worst year on record. Thousands of acres were burning in San Joaquin, seemingly all of Napa Valley was on fire. When I finished it, I opened a *New York Times* forward from Georgia and found the Playwright's face smoldering up at me: following the exposé he'd retreated to his family home in Connecticut and had not responded to requests for comment, but his play was in its second month of sold-out shows. Georgia had sent it Friday afternoon and followed up an hour later: "I shouldn't have forwarded that, I wasn't thinking, chalk it up to heatstroke. Hope he never shows his ugly mug in this town again. Love you." I closed the laptop without writing back.

On Monday morning the burn on my shoulders had crisped and begun to peel, and I picked up an iced coffee from a hungover-looking Ben at the Beanery. Rain was forecast and the air smelled like a hair dryer on high. Back on the street, I pulled my phone from my ratty tote and turned it on for the first time in days. I wanted to check whether Moira had time to meet. No new texts, no calls—a weekend of non-communication. I wondered if she was avoiding me.

When I tried calling Moira, an automated message said to check my service carrier and try again, and in a panic I wondered if she'd blocked me, having realized in the wake of my petulance that I had been in Martin's study, knew I'd taken the photos. Or, worse, that Caroline had finally convinced her I was bad news. Maybe Moira had brushed off earlier attempts at showing her the Playwright play-by-play but, following the short way I'd spoken to her, she was more willing to hear out her daughter's concerns. As I redialed, I realized it was her landline, which I didn't even think had blocking capabilities. Still, the call didn't go through, nor did an attempt at dialing Georgia's cell, and then my mom's, which was when I realized that Hugh had kicked me off the phone plan.

I couldn't help laughing, because whatever else one could say, it was a power move. I walked back toward the Beanery and connected to its wireless internet as soon as I was in range. Texts bubbled up, including several from Georgia: *Call me when you get a sec* elevated to an adamant stream of, *Call call call call call.*

"I thought you were dead," Georgia said when she picked up. "You can't do that, go a whole weekend—"

"Hugh cut off my service," I said. "I didn't realize until just now."

"Hugh also left four wardrobe boxes of your stuff with the door-man. We got back from the Cape yesterday and it was waiting in the basement."

Something cold and hard dropped inside my body. "What?"

"Yeah. A note, too. Sal, I told you to call him."

"Right," I said. "What did the note say?"

"Something very Hugh, like, *Sorry to impose, but you're her In Case of Emergency.*"

I sat down on the bench outside the shop. Underneath my feet a sticky swirl of pink ice cream congealed around a tiny plastic spoon.

"Sal?"

"Yes," I said. "Trying to think. Why didn't he call me?"

"You said he did. And texted. A few times."

I tried to lean my head against the wall behind me but misgauged, jerk-ing back into empty space. "Do you want me to come pick up the stuff?"

"And take it where?" Before I'd thought of how to respond, she pushed on. "Sorry, sorry. You can keep it here as long as you need, obviously, but what are you going to do? Like, long-term?"

"I don't know." I pictured our apartment with its hardwood floors and the desk Hugh had set up for me in the second bedroom. The closets empty of my clothes and shoes. Had he sorted out my books? Boxed up my perfume bottles and old notebooks and the two glass fox figurines my parents had given me, independent of each other, for the first birthday I had after the divorce? The idea of him going through my things was intimate and tender, and for the first time since leaving I missed him, a curdling fizz located at once in my stomach and lungs. Down the street a Prius attempted a parallel park: inching forward, back, forward, back.

"Also," Georgia said, "I don't want to pile on, but that text you sent Bonnie about Hugh having a thing for dumb girls was pretty messed up. I went to her spin class, she started crying when she told me. She really liked you."

"I knew I sent something, I didn't know it was that." I closed my eyes. "I think I actually *wanted* him to be cheating on me, just to see what it would make me do."

"Sal, that's so sad."

I was working at the inside of my cheek again. "I started going through his phone." I hadn't told any of my friends about my bad habit, and the words left my mouth in a rush. "He put my thumbprint in when we drove to Boston last year so I wouldn't have to keep asking for his password to play the next podcast episode. I don't even know what made me look for the first time. I think he went to the gym and forgot it. It was just there. There were lots of texts with Bonnie, but they weren't bad, you could barely call them flirty. But then I just kept doing it. At night he'd leave his phone in the living room and I'd get up at, like, two a.m. so I could read his emails and look at the web pages he'd visited. It was like binge-watching a TV show. Hugh's so fastidious about everything, you would think he'd purge his past digital lives, but he'd kept all these messages from when we were broken up. With Bonnie, and other girls. Stupid things. *You were wild last night, when can I see you again?* So then there was this part of him that I knew about, but I couldn't talk to him about it."

"Oh, Sal," she said, her voice gentler.

"This spring, he took my print off the phone. I don't know why. It just stopped working. Maybe he figured out what I was doing but he'd stopped caring about the relationship enough to fight about it."

"Maybe it was just an update glitch."

"Maybe."

Georgia made a quiet humming noise. "Are you going to come back to the city?"

The Prius, having gotten as close to the curb as it was going to, turned off, and Sawyer emerged from the driver's seat. "I should stay here for a while. It's not like I have a home to go back to in the city," I said. "I'm really sorry about all my stuff."

"Don't worry about it," Georgia said. "What's happening up there?"

"I have the worst sunburn of my life."

Georgia tsked. "That's too bad. When it rains, it pours," she said. "Or the opposite, I guess. I have to run to an appointment but I'll talk to you soon? Are you going to be okay?"

"Yeah. Sorry." I was doing an agitated mental scan for some quip to lighten the mood, to remind her why we were friends, but it was too late, she was demurring again, and then the line was dead.

Sawyer approached, gesturing back at the car. "Did you see that? Spatial relationships, not my forte." They focused on me, quizzical. "You look like you swallowed a lizard. Bad day?"

"My boyfriend dumped my stuff at my best friend's apartment." I got up and followed them back to the Beanery. "Ex-boyfriend, I guess."

"He was sort of bankrolling your whole endeavor, no? What does he do again?"

"He was Employee Nine at a sock disruptor."

Sawyer gave me a look.

"This sock subscription company. They're comfortable and you get a new pair every month. It's stupid. He designs the website, he doesn't even design the socks." It was hard to concentrate. I was acutely aware of my dwindling bank account. "Have you thought any more about whether I could fill in a few shifts around here?"

"I have not," they said.

I sat down at the counter. "Please, Sawyer. I need the money."

Sawyer sighed and pushed the sleeves of their navy coveralls up to their elbows. "Don't you have, I don't know, a trust fund or something, Aspen lady?" I had made the mistake of telling them about my dad's recent case defending one of the resorts against a woman who claimed a waiter spilled red wine on her Birkin bag. I did not have a trust fund, but it was true: if I asked for it, my dad would almost certainly give me money to tide me over for as long as I needed. He would also inevitably tell my mom, who would then get offended that I didn't go to her first, though she never had anything to spare. Pointed silences would follow, which were different and worse than her typical uninterest in my life.

"No," I said.

"You're *un peu pathétique*," they said, looking bored. "Sure. I'll tell Mark"—the absentee owner—"that you're doing a trial period."

"Oh my gosh." I stumbled on the newly adopted phrase, one I'd been trying out recently in case Sawyer cared about using the Lord's name in vain. "That is so kind of you."

"You're around here enough as it is."

And there I thought of what I should have said to Georgia, which was that my best argument for the existence of a benevolent god was that after you suffered through a bad sunburn you were rewarded with the satisfaction of peeling dead skin off your body, like strips of Elmer's glue.

————

I ORDERED A cheap flip phone, the kind I'd had in high school. Without a tiny entertainment center in my pocket, I started carrying books everywhere I went, reading them at the Beanery and on park picnic benches and in the bathroom while I peed. During my sparse work shifts, Sawyer taught me to angle the stainless-steel pitcher so that the steamer on the espresso machine churned the milk into luxurious foam, and the nails of my pointer fingers darkened from scooping out grounds caught in the portafilters. ("This smell," they said, banging the filter's handle on the trash can to clear it, "will never not remind me of my mother's breath, singing on Sunday mornings.") After a visit to Randy's to check on the state of the news—an industry, to hear him tell it, that he was single-handedly upholding—I started writing for him, short pieces about a town hall meeting for a proposed affordable housing complex near the playground and one on a little girl in 4-H whose pig, not yet full-grown, weighed 850 pounds. I'd missed having assignments, I realized, and the feeling of working and reworking sentences until they said what I meant them to. "I can't pay you," Randy told me when he first asked whether I was interested, "but can you even begin to fathom the exposure?"

When two weeks went by, and with them three visits canceled by Moira, I left a message on her machine saying I'd meet her at the farmers' market, her weekly Saturday ritual. I biked there and sat down under a tree to read: Nicholson Baker's ode to Updike, *U and I*, which Randy had recommended earlier in the week. I was wondering whether Updike could actually have described a vagina as being like a ballet slipper, when I glanced up and saw Moira hovering over the edible flower stall. "Chamomile is a sleep aid," the teenage seller was telling her, though surely she knew already. Her rigid multicolored basket bulged with red-leaf lettuce and stone fruits. Blue sat beside her, dejected, her short back legs splayed to the side. I wished, not for the first time, that Moira and I had met under different circumstances, that I wanted nothing from her but her friendship. "You can make chamomile tea," the kid continued, "but they're also pretty on cakes. You can infuse it in honey, or—"

Moira noticed me as I approached. "You weren't joking, then." She pulled a few dollars from her wallet and exchanged them for a berry box of flower heads like tiny fried eggs.

"Did I do something wrong?" I followed her to a stall of breads and canned goods: mason jars filled with buttery lemon curd, raspberry jam, ginger marmalade, apple chutney. They glittered like gems in the sun. "Are you avoiding me?"

"Sal," she said, perplexed. "I've told you that I'm preparing for the conference. I'm busy. You caught me in a lull earlier this summer. I don't usually have time to sit around yakking about days gone by—it's why the house is in the state that it's in. Surely you have what you need for the article?"

"Well, that's the thing," I said. "I'm not sure if I do."

"Perhaps you should seek out other opinions while I get through this, yes? Why don't you try his colleagues in the literature department?"

"I could," I said. I had already met with the head of the Linden literature department, a man who called me six minutes after I pressed send on my email to him. He had told me that, as one of Martin's closest confidants, he could speak to Martin's character and disposition as a professor of writing. I met him at his office on campus and, after I tried and failed for half an hour to nudge him away from his personal theories of adolescent malaise and in Martin's direction, he finally propped his feet on his desk and told me about how he'd once thrown a book party for Martin, and Philip Roth almost came, but didn't.

"Is there anyone else in particular you think I should talk to?" I asked Moira. "His old roommate, Wesley, maybe?"

Moira gave me a calculating look. "You're laser-focused on Martin's early career."

"I'm just trying to figure out how he became who he was."

"Do you suppose one stops *becoming* after the age of thirty?"

"No," I said slowly, masking my real annoyance with camp petulance, though I realized she was right, my fixation on Martin's prewriting life was strange—before uncomfortably thinking that it wasn't strange but solipsistic; of course I was interested in the person Martin was when he was my age. "But it was a juncture, wasn't it? He wasn't an author, and then he was."

"Well, I haven't seen Wesley Gates in decades. I barely knew him. Though he actually lives not far away."

"Really?"

"It's called the Center for, I don't know, Psychological Acuity, or something. Communing with past lives, dreamwork, unlocking your inner artist, all of that. I don't know how much insight he'd give you."

"Okay," I said. "Fine. But I need something, Moira. And I've been thinking: his sending the excerpt to *The Paris Review* is sort of an inarguable sign that he wanted his final manuscript read. I don't see why it would be such a problem for me to read it."

"I don't even know if he sent it," Moira said, turning back toward the parking lot. When she wanted to, she could walk quite quickly, and I was almost skipping to keep up. "I wonder if he sent it to Caroline, and she sent it in. I've never asked her."

"You know that's not what happened," I said, annoyed. "You know he sent it himself, you spoke with his editor there before they published it."

She looked surprised. "I didn't have any contact with the editor. It all went through the lawyer at his agency, handling the estate. Martin had died just a few weeks before, everything from that time is a blur."

"Why would Caroline have had it in the first place?" I said, more peevishly than I meant to. "You said he never showed anyone his unfinished work."

"He didn't show *me* his work, because any response, even a tic of the mouth, he said, would throw him off the project. And he never showed strangers."

Maybe if she hadn't said that I wouldn't have pushed so hard, as though trying to assert that I wasn't a stranger, that I did know him. "Moira, he wanted it to be read. That's what writers want."

"Stop," she said.

"Why do you have the right, though, to decide—?"

"Because I am his wife. And because some stories are only meant for certain eyes."

"Fine," I said again.

We were at her car now, her hand on the door handle. "Would you like a ride?"

"I have my bike."

She opened the door. "Wes was always tricky," she said, as though we were still talking about him. "Martin loved him like family but they had a difficult relationship." She put the bags into the passenger seat. "Call him if you'd like. Who am I to stand in the way of this great journalistic endeavor?"

———

WESLEY WAS EASY to track down. He had a branded online presence, a website for what turned out to be called the Center for Awareness. The forest-green background and scrolling white font advertised private and group dreamwork sessions, soundbaths, and a sweat lodge, alongside photos of the sprawling property: a farmhouse, two barns, a guesthouse converted into a dining hall. The program, the website promised, was aimed at creatives of all kinds, as well as anyone suffering from brain trauma, corporeal or otherwise. "Untangle your Personal Narrative to find your true space in the story," the home page text began. "Work with Dr. Gates, a renowned psychotherapist and the creator of The Program, toward a deep Knowledge." A testimonial page touted anecdotes from "the community" attesting to Wes's abilities, and about weekends that left them "on a path to healing." There were references to Joseph Campbell, to a "ubiquitous power" called energy or mana or Sakti or God.

I called the number on the website three times that afternoon. Nobody answered, and I didn't leave messages. The Center was just forty miles away, but without a car, between a series of loop buses and my bike the trip would take almost two hours.

"Have you heard of the Center?" I asked Sawyer as we executed a changing of the guard a few days later.

"The Center?" They looked tired, and said it like it was a different word, *manure* or *intestine*.

"It's meditation-y, and not too far away. I thought it might be on the radar."

"I don't know, Sal. There are all kinds of places like that around here. Whites practicing magick-with-a-*k*, you know." They inspected the day-olds on the counter and tucked a muffin into their bag.

I was stung and wondered if they'd had a fight with their girlfriend, Valerie, whom I'd never met and was either an EMT or a paramedic. "You okay?"

"Just girding my loins for a meeting with the old lady," Sawyer said, which meant their thesis advisor, Dr. Doefler. "Do you know what she said to me yesterday?" They switched into their Doefler voice, low and nasal, with a myopic squint. "'Sawyer, sweetheart, do you think it's possible that you are procrastinating the inevitable end of this project because you are unwilling to confront the unknown that will follow, because you are directionless, a small herring lost in a sea of aimless fish?'"

"Verbatim?"

Sawyer waved me away. "I can't tell what's procrastination and what's feeding the thesis anymore."

"What's the most recent derailment?"

"This woman who founded a church in Rockland in the 1820s. They have her diaries at the Albany museum." Sawyer massaged circles on both sides of their jaw. "Sometimes I look at all the work I've done and wonder why I decided to spend my life doing this. I started the degree when I was twenty-three, you know? Seven years. I'm an entirely different person. I do have a working title, though. *Weaponizing the Word: Christianity as Subjugation and Savior in Upstate New York: 1899–1935.*"

"Alliteration's good."

Sawyer frowned. "Yeah, and it's fitting. But my worry is that *weaponize* is played out. Everything's weaponized these days. Sloppy degradation of language. I don't know."

———

THE NEXT MORNING, I biked forty minutes to a bus stop one town over. After hoisting the bike onto the rack in front, I sat up near the driver, a man with a face like a bulldog who, when I asked whether he'd ever heard of the Center, said, "Can't say I have," and adjusted a photo of a pair of toddlers clipped to his dashboard.

I might have been more anxious when I arrived at the steep graveled driveway that led to the Center, impossible to bike over, had I not been so hot and tired. The skin between my nose and mouth felt like fine-grain sandpaper and my forehead was gritty with dried sweat. The tree-shaded driveway, full of switchbacks, revealed a small cabin, a wooden sign emblazoned with the Center's name in Gothic print, and a woman between them, hunched over in the dirt. She straightened up as I crested the hill, moving to wipe her hands on her buttery linen coveralls before stopping herself, hovering her hands above the expanse of pale fabric and then rubbing them together like a baker finishing work.

"I dropped my earring," she said. She looked about my age, maybe just older. "Gone, gone, gone."

"What a bummer," I said, trying to sound bright and trustworthy, but also sympathetic.

"Such is life," she said. "Can I help you find anything?"

"I'm looking for Dr. Gates."

"Oh, you're attending the Program?"

"No," I said. "Just hoping for a short meeting. I did try to call but I couldn't get ahold of anyone."

"Sorry about that." She was all angles and artificially tan, with a wide smile that went up to her eyes. "Summers here are busy. Everyone's trying to salve their soul."

"I'm a journalist," I said, in an awkward tone that made it seem like I wasn't. "I wanted to interview him for a story I'm working on."

She motioned for me to follow her. "He'll have time for you, then."

The property, craggy and dark under the trees at its entrance, opened up into a field of long grass with a groomed pasture beyond. The woman introduced herself as Dana and told me about the amenities the Center offered, all of which I'd read about on the site. We passed two horses standing toe to head, shivering their skin and flicking their tails to ward off flies. While the compound possessed none of the sleek modernity that a meditation center in, say, Ojai might, purple and red wildflowers dotted the untended fields and honeysuckle climbed a trellis arching over the entrance to a vegetable garden.

Dana had the intense energy of a self-actualizer, though it was hard to imagine her, with her pristine clothes and tiny gold (now single) earring, at a sweat lodge or discussing dreamscapes. Yoga, maybe, a class in which spirituality came second to the pursuit of a hot bod, and bimonthly sessions with a psychiatrist for a perfunctory hour of talk therapy and a check-in on the current cocktail of pills. Soon, we arrived at a wide brown barn building. "We used to board," she said, as she heaved open the door. "But Mom was the mastermind behind all that, and when she got sick they stopped keeping it up. Now we just have the old fogies out in the field. Restorative riding."

There was something eerie about the empty stables, dark but for faint shafts of light that glimmered with dust motes. "Your mom, you said?"

"Mhm." She reached for a rope that dangled from the ceiling, and a wooden ladder, like a fire escape, pulled down to the floor. "My parents started the Center together. Dad," she called. "You have a visitor."

"No visitors," a man's voice returned, muffled, from the other end of the building. Dana rolled her eyes.

"Wesley's your father?"

She nodded, and I followed her up the ladder.

Where the first floor was dark and abandoned, the second glowed with light and recent activity. We'd popped up in a small but well-outfitted kitchen, marble countertops and stainless-steel appliances, a copper kettle on the stove. "He's this way," she said, leading me through a wide-open room that smelled of cedar. "Wait here a second. It's Sal, right?"

"Sal Cannon," I said. "Here to talk to him about Martin Keller."

She knocked on a door at the end of the room and, without waiting for a reply, opened it and slipped through. Laughter, lowered voice, a grumbled complaint, more laughter. A moment later she reemerged. "You can go in," she said. "He has an appointment in half an hour. Hope that gives you enough time."

Wesley was sitting with his back to me, and so my first impression was of his bald head, backlit by the window he was facing. Both he and the desk between us seemed to emerge straight from the floor. He turned in his swivel chair. Wood and leather, expensive. "Sal," he said, and something inside of me leapt, sounding, as it did, like he'd been waiting for me, knowing that I would come. Then the rapid letdown: obviously he knew my name because Dana had told it to him. "What can I do for you?"

His warmth caught me off guard; I'd been expecting an aloof cultish figure, or an old grouch. "Thanks so much for seeing me," I said.

"You came at an opportune time." Marked-up papers lay on the desk in front of him, a dozen ballpoint pens in a ceramic stand, a plate holding a spent apple core just beginning to brown. "There's an active session this afternoon. You should attend it while you're here. Get a sense of the Center."

"Um, maybe," I said. "That's nice of you to—"

"We're in the middle of a two-week quiet retreat."

"Mm," I said, thinking momentarily of Dana and her eagerness for conversation; how many silent people had she come in contact with that day? "I would love to hear about that, but I know the clock is running, and I had some questions about an old friend of yours."

"Martin," he said, as though supplying a name I'd forgotten. He leaned back in his chair.

"Yes," I said. "I'm writing an appreciation of sorts."

"I read that he died this spring. I was disappointed not to have learned of his death sooner, I would've liked to have gone to the memorial. But Martin and I hadn't been close for a long time."

"Moira mentioned that."

"I haven't spoken to her in even longer."

"I've been interviewing her all summer, trying to figure out how to structure the piece—" I was talking fast, my voice pinched. "I'm interested in how he came to be a writer, the trajectory of his career, and I hoped you could fill in some of the missing pieces."

"You want me to tell you about Martin and Lillian, you mean."

At first the name didn't register.

He looked at me curiously. "Martin's first wife."

"Oh!" I said, excited. "Lillian. Lil. Yes, definitely. I mean, I had other questions, too, but that's definitely a blank I'm interested in filling."

There is a look that certain people get when they realize they are about to have an audience for a story they've been waiting to tell. Calculating and triumphant, but almost furtive, too, as though aware that to become too forthcoming might prematurely shorten the pleasure. There is often a quick, deep intake of breath, a swallowing or clearing of the throat. Wesley, behind his desk, squinted ever so slightly, a tiny contraction of the muscles around his eyes. "How much time do you have?"

"I've got nothing but time, but Dana said you have an appointment."

"That was in case you turned out to be an interminable bore. Come. I'm not one to expostulate across a desk, and the speed of walking is about at pace with that of a good conversation." He picked up his plate. "If your story is about how Martin became a writer, your story is about Lillian, I assure you."

PART III

ONE

Wesley

Wesley was new to Manhattan when he met Martin in 1961, maybe that's what sparked their friendship. The power imbalance tilted in Martin's favor, having already experienced the city for four years by the time Wesley saw him tacking a sign to a deli corkboard. The first of two distinct instances over the course of their relationship in which Martin would have the upper hand.

Wesley had moved to Greenwich Village a few months prior, taking over the lease from an acquaintance who'd gotten married and relocated, as one did, to Ossining. Wes, friendless, was paying a little more in rent than his fixed income—a small trust made available to him the morning of his twenty-first birthday—could reasonably accommodate, and spent long hours scratching out poems that always read angrier than he believed himself to be.

It was one of those days that would stand out, a singular dot on the ever-forking line of a life. Martin under the fluorescents, a flea-bitten calico figure-eighting his ankles as he tacked up a notice. He gestured with a copy of *The Adventures of Augie March* as he joked with the guy behind the counter, a grim man backdropped by canned tomatoes and pickle jars who, in Wes's albeit limited interactions with him, did not joke. Martin—though not yet Martin to Wes—thumped the counter with his open palm and disappeared into the afternoon sunlight. *Single male in search of cheap room for rent.*

Though Wesley had just fled a family of cheerful blonds, on Martin he didn't mind it, was perhaps even drawn to the familiarity. He charged him a nominal rent to move into the living room, and the pair began frequenting readings, gallery openings, a café that smelled faintly of gas, where Martin wrote prose and Wesley wrote poetry, and everyone silently downed charred black coffee until midnight, trying not to notice whether anyone was noticing them.

———

"TELL ME ABOUT where you grew up," Wesley said. They were stoned, Martin lying on the futon couch that he flattened, nightly, into his bed. Wes sat on the deep sill of the window with a cigarette balanced between his fingers, flipping through an old *National Geographic* with the other hand. He took a drag and held the magazine up. "They've opened an underwater park," he said, the *p* sounding more like an *f* around the cigarette in his mouth. "You pay to look at coral."

Martin pushed his glasses down to the tip of his nose as though they might convert to binoculars. Unsuccessful, he lay back down. "There's not much to tell about home. It was no Atlantis."

"What about your aunt and uncle? What about these parents you never knew?"

"My aunt and uncle are wonderful people."

Wes straightened his back. Given Martin's teenage escape to New York, he'd assumed they hadn't gotten along. "Tell me."

"If they hadn't taken us in, I don't know what would have happened. Germany, 1939. Can you imagine?"

Wesley could.

"My mother was sixteen. From what I understand, *her* mother realized she was getting a little fat and dragged her to the *Familiendoktor*, who confirmed I was on the way."

"What was her name, your mother?"

"They called her Gertie." Martin held one hand in front of him and, with his opposite pointer finger, traced the lines of his own palm. "My mother's parents were well off. Involved in the arts. There were anti-religious rumblings, threats of a curfew, the fire at the Reichstag building. Book burnings."

"So they sent their daughter off to rural New England?"

"Probably the most neutered place cosmopolitan Berliners could imagine," Martin said. "Immigration quotas favored certain desirable races, you know. They must have had some connections in government. I can just picture my mother dazzling herself on the sun-dappled ship deck and puking into the waves. Crying at night, her bunkmate praying in some unintelligible language. Ellis Island. New York. My aunt and uncle clutching each other on the train platform."

"And then you were born. And your mother . . . ?"

"My mother was beautiful. I have this memory of her walking up a flight of stairs when I was too young to follow. Though I have no idea if it's an actual memory or a dream. My only photograph of her was taken the year before the crossing, in school." He put both hands behind his head, his elbows pointed up. "In any case, she died when I was three years old. Accident with some farm equipment up the road. Some farmer's adult son was involved."

"Jesus, Martin."

"By the time I was old enough to hear the rumors about her, I was also old enough to wonder what romp with a tractor could have led to her ending up under it. Not that that matters now."

"And what about your father?" Wesley asked softly.

"What about him?" Martin affected insouciance, but Wesley could have sworn he heard his voice wobble. "My aunt and uncle have never exactly been comfortable sharing the details of my patrilineal line—who knows how much they know?—but from what I gather he was bad medicine. Probably died along with the rest of them. My mother's parents and younger brothers escaped to a friend's home in London. A week later that house was bombed."

Wesley winced at his remove, so unlike the gregarious, impassioned friend he'd come to know over the last months. "But I mean, don't you ever wonder who he was? Germany, 1939, as you said."

"No," Martin said. "I don't.

"Martin," Wesley said, speaking in labored tones—he was very high—"here is your story."

"What story?"

"Your story. *The* story. My God, the potential. The ghostly father, perhaps a villain, perhaps the worst kind of villain there is. The wayward mother. A son's search for himself."

Martin made a dismissive gesture. "Stop, Wes."

"Stop what? It writes itself."

"Just stop."

"The sins of the father, all that."

"Wesley," he said, with a horrible expression on his face, "I'm not going to turn my father into a fucking Nazi for the sake of some great narrative. That's not my story."

———

WESLEY GATES GREW up in a sprawling South Carolina family, his father the owner and operator of a homey restaurant off Charleston's main drag, plus a small hotel and a string of storefronts. Family lore held that Gates elders had gambled and drunk away the fortune accumulated in the era of hooped gowns and muttonchops, and that what his parents made, they'd made themselves. ("Convenient way to unshackle the family from the old money," Wesley said as we stopped so he could retie a bit of electric fencing around the horse pasture, "derived, one can imagine, from less than admirable business associations.")

Wesley's four older sisters stayed in Charleston after high school to serve glutinous beige food and flirt with hotel guests before roping in husbands to provide broods of their own. Wes's father hoped he'd take over as head of the family business, but his mother purred to him that he deserved more. It was no secret she loved him best, her only boy. She admired his dark gray eyes and long black lashes. His peachy sisters joked that he was a fairy child switched at birth, and after learning about phenotype in grade school he theorized he was the product of a love affair with some secret, better man than his bland father. When he confronted his mother, she pulled out photos of his grandfather and pointed to the irises so dark they looked black, and told him he'd been reading too much Arthur Conan Doyle—and Tolkien and Hemingway and Wilde besides.

Wes attended Duke, the first university man in three generations of Gateses, and was in the premed track until, while dissecting a fetal pig, he had what he would later compare to a loss of faith. If one only had a single life—if all that separated him from the carcass on the table was an accident of birth—it was a shame to waste it doing anything but what one really loved. Wes wasn't sure what he loved, but he aimed to find out, and soon found he hadn't been reading too much literature, but too little.

———

A SUMMER EVENING. A downtown bar rank with smoke, three stolen stop signs nailed behind the low stage. Martin was there to read a short story he'd been working and reworking for months. He was there, too, for the girls, it should be said; the girls in their Downy-soft T-shirts and gamine hair, murmuring breathy songs into the mic. Martin's milk-fed charm coupled with his literary ambitions were a deadly combination, and in the five years he'd lived in New York he claimed to have had six serious girlfriends, with more than a handful of casual flings in between. But he didn't want just a girlfriend, he had said moodily to Wesley one morning, having returned to the apartment after ushering another young lady into a cab. He wanted a creative partnership; he wanted an ideal reader.

"Maybe you'll have to settle for a good old platonic division of labor," Wes had said. "Men for intellectual fulfillment, a woman to further the family name."

In front of a crowd, Martin held his broad shoulders hunched and high. He stuttered, rushing through some words and mumbling others— it was difficult to remind oneself, through the secondary embarrassment, that Martin was actually capable of stringing a sentence together, and sometimes well. On the subway there, rattling side by side, Wes had mentioned that Martin's penchant for staring fixedly down at the page made for an uncomfortable audience experience. Now his friend was making a weird and concerted effort to dart his eyes upward every few clauses.

Wesley, to cut his own internal tension, leaned toward the slight girl in workman's jeans standing beside him. "Rather like a kidnapped prisoner reading a prepared statement, no?"

She'd been taking a swig of beer and at this she convulsed minutely, the foam climbing back up the neck of the bottle. "That's terrible," she said.

"He, however, is not. Just a terrible reader. But if you listen hard, the effort's rewarded."

The girl eyed him. "You're, what, his representation?"

"Just a good friend."

During one of his furtive upward glances, Martin pinned Wesley in his sights before clocking the girl beside him. When he finished his story—"Yes, okay, thanks for listening"—and flopped, loose-limbed, down the stairs from the stage, she offered her hand. "I liked your story," she said over the music that had resumed on the bar speakers. She was a head shorter than both of them, and the muscles in her arms jumped as she gestured. "The language was lovely. I wish I'd been able to hear better."

"Loud room, bad acoustics," Martin said, puffing up with the glow of the noticed. "Anxious reader."

"I'm Lillian."

"Wes."

"Martin" He tipped an invisible hat. "Some stories are better out loud, but I don't know about this one."

"Just take the almost-compliment and move on," Wes said.

Lillian hooked her thumbs through her belt loops and swayed over her ankles, shifting her hips to the music. "The line about his happiness being like a rusted piston was great."

"Thank you," Martin said, pleased. Wes knew the line she was talking about, and in truth Martin had employed a more worn metaphor, something about the sun, but he could tell from his friend's face that it didn't matter. To hear his words repeated back to him, even incorrectly, was as good as any drug.

When she turned to say goodbye to a passing friend, Martin said, "She's beautiful, isn't she? Sort of feral."

"Yes," Wes said, offering him a cigarette. "Toulouse-Lautrec hair and a Titian bosom."

Wes wasn't surprised when Lillian tagged along with them to a party in an apartment as dingy as the bar had been. Martin climbed out onto the fire escape, and Wes followed, holding a bottle of beer by the neck. "There is probably pigeon shit all over this," he said, peering at the railings.

"It doesn't matter if you can't see it," Martin said.

"My friend the philosopher."

Lillian, a pair of hands and a beetle-black oxford shoe, unfurled last. Then the sudden intimacy of a shared bottle, the ritualistic inhales of a passed joint. Everything moved at three-quarter speed, as though underwater: Lillian reaching over to pluck, with her long fingers, the joint straight from Martin's lips; her sweet ha-ha-ha laugh; his two a.m. smile. Lillian tilted her head, her throat pale in the moonlight, and recited: "The lamp hummed: Regard the moon . . ."

Wesley grinned. "*La lune ne garde aucune rancune.*"

They argued the merits of Tolstoy and Dostoyevsky (Wes and Lillian for the former, Martin the latter). Energized by the warm summer night or Lillian or the pot or the magic combination of the three, Martin climbed high up the escape, howling like a wolf. Down below, Wes leaned into Lillian, nudging her bare arm with his shoulder. "Don't do this if you're not serious," he said, the pot making him grave and protective.

She pulled back her head and eyed him sidelong. "What are you suggesting, Mr. Gates?"

"Don't get involved with him unless you're interested in something significant. He's had a string of love affairs. Now he needs to play for keeps."

"'For keeps,'" Lillian said, testing it out. "You sound like a wise old grandmother in a Harlequin romance."

"He needs stability if he's going to get anywhere with his writing." Wes didn't know what he was saying, but it sounded good.

"'Stability, yes. Romantic. For keeps.'" Every time she said it, it was as if it were the first time. "You know, I spend all day at a department store convincing women that a particular new thing will make them happier. The ones who most fervently believe me are the ones who keep coming back. They're never satisfied for long. Nothing's for keeps." And, maybe because he was so close to her, she'd kissed him, lightly, on the mouth. Then she leaned back and kicked her legs through the fire escape bars, swinging her boyish shoes.

The kiss was nothing, soft and dry. A handshake.

"Nothing lasts forever. Everything changes," she said, and snapped her fingers in front of his nose, startling him. "Just like that."

"Fine," Wes said. But he had seen the way they'd lit up when they spoke to each other, and he knew they were young but getting older; she'd change her mind about forever once she realized it wasn't so far away.

It was Wesley who convinced Martin to call her later that week, after disengaging himself from the latest treacle-sweet romance. In the evenings, while Wes lay in his bedroom, reading or writing or staring at the crack bisecting his ceiling, he would hear the two of them creep into the apartment after Martin's shift at the restaurant. Martin smelled of smoke and grease, Lillian of the department store's oversaturated air, Youth Dew, Rive Gauche, Chanel No. 5. There was the shower turning on and their lowered voices as they soaped each other down, working the suds between fingers and over knees and into curls of hair. They'd lie on Martin's softly creaking sofa bed, behind the chinoiserie screen Lillian brought over to replace the sheet he'd strung up between two hooks in the ceiling, and read to each other. Whole books: *Swann's Way*, *Madame Bovary*, *Moby-Dick*, *Heroides*. In the glow of the lamplight, the shadows of their hands and noses stretched huge on the wall.

———

MARTIN WANTED TO be with Lillian all the time, and when he wasn't with her, he wanted to talk about her. Trailing behind Wesley on St. Mark's, he said he had figured out Lillian's Rosebud, her contrariness for the sake of being contrary, the way she was affectionate and loving one evening and rageful the next. "She was a ballerina," he said as they ate hot dogs beside the fountain in Washington Square.

"Oh yes, I believe you've mentioned that," Wesley said.

"Yes, but, Wesley, imagine the devastation. She was a ballerina and then one year into her position in the corps—"

"The *p* is silent."

"Excuse me?"

"It's pronounced like *core*, not *corpse*."

"I didn't say 'corpse.' Now shut up and listen for a minute; she had just gotten everything she'd ever wanted, everything she'd worked for, and then she *falls*, six months in. Snaps a ligament and her career is done."

"I can't tell whether you sound like that because you're reveling in the tragedy of it," Wesley said, wiping grease off his fingers, "or because you're imagining your girlfriend in a leotard and tights."

"It's no wonder she has this complex, difficult relationship with her body," Martin mused. "She's like a wildcat one night and then for four days—a week!—nothing. Nada. Will barely let me touch her."

"Oh, I wouldn't worry about it, I'm sure it's just because she's oh-so-satisfied by your passionate embrace."

"Maybe," Martin said slowly, considering. Wesley's balled-up napkin hit him square in the forehead.

———

WES AND MARTIN moved into a real two-bedroom, forget-me-not wallpaper in the bathroom and the scar of a burn above the stove. On Wes's initiative, they painted the living room a dusty rose, the bedrooms sky blue. Lillian came over with her hair tied up in a bandanna, wearing already paint-spattered coveralls with legs so long she'd cuffed them into donuts at her bony ankles.

"What are those?" Martin asked as, three steps up the ladder, he held his dripping paintbrush out to the side and leaned down for a kiss.

"My bum-arounds," Lillian said.

"Are you secretly a housepainter in your free time?" Wes asked drolly. "Is that where you disappear to?" Martin gave him a bug-eyed look. He'd been complaining about Lillian's tendency to go hours, sometimes days without returning a call, but this wasn't a preoccupation about which he needed her to know.

"I don't disappear," Lillian said. "I'm home. Writing. You two should try it sometime."

If she'd said it just to Martin it would have been an insult, but directed toward both of them it was just good-natured ribbing; she was the disciplined woman, they were the disappointing, good-for-a-good-time men.

"I might be done with poetry," Wes said. Having masterminded the painting project, he'd gotten bored after the first coat and was now sitting with his back to the only dry wall, drinking a Coke. "I'm thinking about going back to school." But if they heard him, they didn't show it. Lillian climbed onto a folding chair, wobbling as she reached the roller into a corner. Martin, hovering like an anxious parent with an unruly child, told her to get down, to be careful, to not apply the paint so thickly, see how it was starting to form drips? When a huge splat fell from her roller onto the hardwood, she grimaced and lurched into a placating curtsy, from which she shot Wes an almost imperceptible wink.

———

LILLIAN POINTED TO a baby in a buggy outside the restaurant window, all but its face swaddled in a blanket. The baby watched Martin through the lettering printed on the glass and turned its head, hiding one eye in the yellow cotton. "She's flirting with you."

"We could have one," Martin said.

Lillian held her fork like a conductor's baton. One year. Spaghetti and a cloud of parmesan in honor of spending 365 days thinking about each other, pressing lips and teeth to skin. That's why he said it, Martin would later point out to Wesley. He thought it was an anniversary kind of thing to say.

"Is that right?" Lillian said.

"Sure. When I finish the book."

"What about *my* timeline? Maybe I want a baby now."

"You can't have one," Martin said, blinking affably as he pushed his glasses up the bridge of his nose. "Unless you find some other gentleman to beget it for you."

"Maybe I will. Some gentleman who's not so keen to send me off with some other gentleman."

"Oh come on."

Lillian leaned back in her chair and crossed her arms. "I didn't bring this up. I just pointed the kid out."

"Lil." Martin reached across the table, his hands open. "We know this is the long haul. I was just teasing."

"The long haul. I know." She dropped an ice cube into his cupped palm and did not finish the expensive lunch.

———

THEY TALKED ABOUT getting married. "It's sort of irritating, the inevitability, no?" Lillian called from the toilet. Martin, splayed naked in bed, made an *mmph* noise. They'd just concluded an inaugural screw following an inaugural champagne toast in their new apartment. The tiny place on the Bowery was twenty minutes by subway from the midtown offices of Grant Aikens, where Martin was in his fifth month of dangling from the lowest rung on the ladder. It had been Lillian who argued that being near writers might stimulate him in a way that working at the restaurant did not.

They had been at her old apartment, a rarity; Lillian's roommates, a pair of prudish sisters, were away. It was early in the morning and she'd come into the bedroom already dressed and smelling of lavender soap. "You'll thrive on the internal jostling. You love to compete."

"What about you?" he'd asked. "You pick out overpriced clothes for rich women."

Lillian lay down beside Martin, fitting her body to his; she above the covers, he below. "I'm already stimulated," she said. "I write every night. But, love, you haven't been making time." He jerked his head back, slid out of bed. "Martin," she said. "It's not an accusation." But he left for his lunch shift early and in a sulk.

He returned that evening smelling like steak and french onion soup, clutching bodega daisies and a day-old apple pie from the dessert case. She was in the bath, her hair under a puffy cap. He beheaded one of the flowers with a pinch of his thumb and forefinger. It plopped into the water and bobbed by her left breast. "I'm sorry," he said.

"I know."

"I didn't go to school. I'm an autodidact and a peasant. Nobody would take me."

She reached up with one dripping hand and he crouched to hold it. "You have a brain for which those stuffed suits would hang a friend with an Hermès necktie," she said. "And I am cunning and well connected." Her friend was the junior assistant to the publisher Jack Grant, of Grant Aikens. Lillian asked her to schedule Grant a lunch at Portofino, and Martin deployed his slightly bumbling charm. A month later he was hired.

"You were right," he said when he met Lillian and Wes for what they were calling celebratory drinks at the end of his first day. "My menial tasks as a glorified secretary will do wonders for my writing career."

"Give it some time," she said.

Five months later, he was on a lease with the woman he loved, who was washing off after a bout of lovemaking on a Saturday afternoon. He poked his head into the shower steam. "Maybe it's fine to be inevitable."

TWO

Lillian

Two years in and now an assistant editor, Martin was filling the black notebooks he'd been carrying around since Wesley met him with startling speed.

"What are those, your reviews of lunch dates?" Wesley asked as they sprawled on a blanket in Sheep Meadow. "Are they going to congeal into a novel anytime soon?"

Martin shielded his eyes and motioned for the bottle of Blue Nun protruding from Lillian's purse. "I had a dream that Martin Amis wrote my novel," he said. "I opened a book in Schulte's and knew it was mine, but then I realized it had his name on it. I kept trying to scratch the Amis off."

"Classic," Wes said listlessly, flexing his feet and waving a rolled-up *New Yorker* at a circling wasp. He was well aware of Martin's primary bugaboo—that someone else was going to publish his ideas out from under him. Martin had become increasingly suspicious of new manuscripts, terrified he'd open one up and find his ideas translated to the page by some better-known writer. It was an occupational hazard, Wes teased, for someone who read new manuscripts for a living. "Means you want to ravage your mummy and murder your daddy and immolate them both on a smoking pile of great literature." His expression fell. "Shit, Martin. I'm sorry. I'm exhausted. I wasn't thinking."

Martin cleared his throat. "You're sure you've been an intern and not a patient at Bellevue this summer?"

"Ha ha."

The air smelled like suntan lotion and pot, sour garbage, cut grass. Lillian, swaddled in a Mexican serape, lifted a slice of pizza from its box and pointedly said nothing.

Martin rolled onto his stomach. He reached to wrap his hand around Lillian's ankle. "The Mailer," he said.

Lillian sighed and tipped her head up to the sun before slouching back and pulling the wide brim of her hat low over her sunglasses. "That wasn't your book, Mar."

"But that feeling of the city. And the jazz singer. My girl's always been a jazz singer, too," he said to Wes, who nodded, though he knew she hadn't been: she'd been a skier and a mathematician and an artist and a skier again, and only lately a jazz singer.

"There's room for two jazz singers in the whole wide world of literature," Lillian said. She had her own notebook in front of her; on the phone earlier that week she had told Wesley with something approaching giddiness that she couldn't stop writing, that everything was ripe for a poem.

Wes leaned across her legs to see the page and she swatted him away, not hard, not enough to stop him. "*On Thursday night*," he read, voice raised in a movie star's lockjaw, "*I saw a woman, fanged and gnarled with skin hung slack, across the street.*" He continued, giving appreciative *Mm*'s after certain lines and enunciating theatrically. Across the lawn a group of men kicking a soccer ball between them had just knocked it into the middle of a group of hacky sackers; rather than the expected cross-cultural brawl, the two factions joined forces and began a complicated mixed-medium game.

"*The Bard and Redgrave, Millay and Hughes*," Wesley slowed down, preparing for a big finish. "*Tennyson, Carroll, Waterhouse, point meaty fingers at necks and ribs, their brilliant blooms in purples and blues.*" He gave her back the notebook. "Yum."

Lillian mimed a seated bow.

"The meter's wonky," Martin said to her after a moment.

Lillian shrugged. "It's just a doodle."

"Your girlfriend isn't quite so precious about her unfinished work as you are," Wes said. "When do we get to read the great epic?"

"Fiction isn't like poetry," Martin said. "You don't just fling it out. Christ. You have no idea. I can't tell if any of it is any good. And every time I pick up a new book I'm sick, waiting to see whether it's all my ideas blaring back at me."

"One mustn't fling the prose," Lillian said to Wes.

"One mustn't in*deed*."

This conversation followed them everywhere. That fall, Lillian worked on a three-part poem about the men who assassinated Martin Luther King Jr. and Bobby Kennedy (her father, consummate Irish Catholic, thought Sirhan Sirhan should be "dropped on the spot"), and the woman who shot Andy Warhol. Martin tore through *The Arrangement* and *Couples*, looking for his own sentences. He wrote less, read more, raged about salability and selling out and the shackles of a day job.

"If you'd just finish the manuscript you could stop worrying about someone else getting there first," Lillian said the following July as they stood outside Wes's apartment door, she carrying a sweating pint of vanilla ice cream, he a bottle of root beer in one hand and Chardonnay in the other. The moon landing was scheduled for that afternoon, and radios across the city had been crackling with excitement all week.

"Thanks, Lillian. Helpful."

Martin recounted the exchange to Wesley in the kitchen, and Lillian spent the rest of the visit dialing up her charm, putting her hand in spontaneous wonder on Wes's knee as they watched the grainy image of the astronauts descending onto the lunar surface.

"I heard Aldrin brought a chalice of wine with him," Wes said, hoping to break the tension. "All the way from a Presbyterian church in Texas. And some bread. He took Communion before he went out."

"They have to haul their God everywhere," said Martin, staunch atheist. "Even to the moon."

MARTIN WORKED A nine-to-five, but because Lillian had shifts that ranged anywhere from early-morning openings to late-evening closes, and Wes had hours of reading to complete and synthesize in between his clinical studies and training hours, she and Wes had taken to meeting at one of their apartments on Tuesdays and Fridays to work. "When we need a break you can analyze me," she said, and when he said he couldn't do that, it would be unethical, she rolled her eyes. "Presbyterian Hospital's bludgeoning the humor out of you, I see." Wes realized he hadn't slept in two full days.

When she first mentioned it to Martin, she'd thought his poor reaction was born of jealousy that they were spending time together without him. He soon made it clear that it was their shared luxury of time he most resented. "As if I don't spend forty hours a week helping women in and out of silk blouses and lying to them about how the new skirt length slims their calves," Lillian said, though Wes knew she enjoyed her job. She was embarrassed to feel so safe and contained among the Jacquard skirts, the puffs of perfume amid the metal and glass reflections of the cosmetics department; the cool, subservient mask she could don when a customer was angry or dismissive: *What a strange experiment this is, life*, she would think.

The department store offered a complementary stability to her years in the ballet studio. She'd started dancing at age five because her mother thought it would instill femininity and grace while serving as an outlet for her boundless energy. Lillian's elementary school teachers were worn out, her mother was exhausted, her older sister endured her demands to play like an old bloodhound walloped by a kitten.

Her body grew in proportional perfection for ballet: long limbs, average torso, small head, not too tall. The teacher at her West Hollywood studio, a sturdy woman who had danced in the Russian National Ballet, paid more attention to her than to the other girls, and when Lillian was thirteen—sans menstruation and lacking even the suggestion of breasts—she was encouraged to audition for a summer intensive in New York. For two Junes in a row, she and her mother stayed at the midtown Hilton in Manhattan, and Lillian spent her days staring into a mirror at her impractically moving body, and discussing what she and her classmates hadn't eaten that day, and giggling through the studio doors at the boys practicing fencing. At the end of her second year she was invited to join the school full-time.

Lillian liked the independence of leaving home so young, and the soreness of her muscles at the end of a long day. She liked to force the changes in her body, her quadriceps and soleus and biceps and deltoids and obliques rippling, the cool burn in her thighs and hips as she stretched her turnout. She even enjoyed the meditative boredom of sewing ribbons into her Capezios and hearing the *thwack*s of girls breaking in their shoes against the stairs. But as she spun through days that smelled of Pine-Sol and sweat and were filled with the repeating images of her friends smoking out the dormitory windows, youth parts in *A Midsummer Night's Dream* and *Coppélia*, she felt as though she'd fallen into a long dark slide. Each day she skidded down the chute, farther and farther away from the light at the top.

She was nineteen, dancing her first year in the corps, when she slipped on the stage. She didn't hear the distinctive pop of her Achilles tendon giving out, just felt a white-hot pain in her ankle, but later two of the girls dancing Snow alongside her would swear they'd heard the snap as she landed just so on her last *grande jeté*. *The Nutcracker*, unbearably embarrassing. In the days following her initial heaving panic at the doctor's prognosis—six months off her toes—a beatific calm descended. This would be the end, she knew, even as her friends, bearing chocolates and schadenfreude, dropped by to tell her that dancers healed from this all the time.

She stopped performing the manipulations prescribed by the company doctor, allowing the growing tissue to bind together and harden. She lay in her bed and let her kindest roommate bring her salty noodle soup in a chipped pink bowl and tea as though she were a child with a cold. One evening a soloist who had once been out for a year because of a herniated disk stopped by with a stack of books. "You can't stay in your own head the whole time," she said in her bright London accent, plucking her sweater away from her stomach, her forehead glazed with sweat in the apartment's unregulatable heat. "And you can't obsess over your injury. These will keep your mind off it."

She read *A Separate Peace* and *This Side of Paradise*, and then *To Bedlam and Part Way Back*. She'd hadn't read poetry since a dry unit on *Romeo and Juliet* when she was thirteen. This was something else, a tripping, tearing something. At night she read the poems and found she could memorize them as easily as she'd stored away footwork.

> *I have ridden in your cart, driver,*
> *waved my nude arms at villages going by,*
> *learning the last bright routes, survivor*
> *where your flames still bite my thigh . . .*

Lillian hadn't realized that the nightmare thoughts she scratched out could be art in themselves. She collected her crutches and hobbled downtown to the library, her arms shaking by the time she arrived. She dropped the Sexton on the counter. "More like this, please," she said to the librarian. That night she wrote in her journal: *The days drift by, the seasons change, and I, so much in motion, do not move among them.*

THREE

Martin

In the spring of 1971, an anonymous angel plucked one of Lillian's poems out of the slush pile and immortalized it in the pages of *The New Yorker*. Martin threw a dinner party of Chinese carryout and prosecco to celebrate. When Lillian spent a day at the Met and came back shivering, coatless, her notebook filled with new ideas, Martin welcomed her home with a bouquet of quivering pink roses. That December, just before the Christmas holidays, two publishers inquired about the possibility of a book. Martin kissed her left eyelid, her right eyelid, the tip of her nose, and bundled her onto the tarmac at LaGuardia to visit her parents and sisters in Malibu. Martin was not invited, due to it being Jesus's birthday and a particularly bad time to be living in sin, and as usual Lillian offered to boycott. But this year he said she should go. She missed them, she deserved the heaps of familial praise. He would use the time to work.

Back at their apartment he tried to write and could not. A spectral man sat in the corner of the bedroom, one leg crossed at the knee, a red armband vibrant against his double-breasted trench coat. Martin squeezed his eyes shut, banishing him. Although he had told Lillian he didn't mind that she had left without him, he now found that he did. He prowled into the living room and rifled through the papers and books on her desk: the saved acceptance letter from *The New Yorker*, notes on new poems, a UK edition of *The Bell Jar*, out soon in the U.S., which Lillian was writing about for the *Review*. *For the all-but-unknown Plath*, she'd scribbled on the inside cover, *death served as validation*. He turned through a few typewritten pages, scanning down an ekphrasis covered in scratch-outs and angry splotches of ink, about Arnold Böcklin's *Isle of the Dead* painting, which Lillian always beelined for at the Met; how Hitler bought one of the five versions he'd painted; how Böcklin's first young fiancée and later eight of his children had died. *Loam, stone, Rome, gloam, unknown, drone, alone.*

Something about it irritated his molars. He itched to write a note about the off-putting present participle in the second stanza and that she'd changed the rhyme scheme halfway through. Sinking into her chair, he wondered if their differing success was a by-product of work locations. They'd tucked his own desk into a shallow bedroom closet from which they'd removed the door to make a writing nook, the walls tacked up with timelines and notes on characters, a few of Lillian's dresses pushed all the way to the side. It was too cramped. The optimistic blank page in her red Olivetti was a personal affront, and with a boomless *tick-tick-tick* he tore it out, crumpled it up, and hurled it at the wall. It bounced with a crinkle and came to rest half a foot from where he'd thrown it.

Three days before Christmas he stayed late at work, making notes for one of his authors. Freezing rain pattered against the window, and he waited until he was too hungry to think before he slipped on his jacket and hat and pulled the brass ball of his desk lamp, extinguishing the light.

The elevator doors slid open to reveal a dark-coated girl holding a book: a secretary or an assistant, maybe. "Hi, Nathaniel," Martin said to the man operating the elevator.

"Evening," Nathaniel said with an incline of his head. All three were silent, staring ahead at the closed doors, lost to each other in private thought.

"Thomas Hardy," Martin said to the girl without taking his eyes off the blinking numbers above them. "Bleak."

"My father's," she said. They left the elevator. He walked a couple feet behind her. "Give my best to Mr. Nelson," the doorman said as she passed by. And then it clicked. Nelson, of Nelson Literary, who had launched a dozen careers. Emmett Nelson, whose holiday party he had attended years earlier.

Martin felt a flutter in his chest as they stood side by side, waiting for cabs as the drizzle flashed silver in the streetlights. Emmett Nelson's daughter. He turned to her. "Listen . . ."

———

IN THE HOURS afterward, Martin tried to elucidate his emotions about the affair. Not an affair. A blip. A dream. When it became apparent that he could not sit alone with the weight of his own decision he called Wesley, who was leaving the next morning to visit his parents in Charleston.

"Wes," he said, taking a long drink of water to steady himself. "I've done an insane thing."

They met at a faux-speakeasy tucked behind an art gallery on Jane Street. Martin arrived first and slid into a booth, jiggling his foot as he waited. He'd stepped in a puddle and dampness climbed up his sock.

"Goddamn umbrella broke," Wes said when he arrived, shaking his arms violently and ineffectively, scattering drops.

"Take a cab, for once."

"And risk my life in one of those death traps? You know I saw one run a woman right down, right at the corner of Houston? The cabbie wouldn't have stopped were it not—"

"By that logic, you'd be safer inside than out." He motioned for the bartender. "Two more," he said, pointing to his glass.

"The problem with you, Mar, is you're—"

"Listen," Martin said, putting up his hands, two stop signs. "I've got to tell you about this."

Wes settled into the booth with the weary air of an old whaler returned from sea. "So you slept with a girl. And now you're all torn up."

"Not a girl, Wes. Not *a* girl. Moira Nelson. It was like something out of a book. She appeared and it was as though I'd known her all my life. We connected. And in bed, her body—"

"Please. Spare me the details." Wes passed a hand over his face "Are you going to see her again?"

Martin sat back in the booth, sticking his long legs out to the side so five inches of hairy calf showed at the bottom of his pants. "I couldn't do that. Although I can't stop thinking about her."

Wes looked at his watch. "Well, it's only been three hours."

"You've got no romantic bones."

"This is romance?"

Martin slumped forward onto an elbow, resting his chin in his cupped palm. "I didn't know I could be so surprised by my own behavior, but I feel like a new person. It's so the opposite of how I'd expect myself to behave. I feel incredibly inspired. I shocked myself out of a rut."

"Rutted yourself out of it, at least."

"Crass."

Wesley made a frog face.

"Now the question, I suppose, is whether to tell Lillian."

"Unless you want to leave Lillian, I suggest you not tell Lillian."

"I don't want to leave. Only . . ."

"Only what, Martin? Only what?"

"Only I do wonder. If I'm capable of this, does it mean that I'm fundamentally unhappy?"

Wes pinched the bridge of his long, thin nose. "This is so boring," he said. "I can't tell you how bored I am. Do you know how many people step out on their girlfriends? Do you know how many relationships end in infidelity? Or, usually, don't end, but plug unmerrily on?"

"I hadn't planned on my relationship being one of those."

Wes wouldn't meet his eye. "Well, then, leave her. Tell her. Dig your own grave."

"I don't know why *you're* so upset."

"Because I am a friend to you both. Whatever happens, I'll be on your side, whatever that means, but, Martin, she's not just yours, you know. I've loved Lillian for a decade. I love you together."

"Not quite."

"What?"

"Nine years. That's how long we've been together."

Wes looked exhausted. "If I'm honest, I'm surprised. Not shocked, but surprised. I know that accidents happen. But I would've thought that any affair of yours would be emotional, first; some girl at work you fancied yourself in love with, not a teenager you bumped into on the street."

"She's twenty at least."

Wes didn't say anything, just let his head fall back against the top of the booth's cushion.

"It's eating me up, too," Martin said after a pause, with none of his previous gusto. "I had to talk about it so I wouldn't lose my mind inside that apartment. And I can't bear to feel guilty about it. I know it'll hit me soon."

Wes had picked his head back up and crossed his arms high and tight across his chest. "Put it out of your mind," he said. "It's something that happened, and now it's done. If Lillian never knows, what's the difference?"

"But I'll know."

"Then the only person you've hurt is yourself."

"Do you think I'm depressed?" Martin asked, twisting his smudged whiskey glass in quarter-turns on the table.

"Professional opinion, or as a friend?"

"Neither," Martin said, and downed his drink. "Never mind."

That night, alone in the apartment that he lit up with every available lamp, guilt did come home to roost. He was too distracted to write, and when he tried to read, the words skittered out from under his eyes so that when he reached the end of the page he found himself returning to the top, an endless, pointless loop. By the time a razor's edge of sunlight appeared around the bedroom curtains, he was running through scenarios in which Moira found Lillian's California phone number and told her what he'd done.

The sleet solidified into snow, which stuck around just long enough for the plows to come through, and then morphed once more into freezing rain. On street corners, the icebergs forming around the trash cans grayed, then yellowed. Nobody was around, everyone was with their families or nestled together in unbreakable twosomes. The office wouldn't reopen until 1973, and to spend the holiday, which he was supposed to use writing his novel, instead shivering at his desk was a scenario too depressing to entertain. He took the train uptown. The city at Christmastime was surreal, like a reproduction of a television image: Salvation Army Santas ringing bells outside Macy's and Woolworth's, shoppers scurrying down Fifth Avenue, their arms laden with bags. But in real life the lights didn't twinkle as poignantly as in the movies. When he eventually reversed course and arrived home, he tried to make himself write, but nobody talked about the physicality of writing, the way it felt like dragging one's feverish body through deep sand.

On Christmas Day he forgot the time difference and called Lillian's parents' house in California at four a.m. When her father picked up and said, in his charming Irish brogue, "This better be a G-D emergency, whoever ye are," Martin hung up.

Three long hours later, Lillian: "Was that you who woke us all up this morning, love?"

"Woke you up?" he said with false Yuletide cheer. "I don't think so!"

"I miss you," he said.

"I love you," he said.

"Come home soon, I'm going late-stage Tolstoy without you," he said, and she laughed.

———

HE HAD TO tell her. He had to prostrate himself in front of her and let her decide where to go from there. He would not make excuses. (Though it was true that she had abandoned him during the holidays, flown across the country to see her family, who did not like him, leaving him all alone.) But he would fight for her. He was not like his absent father, whoever and wherever he was, who had not worked hard enough to be with the woman he loved. It was Lillian who made his life possible, Lillian who had introduced him to the man who had given him his job, Lillian who encouraged him to write, nagged him not to give up.

The morning of her arrival he Cloroxed the kitchen counters and bathroom floor, even using a wad of toilet paper to specifically address the rank slick of urine around the base of the toilet. He emptied the trash, filled with oiled paper bags emptied of their candied nuts and french fries, and childishly crumpled typewritten pages damp with coffee grounds, a glob of jelly, the mash of a too-ripe banana. He put new sheets on the bed and stood looking at it, his hand pressed to his mouth. The hours ticked by, punctuated by the sputtering hisses and thumps of the radiator, as he stood staring down at the street. When a cab pulled up and he saw, through the clouds reflected in the window, a glint of the green scarf she liked to wear over her hair, he was downstairs so fast he'd made it to the sidewalk before the cabdriver hefted her inconvenient carpetbag over the puddle, two feet wide, that had consumed the gutter.

"Martin," Lillian said when she saw his face, "I wasn't even gone two weeks."

"Marry me," he said. "Right now. Let's go to the courthouse today. It's been nine years. What're we waiting for?"

She made a noise through her nose like a bus coming to a stop. "Come on."

"I mean it."

The cabdriver was watching them through tired eyes. "The fare is—"

"Here, here." Martin pulled some bills out of his pocket and pushed them into the man's hand. He bounded to where Lillian now stood by their building's front door. It was frigid outside, he hadn't put on a jacket, his fingers felt thick and too slow to pick up signals from his brain. "I don't want to spend holidays calling your parents' house in the middle of the night. I want to be there with you."

Lillian, holding her bag in one hand, had been waiting for him to unlock the door; when she saw he wasn't going to, she rooted through her purse for her own keys. "So it *was* you who called."

"I missed you. You can't believe how much I've missed you." He was trailing her up the four flights of stairs, out of breath; he'd left the door to their apartment swung wide, and when they were both inside she dropped her bag and toed off her shoes, the leather damp. He hovered around her as she filled their kettle with water and sparked the stove with a blue hiss. She sat down at the table.

"You really want to do this?"

"I do," he said. "I very much do."

As she untied the scarf from her hair, she looked at him in the flighty, scanning way she had, her eyes roving from his own to his forehead, his mouth, his hands. "Maybe. Let's talk about it."

"Yeah?"

She stretched, feline, her whole body going rigid as she arched her back. Her eyes closed.

"Lillian, I mean it. I want to marry you as soon as you'll have me."

She let herself go slack, her legs splayed in their wide, somehow mannish turnout. "Okay. Yeah. Let's make this thing"—she waggled her finger between them, grinning—"legal."

He had wanted to whisk her down to the courthouse right then, but there was a process—still, five days later they were married. They spent languorous hours in bed, feeling their way toward each other as car head-lights cast their features in pale bright spots and shadows. Her woo-woo sister, five years younger, had given her a deck of tarot cards for Christmas ("Your father must've loved that, a little pagan ritual at Christ's birth") and Lillian pored over the accompanying book, reading meanings for the Moon and the World and the Lovers out loud. She read Martin's cards, and they all pointed to a fresh start. Their life together was nimble again. One afternoon Lillian surprised him on his way out of the office, leaning on a fire hydrant, and he had the pleasure of watching two men in front of him notice her, while she looked past them at him.

He tried to put Moira out of his mind, and for the most part suc-ceeded. But in quiet moments she crept in, tugging with her regret but also a thrill. It had been so long since he'd had a secret. Lillian knew everything about him, knew that when he was a child he couldn't keep German and English straight, that he didn't just brush his teeth but also his tongue and the roof of his mouth, and that onions gave him gas. She knew the women he flirted with, knowing that her knowing meant that nothing would come of it. She was his wife now. It was all so safe. But he had this, his very own bad thing, and when he allowed himself to indulge in the itch of guilt, the satisfaction was as masoch-istically pleasurable as scratching a scab.

In the evenings, when he used to complain about being overtired, or resentfully pull a manuscript out of his bag to edit, he would instead sit down at his desk and bully sentences onto the page. They might not be the right ones, but they were something.

The book he was writing—though he hated to call it that lest the little, magnificent word jinx it all—was dark and murky and covered in slime, but each day it revealed itself more, a sinking ship in reverse.

He wondered if the forward momentum was linked to his newfound ability to deceive, because what was fiction if not a delicious deception? On frost-laced mornings he would whisper to his wife that he was getting somewhere, that he would write this thing and it was because of everything she'd given to him. And when they made love he looked into her fox face, feeling raw with devotion, though sometimes he closed his eyes and thought of Moira.

———

ONE CONCRETE-GRAY EVENING in February, Martin sat at his desk and watched Lillian slip over her head a cobalt dress he'd never seen before. "Where'd you get that?"

She looked down, her hands working the clasp on a strand of glass beads. "I've had this forever."

"I haven't seen it."

"I wore it to the Lohmann wedding last year."

He tried to picture her amid the dancing, the champagne toasts. "Where is it taking you tonight? We don't have plans, do we?"

"I thought I'd leave you alone to write. Go see Melody and Eileen at that new place. You know."

"I don't know."

"With the chandelier from France?" The clasp clicked into place. She smoothed her fingers over the soft, thin skin under her eyes. "And on Friday I'm away for the weekend, remember? To see Joann in Connecticut. You were invited, you'll recall, but you said no."

"I'm banking on the weekend to get this draft done."

"My brilliant husband." She leaned down, wrapped her arms around him from behind; when she was gone he would still smell her shampoo on his collar. "My love."

He had come to trust her so implicitly, so thoroughly, that the possibility of her concealing a secret of her own wasn't a question at all. But now, from the window as he watched her round the corner on the sidewalk below, he wondered. All these friends, these Joanns and Eileens.

Two of her coats hung from pegs screwed into Brighton Beach driftwood. He stuck both his hands into the pockets of her trench, as though pickpocketing a thin person under the pretext of a hug. He came up with a dime and a peppermint candy that he unwrapped with a crackle and put in his mouth. The second coat yielded a scrap of paper, which he opened with grim, rubbernecking delight. *Brown sparrows skitter over the brown leaves—mirage, trompe l'oeil, something better than camouflage.* He crunched the peppermint. Not a letter from a lover, then. At her desk, a quick flip through the datebook. But she would hardly jot down a planned infidelity. He slid open one, two, three of the desk drawers, and there, in that fairy-tale third, he found the thing he hadn't known he was looking for.

He didn't immediately realize what it was. She'd folded a scarf over the typed pages, a half attempt at hiding them. They were facedown, the top page cut off midsentence. He skimmed it, lifted a thin stack, skimmed again. She was writing a story. More than a story. His wife was writing a secret novel. Martin removed the whole thing from its bower and started to read. With a start he realized it was a portrait of himself, a story of a man struggling through life, working in the publishing industry, yearning for his own greatness.

It wasn't his kind of writing, stamped all over with Lillian's influences: Woolf, Hazzard, Dickinson, Plath. Images of dark hallways, milk gone sour in the fridge. There was something witchy about it, grim, and by the time he came to the last, unfinished page Martin couldn't tell whether his nausea was from the dread dripping through the pages, or his own personal sense of betrayal: a slightly sinister husband with an even more sinister past, hinted at in dreamlike dispatches—a Nazi father who'd passed on all his weakness and anger to his mostly unwitting son. Martin dragged himself from the story's gloom. There was the smell of the chicken he'd heated on the stove for dinner. There were his shoes, lined up by the door. Everything was the same. And yet.

When she returned, he was sitting up in bed, a few sheets of his own writing propped on his knees, but he waited for her to come into the room before saying anything. He could hear her taking off her shoes in the hallway, the accompanying muffled thud (welcome mat) and clatter (hardwood) as she let one heel and then the other fall to the floor. She appeared in the doorway, her coat open, her feet alien in stockings.

"You're up," she said. Her lips and nose were so cold they felt wet when she kissed him.

"I've been working," he said primly.

"I knew you'd like a night alone. We had a nice time, too. I think Eileen's seeing someone, but she was being coy."

"That's nice," Martin said, and pulled her down so she was sitting beside him. "Hey."

"Hey, you."

"You're out with your friends so often, are you putting poetry on hold?"

"I'm"—and here she made her voice flutey, officious—"accumulating imagery. You know how it is. Peaks and valleys." She removed his arm from her waist. The hall flooded with a wash of light and then darkened as she shut the bathroom door. Martin lay spasmodically jiggling his foot, livid.

In the following days he tried, under increasingly blatant guises, to weasel it out of her. Would she ever write fiction, did she think? A novel? "Don't be ridiculous, Martin," she said from the desk where she was paying the bills. "I can barely get my poems out these days." But that wasn't true, either: she'd had a set accepted three weeks before. And when he checked the manuscript during her last shift at the store before the weekend, he found that she'd added six new pages. He was full of a dangerous power, knowing this thing about her, this secret thing that she had tried to keep hidden.

———

SHE LEFT FOR Connecticut. The manuscript went with her. Martin met Wesley for lunch at a neighborhood dive, where he waxed unpoetic about her deception, her distance, her imperious expression when he said he'd made progress on his own writing, as though she didn't believe him. "Probably collecting information," he said, his eyes fixed on a pair of men down the bar who were, in turn, watching a woman sitting alone by the window. "Tracking my movements to feed into her story."

"You're being paranoid. You're in a partnership. It's natural that you'd influence her writing." Martin was not interested. He marched around the neighborhood as the sun went down and his ears and cheeks deadened to the cold. He returned to the apartment. He couldn't write, and that felt like her fault, too.

He had to do something to relieve the pressure building between his eyes. He opened his wallet, took out a scrap of paper. A number. He moved quickly, lest he change his mind. Their phone was an old-fashioned contraption, black with gold details, that Lillian had sweet-talked a flea market vendor into giving her for cheap. Now, clutching the earpiece, he imagined all the thousands of men who had made calls like this through the millennia, all the girls on the other side waiting, hoping. He dialed. It rang.

"Hello?" It was her.

Martin said nothing.

"Hello?" she said again, that sweet, low voice.

"Moira," he said, so quietly she might have missed it.

He thought he heard her let out a breath. "Shall I come over?"

And, knowing exactly what he was doing, he said yes.

FOUR

Lillian

There had been other women. (When Lillian said this to Wesley, her feet tucked underneath her on the couch, a glass of wine in one hand, he'd had to work not to react; Martin had told him about flirtations, but nothing serious. Nothing real.) Nine years was a long time, and both she and Martin were people whose desire for applause could never be satisfied by an audience of one. She had watched from across the room as Martin dipped his tall bottlebrush of a head to align his ear with the mouth of one of her friends, another ballet defector, or laughed with one of the tall androgynous women with dark eyes and short hair to whom she so often found herself drawn. The women stared as though hypnotized as he spoke at the near-manic clip he could reach while drinking.

"There are so few people who maintain eye contact like that, while they talk," she said to Wesley. "I've tried it. I can do it when someone's talking to me, but when I start speaking I have to glance off into a middle distance or down at my hands. He's like an unsocialized animal. But when he directs it at you, you feel so . . ."

"Singular," Wesley said.

She thought it unlikely that anything more happened between Martin and these women than longing glances, the occasional kiss in a dim entryway. Only once had she herself allowed an extracurricular flirtation to go too far. Martin had always opined that love and sex were integral to each other. She didn't agree. Sex was most exciting when it was dangerous, unknown. It was why she'd waited so long to marry—she could've gone on forever were it not for his holiday melt-down. The little outside dalliances had likely saved them; kept them on a low burner of jealousy that never boiled over.

She began to suspect he was seeing someone the way she imagined most women did, which irritated her. As the weather tipped from end-less miserable damp to the first blush of spring, he started spending more time away from their apartment—writing, he said. He stared at himself in the mirror, examining the curve of his own jaw, his shoul-ders. She'd been away one weekend, in Connecticut. She'd rung the house and he hadn't picked up, and when he called the next day he sounded removed. At the time she'd assumed it was his usual career frustrations, but perhaps it had started then.

She'd always loved that they could be independent; kiss goodbye before dinner and meet up in bed late at night. But as he drew away from her she clung harder, something she had never done before.

"You'd have a joyless evening," he said one night as he sat on the edge of their bed, tugging a tall gray sock up his long calf. "I wouldn't be going if it wasn't Grant throwing it. It's mandatory for me to kiss up to the boss. I didn't think you'd want to subject yourself to it. You hate how that lot gets when they're boozy."

"I miss you. It seems like I hardly see you anymore, and I've always wanted to ogle the richesse of Sutton Place."

He lowered his foot. "I can't just leave after the first half hour."

"That's fine."

"I suppose," he said, not looking at her, "it could be a good networking opportunity for you. Maybe you'll pitch a brilliant idea for a book to some better editor than me."

"Yes, very likely. Do I have to have an ulterior motive to spend time with my husband?" She handed him the glass of whiskey she'd poured herself, planted a hand on either side of him on the bed, kissed his neck, the ridge of his ear.

"I'm not going to spend all night rescuing you from old Mr. Handsy, so you better stay clear of him." He was smiling now.

"I think, at thirty-four, I may have aged out of his ideal bracket. But he'll get a good swipe if he tries anything."

"You alley cat." Martin tipped his head back, a little cross-eyed because she was so close. "Don't say I didn't warn you. Get changed. I'm going to make a quick call."

"No," she said. Who was he calling? "Stay with me."

"Lil."

"Stay," she said, pushing back from him. "Stay and watch me dress." She turned, pulled her T-shirt off, her arms crisscrossed in front of her.

"We don't have time for that."

"For what?" She shimmied her pants over her hips and stepped out of them. "I'm just getting dressed."

"You'll kill me. Dead at thirty-two. How will you live without me? What will you do?"

"Oh, I'll find someone else." She was in front of the closet now, her back to him, enjoying her nakedness. "Someone rich. Accomplished. Some rich prince who has also won the Nobel Prize in Literature."

Suddenly he was next to her, roughly pushing the glass back into her hand. "Charming," he said, and stalked out of the room.

"Martin," she called. "I was joking. Obviously." She squinted in annoyance and yanked a dress off its hanger, soft, long-sleeved, not suitable for a party, but what did it matter? She didn't want to go to the stupid thing, he'd been right about that.

Martin was in the next room calling whoever it was he'd wanted to call. Maybe he was calling *her*, if there was a her to call.

Maybe it was inevitable that this creeping paranoia should seep into every relationship—maybe she'd conjured a girl with whom he'd betray her, as if from thin air. Martin was loyal. Martin needed her. He'd said so himself days before, his cheek resting on her breast, occasionally tonguing a nipple (which she'd never liked; too maternal). *I need you.* And no, he wasn't on the phone, he was crashing around the kitchen, washing the clean dishes the way he always did when he wanted to demonstrate his virtuous nature. She knew him.

By the time they arrived at Jack Grant's apartment, Martin's funk had given way to jittery throat-clearing. In the cab, he was shaking his foot so hard that one knee, crossed over the other, vibrated against hers. Lillian put her hand on his thigh. At these parties and at work, where editors and agents and writers and patrons intermingled, he inhabited what he believed was an incorrect role. He didn't want to be the editor. He wanted to be writing the novels they all stood around trashing, praising, debating. To be mocked would be better than to be ignored.

And he'd tasted the earliest glimpses of success. That made it harder. When they'd first met he was getting stories published. Not anywhere monumental, but still, there was interest. Somewhere along the way he had lost the frenzied desperation that propelled him forward during those early, hopeful years.

Inside, Martin shifted into his affable, charming self. He had his arm
through Lillian's, as though they had not just been fighting, as though
they'd never fought in their lives. She should have worn something
showier. Something that bared more skin. There was so much glitz in
the room, diamonds glinting on earlobes and necks, glasses catching
the light. The apartment was gaudy but it glowed. Dark wood paneled
one living room wall, the other three were covered in pale green paper.
A weird geometric sculpture, like a piece of big red trash. Chairs that
swelled to meet the bottoms of those who sat in them. Perhaps if Martin had this kind of money he'd be able to finish a book. Or maybe, at
least, he'd stop caring.

"Lillian, Lisbet, Lilith," a voice boomed. "My demon, my joy!"

Martin gave her shoulder a squeeze and beamed at the man pushing his way toward them. "Jack," he said. "We're so glad to see you."

"I'm not so glad to see *you*, my boy, if I'm being honest." Jack Grant,
red-faced and damp-browed, leaned in for a kiss. If she'd written him,
Lillian would have made Martin's publisher secrete a scent of fetid
body odor and beer, but in reality he was always fastidiously soapy.
"Let's run away together," he said.

"Mr. Grant," she said, "not in front of my husband."

"Forget your husband. I own your husband. Come away with me,
I'll make you a star."

"Poets don't make for great stars these days, surely you know that,"
Lillian said in what she knew was a forced, teasing voice.

Two of Martin's colleagues, fellow editors he actually liked,
wandered up. Bart, a decade older than Martin and Eeyoresque in
demeanor, and Gregory, a short, droll man who could not hold his

liquor. "'The poet'"—Gregory attempted a clipped British accent—"'is the priest of the indivisible.'"

"Invisible, I think you'll find," Bart said.

"Absolutely."

"Is that how you see yourself?" Jack asked Lillian, his hand still glued to her back, his eyes on her lips.

"I don't see myself as anything. I just write what comes."

Jack smiled appreciatively. "And how."

"Perhaps she won't confine herself to poetry," Martin said. "Perhaps our Lillian is ready to move on to prose."

Lillian stared at him. "*Perhaps* I will."

"Rachel's brought her fiancé, did you see?" Gregory's eyelids, like a pair of mismatched window shades, lowered independent of one another. "That Trotsky-looking fellow over there. Looks sloshed."

"You're sloshed," Martin said. He glanced around the room. Lillian, following his eyes, couldn't find what he was looking at.

"Well, boys." Jack clapped his hands together. "I must mingle. You." He pointed at Lillian. "I will find *you* later."

"Oh, goody," she said.

"What an ass," Gregory said. "Who's that girl he's gone off to bother?"

"I can't see through the smoke," Lillian said.

"Emmett Nelson's daughter." Bart removed a pack of cigarettes from his breast pocket as though suddenly reminded of them. "The wife was here, too. It's too tragic."

"Nelson knew how to throw a party."

The young woman was standing, hands laced behind her back, in a long, almost mannish navy blazer over a pleated skirt. She was hardly reacting to Jack's jocular tone. Lillian touched Martin's shoulder. "We went to the holiday party at his place, remember? The year we started dating. She was just a little girl then."

Martin nodded, hardly registering. "What is it that's sad?"

"You don't want to believe every rumor," Bart said, "but I hear there's something not right. Apparently Nelson made some off-color remarks to the secretaries."

"Sexual," Gregory said grimly. "Started forgetting meetings. Blowing up at the elevator boy."

"Jack's putting the moves on her," Bart said. "I wonder why she's here."

"His wife, what's-her-name, Nina, she puts on a good show. Should we go save that poor girl?"

Martin ran a hand through his hair, leaving it rumpled. "We shouldn't be gossiping about the poor man's misfortune."

"And she doesn't need rescuing," Lillian said. "Look, she's stepped out of his grasp. So serene, like a Spanish painting in that plain little suit."

Gregory, with an abrupt and unprompted forward lunge, stumbled the length of the room, narrowly avoiding a collision with a man in a checkered suit, and arrived, somehow upright, at the girl's side. With dignity, he placed his hand underneath her elbow and made fawning, self-deprecating movements at the bemused Jack Grant. Then he was whisking her in their direction.

Later, Lillian found herself fixating on this moment. "It would be easier," she would tell Wesley, her mother, the hairdresser, the postman, anyone who would listen, "it would be easier if I knew that that night was the beginning of it all. That they weren't standing in front of me sharing this private secret, that they hadn't already— I can't stand how foolish I feel." She went over how Martin had stuck out his hand like the rest of them and shaken the quiet girl's hand, how she had nodded along to the inane conversation, and eventually made an excuse and slipped away. Had her eyes lingered on Lillian? On Martin? Lillian tried to draw forth the memory, but each time she did, she registered her own edits, shellacking the girl's bare lips with red, ballooning her breasts, letting Martin gape after her as she left.

("It makes me think," Wes said to me as he leaned down to inspect a convoy of glittering ants hurrying over a twig in their path, "about the interviews Martin would later give, in which he talked about meeting Moira on the way out of his office. How he felt a connection unlike anything he'd previously experienced." Wes moved the twig and the line broke, confused by the change. In a second they were back in formation, moving smoothly forward. I was familiar with the interview, the one conducted the week Martin's first book was published. *I knew, immediately, that she would be my wife.*)

A week after the party, Martin stayed late at the office. He'd called home, saying he was finishing an editorial letter and didn't want to be disturbed, and when Lillian called back half an hour later he picked up and said, "Are you checking in on me?" She made something up about wanting to know where the circuit breaker was, there was a set of lights out, and hung up. She lay across their bed, her head hanging over the edge, her arms and legs spread open in an X. She could read. She could go to bed. She rang Wesley.

"Come over," she said.

"I'm working."

"You're not. You're drinking. I can hear it in your voice."

"Lillian, I'm trying to get this paper done."

"Come on, come finish it here. Martin's left me all alone."

He sighed. "You temptress."

"Bring the bottle."

"Nothing left."

"Well, all we have is gin."

"I'll pick something up on the way."

The apartment was best in the evening and at dawn, when the light caressed the living room rather than flooded it. It burnished the wing chairs they'd found on the street half a decade ago and reupholstered in bright marigold, so they glowed like two hot suns in the middle of the room. Wesley sat in the one closest to the couch, where Lillian lay curled in a quilt Martin's aunt had made years ago. The late light caught the clutter of art on the walls, paintings from friends and prints bought from sidewalk vendors.

"Should we become ascetics?" She rubbed a square of the quilt between her fingers. "We have more things than we need. An excess. Maybe with a clean slate Martin could finish his book."

"Always waiting for the thing that will make him do it, aren't we?"

Lillian turned onto her stomach, resting her chin on the back of her hand. "We are. Always waiting." She looked as though she was about to say something else, but stopped.

"When I first met him we were ascetics through no choice of our own, untrammeled by objects and responsibilities, and he couldn't do it then, either." He spoke haltingly, tiptoeing through disloyalty.

"We're all certainly trammeled now."

"I loved that bare little apartment," Wes said. "The three of us banging around in the emptiness. I was sure that you would have a baby as soon as you moved out. I thought I'd get to be the funny uncle."

Lillian reached down for the glass she'd placed on the floor. "I did, too, in the beginning. But Martin didn't want it then, and I don't think I want it now." She'd put on an Ella Fitzgerald record when he arrived but it had long since come to an end and the needle shushed back and forth. "I'm happiest when I have long stretches of time to work, alone. I had a scare, once, and all I felt was dread."

"A scare."

"It was nothing, in the end. Or it was something that took care of itself. The thing is, now I wish Martin would say that he's ready for a baby just so that I could tell him that I'm not."

"Lil."

"I know. But why does he get to decide everything? He'll be ready for the baby when he's done with his book. He'll be happy when he works on his book. But does he work on the book—really work on it, in a productive, sustained way? No."

"I do want children," Wesley said softly.

Lillian propped herself up on her side. "You'll be a wonderful father."

"Oh, it doesn't seem like a particularly likely turn of events."

"Haven't you heard? That's the wonderful thing about being a man. You can keep fathering children until you're on your deathbed."

"It just might take that long."

Lillian reached toward him. "You know that's not what I meant."

Wesley made a collapsing smile and, with his finger, drew a spiral on her palm.

ONE AFTERNOON IN April, Martin told her he would be stopping by Wesley's after work; he hadn't seen him in a couple weeks and wanted to catch up. An hour later she called Wes. "Can I speak to Martin, please?" she asked.

"Oh, he's actually—" Wesley began.

"Thank you. That's all." She hung up.

She poured herself the dregs of an open merlot and then stood, bracing herself on the counter, her hand around the base of the wineglass. The phone rang, and kept ringing for a minute, maybe two. Then it stopped. She was so still that she could feel her heart pumping blood, a minute oscillation of her torso. It was something like stage fright, what she was feeling: not the draining void and panic that other girls described, but a colossal building in her chest, a feeling that if she didn't get onstage, was not able to let that energy out soon, she would blow apart. The wine smelled acrid; she dumped it out. She thought about slamming the glass in the sink but didn't want to have to clean it up. She thought about changing out of her jeans and T-shirt into something more dramatic but didn't want to waste the effort. In the bedroom, she packed a few changes of clothes, her comb, a toothbrush, into the carpetbag she'd had since she first came to New York. Back in the living room, she drowned the pale spring sunlight with a flick of the overhead and sat down to wait.

When Martin got home a few hours later, whistling "Luck Be a Lady," she was perched on the edge of the living room couch with her hands folded over a throw pillow in her lap.

"Hey, darlin'," he called as he hung up his coat.

"I know, Martin," she said.

"What's that?" He emerged from the narrow hallway, carrying a white box she recognized from the bakery down the street: black-and-white cookies, her favorite. His hair was carefully parted and combed.

She almost laughed, watching him trying to keep his expression neutral, but as she flipped through a mental slide deck of other arrivals home and their accompanying tulips, chocolate éclairs, pretty bibelots, she became grim again. "How long has it been going on, exactly?"

His tentative, happy expression disappeared. To his credit, he did not deny it. "Two months."

"God, Martin. Who is it?"

Carefully, he set the box down on the table. "Lillian."

"I have a right."

He cleared his throat. "You don't have a right."

"I'll find out."

"Okay."

"That's it? 'Okay'?" She was clutching the pillow to her chest, and she made herself release it.

"That's it, I guess. What else do you want me to say?"

"I want you to tell me who it is."

He tensed his jaw once, twice. "It's Moira Nelson."

The name didn't register. Then it did. "You're kidding."

"It wasn't all me," he said, his voice emotionless.

"I'm not doing this." She stood up, stretching her shoulders, cracking her neck on each side. "I'm not running through this script with you."

He should have been ashamed, but he kept staring at her in that unnerving way he had. "You have secrets, too."

"Excuse me?"

"You've been lying to me, too. For longer than I have been."

"Don't be ridiculous. Don't try to justify what you did."

"You have a se-cret you have been hi-ding." He enunciated each syllable and lowered his eyebrows as though trying to telecommunicate.

She imitated his diction. "You sound de-ranged."

He didn't say anything. And then she did know.

"This is about the book? You went through my things and found the book?"

He snapped his fingers into a pointed gun, sickly triumphant.

"Just because you can't work, no one else is allowed to? You're pathetic."

"It's me, Lillian!" he said, his cool veneer slipping. "It's my life!"

"It isn't. It's not. It might take the general shape of possible aspects of your life, but there's much more—"

"Is that what you tell yourself so you can sleep next to me at night?"

"I can't believe we're having this conversation," she whispered.

"And you know what? You didn't just steal it from me. You got it wrong, too." His voice transitioned rapidly from a near shout to a tremulous pleading. "I'm not like that. I didn't stifle you, I never asked you to give up your job, didn't pressure you into having children—"

"Yes, Martin. Because it's fucking fiction."

"Fiction." He sneered it at her, as though it were a dirty word, and not the thing around which he had centered his life.

He didn't move when she went into the bedroom and emerged with her bag, didn't move as she belted her trench. She paused at the door, and then she dropped the bags and strode back to her desk, yanked open the third drawer, removed a filing folder of their bills, and pulled out the stack of her manuscript. She wanted to throw it at him—the purgative release of watching the pages hold together in the air and then, just before they hit him, curl and separate, shushing on the hardwood like footsteps through new snow. But she wouldn't do that to her work. Gently, even in her rush, she slid the pages into her bag.

FIVE

Wesley

It only took a month for Martin to move Moira into the apartment. He told Wes matter-of-factly one day over drinks, as though daring him to disapprove. Wes just took another swig of his beer. "If this is what you want," he said.

"It is. It is what I want." Martin raked his hand through his hair. "I'm in love with her."

"Then I suppose I'm happy for you."

"Good," Martin said. "Have you seen Lillian?"

Wesley held his glass from the top and circled it around, watching the liquid cling to the sides. "Please don't put me in this position."

"Have you?"

"Yes."

"That's good."

Wes opened his hands to the ceiling and then clasped them together, dropped them to the counter. "What can I say?"

"I didn't ask you to say anything. You're right. Never mind." He twisted a cocktail napkin into a gnarl. "She's probably sitting around doing tarot readings for her characters or some other horseshit. 'What will the Martin avatar do now?' You know, sometimes I wish—" He stopped.

"What?"

"I wish she had died." He said it bullishly, like a kid trying out a swear.

"Come on, Mar."

"I mean it. If she had died a year ago I could have remembered her as this incredible person in my life. I could have talked about Lillian with Moira, about the things I loved about her and the things that drove me crazy."

"That is incredibly selfish. You don't wish Lillian were dead." He was tired of hearing them complain about each other, and how in those complaints they were always actually just talking about themselves.

"I still think about her." Martin's voice was low, as though speaking through a confessional screen. "I want her, even."

"Don't, Mar," Wesley said, so exhausted—by them, by his clinical hours, by all of it.

"No. I know. Greg's cousin is getting the divorce papers together. I love Moira." He paused, dropping his eyes. "I just have to say it sometimes. Let those feelings out. So I don't actually do anything about them."

———

WHEN LILLIAN ARRIVED at his apartment after her fight with Martin, Wesley had picked a fallen blossom out of her hair and assumed she would be back home by the end of the week. After she'd hung up on him, he was so grateful she'd shown up at all—that she didn't question him about the part he'd played in concealing Martin's affair—that he didn't think, then, about the implications of her staying there. "You *just* got married," he kept saying, as though a piece of paper would protect against destruction. But then Lillian had one of her friends, a male principal at City Ballet with shoulders cut from marble and a nose like a Roman coin, pick up the rest of her things from her old apartment. And then the divorce proceedings began.

The city lost its blossoms, its inhabitants shed their clothes. During the months once cluttered with subway rides to Coney Island and loud, hot nights, Wesley and Martin saw each other sporadically. Martin was wrapped up in Moira, but Wes was busy, too. After listening to his friends work separately through a lifetime of insecurities and bitterness, he'd started wondering whether all his work on the brain could lead somewhere outside the hard old walls of academia, whether he could do something different from simply treating people one-on-one. He wanted to build something new. A therapeutic practice built on community, one that melded science and art.

Lillian made plans to visit her family in California. A few days before she left, she was zipping up a boot before one of her last shifts at the department store when the doorbell rang. The windows were open and Wesley, frying an egg, leaned out.

"Let me up," Martin called from below.

By the door, Lillian mouthed, as though he could hear from the street, *Is it him?*

Wes nodded, leaned back out. "Mar, I'm coming down."

"Let me up, I have to piss," Martin shouted, and then someone opened the front door from the inside and Martin bounded past them to catch it before it closed.

"What do we do?" Lillian whispered.

Wes shrugged helplessly, just before the thunderstorm of knocks.

Martin's face, when Lillian opened the door, assumed something like a smile, replaced rapidly by confusion, and finally irritation. He looked past her to Wes, who was pressing his pointer and middle fingers into both temples, and then he saw the carpetbag beside the hall closet.

Without saying anything, he turned and left.

SIX

Sal

"I went after him," Wesley said.

We were standing outside the second of the Center's farmhouse buildings. As we approached, I'd registered people, all ages, making their way inside. A couple nodded to us before they, too, disappeared through the open barn doors.

"I grabbed hold of his arm just as he made it down the steps of the apartment building," Wesley continued. He spoke evenly, as though he were describing something that had happened to someone else. I felt myself concentrating hard on his face, as though I might be able to see past his story. Whether or not they meant to, everyone was always concealing something. Wesley was a generous storyteller, but I could tell there was a sense of remove, too: these were details he'd repeated so many times that the words had lost their meaning. Or, otherwise, this particular chapter of his life was one he was used to leaving out, and in telling it now he was distancing himself from what he was saying in order to make it through.

"I'd expected him to be angry. But it was hurt, confusion. He accused me, us, of a romantic involvement, which of course I denied. I told him that she was staying there temporarily and I hadn't wanted to upset him. When he didn't say anything I became frantic and said I wouldn't see her anymore. Maybe I expected that to soften him. I thought he'd tell me not to be stupid, that I shouldn't cut off my friendship with her just because their relationship had changed. But he said, 'That seems like the best solution for everyone.' I remember trying to figure out what to tell Lillian when I got back upstairs. But when I did, she was already packing the few items she'd left around the apartment. She straightened up when she noticed me standing in the doorway, and I wondered if she'd been able to hear what I'd said from the open window. 'This is it, then,' she said, and when I didn't reply, she came over and put her hands on my shoulders. 'I'll miss you. Be in touch if you want. But I'll understand if you don't.' And then a few minutes later she was gone, too." Wesley sighed, seeming suddenly depleted. He motioned into the cavernous barn, where a dozen participants sat on the floor. "We're about ready to start."

"Wesley," I said, widening my eyes.

"Please. You don't want to miss this."

I knew that the last bus I could take departed at 6:45 p.m., and that it had to be nearly five already, but now Wesley was pulling two flat pillows from a stack inside the doorway, and before I could think of how to extricate myself we had joined the circle. For a few minutes no one spoke, and the only sounds were the occasional deep breath, the rustle of a repositioned leg. My consciousness split between the story Wesley had just told me and a distracting anticipation—for someone to direct our group as to what to do next; for something, anything, to happen.

When I had come around to the idea that we would be spending the hour in silent, open-eyed meditation, one of the women in the circle began to speak. She was college-age, or just older, with tattoos of lizards sprawling over arms that rolled in pleasant hills, like dough. She described a dream in which she passionately kissed a former lover, only to discover that her feet were tied to a raft that was drifting away. When she finished her description, a man who had what looked like a small radio transmitter attached to his head said that the dream made him think of addiction, and a wiry white man with dreadlocks said that it made him think of what it felt like to lose a parent, and of course it made me think of Lillian and Martin.

They went around the circle that way, sharing dreams; some banal "I was in the office, but it wasn't the office at all," others violent or explicitly sexual: the dreamers penetrated, were penetrated, with strangers, with two other men at once. As the members of the group frolicked in one another's Freudian playgrounds, I imagined Lillian flying back to California, shaking off the disappointments of Manhattan. Summer in Los Angeles, 1974. A sense of heat and color, television studios, long-nosed cars barreling into the future. (The details I filled in later: On Lillian's mother's coffee table, Alfred Hitchcock with a turkey dinner splashed across the cover of *Los Angeles* magazine. Block heels clacking between the clothes racks at Joseph Magnin. Car radios—Joni Mitchell and Bo Donaldson and Steely Dan—competing for airspace.)

She would have thought about all the moments leading up to her departure and wondered if she could have done something differently. Maybe she thought about the small, cutting things she'd said to Martin over the years, or about the times he'd become sullen and she'd let him sulk instead of trying, for the thousandth time, to make him feel better.

Once, in college, when Hugh and I were staying with his parents at their home outside Boston, I'd slapped him in front of his mother. I don't remember what precipitated it, only the sudden, uncontrollable frustration that culminated in my striking his bare forearm. He barely registered it, just rolled his eyes, but his mother, her hair knotted with a tortoiseshell claw clip and her lips crimson, stared at the pale spot my hand had left behind. After that I hated to be around her. "Is it because it's hard to see that we have such a close relationship, when you and your parents—?" Hugh said one night, after I'd made an excuse as to why I couldn't visit them with him. "No, but thank you for the armchair analysis," I'd said.

"Our dreams can reveal to us what we want," Wesley was saying. The energy had changed in the room, reverting to the calm before the oneiric storm. "Some of you are here because a trauma has blunted your personal narrative. Some have sought to achieve a dream state in your waking life through substances or dangerous personal decisions, and you have found that road to be destructive. In coming here, you have chosen to go deeper into your consciousness instead of to diminish it."

I imagined Lillian tiring of Los Angeles, longing for something both new and familiar. Wesley. She'd picked the wrong path, all those years ago, choosing Martin. Wesley had been right there. Theirs was a scalene triangle, ever shifting, but maybe the longest leg was the one connecting her to him. I could see how Lillian's and Wesley's DNA might mingle to make Dana. A child chosen later in life. Something worth losing Martin for. Still in New York State, though it might as well be a different country. The woods. A place to create art, ride horses, live close inside the changing seasons.

"We are our own mythmakers," Wesley said. "We are explorers by nature. Your dreams are an escape, yes, but they can be an escape into, rather than out of, your life."

I stood up with the others and made my way back outside. The sun collected, pink and purple, in the fat cumulus clouds. The dreamers, back in their silence, made their way toward the building Dana had pointed out as the communal dining room; a plume of smoke rose from its chimney. It shouldn't have surprised me that I had enjoyed being lectured to. It was a wonderful break from reality, to have someone else organize the world.

"How was that?" Wesley asked, his hands in his pockets, as we walked back to where I'd left my bike.

"Interesting," I said. "Meditative. Though I did have something of a hard time concentrating."

"There's value in mental meandering."

"I should leave soon," I said, aware of the time, of the bus beetling in the direction of the point I hadn't yet started toward, "but that was some cliffhanger. You have to tell me how you got past all that. When did you see her again?"

"I didn't mean to leave you in suspense. I assumed you knew." His lips tightened into a flat line. "I didn't see her after that. That was the last time I spoke to her."

"Oh." I felt my eyebrows come together. It took a moment to wipe away my Hollywood ending. That's the thing about belief; it can defy logic right up to the end. "Then I don't suppose you know where she is now."

We'd arrived at the front office and my bike, propped against the building like a drowsy pack animal. Wesley rubbed his eye, pushing his finger deep into the tear duct. "She died."

"Oh," I said again, deflating. "When?"

"The summer after the divorce."

"She died *that* summer?" (She *died* that summer? I tried to make sense of it. *She* died that summer?)

"She was in a car accident in Los Angeles. Moira didn't tell you?"

"Moira hasn't told me anything," I said. I exhaled, hard, out my nose. There should be a word for that noise, the center of a Venn diagram between a sigh and a grunt and a moan. "I thought all this . . ." I gestured to the barn, the fields, but I couldn't finish the sentence. It had momentarily made so much sense, why he and Martin had lived an hour's drive from each other for twenty years and yet hadn't stayed in touch. "Then where's *your* wife?"

"My wife?" The change that came across Wesley's face was like curtains opening on a stage. "I don't have a wife," he said, amused.

"But Dana said her mother—"

"Oh, I see. No, no. Dana's mother was a dear friend. We each wanted a child, but lacked the romantic partner or the biology, as the case may be, to make that happen. Together, we had Dana, and three years later her brother, Thomas." As though indulging me with an answer to the question he knew I'd ask next, he said, "I've had my own romantic relationships as well. But I believe that's beyond the scope of your article."

"I had it all wrong." I was laughing, overwhelmed suddenly by the panicked knowledge that I understood nothing. How could I possibly hope to describe the lives of others? "I thought you were in love with Lillian."

"But I *was* in love with Lillian," he said gently. "Only it was philia rather than eros. She was one of the best friends I'd ever had. She and Martin were each a terrible loss. She was gone, and then he left the city, too. Not a happy year, 1974. Or '75, for that matter. But without them to hold on to, I fell in with a new group and in the end I was more myself with them than I ever had been with Martin. Then the eighties hit. It was too much. Too much loss. I moved up here."

"I don't know what I'm going to say to Moira," I said, kneeling down to pull a twig out of the spokes of my front wheel.

He clasped his hands behind his back. "I didn't ever get to know Moira well, but she struck me as something of a sphinx."

"I don't know her, either, I guess."

"I almost forgot," he said, his tone changing. I paused where I'd knelt, waiting for a revelation. "Don't forget to check for ticks. Linings of your socks, armpits, hairline. They're bad this year. Weather patterns are all wonky, you know. The ticks are thriving."

"Right," I said, straightening up and swinging my leg over the bike, tired from the day, ready to be back at the apartment. "Well, thanks again."

"Was he writing anything?" he called.

I'd started down the hill and came to a crunching stop. "What?"

"You don't happen to know if Martin was writing anything when he died, do you?"

"He was," I said. "But I don't think anyone will ever get to read it."

Wes nodded. "Even now, I still imagine he could have been better than he was."

———

I WOBBLED OFF into the twilight. It was half an hour later than I'd planned to leave and I pedaled hard, my calves and thighs aching with the effort. It was twenty minutes before I realized I was pointed in the wrong direction; I'd studied the map before I left for Wesley's, but now I'd forgotten the way. Cars sped by and my chest squeezed in disoriented panic. I did eventually make it to the bus depot, where I perched optimistically on a bench between a pay phone and a trash can, but it was with little shock that I waited and waited and no bus came. Eventually, a lone car slowed down. A man with a red baseball cap and a handlebar mustache leaned out his window. "Last bus left an hour ago," he said. "You need a ride?"

I thought of women's bodies in ditches, on trash heaps, buried out behind woodsheds. "No," I said. "Just waiting for a friend. He's almost here."

He tipped his hat and drove off. I felt a twinge on my arm, slapped it, and left a streak of tiny limbs and blood behind. Inside the pay phone booth were the numbers for two local cab companies, the bus depot (operational between nine a.m. and five p.m., Monday through Friday), and 911.

I pulled my flip phone from my pocket. There was a voice mail from Anna, which I ignored. When I dialed the first number in the booth a gruff voice informed me that Erv's only did local runs. I was anxious and tired and hadn't eaten since Wes handed me a muffin half a lifetime ago. "I'm in a bind here."

The man sighed and clicked around on what sounded like the world's oldest keyboard. "Sorry. Can't do it. We have a couple airport runs. Maybe in three hours."

"I can't wait—" I took a breath, softened my voice. "I can't wait here for three hours. What about Blue Line, near Linden? Do they have more drivers, do you think?"

A snort of a laugh. "Lou's probably at Nine Barrels right now, three deep."

"What?"

"It's Saturday," he said, by way of clarification.

"Well, thanks," I said.

"Anytime."

I had the numbers of two people in Linden saved in my phone. I didn't want to call Moira, and anyway she'd never drive all the way out here at this time of night. I punched in the other number, feeling like a guilty teenager.

"Hello?"

"Sawyer?" My voice came out creaky. "I'm so sorry to ask you this, but I'm stuck—"

"One sec," they stage-whispered, "one sec, one sec, one sec."

"Where are you?" I whispered back.

"Library. It's fine, but I'm getting glared at by all these baby nerds. It's summer break, what are they even—? Okay. What's up?"

"I'm stuck at the bus stop in I don't know where, Walton, it says, and the last bus left half an hour ago and there aren't any cabs."

"No shit there aren't any cabs. What're you doing out there?"

I gave them an abridged recap of the day.

"Why didn't you tell me you were going today?" I could hear the click of a lighter and Sawyer's long inhale. They self-identified as a weekend smoker. "I mean, I couldn't have gone, I'm crushed under this bibliography, but I'd go sometime. What was it like?"

I tapped my nails on the metal siding. "Good. Weird. Good and weird. Listen, I really hate to ask, but is there any way you could come pick me up?"

"Shit, Sal. I've been reworking two paragraphs for the last hour. I'm so caffeinated, you should see me." They made a sort of guttural *aach* noise, and when they continued it was in Professor Doefler's high crypt rattle. "'Step away from the computer, my dear, step away from the screen and let the vines of inspiration grow, grow grow.'" They switched back to their normal voice. "You can pay for the gas and a beer."

"You're an absolute angel."

"Coming to you on wings of steel, baby."

I returned to the bench, still holding my phone. After a moment I brought it back up to my ear to listen to Anna's message. *Hey, Sal,* she said, *I hate to do this, but I think we have to pull the plug on this piece. I haven't heard from you and my bandwidth is about to be completely—* I shoved the phone back into my pocket. "Perfect," I said. I squeezed my eyes shut so hard that something like color billowed along with something like pain. When I opened them, I pulled the Center's brochure from my bag, desperate to displace Anna's words.

At the Center for Awareness, it read, *we work to heal the past and massage the future through reframing, restructuring, and reshaping our personal narratives.* Heal the past; massage the future. Moira didn't subscribe to the notion of a directional temporal flow. I had started thinking about this when I watched the sun set, and in the morning when I noticed the wrinkle, ever lengthening, that had appeared on my forehead the previous year. Was this not the arrow of time? "Just because you observe something doesn't make it so," Moira said when I brought it up one afternoon. "Human perception is limited. You stand on the beach and look out at the horizon line. If no one had told you, would you guess that the world was round?"

Sitting there at the bus stop, I lost time, too. The sky clouded over, a warning rumble of thunder sounding from somewhere far away. The songbirds went into hyperdrive before giving way to the hum of insects. A couple drivers leaned out their windows to tell me the bus wasn't coming. "Just waiting for a friend!" I'd call back. I entertained the idea of writing about Wesley and the Center, for Randy, trying to give my mind a break from everything I'd learned that day, but it kept drifting back to Moira, to Martin, to Lillian. It was disappointment, what I was feeling, the long slide, bottom dropping out. Of course I didn't imagine that Martin and Moira were perfect—my visit to Wesley's was cast in the shadow of my own annoyance with Moira—but I did imagine that they were perfect together, and I kept bumping against the sensation that something was going wrong just outside the frame of my vision. I pictured my edges blurring, the colors of my clothes and body and hair dissolving into the dark. The first drops of rain speckled my T-shirt. And then: headlights.

"I hear someone's looking to escape a cult?" Sawyer leaned over to push open the passenger door of the truck, a twangy pop song spilling out into the night. "Throw the bike in the back."

"Thank you, thank you, thank you," I called. The bike was unwieldy and it took a couple tries to get it into the bed. Once inside the truck, I tapped the nose of a bobblehead dalmatian perched on the dashboard. "This is your truck?"

"My car's on the fritz. This is Valerie's," they said, checking the rearview and pulling out into the road. "For when she's on call for search-and-rescue. So, did you drink the Kool-Aid?"

"Sort of," I said. I told them about the dream workshop, about Wesley and Lillian and Martin and Moira, about the long relationship I'd known nothing about and the way my heart broke to learn of the early betrayal.

The rain was falling faster, in fat drops that splattered on the windshield. Sawyer switched the wipers on, and they scritched across the glass. "And the point of all this is what, exactly?"

"Ha," I said, drawing it out. "I don't know. I seem to have both found and lost the plot. The plan is still to write about it, I guess. Although . . ." I turned to the window and let my tongue loll out in a gag, not quite ready to admit the defeat of Anna's voice mail out loud. "Yeah. Guess I'll just write it all down."

"Moira's fine with having it all aired in public?"

"She agreed to be interviewed. I don't need her permission to write what's true." I said it with more confidence than I felt. The truck smelled like wood chips, coffee grounds, the shea butter moisturizer Sawyer kept in their heavy leather backpack and rubbed into their hands throughout the day. "I sometimes wonder if writing has to hurt the person it's about, if it's going to be any good. Joan Didion wrote that 'writers are always selling somebody out.'"

"Would it be worth it, though? You could hide identities, change things around. Call Moira, I don't know, Phaedra and make her a biologist."

"I think if I could change anyone in this story it would be myself," I said, leaning my forehead against the cool window.

"It's a good place to have a spiritual center," they said a few miles later. "Historically speaking. We're just a couple hundred miles from what they used to call the Burned-Over District."

"Forest fires?"

They laughed. "Spiritual ones. There was a religious awakening in the central and western parts of the state in the 1800s, burned so bright it actually turned the less zealous off religion entirely. Mormons started there. Shakers. Oneida."

"Is that why you ended up at Linden?"

"In a roundabout way. Linden has a good program, probably partly because of the rich history. Fully funded. But I also just wanted to get the fuck out of Florida. My mom actually had some family in this part of the state," Sawyer said. "Way back. My therapist had a field day with that one."

I smiled at their rueful tone. "What do you mean?"

"Seven years studying Black churches in the place my deeply religious mother has her roots in this country? It's a little, you know, on the nose." They went quiet. "I should give tours. Sawyer's Guide to Hellfire and Fury."

I flicked my focus from my own reflection in the window to the trees outside, and back. "I used to be a tour guide."

"Of what?"

"Central Park."

"No shit. Tell me something."

I adopted my perky, professional voice. "Welcome to Central Park, it's six times the size of Monaco, and until twelve thousand years ago it was covered by the Laurentide Ice Sheet, a thousand feet deep. Bird-watchers can hope to see up to two hundred and seventy species each year, from the indigo bunting to the common mallard duck."

"That's cute. You tell the tourists about Seneca Village, too?"

"Mm-mm. What's that?"

They glanced over their shoulder to make a right-hand turn. "Never mind. Where do you live? Where should I drop you?"

Without my realizing it, we'd arrived in the center of town. "Up that way," I said. "Actually, wait." I'd thought I wanted to be alone, but the prospect of sitting in an apartment that wasn't mine with an insomniac night looming ahead of me seemed untenable. "Want to get a drink or something?"

Their eyes went to the time on the dashboard. 9:05. "I don't know. I should, in theory, be working."

"Come on," I said, with false gusto. "You said yourself that I owe you a beer. And you only live once."

Sawyer drummed on the steering wheel. "In this corporeal form, at least."

The Last Resort was comfortingly populated by a crowd that looked as if they'd spent years watching the Linden students pass through, observing their drunken fights and crying jags and makeouts with varying degrees of amusement and disgust. The place was lit by old neon signs for Budweiser and Pacifico, and the smell of spilled beer felt like home.

"Seltzer with lime?" I said, apologetically, to the woman behind the counter. She had pigtail braids and wore a red bandanna tied at her collarbone. She nodded, impassive. "Actually . . ." I said. She turned back and I hesitated. "Yeah, um, can I get an IPA? And"—motioning to Sawyer—"whatever this one wants?"

An old Jack Nicholson movie was playing on the boxy television suspended in a corner above the bar.

Sawyer peered into the back. "It's Ben. I love running into him outside of work, he's such a Martian."

We made our way to where he stood with a couple of his friends around the pool table. It had only been a month since my last night out in Brooklyn, but the loose-limbed magic of that first IPA felt particularly effervescent, the pleasant feeling of defenses and anxieties melting away. Sawyer's girlfriend Valerie showed up, and they both teased me with comfortable familiarity for getting stuck in the middle of nowhere, and I wondered why none of them had ever invited me out before. I bought everyone drinks, liking the gentle ribbing.

I remember huddling under an awning on the back patio while Ben smoked a cigarette, telling him about how my dad had been removed and restrictive while my mom had let me run wild. How I used to hold my breath and press my ear to the bottom of my bedroom door, trying to hear whether they were talking about me. Then Ben was nodding and saying, "Yeah, man, my parents damaged me, too." Stray drops of rain fell on my knees and when I took a drag of his cigarette it tasted like a thousand other nights.

I remember buying a round of tequila shots, salt licked from an already salty wrist, the alcoholic burn and sharp tang of bitten lime, a spin of new faces, the click of the jukebox—Beastie Boys, Michael Jackson, Blink-182—and leaning my head on someone's shoulder as we watched the album covers whir by. "I'm trying to remember the name of a song," I said, working hard to keep my words from slurring. "I want to listen to it so much but I can't—" A kiss. A car ride.

I jolted awake just after five a.m., confused, my clothes tangled at the foot of my bed. I called Hugh two, three, seven times. Finally, his voice. "What is it, what is it? Are you okay?" And then: "What're you doing? I can't understand you. It's been weeks, and now you're calling to tell me you fucked some guy?"

Maybe there was more to the conversation, maybe I just cried, maybe he said *hooked up with* or *kissed* or *fell in love with*, or maybe nothing like that at all. Three minutes and forty-two seconds. Then my own damp weeping, inconsolable, sinking back into bed, to darkness, to sleep.

PART IV

ONE

Sal

A year after college I started a journal in which I tried to write down every detail I remembered about my life. This was some amalgam of a long-held reverence for *Harriet the Spy* and the newly acquired understanding that a human soul is but a collection of its owner's memories. I divided the blank book into years, beginning at age three and a half, with my first definitive recollection: stealing a shiny green rock out of my preschool's succulent terrarium, and lying awake from the guilt, though I never felt guilty enough to bring it back. I started filling out all eighteen sections. A fight with my best friend in second grade about who got to play Pocahontas and who had to be John Smith, embarrassing now for a number of reasons. Dad trying to explain the trick for memorizing the 9 times table. Tense preadolescent Christmases, full of high expectations and disappointments, and then quieter ones stretched out over separate days, in separate homes. Watching Hugh throw a Frisbee, a tug behind my navel. A feverish layover spent in the Chicago airport, a little boy whimpering, "I think we're in hell," six hours into a delay.

I filled the notebook in a couple months and bought another. I'm not sure what made me keep going, but I do know what made me stop: the sudden, overwhelming impossibility of the task, which hit me like a virus one day. I had forgotten so much. I could not, for instance, visualize the bathroom in my college apartment, such a recent image. I couldn't remember the present I received after I returned from a sleepover not to the baby sister I'd been promised but to my mother, putty-faced and holding, instead, a box festooned with silvery ribbon curls. No matter how much I wrote, I could never fill in my entire life. It was fruitless to try.

Likewise, I do not remember the bike ride to Moira's the morning after that bad night at the Last Resort. In my memory, there is no communication with her, no warning that I'll arrive. I am just there. "Moira," I call into the front door, and when there's no response I walk around to the side of the house, wondering what I'm going to say. I'm so frustrated with her for keeping so much of the story from me, and the small, irritating voice that keeps reminding me she doesn't owe me anything just works me up more. Ahead of me, what she describes as "the pond" stretches out toward the trees, her boat out in the middle disrupting the pale reflection of the cloudless sky. I lengthen my stride into long, tripping steps down the hill dotted with puffball clovers and yellow dandelions. As I get closer, I realize that the boat is bobbing some yards out but Moira is not in it. One oar is floating close to the dock but she is nowhere in sight.

Moira was a strong swimmer. I had seen her myself, cutting lengths across the lake. But still, there were accidents. Cramps. A sudden cardiac event. One wrong breath, the struggling lungs filling with water, and no one around to hear the calls for help.

In this sharp, surreal memory, I am aware of a howling. It is Blue, baying from the back deck, trapped behind the baby gate, and this is what shifts the energy. Moira never leaves the dog up there unless she's out on the pond, and all at once I'm crashing into the water, falling forward, water up my nose and in my eyes, doing messy breaststrokes out toward the canoe. By the time I get to it I'm winded, but I plug my nose with my fingers and sink under the surface, scrabbling with my free hand, touching nothing but slimy water plants. *She's gone. How can this be happening? This isn't happening. This is happening.*

It's only once I come up for breath that I hear someone shouting my name.

I jolted upright and found that, standing on tiptoe, I could touch the bottom. I half stood, half floated, coughing up lake water.

"A single trip to Wesley's compound drove you literally off the deep end, I see," Moira shouted as she walked down the back steps.

My clothing billowed around me as I paddled toward shore. I couldn't find the ladder on the dock, so it was with an awkward, seal-like flop that I ended up back on dry land.

"Look at you. Like a drowned muskrat." She pulled her lips into an upside-down smile, trying not to laugh.

"The boat," I choked out.

"It got blown loose during the storm last night."

I stood dripping on the grass. "You should have told me," I said irrationally.

She pushed her glasses onto her forehead. "I was on my way to deal with it when I got waylaid on a call with Caroline. See? Blue's caged. I have my suit on." She pulled up her sweater to reveal the dark latex. On the deck, the dog was lying pitiably, the tips of her claws poking out from under the baby gate, her nose pressed between the slats.

"I'm all wet." I leaned over, dizzy. Moira reached for me—maybe she thought I was falling, or just wanted to comfort me—but as she leaned forward and I instinctively waved her away, the back of my hand knocked her glasses off her head and sent them skittering onto the grass. I reeled back, my hands over my mouth. A thin line of blood appeared on the side of her forehead. "Oh my God, Moira, are you okay? I'm so sorry. Are your glasses—?"

"Stop. Go inside." Her tone wasn't angry, but authoritative, as she shuttled me up onto the back porch. She was steering me into the bathroom, pointing me toward a cupboard stacked with towels and returning a moment later with a neat stack of clothes. Thick black T-shirt, thin slacks that clung at my thighs. I sat down on the toilet lid to blow my nose. My hair hung in damp tangles down my back. My breath returned to normal as I stared, half-seeing, at the cerulean tiles on the walls.

Sitting alone in the bathroom, squeezing the water from my hair, I beat back a memory of leaning in close to Ben's face the night before, and the cascade of mirror images that threatened to follow: drunken nights in high school straddling men in backseats and waking up, home somehow, my hair smelling like a bonfire. That reckless confusion returning my last year of college after Hugh and I broke up, whole nights scrubbed clean from my brain, hours unaccounted for. *I was fine*, I'd insisted to Georgia earlier that summer. But I hadn't been then, and now that bogeyman chaos, looming for months, had finally caught up with me. With it, another version of myself—the clean-living upstate writer—had been torn to sinewy bits. I didn't want to be there anymore. I also didn't want it all to have been a waste.

I leaned against the doorway to the living room, where Moira was sitting at the laptop she kept on her writing desk, her nose just inches from the screen, comparing something there to a legal pad beside her. Her glasses lay next to the mouse pad, one resin arm snapped short.

"Moira, I'm so sorry. I'll pay for them." She didn't turn, just gave her head a minute shake, eyebrows low. In the anxiety of my hangover I couldn't tell whether she was upset with me, or I with her, or both. The day before, I'd thought I'd be on a moral high ground when I saw her, knowing what I did, but now I felt unsure, contrite. I moved into her field of vision, my hand braced against the doorframe. "What're you working on?"

"Hm?" She kept scrolling through the columns of figures.

"What's all that?" I repeated, trying to keep my voice light.

"I'm preparing my data for the conference next week. I'm presenting this paper, and the corrections . . . I don't know what research fellow they had reviewing it—"

"What conference?"

"The biologist and I are presenting our SETI paper at MIT. It's all hinging on huge unknowns, but I'm looking forward to stirring things up."

"What are you talking about?"

"The paper, Sal, positing the feasibility of space-time travel, and that certain inexplicable phenomena known colloquially as UFOs may be future terrestrial life come back to observe their past."

"I didn't know anything about this," I said. It was a simple, tangible reason to be angry with her. "How long are you gone?"

"A few days. A long weekend. I'm sure we'll fall into the same old squabbles. Is the forward movement of time fundamental or is it a question of perspective, et cetera, et cetera. I'm sure I've mentioned this." She was being so rational in the face of my petulance. I wanted her to react, to tell me to cut it out.

"Are you sure?" I felt wild. "Did you happen to slip in any other big revelations while I wasn't listening carefully? Anything else I'm just forgetting?"

She looked quizzically at me. "What's gotten into you?" Her expression shifted. "You spoke with Wesley."

"I did. He told me about Lillian. And about the novel she was writing, and how Martin left her. Martin was married to her when you met him, did I just miss that? She died, Moira," I said, unable to order my thoughts, feeling my tone slide from accusatory to entreating. "How could you have left that out?"

She turned her head slightly, the way a dog cocks an ear toward a sound. "I see," she said without inflection. Like ocean water rushing back out to sea after crashing onshore, any bravado I'd felt drained completely, replaced by the terror that she was going to kick me out and put an end to all of it. There would be no manuscript, no answers, just this last, horrible interaction—the broken glasses, the feeling of seasickness—that I would replay over in my mind for years, wishing I'd done something different.

But that's not what happened.

"It sounds fatuous to say that it all happened a long time ago, though it's true," she said. "It isn't something I think about every day now, or even every month. But it was terrible. Just terrible. You move on, life continues, but it is always there. Martin wouldn't talk about it. Maybe it was too painful. Or maybe he thought I didn't want to talk about it, and I thought he didn't, and so neither of us brought it up. I got used to deflecting." She closed her mouth into a taut line and her eyes traveled to mine, to the laptop screen, to the window. Thinking. "Maybe I've been waiting for you to ask."

TWO

Moira

*H*ow's this for a truth that should be universally known? Moira used to say to her husband: *There is no tense more irritating than the past subjunctive. I know that you love it. I know that what might have been is something you've spent your life thinking about—what was not, is not, but could be.*

As someone whose understanding of life does not make space for the concept of a past subjunctive, I care not for what might have happened; what was *is all that is or could have been. And yet when the past subjunctive enters my life, it does so insidiously. For me, it is the creeping thought that steals into my consciousness when I wake with a jolt at 3:24 a.m. It is the thing that I think about on long drives through the rain when I've exhausted my worries about Caroline's safety and health and happiness, about your creative fulfillment, about whether I fed the dog or turned off the stove, about the reception of my work. Then the klieg lights of my anxiety pivot into the past. The past! Incontrovertible, immutable. Futile. I start searching around for what I might have done differently. Are you listening, Martin? You must do it, too.*

———

SIX WEEKS BEFORE the accident, Moira heard noises outside the door of the apartment. Martin was gone—writing, as he always did on the weekends, at the library. The place still felt like his, not theirs, though Martin did ask her opinion on whether to move a brass lamp from one side of the room to the other, and together they'd bought a blanket at the flea market, a colorful woven throw from the world goods stall.

She'd never been so unproductive, had never spent so many days allowing the hours to slip by. For all her short life, she had been working toward a goal. Now, as time ran irregularly for her father—returning him to a childlike state while speeding him forward into old age—she reveled in the suspended temporality of Martin's apartment. She woke up, made coffee, did some scattered work, took a shower, made lunch, worked some more, and then the day was done. But though the hours shot by, recent months felt like an eternity ago. She had met Martin some six months earlier, which meant that just six months ago her father was lucid enough to request something from his office. The doctors had assured her mother that the sharp decline in cognitive functions was not unexpected; that it was typical for patients to vacillate back and forth between "bad" months and "good." Just because her dad didn't remember her name today didn't mean that he wouldn't tomorrow.

When she told her mother that she'd met someone and that she would be staying with him until she left for Berkeley, Nina said only, "You're an adult. You can do whatever you think is best. But I'm letting you know that I think it's a bad idea, and that I don't want to know about it." Her mother was out nearly every evening now, and had a community of friends Moira hadn't known growing up.

"I thought her assignations were rather more carnal in nature," Moira told Martin, "but it turns out she's been going to the synagogue on Park."

Martin had scoffed—"The opium of the masses, indeed"—and she suddenly felt protective.

"She gave up her family, her religion, her education to be with him," she said. "And now that his memory's gone, it's like hers is, too. Of course she's clinging to this old constant."

"Gave everything up?" Martin said. "She had him. She had you. The two most incredible people in the world."

It had happened so quickly, their coming together. She was tempted to compare it to a reaction, some rapid chemical change. But no. They were human beings; these were choices. Their togetherness was the sum of their decisions, his and hers—though what was a choice, she'd meander on, if not itself a sum of identifiable factors: genetic predispositions, external influence, societal expectations . . .

During the weeks following what she thought of as the elevator encounter, her father had often asked for items from the office. Where was the manuscript they'd sold to Random House? It had been much better before the editor got his hands on it. Where was that book? Where was that ledger? Her mother didn't want the assistants coming to the house, but she didn't want Emmett going back to the office, either. And so Moira returned and returned, sometimes sitting for hours at his desk, preparing for coursework or reading one of his clients' novels or lying on the bristled carpet breathing in the dusty competence of the room and remembering who her father used to be.

She thought of Martin, too, spending each cab ride there idly wondering whether she would run into him, and each one back imagining what would have happened if she had.

It was during one of those trips, on a hard, blue day in February, that she slowed as she approached the building doors to watch a woman on the street, her gray-gloved hands tucked into her armpits, her skin pale, with hot red patches on her cheeks and nose. Waiting. And then, like a nudge to the back of the knees, Martin appeared, striding over to kiss the woman's lips and eyelids, and as he cradled the back of her head, the bright gold band on his ring finger shone. Moira watched them as they hailed a cab, the edge of the woman's long coat disappearing into the car as the door pulled closed, a single motion.

Did she feel guilty when he called and she returned to the apartment she now understood to be not his, but his and hers? Did she imagine that other woman, with her plumeria lotion beside the sink and Baudelaire by the bed? Did she do so when they met for lunch, and dinner; when she returned to the office building late one night not on an errand for her father, but so that she could perch, naked, on Martin's desk? She did. But then she thought: *I am doing this, and therefore it is the only thing that I can do.* That made things easier. And anyway, Martin, for all his comforting warmth, was a temporary distraction. She was leaving for school in a matter of months.

But it turned out she couldn't stop herself from caring. After she and Lillian had actually met at Jack Grant's horrible party, which Moira and Martin had planned to attend together, if only secretly, he'd been spooked, and they hadn't spoken for a week. When he showed up outside her parents' apartment building asking to come inside, she'd told him, for the first time, about the extent of her father's illness; he'd taken a sharp downturn in recent weeks, refused to take his sleeping pills, accused Rita of poisoning him. Martin had gone pale and speechless, and at this empathy something loosened inside Moira.

When he called her one evening in April and said with manic energy, "She knows. She left. I need to see you," Moira told him, though it was difficult, "I think you should be alone tonight, to think about what you want." When he started to protest, she said, "I need to, also. Call me tomorrow night." And before he could call her the next day, she rang him herself. "I'm all in if you are." She understood that there were several sides to every story. She had certainly heard Martin's: about the way Lillian had been feeding off of their life together, *his* life, and turning it into a novel. It was the secrecy he didn't ever want to repeat, because it was the secrecy that made him realize he didn't know her, and that was unbearable.

Moira did not, for his sake and her own, remind him that they had spent their first evening together before he found out about Lillian's own deception.

Martin's small apartment was a welcome escape from the empty rooms at home, her father shuffling in now and then to shout about intruders in the bedroom or to ask her to explain, for the tenth or twelfth time, how he knew her. Martin had already developed a patter around the story of meeting Moira at Emmett's Christmas party, though Moira didn't remember it at all. She wondered, but never asked, if he was disappointed that she couldn't simply pass his manuscript to her father, an easy in with a great taste-maker, an elevator rather than the drudge of the stairs.

———

THAT MORNING, WHEN she heard the muffled steps on the landing outside Martin's apartment, she knew, somehow, that it was Lillian. A knock. A quiet voice. Moira crept across the living room to the hallway and stood, trying not to breathe. Lillian didn't know that Martin spent long hours elsewhere on the weekends. That he was writing—really getting somewhere, he said—for the first time in years. Moira felt a twinge of embarrassment for the woman.

Another knock. And then, softly, "Moira?" It was jarring to hear her own name in that cool, calm voice. She froze, imagining herself opening the door, hearing what she had to say. But as she made herself move, as her fingers connected with the doorknob, an envelope appeared under the door and the footsteps retreated back down the stairs.

Meet me tomorrow, May 9th, at Clarke's at noon.
I have something you want. L.

Moira studied the note. It was, surely, for Martin. Though it was her own name that Lillian had murmured through the door. It was like something out of one of the old novels her father used to read to her at bedtime. Oil sconces and wax seals, fateful missives delivered by unseen messengers.

She realized too late that she'd be able to see Lillian leave the building from the window. Two women pushed a stroller along the sidewalk. A cabdriver, idling down the street, had craned most of his upper body out the window, yelling jocularly at a man on the corner. Lillian was gone, though Moira could imagine what she'd be wearing on a day like today: long flowing pants, white blouse, silk kerchief at her neck. Her unwieldy hair pulled high into a bun or—no, that's where the kerchief would be, holding back her curls. Bones and muscles closer to the surface, somehow, than most people's. Moira's stomach hurt.

———

SHE WAS LATE. Already running behind, stuffing her money and keys and lipstick into her long leather purse on her way down the stairs, she'd waited until the last possible moment before hailing a cab that inched in traffic caught behind an accident at the corner of Tenth and Broadway, the street clogged with sirens and lights. It wasn't particularly warm out, but Moira dabbed at her forehead and upper lip with one of her mother's handkerchiefs, a pair of *N*s embroidered in one corner. Inside the restaurant, she scanned the diners. "I'm meeting a . . ." she said to the neat, bored hostess, trailing off. "I'm meeting someone. I don't know if she's here yet."

"Name?"

"Oh, there. I see her," Moira said, her mouth dry. Lillian sat at a table for two, a cup of coffee and a carafe of water, half full, in front of her. She was watching Moira, her face expressionless. "I'll just—" Moira motioned to where she sat, and then glanced down at her dress, which looked young.

But the woman insisted on one of the busboys showing her to the table. "Madam," he said with exaggerated grandeur, "your guest."

"So she is," Lillian said.

Moira couldn't look at her as she hung her purse on the back of her chair and sat down. "Just coffee," she said to the boy. Her body buzzed; she hadn't expected to be this nervous.

"Well, Moira," Lillian said.

She had leaned forward when Moira sat down and was now resting her elbow on the table, her chin in her hand. She held an unlit cigarette between two outstretched fingers. Her pale eyes were like a particular kind of arctic dog's, and sat wide apart on her small face. Her eyelashes were dark with makeup, her hair pulled back in a low bun. She was serene, unworried.

"I thought it was you," Lillian said, reaching into her pocket and emerging with a matchbook. She cupped her hand around the flame and lit the cigarette with a hiss and pop. Her nails were bitten down to nubs. "Last week I stood across the street from your building and waited for hours. You must have come or gone at some point, but I couldn't distinguish you. You look like a thousand other girls." She said it not unkindly, but with the innocuous tone of someone stating the results of a recent tennis match, or the price of a new pair of shoes. "Although that was your parents' apartment. Perhaps you weren't there at all."

Moira was on an increasingly unstable surface, ice melting on a lake. "How do you know where I live?"

"I've been there before. Excuse me," she said to their waiter as he passed. He bent at the waist. "The shrimp scampi. Green salad to start." She turned, and Moira realized she was waiting for her to order.

"Oh." She scanned the menu, unseeing. "The soup, please."

"Which soup, ma'am?"

"Um," she said. "This one, the mushroom."

"Very good." He disappeared.

It was too bright in the restaurant. "What do you want from me?" Moira said.

Lillian narrowed her eyes as she inhaled. "From you?" she said, her voice choked and stiff. She exhaled, turning her head and directing a smoke stream out the side of her mouth. "I don't want anything from you. You were quite a surprise."

"You left a note under my door. You," Moira stumbled, embarrassed, "you said my name."

"Did I? I left a note under Martin's door. I assumed that if you happened to find it, you'd leave it alone. Throw it away, maybe. But certainly not show up here. Quite a funny trick to play."

Heat rose in Moira's cheeks. She was the child who'd misunderstood the rules of the game. "What did you want from him?"

Lillian rubbed her temple with the palm of her cigarette hand. "When we first met we used to leave each other notes," Lillian said. "Letters wedged into doorframes, or tucked into purses or pockets. It was romantic, thrilling. These last few months have felt like a return to that time. The uncertainty, the physical separation."

"The divorce."

Lillian tipped her head, conceding. "Like a reset. I'm not saying this to hurt you. I'm afraid you're collateral damage." She pulled on the green stone at her earlobe. "I was so upset when I left. So confused. But since then, I've begun to wonder if the distance might be a way back to each other. It's funny, I've always loved movies about divorced couples. *The Philadelphia Story, His Girl Friday.* The sense of history, knowingness." She raised her shoulder in an elegant, lopsided shrug. "Maybe it really is the end. But either way, I wanted to talk about it in the daytime, in a platonic, passionless space. Hence . . ." She made a sweeping gesture toward the room.

The waiter arrived with Lillian's salad, a beautiful green.

Moira crossed her arms. "Why are you telling me this?"

"You asked," Lillian said. She took a bite of the salad, chewed. "I also have to admit that none of this feels real. You seem like a child to me. Maybe it's because you were a child when we met."

Someone bumped Moira's chair. She hunched down like an anxious cat. "At that party? It was just a few months ago."

Lillian frowned. "Oh, you mean at—No, that's not when we met. Is that where you met my husband? No. Don't tell me. I don't want to hear any of this from you." Her jaw rippled; she was, maybe, less composed than she appeared. "I went to your parents' parties for years with the man I was going with before Martin; a painter, a friend of your father's, you'd probably know his name. The last time I attended I brought Martin with me, you know, trying to prove I didn't care about my ex. And that's when I met you. I went looking for a place away from the noise. Away from both of them. You were like a child from a storybook, going on about stars and time. And so, to me, you're still that little girl alone in her bedroom, folding her socks." She drew her brows together, thinking. "I came downstairs and Martin and Wesley were fawning over your father. The kingmaker. He was such an idol for Martin, *is* such an idol, as I'm sure you know."

"That was you?" The words were registering in a strange jumble. She was unusually aware of how often she was blinking. "He said that he . . ."

"He said what?" Lillian sat back in her chair, her eyes roving over Moira's face. "What?" The rest of the food arrived, Lillian's pasta smelling of garlic and warmth, Moira's soup a disappointing porridge.

Moira was going to be sick if she ate even the smallest spoonful. She watched Lillian twirl the pasta around her fork. "I don't believe you," she said.

"Excuse me?"

"He doesn't want to be with you anymore."

"Martin does not know what he wants," Lillian said. "He wants to be understood, but has a fundamental terror of being known. He wants recognition for work he doesn't do. He wants his writing to prove to the world, once and for all, that he is a good person, an artistic person, a high-minded man—never mind that good artists do bad things. As do mediocre ones. The thing is, I know my husband. You don't know him. You are young. You are a blip."

A week ago, Martin was going on about applying the laws of physics to human nature—entanglement, that's what he was so entranced by. The idea that two humans, like two atoms, could become irrevocably connected, that through time and space the connection would remain. He had said, "What are the odds that we'd meet all those years ago and then find each other again? What is that, if not entanglement?" Moira had explained, pedantically, that this was impossible, that humans were not atoms, that quantum theory applied only to the smallest things, and that anyway, entanglement necessitated a lack of independence—not something, really, to aspire to. He'd come up behind where she was standing at the window and wrapped his arms around her, nestling his nose into the soft sensitive place behind her ear. "Look," he said. "We're entangled."

Now, at the table, Moira felt herself running a phrase, a child's memorization, over and over in her mind: *To every action there is an equal and opposite reaction.* "I think I'll go now," she said, bumping the table as she stood. "You should stay. I'm sorry this wasn't the lunch you were expecting." But as she turned to pull money from her purse, she realized her purse was gone. She peered under the table, then looked wildly around the room, as if it might have scurried off on its own. Nothing. She tipped her head back, gazing, unseeing, at the ceiling.

"This one's on me," Lillian said. Moira couldn't tell from her inscrutable expression whether she'd seen someone take the bag. "But maybe you can do me a favor in return." Lillian reached into her own bag and drew out a stack of papers, rubber-banded together. "Can you give this to him? It's my book. I promised I'd show him when I was finished. I'd always planned to—that's what he didn't understand—and it's changed since he last saw it. You can read it, too, if you want."

Moira hardly processed that she was accepting the pages, that she was clutching them as she left the restaurant. Outside on the street the day continued. A man in a baseball cap selling oranges and strawberries on the corner called out, "Why so glum?" as she passed and she smiled mechanically. She walked toward home. Martin's home. Her shoes, taken from her mother's closet and half a size too small, pinched at the soft place beneath her ankle bone; she'd have a blister. She thought about what Lillian had said, about how she and Martin would find a way back to each other. It all sounded absurd and delusional—and yet it also sounded like she'd actually seen Martin. Had been seeing him. They needed a passionless, platonic place to meet because at some point in the not distant past they had met under other circumstances.

Martin was there when she got back, sprawled over their couch with a copy of *A Farewell to Arms* propped above him as if in flight, a mug making rings on the coffee table. "Where have you been, my love? I've been bereft without you."

Moira sat down across from him in the old wing chair that predated her, and that would live in each of their homes, in Berkeley, on the Upper West Side, in upstate New York. She placed the manuscript on her lap.

He closed the book. "What's the matter?"

"I've just seen Lillian."

"What, on the street or something?"

"No. We met at a café."

"Okay." He sat up, irritated. He didn't like suspense unless he was the one administering it.

"She was expecting you. She left a note yesterday, but I got it and thought— It doesn't matter. I went." She watched him for a reaction, but all he did was raise his eyebrows. *And?* "She gave me this, her novel, to give to you. It sounded like you'd asked to read it. Recently."

"Oh?" Someone who had not spent the last months collecting his mannerisms like data points to be logged and analyzed might have missed the stutter of hesitation, the way his eyes darted from where they'd been locked on hers, to the table, to the door. Thinking. Moira felt her breath catch. There it was. At some point, maybe more than once, he'd gone back to her. "Well, I haven't. I don't care about it at all."

"Right," she said. His choosing her, then, should have made her feel powerful, this triumph over Lillian, but instead she was exhausted and numb to what now felt like a pathetic charade.

She stood and placed the manuscript on the coffee table. "And it wasn't you, Martin." Her voice sounded old, ragged. "At the party, all those years ago. It was her."

"What are you talking about?" He looked baffled, genuinely confused.

"My dad's party," she said slowly. "Did she tell you about meeting me? And then you pretended—?"

"No," he said, with sudden comprehension. "I was there. I met you, Mo. When I saw you in the elevator, I knew it was you."

"Martin," she said, on the verge of tears, "don't—"

He was up, cupping her face in his hands. "You can't believe everything she says. She's upset." She didn't think his adamance was something someone could fake, which was when Moira learned that belief could be a choice, too.

———

LILLIAN'S BOOK DISAPPEARED from the coffee table shortly after they spoke, and she was too proud to ask if he'd read it. They circled carefully around each other. Martin, eager to please, spoke of how much work he had gotten done, how it was all because of her. She often felt that she was watching him as though through a telescope—that she could see him up close while remaining impossibly distant. There was comfort in his presence and his tireless devotion, but she was happiest on the weekdays she was uptown at the lab, or the Saturday mornings he wrote at the library and she stayed in bed reading a novel or going over her notes from the night before, puzzling over whether it was possible for a human brain to conceptualize time, making tea in the cranky old kettle.

It was on one of these mornings that, while she was chewing on her pencil eraser and reading a paper on scalar bosons, the phone rang.

She didn't like answering the phone there, in his apartment, on edge at the prospect of being confronted by her mother bearing bad news, or finding Lillian on the other end of the line. She let the phone ring six, seven times, before she picked up.

"It's Wes."

"Oh," she said. In the last few weeks Wes had come over twice for post-dinner drinks. He had an easy familiarity with Martin but treated her with polite reserve, and his quick brain both fascinated and unnerved her; at times, with his perpetual punch lines and vast sphere of references, he reminded her of her father. She wanted to ask him about the work he was doing on the brain—neural pathways, rerouting cognitive functioning—and about whether it might help someone like Emmett. But she knew how close he had been with Lillian, and she felt distrustful around him, self-conscious. "Martin's not home," she said.

"Mm. The muse hath struck, then. I can call later. Or perhaps . . ." He trailed off.

"Yes?"

"Perhaps I'll leave this message with you and you can decide what to do with it."

"Yes, sure. What is it?"

"I'm afraid it's a bit awkward. Lillian was in an accident." He paused, waiting for her reaction.

"Is she—?"

"She's not dead, Moira, no. It happened last night. Los Angeles. I only heard about it through a friend of her sister's and the details are hazy. Questions about whether drugs were involved, whether it was purposeful, but you should have seen her when we went to Vermont one Christmas—she almost crashed three or four times before Martin made her stop driving. And I guess she was borrowing her mother's old Buick, a pontoon boat of a car, but there was also something about a man driving—" He seemed to remember to whom he was speaking and stopped short. "In any case, you can let Martin know as you see fit."

"Got it," Moira said, her voice small. "Thank you."

"Yes." Wesley sounded like he might be about to say something else, but cut himself off. "'Bye, then."

She had to tell Martin. And then, maybe, that would be the end.

In conversations about her impending departure—she was leaving for Berkeley in just under three weeks—Martin behaved as though it would change nothing between them, as though she were not going to live across the country for four to six years but rather taking a weekend away. The imagined death of his ex-wife may be the catalyst Martin needed to end his romance with Moira. Though maybe it was time to think about what *she* wanted. Maybe she didn't want Martin at all, didn't want the musty smell of his body after a weekend spent writing. Didn't want the way her consciousness now split—where was Martin, what was Martin thinking, how was he, did he still want her?

He wouldn't be home for hours. She couldn't sit festering in the apartment. She pulled on her Keds and started walking uptown, following the slanting line of Broadway with the vague idea that she'd stop in at the Hayden Planetarium. She hadn't gone since she was in grade school, but staring up at the rings of planets in the Copernican Room sounded soothing. "They're moving," her father had once told her, crouching down. "They're moving just as slowly as we are." By the time she made it to the entrance, the planetarium was closed.

There were hours of daylight left. She sat down on a bench to watch the people passing by. If life was a series of forked roads, in which each decision closed some options off and opened up others, she had arrived at one of those points. She could stay with Martin, or she could leave. She could go to Berkeley, alone, get her degree, go on to discover some twisting equation that would once and for all determine whether time could turn backward—whether it already had. She could study the stars, study the earth, attempt to make contact with other forms of life.

It was evening by the time she arrived back at Martin's. As she walked up the stairs, she went over, for the hundredth time that hour, what she would say to him. If she practiced enough, she might be able to ignore his stricken expression.

She reached his floor, and had taken two steps down the hallway when the apartment door wrenched open and Martin appeared. He was breathing hard and for one delirious moment Moira imagined pushing past him to find a woman, naked, in the bedroom. It was Wes, though, she saw over his shoulder, his eyes red-rimmed.

"It's Lillian," Martin said, frantic, the room dissolving around him.

———

IN THOSE HARROWING days after they learned the actual outcome of the crash, Martin clung close to her. "Oh, God," he would say in the middle of the night, and Moira would snake her arms around him as though, if she held him close enough, she could force her way inside, extricate his pain. To witness his anguish was unbearable. She made scrambled eggs and buttered toast that they ate at six p.m. Lillian popped up between them, the hundred Lillians of Moira's imagination. Her knobby fingers on her water glass. Her stillness, eyes drilling into Moira from across the restaurant. The way she'd looked that day on the street, rising on tiptoe toward Martin as he bent from above.

There she was, driving fast on the 405, her sandals kicked off on the floor of the Riviera and her bare feet on the pedals, as she'd done every night since she'd come back to Los Angeles. There was no man beside her. There is not always a man. If death was instant, as is so often reported, there was no pain. But nothing happens instantly. There is space and time in between the body alive and the body shut down. A separation.

A three-quarter moon. The cars on the road were just streaming headlights and taillights, and Lillian was an object moving through space. She'd rolled down her window and reached over to crank down the passenger side, too, and the cleansing flood of the night air, the sound of the Santa Anas and the passing cars were almost loud enough to drown out her thoughts. Almost. For the first twenty minutes of the drive she thought about Martin and Moira, and her body hummed with rage. She stepped hard on the gas. Why had she left her manuscript with him? He'd probably burned it or dropped it even less ceremoniously into the trash. What was she trying to prove? Then her mind gave way to streaky images: the moon illuminating the scene in her favorite painting, just outside the frame; the ocean she couldn't see or hear but knew was close; a seabird lit from underneath by a streetlamp; the ragged white tear of her own tendon and the callus that repaired it. Her blood beat at her wrist, her breast, her neck, as though every part of her body were pulsing a reminder that she was alive. In an effort to stop biting them, she had painted her nails that morning in hot Barbie pink. She opened her hands on the wheel, admiring their gloss.

A damp patch, a slick of oil, a glinting distraction over her left shoulder. A hard acceleration to match the energy of her brain and an overcorrecting brake when the car was out of control. A spin and a rotation. Three seconds, maybe, from beginning to end. But as the windshield cracked like ice on a lake and the atoms of the metal car tried hard to connect with the atoms of the highway's cement barrier, perhaps not in that order, time stretched. *This is a car crash*, Lillian thought, taking a deep breath as though she were submerging in water. *My mother will be livid.* The spinning stopped. Wet heat on her forehead, her neck. Confetti snowflakes. Pale boat on a dark river. One entire life. A sound like radio static, with words so close to distinguishable. *I'm not ready for this.* Inside: a cleaving. *I should have written faster.*

THREE

Sal

When Moira finished telling me what she was able to that afternoon, we sat without speaking. Blue's metronomic snores cut through the quiet. I was scratching a dry spot at the nape of my neck and pointedly not looking at Moira, but I could feel her eyes on me; not continuously, but moving up and down from my face to her hands and back again.

"I don't know what to say," I said finally. "I feel like I should tell you that none of it was your fault, but it doesn't matter what I think, and also—" And also, I actually wasn't sure that was true.

"You don't have to say anything," Moira said, her expression like a shrug. But there was something else under her indifference. A vulnerability.

"Okay." I made my tone businesslike and braced myself on my knees in preparation to stand. "Thank you for telling me."

She stood, too. Her face was now almost slack, as though she'd voided it of emotion. "Why don't you come by tomorrow?" she said. "We can address any questions that have come up."

"I don't think I can tomorrow," I said. "I have a shift at the café."

"Of course. Whenever's convenient."

I began the trek home on my bike, but I was so dizzy I thought I might fall off, so I dismounted and escorted it over the gravel. I already regretted my coldness toward Moira. And I didn't have a shift at the Beanery until the following week. My response had been automatic, a lie

I didn't even think about. I could have just said I was busy, and left it at that; or, more truthfully, that I needed a break from her and their story.

Still, it was almost all I thought about for the rest of that evening. The bathtub at the apartment was shallow but the tap was piping hot; something about a hangover always makes me want to be in water. Maybe it was that primal urge, rather than the altruistic hope of saving a drowning woman, that had launched me into Moira's pond. Submergence in water was a popular ending for women both in literature and in life: Ophelia, Lucette Veen, Virginia Woolf, Edna Pontellier, Harriet Shelley. Protagonists and supporting roles and wives and poets and poets' wives succumbing quietly to too much of a good thing. While the tap ran, I retrieved my copy of *Evergreen*, peeled off Moira's clothes, and sank into the steam.

I started the book from the beginning, set on tracking congruences in Martin's life—which were there, it turned out, if you looked for them: the career-ending injury, the current of betrayal, the somber, funereal ending. "She had once crested the slopes like a seabird skimming a wave . . . The blank expanse of canvas stretched wide and white, the windward side of the mountain, and every day she moved further away from me." Lillian, poor Lillian—it felt as though I were mourning the death of someone I had only just met. It was a terribly unfair ending to her strand of the story. I imagined the guilt Martin and Moira must have suffered and my breath turned shallow, as though the feelings were mine.

But these musings were crosscut with others: the ballooning worry about what I'd done the night before; hopelessness that Hugh hadn't felt the need to check on me; mercantile thoughts about whether this new glut of information made for a worse or better story—I tended to think that it was the latter. Forget any part I played in Martin's last novel; I had the dramatic, real-life, long-buried tale that not only inspired a cult classic, but shed light on his final work. I clung to the idea. This wasn't simply a magazine story, this was an introduction to a reissued *Evergreen*. When the water cooled I drained the tub, toweled off, and climbed into bed with my laptop. *The Tragic True Story Behind This Beloved 1970s Novel* or, for the lawyers, *Did One Woman's Tragic Death Inspire Popular Fiction?* I wrote, near-giddy with narrative.

But that sureness dissipated overnight, and in the morning I was bereft, the project seeming ludicrous. Moira had mentioned that Lillian's sisters were still alive and I located one of them, a costume designer in L.A. who'd done one of the National Lampoon movies. I stared at the IMDb picture of her, green eye makeup and a green velvet dress, taken in the early aughts. Maybe Lillian would have become a screenwriter. Maybe she and her sister would have become an iconic collaborative team, now gray-haired and angular, the kind adored by sleek women's quarterlies, THE BODEN SISTERS embroidered across baseball caps.

The next few days passed quietly, mostly in the apartment; I ignored a call from Sawyer, one from Moira, and three from Georgia. Sawyer and Moira left messages, promising to make "the best breakfast sandwich of your life" and asking whether I was going to come by the house that week, respectively. I read and made notes, and in the evenings I rode my bike past a fallen-down barn, and a cow pasture where the big brown animals watched me benignly, and an ominous cement structure surrounded by barbed-wire fencing and signs that read: SHOOT FIRST, QUESTIONS LATER. I began a list of what I wanted to ask Moira and what I never would. When she called on the third day, I let it run to voicemail. I didn't want to think of myself as punishing her, but of course that's what I was doing. *Would you have stayed with Martin if Lillian hadn't died? Would Martin be an author at all? Would he have been a greater writer if he hadn't married you? Did you think about her when you were in bed with him, and did you like that you had won? Do you wish you hadn't told me?* I wrote in luxurious, looping script, and then stared at the page. When she called on the afternoon of the fourth day, I picked up.

"Oh, Sal," she said, as though surprised to hear my voice. "I wondered if you'd gone back to Manhattan."

I was in bed with my laptop propped on my knees, combing through Bonnie's social media in search of traces of Hugh. "You thought I'd just leave, without saying anything?"

"You seemed quite upset by the end of your last visit."

"It was a lot to process. I've gone the whole summer thinking one thing, and now—"

"Would you like to come by and talk?"

"I could be there in an hour," I said. I glanced down at the sweats I'd been sleeping in. "I have to give you back your clothes, too."

———

"DARLING," SHE WAS saying when I pushed open the front door, Blue shifting back and forth in her happy waddle, "you haven't lived with anyone for years. You have no idea what kind of roommate you are."

Caroline. It struck me how startlingly intimate it was to be privy to the private discussions between a mother and her daughter—made more intimate, somehow, by knowing what Caroline thought of me. And yet, only getting half of the conversation prompted a lurch of discontent, too; I often found myself picturing what Caroline was doing on the other end of the phone.

"Don't be silly." Moira wandered past, returning a throw pillow Blue had carried into the kitchen to its proper chair. "I tried California. It didn't stick. There are earthquakes and fires and marijuana and free love." She raised an eyebrow for my benefit, and even after everything, I still felt a certain thrill in being there with her, while her daughter was three thousand miles away. "No, I know it's nothing to joke about." She grew quiet. "Yes, I know you do. But, Caroline, it's not a question of personal choice, you know that. Of course we all have to do our part— darling, why don't you call Priya? There's no need to take your annoyance out on me. All right. I love you."

She returned the phone to its receiver and ran the sponge under the tap. Her sapphire anniversary ring clacked the counter as she wiped it down.

"Is anything wrong?" I asked tentatively.

"Oh, Caroline's worried about the fires, she's arguing with her girlfriend. She picks fights with the people she loves when she's low. It happened quite a lot in the weeks after Martin died. So much bubbled up to the surface. How I wasn't around when she was little, how I chose my career over her."

"That's what she was just saying?"

"No." She drew out the word. "Now she's angry at me for the fires."

I laughed. "What do you mean?"

"She read a report a few months ago about how many tons of carbon emissions physicists produce each year as a by-product of research: flights to conferences, the supercomputers. She has some idea that the world's scientists should be diverting our attention toward the climate crisis. That it's immoral to pour resources into studying extraterrestrial phenomena when our own planet is in peril. But it's a limiting argument.

Our understanding of atmospheres on other planets, those hotter and colder than our own, inevitably impacts our understanding of earth's atmosphere, the implications of terrestrial warming—" She squeezed out the sponge. "And does she think we would understand the trajectory of greenhouse gas warming were it not for quantum mechanics? Where does she think radiation transfer codes come from? There's no arguing with her when she's in that kind of contrarian mood, looking for someone to blame. Your children never grow up, not really."

"That sounds exhausting," I said.

"It is." Moira nodded, holding her wet hands gingerly in front of her. "And it isn't. Caroline went through a very fierce phase when she was around four years old. When something happened that she didn't like—stubbing her toe, a rained-out soccer game—she'd throw her head back and shout, 'Do you think this is a funny joke?' Not at anyone. Just sort of at the world. She must have picked it up from a teacher or a babysitter. Martin and I loved it; we started calling the recipient of these chastisements Caroline's God. The God of Funny Jokes."

I handed her the dish towel I'd been leaning against. "Does Caroline know about Lillian?"

"You are a terrier, Sal," Moira said, drying her hands. "She knows that Lillian was her father's first wife. She knows that it was an unhappy time. But it's ancient history to Caroline, it doesn't involve her. How much do you know about your parents' lives before they had you?"

It was hard to fathom the people my parents used to be. They had met at the University of Colorado, but I'd never been able to understand why they'd gotten married in the first place. They had so little in common. They enjoyed the outdoors and were descendants of cultures that liked to plant flags in other people's home soil, I had once joked, self-consciously, to Georgia. I had to assume that they started closer together, and it was just time that wedged between them, but maybe it was as simple as a physical attraction that had faded. They were both closed off, in their own ways, my dad talking about his youth in bland generalities, my mother telling stories about wild adventures that I found difficult to believe.

"Not much," I conceded. "But, Moira, the way you told it made it seem like you'd decided to end the relationship with Martin, before you found out—"

"When he told me what had happened, I was sure that that was the end for us, regardless of what I'd decided. For Martin, though, I think the idea of going through all of that only to let our relationship fail would have been too tragic. He needed it all to have meaning."

"Do you think about that time often?"

"No."

"Moira, that sounds so callous."

She sucked in her cheeks the way she often did when thinking; her expression was almost stubborn, and I could picture how she must have looked as a little girl. "At your age," she said, "everything has more weight, more importance. I'm not condescending, it's a truth: the telescope of time. I've accumulated nearly half a century of experiences since that year with Martin and Lillian. Did that time matter? Of course, but the number of mistakes and triumphs and heartbreaks since then—there's a certain temporal smoothing that comes with age. Maybe that's what people mean when they talk about wisdom."

"That seems very sad," I said.

"It's not. It's liberating. Would you want to spend your life devastated by the balloon you lost when you were four?" She let the smile fade from the corners of her mouth. "It isn't that I never thought about her. If I'm honest with myself, she consumed my mind for a long time, in different ways. Her death. Her relationship with Martin. The more often one recalls a memory, the more warped it becomes, the more subject to mental manipulations. There's a sharpness to my recall of that time, but I do wonder how accurate it is."

The telephone rang.

"Leave it," Moira said. "Telemarketers." The machine clicked on and the caller hung up. In the living room, her cell phone buzzed. "That's funny," she said. "It must be Caroline again."

Slowly, I began wiping down the counter, for something to do and because it gave me a sight line across the hall to where Moira stood with her back to me. Her voice softened and lowered into the register she used only when she spoke to her daughter. "Is there an official direction?" I heard her say. "You said they restocked the N95s, yes?"

Phone pressed between shoulder and ear, she opened the television cupboard and clicked through channels until she found the news: an amber alert in the Bronx, a hate crime outside a movie theater a few towns over, blue skies for days. Without thinking, I drifted to stand in the doorway.

"There's nothing on TV about it here, I'll have to check online," she said, but then the screen flicked to an aerial shot of a fire blazing through woodland. "Found it." The anchor, an unblinking bottle-blonde, described the two fires that had joined together, the dangerous winds. "It's north of you," Moira said. "Right?" She listened, and I could hear the muffled sounds of Caroline's voice through the receiver. "Please do stay at Priya's tonight. I know you are, but I have to say it. Call her on your way in. Sooner rather than later. Yes. I'll be here, call anytime. I love you." She hung up. The television flicked through shots of a decimated town from the year before, billowing smoke, the view from car dashboards as people drove down roads that were winged with flames.

"This looks pretty bad," I said.

"It's miles away, but she's going to drive into the city. Just in case."

"I'll get out of your hair," I said. "Unless you want some company?"

"Mm." She was standing so close to the television that her face glowed pink from the flames.

"I'll head out, then. But I'll keep my phone on . . . Moira? I'll keep my phone on. Call if you need anything," I said, simultaneously thinking, *What could she need from me?*

"Thank you, dear," she said. She'd never called me that before. Something about it was awkward, embarrassing. "You know, I have thought about something, over the years," she added.

I'd already opened the front door; Blue was snuffling the air, and in the distance I could hear cars and the low hoot of a passing train.

"That poor woman's mother," Moira said. "She's who I think about the most. I can't imagine living with that; knowing that your child died such a violent, solitary death."

"Would you do it differently?" I said, breaking in. "Knowing how it all ended, would you stop yourself from going to your dad's office that night?"

"You mean," she said with a wry expression, "would I give up Martin if it meant keeping Lillian alive?"

I nodded.

"If I hadn't been with Martin she wouldn't have left for California. She wouldn't have gotten in that car. I could never have foreseen that trajectory of events. But still, what I did was wrong, in a larger ethical schema. One could argue that I knew I was inflicting harm, I just didn't understand what kind. At one point I could have said that, if given the chance, I'd do things differently. I love Martin. It's hard to imagine my life without him, but it's possible, and if it kept Lillian alive I think I would be strong enough to sacrifice that love. My career, too. After Caroline, though, I couldn't imagine it. I cannot become so selfless, even in my own imagination, as to give her up."

FOUR

Caroline

C aroline's house, with its weathered front porch and falling-down greenhouse and single room serving as kitchen and living room and dining room combined, had been on the market for weeks by the time she first walked in the door. The realtor, an impressively muscled man with expensive lavender socks, was unable to frame it as anything other than an "exciting project" or "a great piece of land." Caroline, at age thirty-five, hadn't had the money to overhaul anything—that she was able to buy the house at all was because her maternal grandmother had left her not an enormous sum, but more than she'd ever imagined she'd have in her bank account. But the kitchen window looked out over the garden, which had been left to grow wild with the brushy grasses that covered the hillsides, and she imagined planting a lemon tree with her mother, an orange tree, plums. Hibiscuses, hydrangeas, daffodils, irises, tulips.

She spent months painting the bedroom upstairs, the bathroom, swapping out the plastic switch plates for pretty enamel ones she'd picked up at flea markets and estate sales. The house was all her own, a singular happiness.

At work she encouraged the children to play. Not to play pieces, though they aimed for that as well. It had been her dad who'd pointed out the sweet double definition to her: "It's nice. To play, as in the instrument, but also to *play*, as in to enjoy without necessity." Pleasure for pleasure's sake. At the time, because she'd been fifteen and moody, she'd taken what he said to mean that he thought music was unnecessary, which was a sentiment he often imparted. But eventually she understood.

In her first sessions, the goal was simply for her students to enjoy the experience, to give themselves over to the rapture of striking a key and producing a sound. She shouldn't have had favorites, but she had favorites, and the top of the bunch was Arthur, whose big eyes projected his terror half the time, and wonder the rest. He was seven years old; she'd met him when he was five. And while his mother, Nadine, assured her that he did speak to his family when they were alone together, enough to let them know that he liked peas but hated broccoli, and that he wanted to visit the bus depot, and that he wanted a pit bull puppy, Caroline had never heard him say a word.

The first time they sat together at the piano, he looked down at the keys and up at Caroline and let out a growl that Nadine had warned her often preceded his rare but explosive tantrums. No piano, then. It turned out that he loved the xylophone, which Caroline used to help kids work on colors. Arthur was more attached to the percussive sounds it produced, and liked to hand the mallet over to Caroline so that she could strike it while he lay on the floor, his curls an inch from the instrument. Nadine had a reputation at the elementary school for being pushy. *Here she comes*, Caroline had heard the secretary whisper to another teacher one afternoon. *Batten down the hatches.* But she wondered how a mother was supposed to behave when she was navigating the public school system with three children, one of whom had been diagnosed with autism spectrum disorder when he was two years old. She'd been anxious to meet Nadine until the woman arrived with Arthur clinging to her hand, her leg, anything he could get ahold of, and she'd whispered into his ear and he'd nuzzled his face in her neck before letting himself be unpeeled from her.

"I wish I was half as good at anything as Nadine is at mothering those kids," Caroline said to Priya one evening.

"You see her in limited circumstances," Priya said, taking a swig from her Jarritos. Caroline had driven into San Francisco to meet her at one of their favorite places in the Mission, a taqueria that Priya, who had moved to the city as a teenager, had been going to for years. "She probably snaps at the kids when she's tired, and screams that she isn't their maid when they leave piles of dirty clothes on the bedroom floor."

"I don't know."

"If you had kids I'm sure you'd be kind to them, too." Priya laced her hands behind her head. "What am I saying? You're terrific with *her* kid."

"That's not the same. I'm not on all the time."

"Roro," Priya said, looking at her curiously, "have you changed your mind?"

"About kids? No. I have not changed my mind about that. Have you?" Priya was younger than Caroline, but on their second date she'd said in the measured tone Caroline would fall in love with that she didn't think she ever wanted children. Caroline once thought, uncomfortably, that she was drawn to Priya for all the ways she was different—she was a marine life researcher, with South Asian parents, who'd grown up all over the world—but increasingly she wondered whether it wasn't a dazzling familiarity that had pulled her in. Perhaps because they shared a scientific mind, like her mother, Priya could discuss emotions without becoming emotional..

Priya shrugged. "I wonder whether it's something I'll miss," she said, as she'd said many times before. "But I don't want to have a child out of curiosity."

That night, back at Priya's apartment and uncomfortably full from the burrito she always said she wouldn't finish, Caroline cracked the living room window and sparked her pipe, listening to the street noises, the rattling and sighs of the 22 Fillmore bus, voices ricocheting from the bar across the street. The air smelled like campfire, and then like weed. By the time she climbed into bed next to Priya she was relaxed, her low-grade nighttime dread blown away like vapor. Priya had her glasses propped up on her head to keep back her long hair, which, at thirty-three, was starting to streak through with gray. She loved stories about famous shipwrecks and plane crashes—*Titanic*, obviously, but TWA Flight 800, too, Delta 191, the *Lusitania*. On the screen, the camera bobbed above the water before sinking into dark bubbles below.

Caroline slipped her hand under the covers and onto the soft warmth of Priya's stomach. She outlined the curve of her rib cage and felt Priya's abdominals jump.

Since she'd met her, Caroline had yearned to write a piece for Priya—she needed to divest herself of some of the intensity of her feelings. She imagined playing it on the beautiful old piano as sunbeams dappled the framed posters in her living room: the New York Philharmonic 1987 season, a 2007 Mark Adams show at the Berggruen Gallery. She could hear the kind of melody it would be, but like the childhood days she'd spent trying to plink out the Chopin tune, her imperfect attempts left her so frustrated that she'd give up for weeks. Then the ghost of a melody would return, prodding at her.

She slid her hand back down Priya's skin, its smoothness and tiny bumps and ripples and errant hairs, until she reached the elastic waist-band of her cotton shorts. Priya was still watching the show, but her lips were pursed in a smile. Caroline pressed the laptop closed, hoisted one knee over her hips.

When they'd turned off the light and Caroline had nestled her head into the soft dip underneath Priya's shoulder, Priya said, "Have you thought any more about what we talked about?"

What they'd talked about was Priya moving in with Caroline, or Caroline selling her place and buying something together. Caroline was out of breath as she imagined giving up the solitude of her home. A home that, to be fair, Priya often already shared.

"It's been five years, Caro. It's tiring, the back-and-forth."

"I thought we liked being one of those chic independent couples with separate dwellings. Like Tracy and Hepburn."

"We could be one of those chic independent couples that live together. Like everyone else." When Caroline didn't respond, she added, "It won't change us."

Sure it will, Caroline didn't say. She rolled over onto her side, her back to Priya but the soles of her feet pressed against her calves.

Priya kissed the nape of her neck. "I love you. We don't have to have this whole talk tonight. But we will need to have it."

Part of Caroline wanted to have the "whole talk." She was too anx-ious to sleep now. She wanted Priya to demand that they live together, to put forth an ultimatum that would make Caroline bend to the plan or depart. But in the dark, the rise and fall of Priya's ribs changed and lengthened and Caroline knew she was counting her breaths. She would be asleep soon.

THE WEEK SHE'D traveled to California for the open position nearly fifteen years earlier, Caroline already knew that even if she didn't get the job (and she wouldn't), she could never leave this place with its neat pastel houses, its crashing waves, its craggy shoreline and gray-green trees that stretched out flat like stratus clouds, the smell of sea salt and eucalyptus and dirt and rain.

The breakup had been hard, especially when Julie had listened so calmly as Caroline laid out all the reasons why she wanted to move, how alive San Francisco made her, and then said, "We can do long-distance. We're solid. And I'll start taking auditions again. Between L.A. and the Bay Area, the state's swimming in orchestras. Something will come up." When Caroline didn't reply, Julie's eyebrows swooped low over the bridge of her nose. "Oh," she said. "This is a shitty way to do this, Caroline."

It took five years for Julie to forgive her, and then, after all those dozens of months of silence and abortive attempts at connection and one misguided romantic reprise, they fell into something new. When Caroline flew out to see her, Julie had a tenured position in Philadelphia and was embarking on the long, arduous process of adoption applications. Being in Julie's warm two-bedroom was like being back home. Late nights drinking hot toddies in the living room, catching up on the memories they'd missed: Julie's two years in an emotionally abusive relationship with a harp player, her summers in Brussels playing a festival there; Caroline's struggle to get gigs, an accompanist job at a ballet school, her eventual decision, arrived at in a flash during one of her long, ponderous walks, to get a degree in music therapy.

She would call Julie from the parking lot of the charter school when one of the fifth-graders she'd been working with was expelled for attacking another girl in her class, and when a six-year-old showed up with bruises like fingerprints all up and down his arm. She would call when her landlord renovated the apartment lobby to look like an IKEA showroom and the building was sold and the rent tripled and her neighbors were suddenly all twenty-five-year-olds in Patagonia vests and sneakers and you couldn't go to the bar down the street without hearing someone's conversation about app patents and market disruption, which was when she started applying for those jobs outside the city.

Priya had a daylong research trip the morning after they hadn't fought about moving in together. She left as the first pale streaks of day lit up the bedroom, kissing Caroline on the cheek and disappearing with a quiet click of the front door. Caroline drifted back to sleep, waking a couple hours later to a bank of fog rolling in. Outside, a fine coating of ash had covered the Honda. She shivered, climbing into the car. Once she hit the bridge she phoned Julie out of habit.

"Sweet Caroline," Julie sang, and in the background one of the girls shouted, *Dun dun dunnnn.* "We're having pancakes, I can't talk long. What's up?"

"Just missed your tranquility."

"You would not say that if you could see the current state of my

kitchen. Gem's in an operatic phase. Into belting Andrew Lloyd Web-
ber, I'm sorry to report."

"No."

"Yes. All *Phantom*, all the time. She watched it at a friend's house.
I could kill those parents. The irresponsibility."

Caroline forced a laugh.

"Caro. What's wrong?"

The fog that socked in the city fell away as she wound up through
the Berkeley Hills. "It's Priya. She wants to move in. Or for us to move
somewhere."

"Good. She's perfect. She's smart and thoughtful and interesting
and interested. The mobile she made for Olivia is incredible. She keeps
you from catastrophe-spiraling. What are you worried about?"

"I like my space. I like living alone."

"So when you need space you go to the living room. Don't close
her out."

"Did I do that to you? I was so difficult."

"Sure you were. So was I. But look at us now, so wise, so mature.
So capable of love and self-expansion."

Caroline let out a wet laugh. "I don't want to throw myself a pity
party. And I know you have to go, so give those girls a big squeeze
from me. Tell Gemma to get better taste."

"You'll be okay, you know."

"I know."

They said goodbye. She kept driving, the car working hard on the
final hill up to her house. The wind chimes beside the front door, a
present from Priya, tinkled in the breeze. Her skin itched.

———

WHEN CAROLINE WAS a child, her mother would play a game with her before she fell asleep: Pick a star, beam yourself there, look back toward earth. What do you see? Now Caroline imagined herself looking back from Alpha Centauri, almost five light-years away. Two pinpricks of light and color, as yet unconnected. Priya and Caroline, 2013. That late-September day, as Priya's silver Prius wound its way toward the Headlands Center for the Arts, Caroline's beige beater putted along from the opposite direction. Priya, a speaker at the event, arrived first. Caroline, in the audience, slipped in during the introductions and, folding her sweater over her arm like a waiter's white napkin, found a seat at the back.

The roundtable was part of an ongoing series that brought together experts on each of the five senses: this month's was on sound, moderated by Caroline's grad school advisor, a pioneer in the field of music therapy with a penchant for jackets in clashing tie-dye, crimson jackets emblazoned with lime-green polka dots. The panel comprised a physicist (Caroline circled his name on the flyer, for her mother), a composer with a froth of dark curls, a sound engineer, and Priya. That day she wore a pale blue dress shot through with silver threads and her hair hung in a fat braid down her back. Onstage, Caroline's advisor introduced her as a marine life researcher who tracked humpback whale pods through their songs.

Priya made a joke about going into her line of work because people often had a difficult time placing her accent: her father worked at a bank and she'd grown up all over—Ahmedabad, where her parents had met and married, London, Salzburg, San Francisco. Now she traced the origins of whale accents, more or less. Male humpback whales were the ocean's composers, she said, their mating calls traveling like pop songs from pod to pod over the course of each season until the whole ocean hummed with that year's tune. On the projector screen behind her, the whales slid through a thousand shades of cyan, their backs curving and turning to reveal bellies glimmering with remoras. Priya talked about the impact of increased oceanic noise pollution from offshore drilling, cargo ships, military sonar. Humpback whale calves and their mothers whispered in tones forty decibels lower than the big singing males. Their quiet chatter kept them concealed from would-be cannibals passing by, but it was also vulnerable to being drowned out by the ships. Mothers and calves could become separated in murky waters during their migration. As the physicist joined in to explain the vast difference between the speed of sound traveling in ocean water versus the air, Caroline was surprised to feel the wet prick of impending tears somewhere behind the bridge of her nose.

In the parking lot after the presentation, the waves audible in the still afternoon, Caroline approached the clustered group of presenters and touched her old teacher's elbow. "My dear!" she said, turning around and pulling Caroline into a hug. "It has been too long." She introduced Caroline, and the conversation resumed. "I like to teach," the composer said in a *don't get me wrong* voice. "But somehow, as a younger man, I never expected that it would be a necessity in securing a basic income in the arts."

"Or sciences," the physicist said.

Priya grasped opposite elbows as though clutching a baby or a loaf of bread. She had a tiny tattoo of a praying mantis on the indentation where her thumb bone met her wrist and a single gold hoop earring tucked inside the seashell cartilage of her left ear. "I don't teach," she said, turning to Caroline with a shrug.

"I loved your talk," Caroline said, extending her hand. "It reminded me of my parents taking me to see that huge blue whale at the Museum of Natural History in Manhattan when I was little. I hadn't thought of it in years."

"I've never seen it." Her hand was solid in Caroline's. "I don't heart New York, I have to admit. It feels so cold and confined. But I've lived in San Francisco for almost twenty years, so maybe the state's just too much in my blood at this point."

"Fair." She was usually annoyed by anyone not from New York who cast aspersions on the city.

"And are you a teacher?"

"Not college. Little ones. I don't know anything about the trials of tenure committees, outside of what my parents used to complain about. Both professors."

"A family of scholars."

"They'd be interested in what you do. My mom would love the science of it and my dad would love the emotion. The idea of the calves learning to sing. It's so . . ." She didn't bother trying to find the right words. She spread her hands to encompass all of it, everything.

FIVE

Sal

It was three in the morning when the call came in. I dropped the phone while scrabbling for the button to answer, but could still hear Moira speaking, muffled and fast, from the floor.

Caroline had left for Priya's four hours earlier and hadn't ever arrived. "Her cell phone is going straight to voice mail. AT&T cut power in the East Bay and the fire knocked out other towers." Moira sounded out of breath, but her voice was calm. The traffic was bad going into the city, she explained, given the evacuation order and general Saturday evening traffic. But she should have been there by now. "I've booked a flight," she said.

"A flight?" My own heart was pounding in the panic of waking from a deep sleep.

"Out of Newark. But I don't think I can make it there on my own. I tried the cabs, and Ming and Roberta, but no one is answering. If I come to your apartment now, could you drive me the rest of the way?"

"Yes, yes," I said, disappointed, even in my confusion, that I hadn't been her first call. Who was Ming? Who was Roberta? "I'll be outside."

A white cat loped down the sidewalk as I waited for Moira. She was grim when she put the car in park, not bothering to turn it off, and handed the keys to me before getting into the passenger seat.

"I might need help with directions," I said, and she plugged the airport into the map on her phone.

"In one thousand feet, turn left," the phone said cheerily.

We made it out of Linden, sailing down the roads I'd come up weeks before. I kept thinking Moira might want a distraction, then tried to come up with something to say, before deciding there was nothing to say, only to start the mental cycle over again.

"The night before Martin's memorial service," Moira said suddenly, as I navigated around a Kroger's semitruck, "Caroline still hadn't decided whether she wanted to be an active participant, as it were. We knew there was a piano at the community center, and I thought she might like to play something. Right before it all got started, she told me she did. There wasn't a microphone at the piano, so when she sat down on the bench and started speaking, her voice was stronger than usual. She said, 'There are a lot of pieces that would make sense to play today, beautiful ones that Dad would have absolutely hated. I would like to say that maybe music sounds better to him wherever he is now, but he wouldn't like that, either. So I'm going to play the only piece he ever really liked. It's by John Cage. It's called 4'33".' Someone in the room got the joke before the rest of us and laughed. And then she sat there, not playing, for four minutes and thirty-three seconds."

"It must have been so terrible for both of you," I said, nauseous with how much I wanted to put my hand on her shoulder, pull her into a hug.

"It was almost unbearable," she said, as though to herself. She was quiet again until we passed under the first sign for the airport. "Shit," she said. "The dog."

"I'll watch her. Don't worry about that."

"Would you? Stay at the house. You can have the whole place to yourself."

"Stay there?" I kept my voice steady, my eyes on the road.

"Here. Take the keys." She dropped them into the center console. "The fridge is stocked, there are clean sheets on the guest bed. It would be a big help."

"It's nothing, really." We pulled into the winding expanse of the airport, into the backup of cars that, thank God, slowed but did not stop. The sun was starting to rise. "Don't worry about a thing."

For the first time since I'd gotten into the car, I really looked at Moira. She was gazing, unfocused, straight ahead. Her chest rose and fell in quick, tiny movements, and with each breath her nostrils flared.

"I'm sure she's okay," I said, trying to keep a frantic edge from creeping into my voice. This all had to be a mistake. Caroline had to be somewhere safe, there had to be an explanation. "I'm sure she just got stuck in terrible traffic without a signal, and ended up staying with a friend, or—" Moira turned. Her features were set, but her eyes were liquid, reflective, and for a moment as we stared at each other a softening fell along her jaw.

I'd inched the car barely parallel with the curb when Moira opened the door, gave a curt "Thank you," and hurried across two lanes of traffic carrying nothing but her purse.

SIX

Caroline

Caroline thought she had more time. She spent half an hour, more, forty minutes, watching the news as the splotch on the map denoting affected areas spread like an oil spill, the itch of a rash. Like a wildfire. An inertia set in.

She was still in front of the television when her cell rang.

"What's wrong with you?" Priya said, her voice near a growl. "Why haven't you called? Why aren't you on your way here? Are you not seeing what's happening?"

"I think we might have to have a fight," Caroline said. "I think you might have to yell at me for being stupid about moving in together, or I have to yell at you, or something—"

"Stop it, Caroline. Get in your car. Have you been listening to the traffic reports? It's going to take you hours. I already called Jim and Norah and they're in Tahoe this weekend, or I'd say go to their place."

"Yes," Caroline said, heaving something between a sob and a laugh. "Yes, okay. I'm on my way. I love you."

"I love you, too. This is the worst."

Caroline had her hand on the door of the car when she started to think about what it would mean if the fire reached the neighborhood. If she was kept out of the area for weeks, as she'd seen with other communities. If it made it to her house. It was something she'd imagined a thousand times in her waking nightmares, the beautiful structure going up in flames, but now, at a more likely time than ever before, it seemed impossible. She had safeguarded against this: she had imagined the worst; the worst would not come. And yet. She had her mask hanging under her chin and the back of her throat was raw. She went back inside.

She gathered the things she thought she could not live without. The photo albums, five of them now, fat with memories. A cardboard box filled with sheet music she'd had since she was a teenager, Bach and Handel. A box of keepsakes that she kept in her closet, love notes from Julie, one of Moira's notebooks from when she was a teenager, postcards from Priya, a manuscript Martin had had bound, just for her, a year before he died. A handful of blue and green pebbles she'd picked up on a walk with Priya by Battery Townsley a few weeks after they met. "These formed in the subduction zone of the San Andreas Fault," Priya had said, running her fingers over the shards in Caroline's palm. "Serpentinite, blueschist, limestone. They're young rocks. Some are only eighty million years old." They were in an old Macy's box, just another quick trip from her front door to the car. The sun was going down and the air smelled of smoke, but it had smelled like smoke all summer. Every day was a Spare the Air Day, as though anyone needed to be dissuaded from lighting a fire. Everyone had had enough fires.

She spent four minutes—240 precious seconds—calming herself at the piano, playing her favorite section of her favorite Graham Fitkin piece. Another one with a home note; she'd have to tell her mother.

On her last trip to the car, after locking the front door and then turning back, unlocking, peeking in to check that everything was still in its place, and then relocking it a final time, she could hear sirens, a man's garbled, distant voice projected over a loudspeaker.

She drove down the eerie, empty streets; she was ten, fifteen minutes from the bridge. There was no mistaking the haze; not pollution, not the wet Bay Area fog to which she'd grown accustomed. It was smoke and it was getting thicker, though perhaps that was her paranoia. It had become dark more quickly than usual, and maybe earlier, too. She tried to call Priya but her phone couldn't connect, flashing *Calling P* for twenty seconds, thirty, before flickering over to *Call Failed*.

Before she ever saw a whale breach up close, she had seen videos online. The difference was incalculable, the former too dazzling to occupy the same description as the latter. She went out with Priya on a drizzly day, buckling an orange life jacket over her rain slicker. Her face was wet with spitting rain, and as the boat cut through obsidian waves, one of Priya's colleagues pointed toward the horizon. All at once an impossible animal was rising out of the water twenty yards away, and her brain was so awed it almost couldn't compute the information.

That was what the first glimpse of fire was like in her rearview mirror. She couldn't believe it was real. But then the flames filled the mirror, and she was driving fast down streets that all looked alike. She was cold, she was shaking, she was driving in a direction that could have been toward the bridge but also could have been back toward the house—all she could tell was that it was away from the fire, and then she lost sense of where the fire was altogether. There was an intersection up ahead. If she stopped she would be able to figure out where she was, where she needed to go. In an unreasonable attempt to avoid traffic on 24, she had made an early wrong turn, shooting herself out into the winding hills of Orinda. The trees on either side of the narrow street whipped in a wind that had not existed an hour earlier. She had read the statistics, knew that the flames could devour towns at the speed of four, five, six miles per hour. She was not so much thinking as experiencing waves of thought breaking over her.

She was out of the car and over the sound of her panting breath and her loafers slapping against the pavement she could hear the bizarre, enormous sound of heat incarnate. She needed shelter. A basement. She ran up a driveway, around the back of a house. Locked. Another. Locked. She considered smashing a window, looked around for a paving stone, and then she saw the sunken hot tub, empty, its bottom filled with leaves. A pool. She needed a pool. There had to be one; what else could be hiding behind these big, flammable wooden fences? She'd seen them, big blue circles, on Google Maps. Her lungs were burning. She was delirious with fear. She could jump from pool to pool like in the Cheever story her father had loved. She could get all the way to the beach that way. The big house on the corner had a gate that swung open to reveal a set of stairs leading to a backyard, but when she got to the top there was just a patio, a manicured garden. She fought off the mounting feeling that she had made a terrible miscalculation. She ran back down the stairs and up the street to another driveway, another huge house, and when she got to its gate an automatic light flicked on and she could see well enough to hoist herself up and over. When she jumped down on the other side she felt a sharp zing in her ankle. But it was okay because there was the promise of a pool, a covering that stretched in a circle like a dark green web. Caroline unhooked the metal loops and the rubber sagged into the water. She stripped down and lowered herself in, gasping at the cold, and it was as she was pushing the heavy cover over to the side so that she would have the greatest possible surface area of unfettered water space that the world went from dull dark purple to red to orange, and then the smell and sound and heat were so huge that something down the street had to be burning, and she took a deep breath in.

SEVEN

Moira

M oira had spent a lifetime chastising Martin for his analogizing scientific properties with human existence. (No, she would tell him, entanglement does not and cannot and could never apply to human beings.) Still, he would insist on inserting them into his stories, like a child sneaking cookies from a box. "What is the difference between my comparing the limbs of a person to the limbs of a pale birch tree, and my comparing my love for you to the properties of two unique particles, separated by space, that have formed an unbreakable bond? We *are* entangled, my love." But their bond, she wanted to tell him, *was* breakable. That's what made it different. Their bond was not a property but a mutual choice.

Hurtling across the sky toward a fast-moving sunrise, she found herself, as she so often did, imagining her husband beside her. He was telling her that while yes, he did understand that the thought experiment of Schrödinger's cat relies on two specific variables—one: a radioactive substance inside a box; two: a catalyst that, at random, triggers a release of the substance—it seemed to him there were multiple moments in a person's life in which loved ones were both alive and dead, this flight, for instance, being one obvious example. (Here Moira shushed him because the death of their daughter could exist in no possible world, not one.) But he went on: there were so many moments in which you are not with the person you love, and so to you they may be dead, or they may be alive.

She imagined a tiny spaceship orbiting Sirius, beaming an ultra-strong telescope back toward earth, peering into the past. When would that be? Christmas 2008? She and Martin in California, splurging on two rooms at the Fairmont. Waking up to a wall of ocean and sky and Caroline tapping at their door in her music-note pajamas and a thick hotel robe, rubbing sleep from her eyes. Moira's spaceship zipped to TRAPPIST-1: she and Martin, their Berkeley city hall wedding four years in their rearview, packing up to move back to New York, her diploma nestled in a moving box and the cells that would become Caroline blooming in her pelvis. To 51 Pegasi: she's fifteen years old, splayed beside a Clear Creek pool in Celia's oversized sunglasses. Pie Mensae: Moira and her parents on the dock in the middle of a lake, looking through her first telescope as the water around them glitters with reflected stars.

But Caroline kept rushing in. Age two, twelve, fourteen, thirty-two. Caroline and her solemn brown eyes flecked with gold, like her father's. Caroline making a blanket fort under the piano with Martin's old quilt. Caroline teaching Martin about musical cryptograms—about Bach spelling his name into *The Art of the Fugue* with the notes B-flat, A, C, B natural—and Martin's sudden and total expression of delight. Caroline trapped in the house when the fire consumed it. Each time that image tried to push its way into her brain she clamped down. She hummed. *Our baby*, Martin said from the seat next to her, and reached out to hold her hand.

EIGHT

Caroline

Time is gone. So is space. It is just Caroline alone in this stranger's pool under the heat and sound of the fire, a loudness so huge it cannot be described, not through words, not through music. A rending. The smoke is so dense in her lungs that each time she emerges from the water, each time she lets her mouth open to the air, a koi fish gulping, the fire climbs down her throat. In the beginning there is fear, and pain in her ankle, but as she stays in the pool and the world burns around her something changes. She has never spent so much time awake without sound, without music. At first she can hear the pretty opening notes of the piece she was playing before she left, but soon she cannot hear even that, she cannot hear the fire, the world sounds the same above the water as it does below. She loses all sense of the leaves, the dirt, the hunks of wood that have blown into the pool. The pain in her ankle, an ache in her shoulder from wrenching it along the way, those feelings dull and then disappear. There is no time, but it speeds up. It slows down. She thinks, without thinking, that it might be running backward.

She goes under. She comes up. Goes under, comes up, goes under.

NINE

Sal

On the way back from the airport, half-dazed with exhaustion and following several wrong turns, I stopped at the apartment to pick up my laptop and clothes. At Moira's, I fumbled with the key in the lock before realizing it hadn't been locked in the first place, and Blue gave a couple of low, huffing barks. When I pulled off my shirt and pants in the guest room she watched from the doorway and then lumbered down the hall. I found her lying in a corner of Moira's room, her chin on her paws. We watched each other for a minute in the dim light, her eyebrows cocking left and right and left.

"It's okay," I said. The dog thumped her tail. "She'll be back soon." I didn't want to leave her alone. Didn't want to be alone myself. And so I pulled back the covers on the bed and climbed into it, imagining, during that liminal moment between waking and sleep, that someone— Martin? Moira? (Hugh?)—lay down with their head on the pillow next to me, smelling of mint leaves.

I slept late, later than I had in years, and when I woke up I forgot, at first, where I was and then why I was there. Downstairs, a puddle of urine pooled on the tile beside the back door. Blue was lying across the room from it. "I'm so sorry," I said. "It's not your fault." I pulled off a wad of paper towels and sopped it up, dousing the spot with the lemon floor cleaner I'd seen Moira sprinkle beside the sink after cooking. Moira hadn't called, and I didn't have her cell number, I realized

only when I picked up her house phone and prepared to dial. I found
Priya's in a Rolodex on Moira's desk, but I hated the idea of intruding
on this woman I'd never met; it would be unspeakably terrible if the
news was bad. It had already been reported that a man and his grand-
son had died, and the details of three other fatalities were yet to be
released, as authorities waited to confirm identities and inform next
of kin. Several people were missing.

As I drank a cup of Earl Grey at the kitchen table, I imagined
Moira standing in the aisle at the end of the flight, waiting to deplane,
and receiving a call from Priya that her daughter's body had been
found inside her charred house. My eyes filled with useless tears. I
imagined her standing in the aisle and receiving Priya's call saying
that there was still no news, and Priya picking her up at the airport
and bringing her back to her San Francisco apartment to decide what
to do, and the doorbell ringing, and the door opening to reveal two
members of a coroner's team. I hoped that by imagining these things
I might keep them from happening, and I feared that by imagining
them I might make them come true. We went for a walk, Blue sniff-
ing patches of grass, pausing to squat every now and then, her nose
twitching in the breeze.

I told myself I wouldn't paw through Moira and Martin's things in
search of the manuscript. (I would be good, and Caroline would live,
I bargained.) Instead, I curled up on the couch with my rumpled copy
of *The Paris Review*. The cover was ripped half off and the pages were
so dog-eared that some of the words were illegible. I searched for the
sentences that had so reminded me of myself, for the conversation that
mirrored ours, and found instead pale imitations of what I had been
carrying around in my head. He had woven allusions to Petrarch and

time into all of his work, not just this; the girl's edges were blurred, less sharply defined as the person I'd hoped I projected that night.

But. But! I couldn't quite see Moira in the descriptions, either. She was a young girl obsessed with the sky, but she didn't look like Moira, didn't sound like her. And there was that rose barrette glinting back at me as the man, tipsy, says goodbye to the girl: "It was as though I'd met her in some other dimension—she was a former guide in a future life with a name I'd know immediately."

I lay back on the sofa to watch the gentle whirring of the ceiling fan, the slow spiral of its chain. I turned on my recorder and listened to Moira's voice while tapping away at my laptop, adding to the now thousands of words of notes. Then I turned the recorder off, looked back up at the fan, and opened a new, clean document. The cursor blinked.

TEN

Moira

U pon landing in San Francisco, Moira woke with a sharp, disoriented start, not remembering where she was or why she'd
come—but then it hit with the bone-crushing weight of a rockslide.
She doubled over in her seat until the blood returned to her head.
She'd left her phone on and had checked it relentlessly on the drive
and during the first hours of the trip, until finally it died. It felt heavier,
somehow, without power. She stood in the line of passengers, a baby
caterwauling a few rows back and a man in a baseball cap shouting
something about mergers into his phone, and it was only once she
pushed her way off the plane and found an electrical outlet that she
realized she'd left her purse on her seat. Her phone charger, Priya's
address, the numbers of two other friends and the four hospitals
nearest to the fire were all written down on a yellow sticky note left
behind in that purse.

Back at the gate, one of the attendants was carrying the bag up the
gangplank. "That's mine!" she called, aware she was shouting too
loudly, a loony old woman. "Hello, that purse is mine!"

"You should check your seat before you deplane," the woman said.
"We were going to destroy this."

Moira didn't care. She had her phone charger, she had her phone.
She thought she might die as the screen flickered first its battery symbol

and then a flood of white. Five notifications popped up, bubbles from the deep. Two voice mails, three texts, all from Priya.

They found her and she's ok

We're at Alta Bates on Ashby

Call when you can

Moira's vision contracted until it was a single star of light. Her forehead connected with the palms of her hands, their backs on the cool plastic table. The waiting area filled with a heaving noise. It was coming from inside her, this hoarse, high-pitched wheeze. She couldn't tell if anyone else could hear it, this ghost scream. It was like a dog whistle, a whale call.

ELEVEN

Sal

Two days after she'd left, Moira called her own house phone and started leaving a message. "Sal, I'm at the hospital with Caroline," she had said by the time I snatched up the receiver. Her voice was haggard, as though transmitting from ten years in the future.

"Oh, Moira," I said. "Is she okay?"

"She will be. There were thermal burns and they had to intu—" Her voice cracked. "Intubate. Oxygen. All that. But she is on the mend."

I imagined Caroline's face covered in hairline scratches and rippling scars. Her house falling in around her, a growing wall of flames.

(It wasn't Moira who would replace my imaginings with the details of Caroline's actual night in the pool, but Caroline and Priya, when I eventually made my way to San Francisco and met them for coffee. They were looking for a place out by the beach. "Somewhere fire-safe," Priya would say to me. "With good storage," Caroline would add. "And a big guest room." They'd been talking about one of Caroline's students when I arrived, a boy, almost entirely nonverbal, who had been on the news because he'd demanded—screamed, hit his head against the wall, bit his mother—that his mother and sisters visit his grandmother just a few hours before the flames took a freak turn and burned through his neighborhood. His dad had stayed behind and was in critical condition. The street was leveled. Four people died.

Coincidence? the anchor had asked with a meaningful look into the lens. Maybe. Maybe not.)

Moira planned to stay another week, ten days at the most, she told me. Could I watch Blue until then? Was it a terrible inconvenience? I stood in the soft light of the kitchen, Blue on her mat, the birches stretching down the road. "No," I said. "Please don't worry about anything but getting her well. And I can only begin to imagine the toll this has taken on you. I hope you're getting rest. And eating well."

"We're all drinking a lot of chamomile tea."

———

AT MOIRA'S I dropped even further out of my life. I ignored the bottles of red wine in the kitchen rack and didn't respond to texts or emails, though Georgia's missives grew increasingly irritated.

Let's catch up soon.

Earth to starstruck Sal—call when you have a second?

Fucking RSVP.

I didn't want to talk to Georgia, because if I talked to her I'd end up telling her about the night at the bar, which I didn't want to think about. When I did finally send her an email I explained, briefly, what had happened with Caroline, and that I was staying at Moira's and taking some time to be alone with my thoughts. In an epistolary mood, I wrote a thousand-word message to Hugh trying to explain why I'd left the way I had. "I've never known if you were with me because of love or convenience," I wrote. "I am sure this is my failing and not yours, and I wonder now whether it's the right question to be asking at all, if all love isn't born of convenience and comfort and hormones, of upholding generational patterns or trying, however unsuccessfully, to break them. I left because I was looking for a different kind of love than what I've found with you. An idolatrous love, one printed and permanent. In the end, I haven't found that, either. And I realize how much I miss that other, less certain kind." Then, because the whole thing was so overwrought and self-involved, I deleted all but a couple sentences of apology and pressed send.

––––––––––

A WEEK. AT least a week alone with their things. I really did try to exercise self-restraint. For the first three days I stayed out of Martin's study like a well-trained dog, lingering outside the door as I passed it but not opening it, then opening it but not going in. On the fourth day I realized that I still had the photo album I'd pinched; that had to be returned. I went in. I sat down at his desk with the album on my lap and swiveled back and forth in his chair. Blue, who'd gotten used to me by then, jutted her nose into the room, panting from the walk up the stairs.

"What?" I said. "I'm just sitting here." I slid open one of the desk drawers, as though it might have been filled with new objects since the last time I checked. "There isn't anything to find." Blue moseyed in and lay down beside the desk, her tail sweeping the carpet like a windshield wiper. I rolled the chair to the big filing cabinet in the corner from which I'd seen Moira pull notebooks and letters. I flipped open a box beside it marked *m's work*. As though there were not two Ms in the house. Sheaves of his handwritten drafts, including early notes for the third novel.

I guess it was, as they say, all downhill from there. I found one of Moira's datebooks from the year she left for college and a box full of cassettes with labels like *Caroline Recitals 1994–1997* and *Juilliard Audition Tape Copy*. There was a small, portable player there, too, which the audition tape slid into with a satisfying click. I don't know enough about classical music to judge the teenage Caroline's playing, but it was nice to listen to, and one of the pieces was ubiquitous enough that I was able to identify it as Bach. A letter from Moira's aunt Celia seeming to respond to her concerns about the ethics of the moon program. An old tally of Martin's short story submissions from the seventies, lists of rejections (personal or form) and the occasional acceptance. There was, alas, no fated appointment book, the date of the library party circled with a loopy heart. There was no final manuscript.

But in a filing cabinet drawer, second from the bottom, beneath notebooks and fat pink erasers, my hand found something small and cool.

It had been almost six years since I'd seen the barrette. It was darker than I remembered—perhaps due to oxidation, or maybe my memory had brightened it into the gleaming thing I remembered—but just as heavy. It provokes a melting sensation, finding a lost object, the weight of expectation for once syncing up with reality. I turned the rose over in my hands. I could feel the muscles around my eyes and cheeks working hard. I took it into the bathroom, where I clipped it into my hair. I danced back into the office, twirling not, I think, because people dance in movies when a good thing happens, but because my body felt like it was the right thing to do.

SAWYER TEXTED AGAIN, asking if I was on a bender. I was scheduled to close the next day and, they hated to remind me, I had literally begged for the job. I said I'd be there. I pulled on the jumpsuit I'd worn the day I left New York for Linden, and washed and dried my hair. I patted Blue on the head and drove into town with an increasing flutter in my stomach, the radio fizzing in and out of a bouncy pop song. I hummed along, belting the few words I knew in an effort to stave off the mounting anxiety about seeing Ben, whom I'd thought about as a human being almost not at all. The sun was out, everything smelled green and new.

But it was just Sawyer behind the counter when I walked in, a red bandanna tied around their head and one of their "special drinks," a blended smoothie comprising four shots of espresso, a banana, and some peanut butter, sweating on the counter. "The prodigal daughter returns," they said, not entirely friendly.

"I'm sorry," I said.

They untied their apron. "For what?"

"Come on, Sawyer," I said. "For flaking on you. For being shitty at the bar. I'm sorry for all of it."

"You were very drunk."

"I bet."

"You were being pretty funny. Until you started crying, then it was sad."

"I was crying?" I'd forgotten this feeling, the perverse fascination in listening to someone else tell you about something you've done but do not remember.

"Mm-hm. And then you got a little crush on Ben, I think. When he got back from dropping you off, he said—"

"He came back to the bar?"

"It wasn't even eleven by the time you were out of commission. And when he came back, he said—"

"How long was he gone?"

They frowned at me. "The interrupting cow says *moo*. Fifteen minutes? Twenty? What's the matter?"

I didn't want to tell them I didn't remember any of it, that though I had never previously found Ben attractive I assumed I'd slept with him. "Nothing," I said. "What did he say?"

"He said he had to run out of your place to keep you from giving him a striptease."

"Oh God," I said. I wanted to believe this was true even more than it mortified me. "Never mind. I don't want to know."

"It happens to the best of us."

"Too often, for me." I tried to keep my voice light. "I was trying to stop."

"Getting naked?"

"Drinking."

"Oh." They looked concerned. "You should've said so."

"It's not, you know, addiction. But when I start I can't stop."

"Call a square a square."

"Right."

"You could always try a meeting," they said. "You do love to tell a story."

It certainly wasn't a compliment, but I could tell it wasn't entirely a dig, either. Even in such a context, I was pathetically touched by their identifying anything about my character, by being seen at all. "Maybe," I said.

I made lattes and iced teas, and apologized for a breakfast sandwich with a rubbery egg and a blueberry scone with too few blueberries. As I had so many times before, I told myself I would never drink that much again. I was aware of the monotony, but I was also aware that every person who had made a change in their life was stuck in that other old way until one day they weren't. A car pulled up and a girl got out of the driver's seat and ran for a group of kids sitting in front of the café. A peal of laughter and shrieks. School was starting soon. I missed it, all that structured purpose. Such clear goals. I closed and locked the café, and on the drive back to Moira's, the crescent-moon Christmas ornament that Martin had hung on her rearview mirror swayed back and forth like a pendulum.

I wrote for the rest of the day and woke with the sunrise the next morning. I lay on the floor in Child's Pose for a long time. I pictured Sawyer in their own apartment half a mile away, hunched over their own computer, weaving the threads. A bird outside was calling. Three bright notes, like bells.

On a sticky walk through the woods I had the not particularly original or enlightened thought, though it felt both original and enlightened at the time, that a story about my life could begin at any point within it. There was one about my relationship with Hugh, which began with our meeting outside the dining hall and ended, perhaps, with my climbing up into a Greyhound bus. Or it could end sooner, just before we kissed for the first time after those two years apart. Hopeful, full of potential. Or earlier still, the night at the library, romantically unattached and standing next to Martin as everything felt like it was teetering on a precipice between childhood and adulthood: I had gone to the reading looking for love, and found something else instead. All of those were stories, and all of them were splits in the narrative, a forking road. I just didn't realize it at the time.

I had filled Blue's water bowl at the kitchen sink, and was splashing water on my own face upstairs when I heard the crunch of a car, a knock on the door.

All my life, I have pictured someone coming to save me. In high school I sat in the wings of school plays, picturing that year's crush surprising me afterward with a bouquet of roses and a sheepish grin. After wearing myself out listening to my parents' fights I'd lie in bed, thinking about a boy throwing pebbles up at my window. *Come down. I choose you.*

Standing in the bathroom, I imagined Hugh's sweet, familiar face awaiting me downstairs. He had gotten the email. It had worked. But all I felt was unease. I wouldn't be able to resist a gesture as grand as this; all it takes is thinking you've gotten something to realize you don't want it after all. I wiped my palms on my shorts as I walked heavily down the stairs, opened the door, and found Georgia standing on the porch.

I was so surprised I started laughing. "You came to rescue me," I said.

"I have not." She'd chopped her hair into a pixie cut and her face was uncharacteristically stony. "I got an abortion. And I don't regret it but I wish it hadn't happened, and you have not fucking been there for me."

"Georgia," I said, aghast.

"Yes, Georgia. Yes, me." Her face crumpled, and when I reached for her she swatted my hands away. "It's just the hormones. Get me some water or something."

"I'm so sorry," I said, leading her into the kitchen. "You should've said."

She looked at me like I had suggested we start wearing tinfoil hats. "I tried, dude, I tried."

"Georgia," I said again, shaking my head, because there weren't words to excuse myself.

"It really sucks. I took the week off from work, but I didn't want to just sit in the apartment. Michael offered to go somewhere with me, but honestly I thought he could use a break. I'm turning into you," she said sarcastically. "I keep picking fights for no reason."

It hurt, but she deserved to get a stab in. "Seems like you have more of a reason than I did."

Georgia shrugged. Blue was bumping her nose relentlessly against her knees. Georgia squatted down to hold the dog's head between her hands. "Look at this sweet girl, look at these big old ears." She looked around. "Nice place."

I was reminded of the day I'd arrived, Moira opening the door. So much had changed since then, but still there I was, stuck navel-gazing.

"I'm horrible," I said, as I ran the tap and Georgia sat down at the kitchen table, not contradicting me. I handed her the glass of water. "I had a bad drunk night and it felt like the end of the world. And at the same time you were going through this huge thing."

"It was a quick, practically painless thing. But it's throwing me for a loop. I could've had the kid. But I didn't want to do it just because I could."

We sat across from each other and she described the Planned Parenthood clinic, where Michael read a *National Geographic* in the waiting room. Nobody had been picketing that day, which disappointed Georgia. She'd been in the mood to scream at a stranger. They got gelato afterward from their favorite place, and three days later she went back by herself and ordered grapefruit and dark chocolate, so it wouldn't turn into the gelato-she-ate-after-her-abortion place. They were thinking about fostering a kitten.

Georgia drove us to an overpriced Italian restaurant that catered to parents of college students and weekenders. Afterward, we did a loop around the town. At the playground, we sat side by side on the swings, my toes in the gravel. A few boys in muddy rugby uniforms jogged past, and a couple with a stroller.

"How're you feeling?" I asked.

"I miss Michael already," she said, swinging back and forth. "And I'm glad we did what we did. And it's nice to be here with you. That is how I feel. How do *you* feel?"

"About what?"

She opened her hands like she was tossing powder into the air.

"Oh, you mean my directionless life."

"Yes, that."

"Terrified."

"You can stay with us for a while, if you need to."

"I think I might have to go home to Colorado." My dad and his girlfriend had visited New York once the winter before, but it had been two years since I'd been to Telluride. "Stay with my mom for a bit. Figure out what to do next, rent-free. Doesn't sound so bad."

"I'm shocked."

"Me, too. But life is short, and we have tears to mend, yadda yadda.

Plus, she loves nothing better than a damaged creature. I lost my job, I lost my boyfriend—she'll probably never be happier to see me."

"No Hugh, forevermore?"

"I should probably figure out how to be a human on my own." I let out an involuntary, embarrassed groan. "This is so stupid, but when you knocked, for a second I thought it was him. I felt sort of triumphant that he was coming to fight for our relationship. But also so disappointed."

"Hugh is the gun that shows up in the first act, gets left outside in the rain, and never goes off. His name sounds like a pejorative." She gave herself a push and pumped her legs to get going. "Michael ran into him on Bedford. He said he seemed good."

I considered how this made me feel. "That's good. I think that sometimes I can't tell the difference between not knowing what I want and wanting everything, all at once."

Georgia whizzed past. "I haven't thought about it like that," she said, her hair floating like she'd touched a staticky balloon, "but I feel exactly the same way."

———

WE ROAMED AROUND for five days. We toured an old Rockefeller mansion nearby, worked on our laptops at Moira's kitchen table. I flipped through Martin's fat old dictionary, falling in love with words, tucking them away.

I opened at the Beanery—my last time there, it turned out. "You didn't exactly find your calling here," Sawyer said, tossing me a bag of beans to refill the grinder. "I'd tell you not to quit your day job, but." Their thesis defense was in the last week of the summer session; afterward, they were moving with Valerie to Chicago.

With Georgia, Sawyer dialed up their charm to a degree they never bothered to with me. When she asked about their thesis, Sawyer looked uncharacteristically shy as they described the project: the ways in which Christianity provided community and a framework for abolition, while at once being wielded as justification for slavery and segregation.

"Oh," I said, "are you still looking for a title? I found a word for you."

"Shoot."

"Cleaving. It's a contranym, which I thought you'd like. It means a separation, obviously, but it also means an adhering to."

"*The Cleaving*," Sawyer said. "That's pretty good. I don't hate it."

"Just trying not to be a total net negative," I said, only half joking. "How does it feel to be almost done?"

They flattened their hands against their cheeks. Their mouth fell open à la Edvard Munch.

———

MOIRA CAME HOME ten days after she'd called, the car service dropping her off in the late afternoon. Georgia and I had jumped in the pond an hour before, and I was aware of our bras and underwear still dripping over the back porch railing. "How is she?" I asked, as I held back Blue, who was snuffling so hard I worried about her cardiac health.

"Okay," Moira said. She was carrying her purse, wearing the same black slacks and navy sweater she'd left in. I wondered if she'd borrowed clothes from Caroline, before realizing Caroline likely hadn't had any to lend. "Better."

She was distracted and businesslike as I introduced her to Georgia; when we'd spoken on the phone a few days earlier I'd mentioned she was staying at the house, too. "Oh yes, your girlfriend?" she said, shaking her hand, and I said, "No," at the same time Georgia said, "Wife."

Moira led us into the kitchen. "How can I thank you? Let me give you some money." And then to Blue, trailing behind her: "Hello, old lady, I missed you, too."

"No," I said, horrified. "Please, I was glad to help."

"I want to," she said. "Your accepting it would be a charity to me." She pulled out a stack of folded twenties.

"I can't, Moira."

"You can."

"No, I mean, I really can't," I said, embarrassed to remind her of our other, journalistic transaction, "if I'm going to write—"

"Oh, of course." She tucked the money back into her purse.

She told us we could stay as long as we wanted. A couple days earlier I'd vacated my sublet, leaving the keys on the kitchen table. But after a whispered conference with Georgia we decided we'd drive back to the city the next day. We made pasta and a salad for dinner and Moira loosened up a little, asking Georgia about her job at the gallery as she shredded carrots and telling us Caroline had been discharged five days earlier and was staying with Priya. But there was still something brittle between us, I thought.

It wasn't until late that night as I lay in bed listening to Georgia snoring lightly beside me that I realized my insecurity was probably brought on by the impending loss of Moira, Linden town, this summer, full of hope. Maybe anticipating our separation was making Moira uneasy, too. Maybe she would miss me.

Or, more likely, she was still reeling in the aftershocks of nearly losing her daughter. Probably it had nothing to do with me at all.

The next morning the three of us ate Moira's six-minute eggs with soldiers.

"What's on deck for you?" I asked her.

She drank from her glass of orange juice and refilled it from the carton on the table. "The conference is in six days," she said. "Lots of work to be done."

"I thought you'd skip it."

"Why would you think that?"

I raised my eyebrows at Georgia.

"Do you ever think of moving to California?" Georgia asked. "To be close to Caroline?"

"Georgia," I said, embarrassed, but Moira didn't seem to mind.

"My daughter wants me to. So she can force-feed me"—she gestured at the juice carton—"fresh-squeezed orange juice and macrobiotic such-and-such."

"Moira, you love those things," I said. "You'd be in heaven."

"Heaven. I certainly hope not. Not for a decade or two."

"You don't believe in heaven, do you?" Georgia leaned back in her chair and crossed her arms over her stomach. "You're a scientist."

"No, I don't. But of all the sciences, quantum physics is perhaps most friendly to God, an afterlife. I argued with Martin about it all the time. He was totally unwilling to entertain the idea of religion having some basis in truth, though he was glad to attribute all kinds of coincidences to what he called fate. He argued that science and religion are fundamentally at odds, when really it's materialism that can't square with God, not science writ large."

Georgia looked quizzical. "Materialism is . . . ?"

"Only matter makes up reality," I said, surprising myself. "Intangibles—behavior, emotions—are products of matter acting upon matter. There's no God in a material world. But quantum mechanics undermines materialism, right?" I said to Moira.

"For the most part, yes. To many minds, quantum mechanics implies that the mere act of observation affects outcome. Matter isn't all that matters. The tree falling in the forest hasn't fallen until someone's seen it. And while it doesn't go so far as to *support* a theory of a deity, it does give materialism a run for its money," she said. She pursed her lips, as though weighing whether to say whatever she was thinking. "If Martin were here, he'd think you were a good analogy, Sal. Your observing my existence has almost certainly changed it."

I touched my palm to my cheek as though that might stop it from reddening. We moved on to other, terrestrial matters. Georgia told us about an ancient ink dish expected to sell for millions of dollars that fall.

Blue made a grumbling noise at the front door. "She's late for her walk," Moira said, glancing at the cat clock.

"Why don't you two take her?" Georgia said. "I'll clear up."

Moira stood and picked up the landline to peer at its rudimentary, old-fashioned screen. She was checking, I realized, for a missed call from Caroline.

The worn path was narrow and we walked single file: Blue, Moira, me. Moira was in one of Martin's old sweatshirts, so soft and threadbare that the yellow cotton fell more like an expensive fabric than the nineties tourist garment it was, BARCELONA! scrawled across the front. Blue squatted, her face tipped toward the sun.

"This summer has been so important to me," I said. I became aware of my thumbnail digging into the spongy pad of my pointer finger and made myself stop.

"You have more than enough for your article, I think." She was a few steps ahead of me. "I can't imagine what you're going to write."

I wished she hadn't brought it up. I thought of the thing I'd started scratching away at, and how it wouldn't pass muster through even the most dubious fact-checker. Embellishments. Imaginings.

"Moira, I mean it. When I met you I was in a"—I waved a mosquito away—"not good place. You inspired me. And having the privilege of being close to Martin's work, the way I did. It's like I really knew him."

"He would have liked you. Well, you met him. I'm sure he did like you."

I took a deep breath, feeling nauseous, but it felt easier to say what I was going to say to her back. "This is going to sound ludicrous, but when I first read that excerpt, I thought it was about me."

She kept moving. "In what way?"

"It's about meeting a girl at a book party; I'd met him at a book party." I was still walking behind her, and she didn't turn around but I could tell she was listening. I rushed on. "I didn't know anything about him then, obviously, or about you."

Moira started to say something.

"I can't hear you."

She stopped, one boot on a steplike stone. "I'd wondered why you were so set on seeing that manuscript."

It felt imperative to correct her. "It wasn't just because of that. I mean, it was, in the beginning, but so quickly it became so much more. I want to be able to fit the puzzle pieces together, to understand why this was the last story he chose to tell. About you, about this difficult and life-altering time in his life. I think it would be informative to see how he fictionalized it. Especially knowing everything I know now, about . . ." I trailed off.

"About how he was married to someone else?"

"Yes, but everything else, too. How he felt about using life in fiction." I barreled on awkwardly. "That it wasn't actually him who met you at your father's party."

She gave me a long, inscrutable look, as though she might be about to say something, but then she started walking again. Her gray hair was luminous in the flat morning light.

I scrambled to keep up. "If what he wanted most was to be remembered, wouldn't the best way to honor his legacy be to try to have his work published? Let it, and him, live on in the minds of strangers?"

"This posthumous publishing; people treat it like it's a note from the beyond. But it doesn't bring anyone back."

"But it almost does," I said. "It keeps a part of them here."

"Do you think that's true?"

"Of course I do," I said, working myself up. "It's this slice of time, a piece of the past that beams forward into the future, like light from a star."

"The stars don't care what happens here on earth," Moira said. "Much to Martin's chagrin."

"But if the universe is indifferent, then offering each other the opposite of indifference—not just empathy but true attention and care, even in death—wouldn't that be one of the most powerful exercises of human will?"

I couldn't tell if she was listening to me or thinking hard about something else. "Hmm," was all she said.

We walked on through the woods. Moira pointed out bits of moss, the calls of a warbler, a woodpecker's hollow taps. Back at the house Georgia had loaded my bags into the back of the car. "Take a last look-round," Moira said, starting up the stairs. "Make sure you haven't forgotten anything. I'll be right down."

"It was lovely to meet you, Moira," Georgia said, and then, to me, "There's a duffel bag in the guest room, is that yours?"

It was; Moira had given it to me for the overflow of things I'd accumulated over the summer, the papers, various books ordered, some clothes. Upstairs in Caroline's old room, I hefted the bag over my shoulder. I couldn't hear Moira, wasn't sure where she'd disappeared to. I checked the bathroom, and then went back downstairs. The light slanted through the big living room windows; the smells of that morning's toast and eggs still lingered. Blue lay down on her mat. Through the screen door, ever efficient, Georgia turned the car around, pointing it down the driveway.

I was crouched beside Blue, looking into her wise and goofy face, when I heard Moira coming down the stairs. It took a moment to register the hefty manila folder in her hands. As I stood up, I'm not sure if I actually said, "Is that the book?" or if I just stared at her and held out my hands to receive the bundle.

"You made me see something I'd been missing," she said. "Try not to go into it with too many assumptions."

"Moira." I was dumbfounded, and worried if I said anything else she might change her mind. "Okay," I said. "Okay, thank you. Thank you." I backed out of the house, tripping over the ledge onto the porch. I turned as I walked down the steps, trying to cement her in my mind: the buttery yellow of the sweatshirt, her fine hair blown like hay. When I got to the car and opened the passenger door, Georgia gave me a baffled look. "Hello?" she said, raising her eyebrows. "You had one job? Your duffel?"

Moira was out on the porch with the bag at her feet by the time I bounded back up the steps. I leaned in to give her a one-armed hug, the manuscript still tucked into my armpit. She hugged me back. Her body—the ropy muscle, the bones—was small under soft flesh. "I'll miss it here."

She gave the nape of my neck a squeeze. "I'll miss you, too."

Then we were rolling through town, down a road between cow pastures and fields of grain. I was holding the package on my lap, not daring to open it, terrified it would, somehow, leap out the open window and scatter its pages down the road, white blossoms, lost forever. Georgia drove smoothly, checking her rearview and side mirror and talking about a movie she'd seen recently, a pair of man-eating mermaid sisters working at a nightclub, but I barely heard her. All I could focus on was the thing in my hands.

"Georgia," I said. "It's the book."

"What's that?"

"The book. She gave me the book."

"The Book of Sal?"

"I don't know. We were talking about Martin and what he wanted for his writing, and I said—well, all kinds of things. I can't believe it worked."

"You look like you're going to be sick."

I bloated out my cheeks. "Ninety-nine percent of me knows this book is not about me. But I still have the teeniest hope that I meant something, that I gave a big enough impression to warrant the creation of, like, art."

"Salale," she said, her voice dripping exasperation. "You're being insufferable. Just open it and see."

"I can't." We were on the parkway now, gliding between trees that, in a few weeks, would light up like a fire, covering the hills in reds and golds. I leaned into the backseat and opened the duffel bag, slipped the manuscript into it, zipped it back up.

"Fine. Tell me about this thing you're writing," she said. "Give me the elevator pitch."

There was a quiet lag as I dragged my mind away from the package behind me. "The elevator pitch. I guess it's about love and ambition and betrayal." I thought about Moira and Lillian, and Moira and Caroline, and Moira giving me the manuscript, giving me the story of both of us, putting it right into my hands. I tried not to envision literary success. I tried not to think about financial gain. I touched the hard outline of the barrette in my pocket, reassuring myself that it did indeed exist.

"Betrayal, yeah. But what's it *about*?"

"I think it starts out as a story about my connection to the manuscript, and then it peels back layers to these other stories—about Martin and his life, about all these things that have nothing to do with me—but then comes back around, in the end, to the novel draft. This story about meeting the girl at the party."

"Martin meeting Moira, you mean."

"Yes," I said reluctantly. "Though it's complicated, because Martin didn't actually meet Moira that night. Lillian did. He took her story and made it his own." The radio crackled. It was incredibly unfair. Nobody would ever know what she could have accomplished. She was all perfect potential. Someone had said that before. Maybe I'd just written it. Maybe—

"Georgia," I said. There was a ringing in my ears.

"Sal."

I wrenched my body back around and yanked at the zipper on the duffel bag. It was stuck; a piece of the manila folder was wedged between the teeth.

"Chill out," Georgia said.

"Oh no, oh no," I moaned. I got the zipper free, lifted the file out of its cozy home like an obstetrician performing a C-section. I sat forward in my seat and tugged out the papers, bound together with two oversized rubber bands. It was a manuscript, yes. It was a novel, yes. It was two sets of pages, one crisp and printed, the other typewritten and time-worn.

If I had thought of it—if I hadn't been so utterly stunned—*Do you think this is a funny joke?* I would have shouted up at the sky.

EPILOGUE

In New York I kept asking Georgia if I was making the wrong decision by leaving, and she kept saying, "New York's not going anywhere," with an expression that suggested I was. Of course I fell in love with the city again, with Showtime on the subway and streets lined with TV show production trailers and the smell of car exhaust and bacon frying and cigarettes and sun-baked pavement. We went to the ballet to see Twyla Tharp's *In the Upper Room*, one of Georgia's favorites. The dancers hurled themselves through the fog, their bodies loose in their soft costumes, the girls in red shoes.

The Playwright's run finally ended and, as of this writing, his whereabouts remain hazy. The rights to his debut work were recently optioned for film. He is probably doing just fine.

I unboxed the items Hugh had carefully packed up for me—clothes, dozens of magazines, high heels I hadn't worn in years. On a hot Saturday morning I laid almost everything out on Georgia's front stoop, and we watched people try on the different versions of the person I'd once wanted to be. With the money I made selling my things, I shipped my remaining belongings to my mom's house in Colorado.

I almost succeeded in leaving Hugh entirely alone. But the desire for closure runs deep.

The Saturday before my flight, I took the subway to my old neighborhood, timing my arrival to when Hugh typically came back from his soccer game. I walked up and down the block in all its August glory, the maples and ash casting short shadows on the sidewalk. Fifteen minutes. Twenty. My timing was off, or he'd met up with friends. I would wait just a couple minutes. Just a few more.

But then, from far down the street, I saw him. He was walking in the unfettered, loping way he had when he was happy. He'd let a shadow of a mustache and beard grow in and he was wearing a shirt I'd never seen before. I'd forgotten the electric jolt his presence used to elicit. There it was. We were still two blocks away from each other when his step hitched and he held his hand up to shield his eyes from the sun.

My excitement pivoted to panic. I had emailed him. He hadn't replied. And yet here I was, cruelly imposing myself on his weekend. I crossed the intersection and power-walked to the corner, ducking around a brownstone. Then I turned to watch him proceed down the street. Soft gray T-shirt, black jeans. He reached the spot where I'd stood and took out his phone as he continued on toward the apartment, smiled at something on the screen, tapped a response. He pulled his tidy key ring from his pocket, pushed open the door to the building we had once shared, and disappeared inside. I closed my eyes, picturing the four or five steps that would take him to the row of mailboxes, the creak as his opened. An issue of *New York* magazine, maybe, the only subscription he hadn't canceled. Up two flights of stairs past cooking smells from 2B, the Monet *Water Lilies* poster in the third-floor hallway. Just before he let himself inside his own apartment I began making my way back down the street.

The next morning, Georgia and I hugged a weepy goodbye on the subway platform. Then I boarded the A train to JFK, and left.

I WON'T EVER know what Martin had in mind when he sent that first chapter to Anna. As I read and reread the manuscript I now understood to be Lillian's, it pained me to contemplate his betrayal of his former wife, his passing off her work as his own, after all those years. A final, desperate bid for notoriety. But during my flight and the long drive that followed, I considered how he had asked Anna for time to talk about the story. Maybe he had wanted to tell her the manuscript was his dead wife's. Maybe, as his life was coming to a close, he wanted to redirect some small part of his singular universe, to right one aspect of a trajectory he'd had a hand in knocking off course. In comparing the two drafts, I found small details woven into his more recently typed version, details—*like the rose, like the rose, like the rose*—that did not exist in the original. He hadn't been able to leave it alone, an editor to the end. He'd woven glistening threads of his own imagination, his own experience, into her story. Surely that wasn't right. But what is effort if not failure, and better failure?

Her book was good. The first section began with the excerpt I knew so well, dwelling in the mind of the husband as he thought about his own past, with its faint shadows of Martin's biography, and of the girl as she sped off into the rest of her life. But even in that early section I could now see the signs that someone else was in control of the narrative, parentheticals and asides that interrupted the story of the pair, so that by the end the narrator, while not entirely in focus, had at least partially revealed herself. Though written in 1974 and placing its central character amid the world of future space exploration, it didn't feel dated, dwelling primarily on the psychological implications of a

life dedicated to the pursuit of knowledge above all else. Relationships
suffered in the service of soaring discoveries. But there was contentment,
too. It was probably never about Martin, not really.

I thought of Lillian willing herself into Moira's brain. Giving her the
fictional future she thought she deserved: one without Martin. Though
surely the girl in her story wasn't all Moira. She was a conversation
overheard on the street, a stranger seen stepping to avoid a puddle,
the headstrong will of a long-dead figure dredged from the pages of
some other book. She was Lillian, too. Lillian's own maybes, her solo
future self. I wondered whether a part of Moira had known all along
that the manuscript was hers and not Martin's—if that had been the
real reason she'd been reluctant to hand it off—or if it had only clicked
in her retelling her stories to me. Whether Lillian's empathetic leap hit
her like the shock of a cold-water plunge or settled in slowly, a chain
of minuscule realizations. Whether she found herself picking through
the words for the truths that landed, and the details that skittered far
from her own reality. I wrote an apologetic email to Anna, the first
half trying to explain why I had never turned in the draft, the second
describing what I'd learned.

I flew from Manhattan to Los Angeles, burning through close to
three tons of jet fuel. I passed through the same stretches of air Moira
must have during that terrible early-morning journey toward Caroline—
the same ones Lillian did decades earlier as she traveled away from
Martin. On the plane I received an email from Anna. "This is one hell
of a correction. And it looks like you've found your story. Let's talk."
The plane's shadow was sometimes visible on the ground.

The rental car I picked up at LAX smelled overwhelmingly of an
industrial cleaning agent, but I rolled down the window and drove thirty

minutes to Seal Beach, listening to a scratchy golden oldies station, and feeling less anxious than I'd expected. Lillian's sisters have condos in a place called Leisure World, a retirement mecca where golf carts bump over the groomed grass and everyone wears visors and sports a bald patch slathered in zinc oxide.

Tegan and Effie live across the street from each other, Tegan with her second husband, Effie with her corpulent orange cat. Through Tegan's old creative agency, I tracked them down to let them know I had their sister's unpublished manuscript. When I arrived at Effie's condo, a one-story beige unit with flowerpots sprawling in front of it, I carried the folder with reverence to the front door.

Though we had discussed it on the phone days earlier, it took a while to explain what I was doing there. "I'm going to have to speak to my lawyer about this," Tegan said as we sat with the manuscript between us on the coffee table. "I don't know the legality, but I would have thought that, as next of kin, these rights are ours."

"Yes," I said quickly. We were in Effie's living room, the sun bringing out a faint musty smell from the already sun-faded furniture, the cat sprawling on the floor, tail twitching. "You definitely do, or at least I'm certainly not claiming them. I've been in contact with an editor at *The New York Review of Books* who's interested in reading the novel. I'm happy to connect you. If you decide to look into publishing it, I hope you might consider me for the foreword."

They watched me carefully. "The foreword," Effie said. I think they had assumed I was looking for money, or that I wanted to make a movie of Lillian's life.

I pushed away images of a three-volume set, painterly covers, a modest typeface in rich tones: a reissued *Evergreen* with a foreword by Moira, Lillian's book with my introduction, and lastly, my own story. "I just want to try to understand it all. I'd like to learn more about your sister."

"You want to know about Lillian? Everyone loved her," Effie said. "She was so amusing."

"Irreverent," Tegan said. "Comfortable in her skin."

"And good at just about anything she tried. I always thought she'd stay here and become a movie star. That mess of curls. Like Tegan's. At least, like it used to be."

"We had this at the memorial," Tegan said, pulling a square of cardstock out of the patent leather purse she'd been holding on her lap. "You can have that, I have a few."

Lillian's face beamed out at me. She was sitting on the front steps of a house far from New York, her arms wrapped around her knees. "She's beautiful," I said. "I'm so sorry. It must have been so hard to lose her."

"It was awful," Tegan said, but her voice was neutral, polite. "All these years later, everything comes back."

"The phone call," Effie said.

"Mom never should have let her take that car out."

"How could she have known, Tegan?" They'd had this argument before.

"Where were you when you heard?" I asked Effie.

"It was morning. The girl I was rooming with answered the phone. She could tell something was wrong, from Dad's voice."

"I was at home," Tegan said. "I still remember Mother's scream."

"The police came to the house?" I asked.

"Police?" Tegan repeated.

"After the accident. To tell your parents—"

"No, no. She went to the hospital after the accident. They checked her over, gave her some stitches, said she was fine."

"Oh, I didn't realize," I said, stumbling. "I was under the impression it was more immediate."

"No," Effie said. "She came home."

"They'd have found the bleed, these days."

"You don't know that, Tegan."

Tegan carried on, ignoring her sister. "She came home around midnight. Mother and Dad fussed over her. Dad made her a grilled cheese sandwich slathered in ketchup. Lil said she wanted to read, but it made her dizzy, so Mother went in and sat beside her bed and read—"

"*Mary Anne*," Effie said.

"Du Maurier, though not her best." Tegan nodded. "And then she jotted a few things down in her journal, the way she always did."

I thought of final words, of liminal thoughts between life and death, dreaming and waking. "What did she write?" I asked, my voice low.

"A shopping list." Tegan rubbed at the corner of her mouth, as though to fix her lipstick. "Moisturizer, new stockings."

At this, unexpectedly, my eyebrows lifted and I swallowed hard to stop the tears. I wanted them to be emotional, too. Effie looked kindly at me. I cleared my throat. "So then—?"

"She didn't wake up in the morning," Effie said.

"Just slipped away."

They showed me a few more photos: Lillian onstage in a dark leotard; the three of them as little girls in puffy church dresses; Lillian hanging an ornament on a Christmas tree. They told me family stories, bickering gently throughout.

"Did you know her husband well?" I asked after a while.

"That man," Tegan said without malice. "He really fooled us."

"Everyone is human. We all make mistakes. But she deserved better," Effie said, and they both, at the same instant, folded their hands in their laps as though closing the matter. "Who needs a husband anyway?" Effie leaned down and scratched behind the cat's ears. "Isn't that right, Marmalade?"

———

EARLY THE NEXT morning I drove north to see Caroline, taking the coastal route through mission towns. I'm not sure what Moira had said to get her to agree to talk to me. Maybe something about preserving Martin's legacy. Maybe that I needed some help right now. Or maybe Caroline was just curious about the person who'd spent so much time with her mother.

I stopped at lookout points where sea lions lolled on the rocks below, and gulls and slope-necked pelicans wheeled over the waves, and rolled into San Francisco in the early afternoon. The sky was a low, billowing gray, and as I walked through Golden Gate Park, pinpricks of moisture appeared on the hairs that jumped out from my arms. I arrived at the California Academy of Sciences forty minutes before closing time, and the woman at the front desk let me in for free. Dim, muffled rooms illuminated by small aquariums; models demonstrating how tectonic plates moved. I spent most of the time at the Foucault Pendulum, watching the huge brass orb swing back and forth in its forever revolution, another victim of gravity set in perpetual motion. I fell asleep that night with a vision of it swinging, swinging.

I called Moira the next day, right before I saw her daughter. "The

Doubter and the Interloper, meeting at last," she said, and from the tone of her voice I could tell she was smiling.

"I met with Lillian's sisters," I said, preparing to tell her what Tegan and Effie had told me—that Lillian hadn't died alone in her car, but at home.

"You'll like this," she interrupted me. "Just as they're going out of season, I found a delightful recipe for a chamomile and lemon cake."

"Oh yeah?" I wondered if she already knew the actual circumstances of Lillian's death. Maybe she needed, for some reason, to believe in the most devastating version, in the one that more accurately depicted her feelings about the event. She may not have been guilty, but she didn't want to be absolved, either.

———

THE REAL-LIFE CAROLINE was like a projection out of my imagination. Maybe because, in ways both subtle and obvious, she was so much like Moira. She had her gestures, her dichotomous coupling of warmth and remove.

She and Priya met me at a coffee shop on Valencia and then, after dropping Priya at her office, we drove across the bridge together. She told me about the stories Martin had been writing for her since she was in college, imagined monologues by her favorite composers. A year before he died, he had them bound and sent them to her for her birthday.

Caroline was allowed limited access back into her neighborhood. We had to wear N95 masks and could only stay for a short time due to the risks: Airborne carcinogens, ash inhalation. The structures were unsound. Benzene in the water. Toxic waste. FEMA was working on cleanup; it could be another year before anyone was allowed to rebuild.

I had watched so many videos of families fleeing through walls of flames, and then families returning to their homes, or what had been their homes, for the first time in the days after the area had been declared safe. Everything black, smudged out. The ocher skies in San Francisco and L.A. But the videos hadn't prepared me for the dark hill faces. The dust and ash filtered the light into a sickly yellow-gray. Pieces of framework jutted up like bones bleaching in the sun.

We drove to the neighborhood where Caroline had spent the night in the pool. Many of those houses had flame-retardant roofs and sprinkler systems. A team of private firefighters, contracted through the expensive home insurance held by several people on the street, had formed a task force. While Caroline was submerged in the pool, there were twelve men and two fire trucks three hundred feet away.

At what had once been her house, Caroline had found the remnants of her piano, melted wire strings.

"So much is gone," she said. "Whole towns leveled. Sometimes the only things left standing are chimneys and churches."

"Churches?" I imagined them looming above the wreckage, swaddled in divine protection.

"Yeah, that's pretty common, the churches staying up. Mosques and synagogues, too." She said it casually, toeing something on the ground. Then she glanced at me and caught what must have been my awed expression, and the look of quiet entertainment that flicked over her face so mirrored Moira's that it shook me out of the chills shivering the back of my neck. "It's just because they're so often surrounded by parking lots, cemeteries." She sounded amused that she needed to spell it out. "It protects them. There isn't much there to burn."

I thought about that—those churches staying up; the story I wanted versus the one that was true—during the long hours driving up Interstate 80 and then U.S. 50, through Tahoe trees and Reno's industrial hotels and the flat, brown desert of Utah stretching on and on. At a gas station outside Salt Lake, I found a brochure for Goblin Valley State Park ("one of the darkest night skies in the world!") and made the slight detour.

Moira, early on, had told me she'd always wanted to see the stars from Chile's Atacama Desert. The finality of how she said it devastated me, as though it were already something she had given up. She had so many years left, decades, I wanted to tell her. But maybe this was only my projection, maybe the Atacama was just one of a hundred thousand things Moira didn't do, because of the hundred thousand things she did. Maybe she wouldn't trade any of it. Over the years, several of her colleagues had made the trip and described it to her. She, in turn, had given those images to me. I had the thought that maybe this was the point of everything—this was the point of relationships, of friendships—to live vicariously through and give ourselves to the other humans we brush past. That we are all fogged mirrors, refracting and enlarging each other's lives.

———

GOBLIN VALLEY WASN'T the Atacama, but it was good enough. The rock formations loomed rust-red. They were like Mars, or some self-cleansing phase of our planet still to come: humans eradicated, earth waiting for the next accident of life. The sun sank below the horizon, and the sky went indigo, mauve. The Milky Way appeared in single pinpricks, then all at once.

At some point if I call Moira's house nobody will pick up, or Caroline will send me an email, or I'll read the obituary in the *New York Times*. (Where will I be? Still sitting in the sunlight filtering through the dusty windows of my mother's kitchen, my fingers resting on my laptop keys, attempting to translate thoughts into words. At a bookstore in Iowa or Portland or back in Brooklyn, shyly searching the shelves between Camus and Capote for my own name.) All lives have an end point, but it's almost physically painful for me to imagine hers. Cancer, heart disease. The recipe for forgetting that may be, already, buried somewhere in her genetic code.

It came to me recently that if I had to write her an ending, I would give her this: someday, long from now, she'll sense an inner faltering, which science will confirm. She will decide it is all under her control. When she's ready, she will buy a plane ticket, stopping first in San Francisco for a week—no, not long enough, a month, a year—to say goodbye to her daughter. From there she'll fly to Santiago, Chile, and then take a smaller plane to Calama. She'll board a bus. She will walk into the desert, where the sky will open above her like a metaphor, and whether she remembers her name or Martin's or mine won't matter under that riot of stars.

ACKNOWLEDGMENTS

Everlasting gratitude to my agents, Michelle Brower and Jen Marshall, and to my editors, Marysue Rucci and Anita Chong, for believing in, untangling, and burnishing this book. Thanks to Andy Tang, who not only kept the ship sailing smoothly but offered true kindness and writerly commiseration. Thank you to Dave Cole, Zach Polendo, Elizabeth Breeden, Ingrid Carabulea, Yvonne Taylor, Jaya Miceli, Katie Rizzo, Jonathan Karp, Richard Rhorer, the rest of the fabulous Marysue Rucci, Scribner, Simon Element, and McClelland & Stewart teams, and to Katie Freeman—without all of whom this book would be less accurate, less physically beautiful, and on fewer bookshelves. Thank you to Wyatt Mason and the much-missed Paul La Farge for, respectively and reductively, teaching me to read and write. Thank you to Ryan Chapman and my dear friend Lucy McKeon, who each read a version of this book and provided invaluable feedback. Heather O'Neill's class at Sackett Street got me past the first chapter. Writing "The Retreat," edited by Medaya Ocher and Sara Davis and published in the *Los Angeles Review of Books* in 2019, unlocked a significant story line. Jennifer Ross-Nazzal, PhD, of the NASA Johnson Space Center, provided helpful historical color for Moira's time in Houston; Moira's paper on UFOs was inspired by the work of Stephen Barr. (Any inaccuracies are all my own.) Thank you to my wonderful colleagues at *Elle* and *Vanity Fair* for years of support, inspiration, and a career that could not differ further from that of this book's narrator. I am deeply grateful for the longtime and ongoing encouragement of my friends, in particular: Mimi Wendel-DiLallo, Emma Wolff, Amy Pedulla, the beloved mimes, and most recently an expanding circle in Maine. Thank you to Lydia and Bruce Feller for not just becoming my family but also planting the seed for Moira and Caroline's telescope game. Thank you to my brother, Jacob Weir, for being our beautiful in-house photographer. Infinite love and thanks, forward and backward in time, to my parents, Barbara Chaffe and Rob Weir, who have given me everything, including music and material. To the dog, for getting me out of the house. And to Dan Feller, who has talked me through scenes and anxieties, doled out endless encouragement, shouted praise from every rooftop, and provided levity in spades: I love you, thank you, thank you, thank you.